A heartwarming anthology from nine northern romance authors

Mary Jayne Baker • Sophie Claire • Jacqui Cooper
Helena Fairfax • Kate Field • Melinda Hammond
Marie Laval • Helen Pollard • Angela Wren

Published by OPS Publishing



ISBN 978-0-99303-561-6



Cover design and typesetting by Oliphant Author Services
(cover illustrations © Shutterstock)
Edited by Helena Fairfax and Mary Jayne Baker
Printed and bound by Kindle Direct Publishing



A CIP record for this book is available from the British Library.

# CONTENTS

words came back to her. It was indeed a strange sort of shop, for the windows, though large, began at least four feet from the ground. A lamp burned in one of the windows, its golden light glinting on the objects displayed. A Malacca cane with a chased silver top was propped against the glass in one corner. In front of it was a metal birdcage and a bronze desk-set that appeared to be missing one of its inkwells. In the centre of the window was a small shepherdess figurine that could be French. Meagre fare to entice customers, she thought.

'But that is none of your business,' Diana told herself, taking a firmer grip on her portmanteau. 'All that concerns you is getting a room for the night.'

In the near corner of the window, next to a very ugly Toby jug, was a tiny brown dog. At first she thought it was another ornament, until she saw its ears prick up. It was watching her with huge, dark eyes as she surveyed the property, but as she walked up to the black door it began to bark before jumping down and disappearing.

It did not look like the sort of shop where one could just walk in, and besides, it was growing late. Diana raised her hand to the knocker, but before she could reach it the door was opened by a petite, white-haired lady in a silver-grey gown. She was cradling the dog in one arm, shushing it gently while smiling at Diana, her hazel eyes bright and inquisitive. Diana thought that she must have been a very beautiful young lady. Her hair beneath the lace cap was silver and the delicate features a little lined now, but Diana found it impossible to put an age to her.

'Napoleon always informs me when there is someone at the door.'

The soft voice captured Diana's attention and she blushed a little, realising she had been staring.

'Miss Moonshine? My name is Diana. Diana R– Riston.'

'You are here about the room.'

'Why, yes. But how did you –'

The little dog barked, interrupting her, and the older woman smiled.

'Napoleon wants to greet you.'

'He is quite delightful.' Diana put her hand out and after a cautious sniff, the tiny creature licked her fingers. 'I have never seen a dog quite like this before.'

'He is from the Americas,' replied the old lady, stroking the tiny head. 'He was originally called something quite unpronounceable, so I renamed him. I hope you do not think it very bad of me, but with Bonaparte now safely put away on St Helena, I thought it could not hurt to call him Napoleon. But let us not stand on the doorstep, Miss Riston. Come in, do.'

Diana stepped over the threshold and found herself in a large, high-ceilinged room, where the candles had already been lit against the impending gloom of the evening. It was like no shop she had seen before. In the centre of the floor stood a large mahogany table, its smooth surface gleaming a deep red-brown in the candlelight. A few chairs were dotted about, but whether these were for sale or for the comfort of customers, Diana could not be sure. Against the walls stood highly polished desks and sideboards, their surfaces covered with an assortment of items, from mundane objects such as books, wicker baskets and pewter candlesticks, to toy soldiers, oriental porcelain and strange ornaments that she could not identify.

'Heavens, what a, a varied collection,' she murmured, trying to be polite.

'Well, I take whatever people bring to me, and my customers come and buy.'

'So they never know what they will find?'

'No.' Miss Moonshine gave a small, enigmatic smile. 'But they mostly find what they need. Now, what *you* require,' she continued, suddenly brisk, 'is a room. I have just the one, and that is very fortunate for you. It is on the first floor, across the landing from my own apartments. One day I shall expand my shop to include the upper floor, but that will not be for a while yet.'

She went on to set out her terms, which were indeed very reasonable, and Diana accepted with alacrity.

'I do not know how long I shall need the room, Miss Moonshine. That rather depends upon the employment that I find.'

'Naturally. Shall we begin with a month's rent? And of course I shall require a bond.'

'A ... a bond?'

Miss Moonshine frowned a little. 'I am not well-versed in the ways of business, but I believe it is customary for a tenant to provide some sort of surety to the landlord. Usually in the form of a lump sum.'

'Oh.' Diana's heart sank as she thought of the contents of her little purse. 'Until I can find some work, I am afraid I do not have a great deal. However,' she rummaged through her reticule, 'I do have one item of value.' She pulled a small hip flask from the bag and held it out. 'It is silver.'

Miss Moonshine put the little dog down carefully on a chair and took the flask. Diana watched as she turned it this way and that, the light catching on the delicately engraved ivy leaves around two initials, "A.S."

'Andrew Sturton.' Diana was unable to keep the slight tremor from her voice. 'My fiancé. He was a soldier, and I intended to give the flask to him when he returned from the Americas, but he was sent directly to Waterloo. He did not come back.'

'I am so very sorry.' Miss Moonshine's bright eyes held Diana's for a long moment, then she nodded and held out her hand. 'Of course I will take this as surety. I shall lock it in here. It will be quite safe.' She pulled up one of the keys from the chatelaine around her waist and unlocked a drawer in the nearest sideboard. When the flask was safely put away, she turned back to Diana, smiling. 'Now, I suppose you would like to see your room.'

'Thank you, it is very kind of you.' Diana followed her up the stairs. 'I hope I shall not impose upon you for too long.'

Miss Moonshine looked back and smiled.

*

The chilly spring was eventually replaced by a cold, wet summer, and Diana was still at Miss Moonshine's. She had settled in well; her room was comfortable and she had found enough work to pay her way. Mrs Lomax, the wife of a local mill-owner, had had a baby in the spring but she had not recovered sufficiently to look after Edwin, her seven-year-old son, who was too sickly to go to school. Diana was employed to give him three hours of lessons, six mornings a week.

Miss Moonshine had also introduced her to Mr Philip Booth, the local vicar. He was a young, energetic man who wanted to open a Sunday School and needed a teacher.

'It will only be for a few hours each Sunday,' he told Diana, his blue eyes shining with enthusiasm. 'But it could make such a difference to the lives of the poorest children here. If we can teach them to read and write, their prospects will be greatly improved. We are dependent upon subscribers, so the post will be poorly paid, at least at first, but it is a very worthwhile cause. I would be delighted if you would consider it, Miss Riston.'

Diana did not hesitate. The payment might be small, but it would supplement the wage she received from Mrs Lomax and would enable her to keep her lodgings with Miss Moonshine. It would also give her more to think about, and less time to dwell on the past.

Naturally she missed her home, but her landlady was very kind, and often invited Diana to take tea with her in her own little sitting room on the first floor. It was on one such occasion that Diana found herself telling Miss Moonshine how she had come to be here, and how her fiancé, Andrew, had been killed at Waterloo.

'I read all the reports about the battle, looking for news of his regiment. They were defending La Haye Sainte and were under attack from the French. The artillery bombardment was fierce.' Diana blinked away a tear. 'We read about the action in the newspapers, but there was no news, until Andrew's parents received a letter from his commanding officer.'

'How dreadful for you, my dear. But what made you leave Shawton and all your friends?'

Diana put down her cup. 'My father died of a putrid sore throat during the winter, and I was obliged to move from the rectory, which was needed for the next incumbent. Andrew's parents took me in and were very kind to me, but they were struggling with their own grief. My presence only reminded them of what they had lost. Also, they have very little, and although they welcomed me into their home, I know my being there was an added burden on their limited funds. I could not live on their charity.'

She did not elaborate, not wanting to explain that Mr Moulton, one of the churchwardens, had become very particular in his attentions. So much so that one day she had packed up her few possessions and fled to the crossroads, climbing on the first coach to come along. It had been a wrench to cut off all ties with everyone she knew, but her persecutor was the main employer in Shawton, a man of influence, and she was very afraid that he would discover her direction and come after her.

Diana worked hard with the vicar to set up the Sunday School for the poorest children. She discovered she had a gift for teaching, and the school, plus her work with Mrs Lomax, kept her busy for most of her days. When she had any free time, she was happy to run errands for Miss Moonshine and to assist in keeping the shop clean and tidy. It all helped her to endure the overwhelming grief of losing both her fiancé and her father the previous year. Those six months had been almost unbearable. The pain of it was still there when she woke every morning, sometimes so sharp it was like a knife in her stomach, and she wanted to scream with hurt and despair.

Diana soon came to regard Miss Moonshine as a kindly aunt. Mrs Lomax treated her with kindness and respect, and the vicar was very pleased with her work in the Sunday School. It was a comfort, knowing her efforts were appreciated. Diana would always miss Andrew and her father, and her heart ached whenever she thought about them, but gradually, as the summer wore on, the constant, aching loneliness that had wrapped about her for so long began to ease.

'I should be thinking about the future,' she said to her landlady one afternoon.

It had become a habit to take tea with Miss Moonshine in her snug little parlour, and Diana knew she would miss the cosiness of these regular meetings when the time came to leave, as it surely must.

'Oh, there is no rush, my dear.' The old lady broke off a

piece of cake and dropped it on the floor for Napoleon, who was sitting at her feet.

'Mrs Lomax is recovering well now,' Diana went on. 'Soon I shall no longer be required to teach little Edwin. And the Sunday School has proved such a success that the committee want to open a poor school. Mr Booth tells me they are even now setting up a subscription to raise funds to buy Lees Hall, on the edge of the town. It needs a little work, but it will provide schoolrooms and a sizeable house. He mentioned outbuildings, and enough land to be farmed for additional income.' She sighed and plucked at her skirts. 'So you see, they will be looking for a husband and wife to run it.'

'Yes, yes, but none of these things has yet come to pass,' replied Miss Moonshine, refilling the teacups. 'You are still needed here in Haven Bridge at present, and you are free to keep your room for as long as you need it. Indeed, I am glad of the company.'

Diana thanked her, grateful for the older lady's kindness. She remembered when she had arrived, and Miss Moonshine had told her how she planned to expand her business into upstairs rooms. Upon reflection, however, Diana thought that perhaps she was right, and there was no rush for her to move out. After all, in all the months she had been here, and although she often helped Miss Moonshine to tidy and rearrange her shop, she had yet to see a single customer.

*

The village of Shawton lay beneath a blanket of cloud, and the rain poured down steadily, turning the roads into muddy rivers and keeping all but the hardiest souls indoors. Late one afternoon, anyone peeping out of their window might have seen a solitary traveller walking along the high street, a knapsack thrown over one shoulder. The collar of his greatcoat was turned up, his hat was pulled low to keep off the worst of the rain and he walked slowly, leaning heavily on a rugged stick. At the corner of Church Lane he hesitated, looking towards the church and the rectory beyond it, then he settled his knapsack more securely on his back and continued on his way to the little house with grey shutters, between the basket-makers and the general store. He beat out a firm tattoo on the locked door.

It was opened by a stooped gentleman with white hair and tired blue eyes set in a gaunt, lined face.

The traveller took off his hat and smiled.

'Father.'

*

Half an hour later, Andrew Sturton was seated at the table with a bowl of broth before him and his outer clothes spread around the fire to dry. His parents had joined him at the table, gazing at him as if he might disappear in a puff of smoke at any moment.

'But how? When?' His mother stopped and began again, saying simply, 'We had given you up for dead.'

'I know, and I am very sorry for it.' He reached across and squeezed her hand. 'It was a tragic, most unfortunate mistake. My comrade James Illingworth – you will remember I mentioned him several times in my letters to you – he was mortally wounded, but before he died he asked me to take charge of a letter he had written to his wife. I put it in my pocket and thought no more of it, for the shells were raining down upon us thick and fast. We had formed square and stood firm, but the bombardment was terrible.' He frowned, almost wincing at the painful memories. 'I cannot describe it to you; indeed, I am glad you cannot know the awfulness of that day. All clamour and stench and carnage! But the noise. The noise was the worst. It was almost unbearable, as if all the monsters of hell were shrieking at once, and it left one's head ringing for days, weeks, after. One shell exploded so close it killed those nearest to me and knocked me clean out of the square.'

He drew in a ragged breath.

'I was one of the lucky ones, because I was taken to a field hospital. Unfortunately, I was too ill to tell them who I was, but they found the letter and thought I was James. When I came to, I was so confused I could not deny it. I began to recover, and although I could not remember my name, I became convinced of one thing, that I was *not* James. I was shipped back to England and spent the winter in Portsmouth. I was in a truly sorry state and too sick in my mind to do any more than get through one day at a time. Spring was well advanced before I was sure of who I was, and it took some time to get that little matter sorted out, I can tell you. The army discharged me, but before I could think of coming home, I had to deliver James's letter to his wife. Poor woman, when I met her she had heard nothing from the regiment and was still hoping James might return.' He finished his broth and pushed the bowl away. 'So, I am come home at last, Mother, Father, and apart from a few scars and this damned stiff leg, I am well enough.'

'Aye, and I thank God for it,' declared his father, his eyes unnaturally bright.

'So, too, do I.' Andrew pushed himself to his feet and reached for his stick. 'Now, I must go to the rectory.' He frowned when he saw the look that passed between his parents. 'What is it?' A cold hand clutched at his gut. 'Has something happened to Diana?'

*

The route up the hill to Lomax House was now familiar to Diana, as was the sight of the morning sky, heavy with the promise of rain. So far this year there had been little warm summer weather, and along with worries about a poor harvest, Diana knew the townspeople were anxiously watching the river that ran through the town. She was dismayed, therefore, when the rain began in a steady, relentless downpour soon after she sat down with Edwin. She had moved the schoolroom table to the window to take advantage of what little daylight there was, and, as she listened to Edwin reading, she glanced frequently at the rain lashing the glass.

By the time Diana returned to Market Street the river was already a torrent, thundering between its banks and creeping ever higher. She hurried to the shop and helped Miss Moonshine to move as much stock and furniture as she could upstairs. As dusk fell, they stood on the staircase and watched the first floodwater trickle under the door.

'Now we must sit and wait,' said Miss Moonshine, tucking Napoleon more securely under her arm. 'The rain has eased, thank goodness, and once the water stops running from the hills into the streams that feed the river, the level will begin to drop. I am hopeful that by the morning we shall be clear.'

'You are very cool about it,' remarked Diana, following her landlady up the stairs.

'It is not the first time the river has burst its banks, and it will not be the last. We shall come about. Now, I have a good fire in my sitting room; we shall have a supper of toasted muffins.'

As Miss Moonshine had predicted, by the following morning the floodwaters had receded, but they had left their mark, a dark stain six inches deep around the walls and a noisome smell. Diana wanted to stay and help clean away the silt and mud but Miss Moonshine sent her off, saying she could cope perfectly well alone, and indeed, by the time Diana returned from her teaching duties the only sign of flooding was a shadow on the walls and a faint mustiness in the dank air.

'But that is nothing,' said Miss Moonshine airily. 'We shall leave the windows open, light a good fire in the hearth and it will be as good as new. Let us instead go and attend to our neighbours. Some of them fared much worse than this.'

By the end of the day, Diana was exhausted and could only marvel at Miss Moonshine's energy. They had spent the afternoon scouring out the room of a widow with two young babes to care for and had used the last of the daylight helping a fellow shopkeeper to restock his shelves ready for the morning. Diana retired to her room, almost too tired to undress, but as she slipped between the sheets she could hear Miss Moonshine still pottering around below. Despite her age and diminutive size, the lady appeared to have boundless energy.

The following days took on a pattern as Diana worked with the townspeople to help those who had suffered most in the flood. She was shocked to discover that some houses along the riverbanks had been washed away. She went to see Mrs Lomax, who rallied her wealthier friends to provide extra food and dry clothing, while the vicar toiled to find shelter for the homeless. The hard work and long hours took their toll, and each night Diana dropped into bed and fell into a deep, dreamless slumber.

*

It was the end of August, and Diana was in the little room set aside for the Sunday School, tidying up, when Mr Booth came in and greeted her cheerily.

'Another busy afternoon, I believe,' he remarked, looking about him.

'Yes, sir, the class was full again.' She placed the last of the slates on a shelf and began to collect up the chalks. 'The parents are eager for their children to attend.' She placed the chalks in their box. 'I am particularly pleased with the number of girls who come to class. Some of them are very bright, and all of them eager to learn. It is most satisfying.'

'You are a very able teacher, Miss Riston. You have done very well with the children, and the success of our Sunday School is in no small part due to your skills. And the numbers continue to grow, which convinces me we are right to expand.' He picked up a stray piece of chalk from the floor and turned it between his fingers. 'You will be pleased to know that the committee has now raised by subscription sufficient funds to set up a proper school for the poor, rather than merely a Sunday class.'

'Why, that is excellent news,' replied Diana, even though she knew it would mean the end of her time here.

'It is indeed. I have been considering John Hesland's cottages, next to the church. You will have seen them, of course. They are in a parlous state and Hesland is looking to sell, as he does not have the funds to restore them. One is already empty, and the other will be free at Michaelmas. They could be knocked into one to make a suitable schoolroom –'

'But there is no land with the cottages,' said Diana, frowning. 'I thought the committee had decided upon Lees Hall.'

'We had, but I thought, perhaps, a farm might not be necessary.' He stopped and cleared his throat. 'I thought you might like to continue, as teacher for the poor school.'

'I?' she looked up at him, startled. 'I wish it were possible, Mr Booth. I cannot tell you how much I enjoy my work here, but you said yourself the salary would be low. Certainly not enough to live on.'

'I did say that, but I have another plan now that I would like to put to you.' He held out the chalk to her, and as she took it he grasped her hand between both of his own. 'Miss Riston – Diana – I thought, hoped, that you might consider. That is, I would be honoured if you would consent to be my wife.' He fixed his eyes upon her and continued eagerly, 'The living here is sufficient to support a married man, but from what I know of you, I do not believe you would wish to be idle. If we bought the cottages, you might run the school while I continue with my parish duties. I would not ask this of you if I did not think it would be to our mutual benefit. After all, you are a clergyman's daughter, and as such I believe we are ideally suited.'

'Wait, wait,' she cried, pulling free and pressing her hands to her burning cheeks. 'Mr Booth, this ... this is most unexpected. I had not thought, had not considered such a thing.'

'And that is part of your charm,' he told her, smiling. 'You are intelligent, accomplished and any man would be proud to call you his wife. And there is no doubt that my parishioners would approve. Your efforts after the flood were much appreciated, but even before that you had gained their respect by your diligence and hard work.' He paused. 'So, what do you say, Diana, will you throw in your lot with me?'

Her head reeling, Diana turned and walked to the window. 'This is all so sudden and ... and unexpected. I must have time to think.'

'Of course.'

'No.' She turned towards him. 'No, I *have* thought, and I regret that I cannot marry you. You see, much as I esteem and respect you, Mr Booth, I do not love you. Perhaps I should explain. You know of course that my dear father died last year, but there is more. I have told no one of it, save Miss Moonshine, but I was betrothed, you see. To a young man, a soldier, who perished at Waterloo. I think my heart died with him.'

Diana twisted her hands together nervously, waiting for his reaction. She had said much the same to Mr Moulton, the churchwarden at Shawton, when he had proposed. He had responded by trying to take her in his arms, thinking he had only to kiss her and she would submit. Now she glanced towards the door, planning her escape, but it was not necessary. The vicar made no move to approach her, he merely nodded.

'I am very sorry for your loss. So many good men have died in the recent wars, it is quite, quite tragic. But you must believe me, my dear, I have seen other young women in a similar case and I know you will recover. Many marriages begin with nothing more than esteem and respect; mutual affection and even love can follow.' He smiled, nothing in his face but understanding and compassion. 'Of course, there is plenty of time for you to fall in love again, so perhaps you would rather not tie yourself to a humble vicar. You need not give me your answer now. Think it over. I hope you will not think me arrogant when I say I can offer you a comfortable, fulfilling life, Diana. And you would make me the happiest of men if you would marry me.'

She looked at him, at his cheerful countenance and smiling blue eyes. There was no doubt he was a very personable man, with a good and kindly nature. But he was not Andrew.

'I see you are going to refuse me,' he said, putting up one hand. 'I beg you will say nothing yet. Instead, promise me you will at least consider my offer. The committee does not have to make a decision on which of the properties to buy until Michaelmas, so there is a little time.'

'Very well, Mr Booth.'

'Call me Philip, please.'

But that she could not do. To use his name would be too intimate and perhaps raise hopes that might not be fulfilled. That she was almost sure could never be fulfilled. Instead she gave a little shake of her head, smiling. Then she picked up her shawl and left him.

*

As the summer waned, so did the numbers in the Sunday School, every child being needed to fetch in the harvest, such as it was. Diana knew they would be back after Michaelmas, and Mr Booth would require an answer. She observed the vicar as he delivered his sermon at the Sunday service, although she was too distracted to pay heed to his message. His manner towards her had not changed at all since he had surprised her with his proposal. There had been no sly looks, no sighs or attempts to win her sympathy. He had continued to be his usual, amicable self, treating her in a respectful and friendly manner that set her at her ease. In so many ways it would be easy to accept the safe, comfortable life he was offering. She must make a decision, and soon, for it was but three weeks to Michaelmas.

Michaelmas. One of the Quarter Days, when rents were due and servants were hired. And yesterday she had learned it would be the end of her employment with Mrs Lomax.

'I am well enough to take over Edwin's tutoring again now,' she had told Diana, adding, with genuine regret in her voice, 'For myself I would very much like to retain you, but we have had the new steam engine installed in the mill, you see, and with the continuing decline in trade, Mr Lomax is anxious that we should economise...'

Diana quite understood, but she was well aware that there was no other work for her locally. She would have to advertise for something farther afield.

*Or you might marry Mr Booth.*

She glanced up at the pulpit, where the vicar was coming to the end of his sermon. Why not? Why should she struggle to support herself when he was offering to look after her? Philip Booth was a kind man, a good man. He would take care of her, and she would not need to move away from the friends she had made in the town. Perhaps she should accept his offer. Perhaps it was meant to be.

The vicar was waiting for Diana as she came out of the church. One word from her, one hint, and she could be his wife. She would be safe, secure. Comfortable. But something told her it was not enough, and now she could only bring herself to throw him an apologetic glance.

She would have hurried past but he stopped her with a word. He said quietly, 'I would not for the world have you avoid my company, Miss Riston. If you do not want to accept my offer, then so be it. But believe me when I say that I shall honour your decision and not hold it against you.'

She looked up at him, thinking how different he was from Mr Moulton, who had hounded her mercilessly.

She smiled. 'Thank you, Mr Booth. I hope we can always be friends.'

'Indeed, I hope so,' his eyes twinkled. 'But I have not yet given up hope that you will change your mind by Michaelmas Sunday.'

*

Andrew sat down at the table and looked at his parents.

'I do not know what else to do, Mother. We have advertised as far afield as the *Leeds Intelligencer* and the *Manchester Mercury*, all to no avail. There is no word of Diana.' He dropped his head in his hands. 'It is as if she never existed.'

'I am sorry, my son.' His father patted him awkwardly on the shoulder. 'I wish to heaven she had never left us, but she gave us no notice, just disappeared one day.'

'She did it for our sake,' his mother was quick to add. 'She knew Mr Moulton would be asking, nay, *demanding* that we tell him where she had gone.'

'And all the money I have spent on notices to the newspapers has done no good at all,' muttered Andrew. 'Money we can ill afford.'

'You must not think we begrudge a penny of it,' his mother told him. 'Diana was like a daughter to us.'

'But we cannot continue like this, can we?' Andrew rubbed his eyes. 'I must get work, Mother. I have tried everywhere in Shawton and there is nothing for an able-bodied man, let alone a cripple.'

'You are not a cripple,' replied his mother fiercely. 'Your leg is getting stronger with every day that passes.'

'It makes no odds, if there is no work.'

For a while they remained wrapped in the gloomy silence. Then his father stirred.

'There is one thing we have not tried. I have an old school friend in Halifax. He has a business and might be prepared to take you on. As a clerk, perhaps. Your bad leg would not matter if you were sitting at a desk.'

'Halifax!' Andrew exclaimed. 'But that is so far away from Shawton.'

*So far away from Diana.*

The heavy band of iron about his heart tightened. He exhaled slowly. 'I beg your pardon, I am being foolish. This is an opportunity that must be pursued. Thank you, Father, I would be obliged if you would write to your friend. Any work is better than none.'

In truth Diana could be anywhere, so what did it matter where he went?

*

'Goodness, it is Michaelmas in a se'ennight.' Miss Moonshine poured tea into one of her pretty porcelain cups and handed it to Diana. 'Where has this year gone?'

'The time has flown past,' Diana agreed. She bit her lip. 'And I must make a decision.'

'Perhaps I can help you.' There was understanding in Miss Moonshine's delicate features, and sympathy in her hazel eyes. When Diana hesitated, she said softly, 'Tell me.'

And Diana told her all about the vicar's proposal.

'He has been all kindness, ' she ended, putting down her cup. 'And patient, too. He has given me until Michaelmas to decide.'

'From what you tell me, Mr Booth is offering you a comfortable home and a worthwhile life as his helpmeet.'

'He is indeed,' whispered Diana, hanging her head.

'Then why do you hesitate?'

'Because... because I do not love him. I do not think I could ever love him.'

There was silence in the little sitting room, broken only by the crackle of the fire and the relentless drip, drip of rain outside the window. There. She had admitted it. Andrew was her one and only love and her heart was buried with him. Wherever he might be. Miss Moonshine reached across to take Diana's hands.

'If you have doubts, then you should not marry him,' she said quietly.

In her heart Diana agreed, although the uncertainty about her future was quite terrifying. She sat up a little straighter.

'Then I must advertise in the newspaper. I thought, with my experience in the Sunday School, I might find employment as a teacher.'

The difficult decision made, they spent a little time discussing where best to place an advertisement and the type of salary she might expect. Diana went off to her room, her heart lighter than it had been for days.

She spent the evening composing the notice she intended to send out and, in the morning, she went in search of Miss Moonshine, to ask her opinion of her efforts.

'I thought I should send it to Leeds, for the *Intelligencer*,' she said. 'After all, the wider the area the more likely I am to find a suitable post.'

'You are quite right, my dear,' murmured Miss Moonshine, scanning her letter. 'This is very good. But I would not send it off quite yet.'

'But surely, Michaelmas is the best time to advertise, being a Quarter Day.'

'That is the point, my dear. We are so close to the end of the month now that this will not reach the newspaper office in time for them to publish it before Michaelmas.' Miss Moonshine folded the letter and held it close. 'I will keep it safe for you, my dear. Trust me, you had much better wait a little.'

'I will, if you think it best,' said Diana, doubtfully, 'but how am I going to pay my rent?'

Miss Moonshine regarded her for a long moment, her head tilted on one side, like an inquisitive bird. She said gently, 'Perhaps it is time we put the silver flask in the window.'

*

The light was fading by the time Diana left the Sunday School, the gloom only adding to her lowering spirits. It was Michaelmas Day. Her work with Mrs Lomax was already finished, and she had endured a painful meeting with the vicar. Not that Mr Booth had been unkind – quite the opposite, which made Diana feel all the more unhappy.

Philip Booth was disappointed, but not, he said, surprised.

'You would make an admirable vicar's wife, my dear, but I must respect your decision, if your heart is not in it. As for the poor school, the committee will go back to its original plan. But enough of that. What will you do now? I suppose you will have to find other employment.'

'Yes.' Diana tried not to sound despondent. 'I am going to look for a teaching post of some kind, but I doubt it will be close by.'

'You will be sorely missed, my dear, and not only by me. However, you may be sure I shall be glad to furnish you with an excellent reference.'

His kindness warmed her, but it humbled her too. Her spirits were further depressed by the fact that after Michaelmas she would no longer be teaching Edwin Lomax and would therefore not be earning any money. If she was not going to marry Philip Booth, she had no option but to leave.

As she turned onto the path leading up to Miss Moonshine's front door, she glanced at the window with its odd assortment of items for sale. There, pride of place in the centre, was the silver flask she had bought for Andrew. She had reluctantly agreed to sell it, but knowing how few customers passed through the shop she thought it unlikely that it would go soon, and if it did, the money would do little more than pay her rent for a few weeks. She had best ask Miss Moonshine to look out the advertisement, and she would take it to the post office in the morning.

She went in, only to discover that Miss Moonshine was not at home. A note propped against the candlestick on the sideboard informed her that she had gone on an errand of mercy and had taken Napoleon with her. There was nothing unusual in that. Miss Moonshine was often abroad, helping the needy. Diana suspected she had some private income, because she was always ready with a basket of food for the family of a sick millworker, or a parcel of clothes to distribute to the poor. Diana went to her room and after heating a little soup for her supper she retired to bed, exhausted by her anxiety.

The following morning, Diana was getting dressed when Miss Moonshine knocked on her door.

'My dear, I am obliged to go out again,' she said, buttoning her pelisse. 'I wonder if I might ask you to mind the shop for me?'

'Why yes, of course I will, but – how do I know what price to charge for things?' Diana thought she should ask the question, but it was unlikely to matter. After all, she had never yet seen a customer in the shop.

'Things will fetch what people are prepared to pay, my dear.'

'Oh pray, do not ask me to haggle over prices,' Diana begged her. 'I have no idea what anything is worth.' She followed the landlady down the stairs. 'Could you not write out a list?'

'There is no time,' declared Miss Moonshine, scooping Napoleon up and putting him into a basket. 'It is only for a few hours, my dear.'

She picked up the basket and was gone, leaving Diana with a head full of questions. What if someone came in to buy the Toby jug? Diana thought it quite grotesque and had no idea of its value. She would not give more than a few pennies for it. Or even worse, what if someone wanted the silver flask? Her throat dried. The flask was engraved with Andrew's initials, and she was not sure she could bring herself to part with it. Hot tears prickled at the back of her eyes. No, she most definitely would not be able to let it go.

Suddenly it was all too much. The tears welled up and she could not stop them from falling.

'Oh Andrew, Andrew.' She sank down onto a chair and covered her face with her hands as a wave of loneliness and desolation swept over her.

She cried for some time, but then she wiped her eyes and blew her nose. Andrew would have teased her for being a watering-pot. She could almost hear him, asking her what sort of soldier's wife she would make, if she fell into hysterics over a trifle. Not that Papa's death, nor Andrew's, could be considered trifling, but here she was, almost a year on, and still feeling sorry for herself.

'It will not do,' she sniffed, trying to find a dry spot in her handkerchief. 'I must think of the future. Really, it was very foolish of me to stay here with Miss Moonshine for so long. I should have set about seeking a good position weeks ago.'

Diana looked around the room, wondering where her landlady had put her advertisement but reluctant to pry into the drawers and cupboards. Well, that was easily remedied. She would write another notice and take it to the post office directly. She turned and hurried up the stairs. She had no idea what time the Leeds mail might pass through, but that did not matter as much as the conviction that it was time to act.

Diana had only written a few lines when she heard a noise from the shop below, and a man's voice calling for service. A customer! Carefully putting down her pen, she went down the stairs.

A gentleman was hovering just inside the shop, his figure a black outline against the light from the open door. He was leaning on a stick and she thought perhaps it pained him to walk so she hurried towards him.

'How may I help you, sir?'

'Good day to you, ma'am. I noticed the silver flask in the window. May I look closer? I could not quite make out the initials but I *think*...'

His voice trailed away, but Diana had not heard one word. She stopped and stared at him, taking in the fair hair and the lean, handsome face that she remembered so well.

'*Diana?*'

'Andrew?' She put her hand on the table to steady herself. 'I... I thought you were d- dead.'

He recovered first from the shock and limped forward, dropping his stick and holding his arms out to her.

'As you see, I am very much alive.'

*

It was dusk, but with the curtains drawn against the night and a fire burning brightly in the hearth, Miss Moonshine's little sitting room was very cosy. On her return, when she had found them together, the landlady had insisted Diana and Andrew should make use of it.

'I need to work up my accounts and can as easily do it down here at the table,' she had told them, her eyes twinkling.

They had taken Miss Moonshine at her word and were now sitting together on the little sofa. Andrew stared at the silver hip flask, turning it over and over in his hands.

He said, with more than a hint of wonder in his voice, 'If my leg had not been paining me, if I had not decided that a walk would do me good before continuing my journey, I would never have seen this. I might have gone on my way and never found you.'

Diana leaned against him. 'I shall always be grateful to Miss Moonshine for putting it in the window.'

'But one can scarce see it from the road,' he told her. 'No, it was the cane that first caught my eye. It is so much finer than the stick I use and I thought it might make me look less like a cripple, so I stepped closer to take a look, and that is when I saw the flask.' He put his arms around her. 'I had quite given up hope of finding you, but when I saw the engraving I remembered you telling me you had bought such a thing for me, and I had to come in and find out.'

'And I am so glad you did,' she said, smiling up at him mistily. 'To think you might have passed so close, and I would never have known.'

'Ah, don't. I cannot bear the idea of it, my dearest. My fair fugitive.' He pulled her closer and kissed her. When at last he raised his head, he said, 'You must believe me, we tried *everything* to find you.' He settled her more comfortably against him. 'We put notices in all the newspapers, asking for news of you.'

'But you were looking for a Miss Pennystone, not Riston,' she replied. 'You were not to know I had taken my mother's name. Oh Andrew, I am so very sorry that I left no word, but I was so afraid –'

'Hush, my darling. It does not matter, now that we have found each other again. My mother told me you had gone away to escape old Moulton's advances, damn him! And she said he had been making himself rather unpleasant, threats and so forth, trying to discover your whereabouts.'

'Then I was right to tell no one. I would not have anyone lie for me, least of all your parents.'

'Moulton is nothing but a bully,' he replied. 'He would not have dared to harass them if I had been there!'

She put a hand up to his cheek and repeated his words back to him. 'It does not matter now that we have found one another again.'

He drew her close and captured her mouth for a long, languorous kiss that sent little thrills running through Diana, right down to her toes. She never wanted it to end, but at length he gave a groan and put her away from him.

'Alas, it will not do, Diana,' he said wretchedly. 'I have nothing to offer you. I have little money and no prospects at all. The army doesn't want me, and there is no work in Shawton, even as a farmhand. The summer has been so bad, even experienced men are being laid off, so who will want to hire a cripple? That is why I am on my way to Halifax. My father knows a fellow there, a millowner, who might set me on, even though I have no skills. He has agreed to see me tomorrow. A clerk's wage is all I can expect, and that will not be enough to keep a wife. At least, not at first. I might be able to work my way up, but that will take years.'

He dropped his head in his hands. Diana heard the desolation in his voice and laid a hand on his shoulder.

'Let us not despair, my love. I am sure we will think of something. And if we have to wait a little while before we can be married, then so be it. I thought you were dead, and that was much, much worse.'

'Yes, yes of course, you are right.' He turned to her, but in the candlelight she could see his smile was strained. 'I must go, if I am to catch the last coach to Halifax tonight. I cannot afford to give up even this small chance of work.'

Diana picked up her shawl. 'I will walk with you to the inn.'

She tried to sound cheerful, to hang on to the thin thread

of hope, but in her heart she knew it would not be easy for Andrew to find employment. Thousands of men had returned from the war, and even those without injury found it difficult to support themselves.

Miss Moonshine was sitting at the table, several ledgers open in front of her, and Napoleon was asleep in his basket at her feet. She looked up as they came downstairs.

'Are you going so soon, Mr Sturton? I hoped you might join us for supper.'

'Alas, ma'am, I cannot stay. I must catch the night mail to Halifax.'

'Mr Sturton is going there to look for work,' added Diana.

'Ah. What sort of work are you looking for, sir?'

Andrew spread his hands, 'Whatever I can find, madam. Unfortunately, I am not trained to anything but soldiering.'

'Ah,' she said again, regarding him for a moment before turning her bright gaze upon Diana. 'I met the vicar on my way home this afternoon. He tells me the committee has agreed the purchase of Lees Hall and its land.' Miss Moonshine looked from Diana to Andrew and back again. 'He told me all he needs now is a suitable married couple.'

Diana's head came up and she exclaimed, 'Of course, it would be perfect!' Almost immediately her hopes faded. 'But – but would Mr Booth even entertain the idea, would he consider me, consider *us*, when I have rejected him?'

Miss Moonshine patted her cheek. 'Bless you, my dear, there is no need to colour up so, just because you refused the vicar's offer of marriage. Mr Booth thinks very highly of you. I am sure he would be delighted if you would take on the school. With a husband to help you and to farm the land, of course.'

Andrew was looking from one to the other, a faint look of bemusement in his eyes, but now he said, 'A school and

Evie needs.' She put the medical book back in the cabinet where it had come from, beneath a shelf of smiling porcelain dolls and tin soldiers, and pulled on her gloves. 'Here's the doctor making Sylvia pay for all sorts of ointments, when all her baby needs is to be taken outdoors.'

She flew down the stairs, her laced boots making a clattering sound on the stone steps. It felt good not to have to tiptoe around a sickroom, for a while at least. In Miss Moonshine's shop, Beatrice always felt she could be herself. It was wonderfully liberating. She jumped the last few steps, narrowly missing a table piled high with sweetly scented soaps and sachets of lavender. Miss Moonshine's tiny dog, Napoleon, raised his head from his basket in the corner and gave a little yap, disgruntled at having his sleep disturbed.

Miss Moonshine was wearing the most astonishing felt hat, with such a wide brim Beatrice wondered how on earth she'd managed to lift it onto her head. A bunch of real cherries dangled precariously over its edge. One of the cherries threatened to drop off with every movement of her birdlike frame. Her hazel eyes twinkled as Beatrice approached.

'Did you find what you were looking for, dear?'

'I did, thank you so much. And I'll tell you something, Miss Moonshine, I'm never letting Dr Sandbone near my sister and her baby again. He's made them both much worse. These doctors! They're nothing but quacks, all of them.'

Miss Moonshine darted a glance towards the far end of the shop, where a man in a dark grey suit stood in the window, examining the postcards and bric-a-brac. The man turned over the card in his hand and carried on reading.

The cherries on Miss Moonshine's hat did a little dance as she turned back to Beatrice.

'Dr Sawbones is an old soak,' she said. 'The last time he was in my shop, he reeked like a whiskey distillery.'

Dr Sandbone – or 'Dr Sawbones', as Miss Moonshine called him – was the most fashionable doctor in the town. He was a frequent visitor to the large stone villas on the outskirts, where the wealthy manufacturers, the lawyers and the bankers lived. His portly figure was never seen in the slum dwellings where the poorer people were housed.

Beatrice sighed. 'I wish Sylvia wouldn't send for him. But Captain Osborne made her promise to see him regularly while she was expecting. It was the last thing he said before he left for India, and Sylvia would never dream of going against his wishes. But I can't tell you how worried I've been. She's been so wretched since the birth. She lies on her bed most of the day, and I know she's weeping when she thinks no one can hear her.' Beatrice gripped her purse. 'And poor baby Evie is a terrible colour. Yellow, like a piece of old silk. And all Dr Sawbones did was prescribe an expensive tonic for Sylvia, and the old *fathead* told her to keep Evie indoors, with the curtains drawn, away from "foul air".' Her eyes flashed. 'And the book you lent me says what the baby needs is *sunshine*. I'm going home to draw back the curtains at once and let in some light. And I'm never letting another doctor over the threshold again, no matter what my brother-in-law may say.'

In Beatrice's frustration and distress, she hadn't noticed the man in the window draw near. She turned to go and almost bumped into him. Beatrice registered a dark moustache and neatly trimmed beard, and a pair of serious brown eyes meeting hers.

'Beatrice, dear, this is my godson, Edward,' Miss Moonshine said. 'Edward Lawrence, the son of a very old and dear friend of mine from over the Pennines.'

Beatrice held out her gloved hand, gazing up at the handsome features with frank interest. She had never heard

Miss Moonshine mention any friends or family. Indeed, sometimes it seemed the kind-hearted lady and her shop had simply arrived from nowhere and had been a part of the town forever.

'Beatrice Diamond. Pleased to meet you, Mr Lawrence.'

The young man took her hand in his and hesitated, before giving a wry smile. 'I'm afraid I must disappoint you, Miss Diamond. My name is Dr Lawrence. Not Mister. I'm one of those quacks you dislike so heartily.'

Beatrice reddened. She would never have taken Miss Moonshine's young godson for a doctor. His open expression was so unlike Dr Sawbones' smug arrogance, and he had a rugged vigour about him. Then she took in the fine tailoring of Dr Lawrence's worsted suit, the gold pin in his tie, and the hint of expensive cologne. Her eyes narrowed. No doubt Dr Lawrence charged the sick a tidy sum for his medical fees. She withdrew her hand and would have made her excuses and left, but the young man detained her.

'Would you allow me to give you some advice? You see, I couldn't help overhearing your conversation. I believe your sister's baby may be suffering –'

'From jaundice, I know,' Beatrice finished for him. 'My niece shouldn't be kept indoors. A walk in the perambulator in the sunshine will do her the world of good.'

Beatrice's tone was cold. Now it was Dr Lawrence's turn to redden. He gave a stiff bow. 'I beg your pardon.'

Miss Moonshine broke in cheerfully, 'There's not much Beatrice hasn't taught herself, Edward. She pores over my medical books whenever she gets the opportunity. The mill girls often come to you for advice, don't they, dear?'

Beatrice thought of her hours of self-study. It was true, she was now able to diagnose many illnesses, but there was a limit to what one could discover just from reading. At the university in Manchester, the male students had proper clinical instruction. They carried out dissections in the lecture theatre, and they observed the latest surgical procedures. There was no comparison between their practical training and Beatrice's haphazard reading.

She gave a wistful sigh. 'What I'd give to be able to study *properly*.'

The cherries bobbed on Miss Moonshine's hat. One of them rolled off and fell to the floor.

'Here's Dr Sawbones killing people,' she cried, 'and an intelligent young woman is barred from clinical instruction and left to scrape what knowledge she can from borrowed books. It's a criminal waste in this day and age, in - in -' She brought her arched brows together, momentarily thrown. 'What year is this?'

'1908.'

Beatrice and Dr Lawrence spoke together. Beatrice caught the doctor's eye. Miss Moonshine was often eccentric about time, believing herself sometimes to live in Regency days, when she attempted to persuade her female customers to buy patches and hair powder. At other times she talked about fashions that were outlandish, with skirts well above the knee. There was affectionate amusement in the doctor's eyes as they met Beatrice's. He had a nice smile. Beatrice was surprised to find how warm it made her feel. Then she remembered what had brought her into the shop. She cast a hurried glance at the clock on the wall.

'Is that the time? Sylvia will be fretting if I stay too long, and I have a long walk up the hill.' She gave Miss Moonshine a grateful smile. 'Thank you so much again. I'll take Evie out in the sun as soon as I get home.'

She gave Dr Lawrence a small nod and hurried to the door. Beatrice was anxious to get home, but as she stepped under the arch of roses outside Miss Moonshine's shop she came to a halt, her eyes wide with wonder. There, drawn up at the side of the road, was a *motor car*, gleaming black in the sun. A group of children were clustered round it. Beatrice had seen a motor once or twice before, but never this close. Who could be driving such a dashing vehicle in Haven Bridge?

She placed her gloved hand on the warm bonnet. The car had a hood which had been folded down so the driver could enjoy the sun.

'Miss Diamond,' one of the boys said, his eyes round. 'It's got leather seats, an' all. Ah've never seen nowt like it.'

She hurriedly lifted her hand from the shining metal. 'Perhaps we'd better not touch it, Alfie,' she said. 'I'd hate to think we'd scratched it.'

There was a quick tread behind her. Dr Lawrence appeared from beneath the arch of flowers. He looked from Beatrice to the group of children, his brown eyes alight with the same warm amusement he and Beatrice had shared in the shop.

'Thank you for looking after the motor.' He put his hand in his waistcoat pocket and drew out a penny, handing it to Alfie. 'Perhaps another day I'll take you out for a drive.'

Alfie's eyes bulged. There was a chorus from his pals. 'Us an' all, mister!' and 'Tin't fair. Alfie 'as all t' luck.'

Dr Lawrence waved the children away good-naturedly. 'You can all have a turn in good time.' He turned to Beatrice. 'But just now I'm going to drive Miss Diamond home.'

Beatrice stared at him. His fees must be extortionate if he could afford to own a car. And was he seriously offering to drive her in it?

'You mentioned you had a long walk,' he explained, when she failed to answer.

Beatrice felt a strong desire to tell him she'd prefer the walk in the sun. But the car gleamed invitingly, and then she remembered how much her sister loved engines. Sylvia was nutty about anything at all mechanical. Her spirits had been low for far too long, and it would be wonderful to see her eyes light up when Beatrice drew up in a car at their front porch.

'Thank you,' she said, trying to sound as though she was accustomed to being driven every day of the week. 'I would love a drive home.'

Dr Lawrence held the passenger door wide, and she climbed gingerly inside. The doctor proceeded to crank a handle at the front of the car - an operation which appeared to require enormous strength. Beatrice caught a ripple of muscle beneath his smart suit. Then the motor fired into life, and the car began to judder. Beatrice was filled with a thrill of excitement.

Dr Lawrence slid in beside her and took hold of the wheel. When he moved a lever, the car moved forward. She caught hold of her hat with one hand as the motor picked up speed. They were trundling over the packhorse bridge when they passed the vicar's wife, a shopping basket over one arm. Her mouth opened in astonishment at the sight of Beatrice bowling along beside a young man. Beatrice wanted more than anything to let out an unladylike whoop as she passed, but she restrained herself and merely lifted her hand in a polite wave.

Dr Lawrence caught Beatrice's eye and grinned. The car began to go even faster, the wheels jolting over the cobbled street, and Beatrice was thrown against his solid frame.

'Oh, it's just as well Charles can't see me,' she breathed. She imagined her brother-in-law's rather stern expression, which always softened at the sight of Sylvia, but was often puzzled and sometimes even disappointed when it rested on his boisterous sister-in-law. 'Charles wouldn't approve,' Beatrice went on. 'He would tell me I'm too "fast".'

Dr Lawrence glanced down at her. 'Who is Charles?'

'Captain Osborne. He's my sister's husband. He's in India with his regiment. Poor Sylvia has been very low.'

Beatrice caught herself up. She hadn't meant to confide in Dr Lawrence, and was surprised how easy she'd found it to tell him of her worries.

'I see,' he said steadily. 'You must be a great comfort to your sister. But it's not unusual, you know, for women to feel very low in spirits after giving birth. It can happen even to the happiest of women.'

'Really?' Beatrice raised her face to his. 'Is such unhappiness common for mothers?' She gave a sigh. 'Oh, how little I know, and how much I want to help her.'

Dr Lawrence didn't reply. He was frowning a little, but the next minute the car bumped over a stone on the road, and Beatrice was forced to catch hold of the side of the door.

They were climbing uphill out of the town, away from the smoke of the mill chimneys, where the moors spread out around them, lush and green in the sun. Beatrice twisted in her seat to enjoy the glorious sight. As she did so, she caught sight of a young girl running behind them, dressed in the clogs and pinafore worn by the mill girls.

'Stop, Dr Lawrence, do stop,' Beatrice cried.

The doctor brought the car to a rumbling halt and turned, surprised, but Beatrice opened her door and jumped out.

'Mary Collinge!'

The girl lifted her head but didn't slacken her pace. 'Miss Diamond,' she panted.

'Are you late for school, Mary?'

'Aye, miss.' The girl's breath was laboured, and it became obvious as she reached Beatrice that she was near tears. 'Me mam were badly this morning an' I were late for t' mill.

Overlooker said I could mek up time, but now I'm late for class, an' all, an' Miss Clarke'll bray us.'

Beatrice took her hand. 'Dr Lawrence here will take you up as far as the school.'

The girl came to a halt, eyes wide. 'In t' motor, miss?'

Dr Lawrence readily agreed to the proposal. 'Yes, indeed in the motor, young lady. Jump in. It won't do to have Miss Clarke "bray" you.'

Beatrice beamed her gratitude. The doctor returned his attention to the road, and the car was soon rumbling forward, with Mary Collinge now installed in the back seat. Beatrice cast a quick glance over her shoulder. The young girl was staring about her as the road disappeared beneath their wheels. Beatrice saw that despite her recent exertion, she was deathly pale, and there were dark shadows beneath her eyes.

Soon they reached the entrance to the school - a small, squat building set back a little from the road.

'There.' Beatrice turned and touched Mary's hand. 'Tell your mother our hens have been over-laying again and I'll bring her some of our eggs. And some chicken liver for you.'

A comical expression of dismay crossed Mary's face.

Beatrice laughed. 'I know. It's hideous. But liver is very good for you. Think of it as medicine for your tiredness.'

The girl scrambled out of the car. 'All right, miss.' Her pinched features spread into a grin. 'Ta, doctor. Worth a braying to tell t' lads I were fetched to school in a motor car.'

She darted away through the school entrance, her clogs ringing on the stone flags.

Dr Lawrence set the car in motion again. 'Poor mite,' he said. 'She looks worn to death.'

Beatrice sighed. Miss Clarke's school was full of "half-timers" like Lucy - children who spent half their day working in the mill and the other half in the classroom. The headmistress said that by the time they got to school, the mill girls were ready to put their heads down on their desks and sleep.

'Mary's very bright, but her mother is a widow and the family needs her wage.' She paused, biting her lip. 'Did you see how pale she is? And her complexion has a greenish tinge. I wonder if it might be chlorosis.'

She cast Dr Lawrence a quick glance and looked away. She remembered she was talking to a medical man – a man who had had every opportunity to study in a university. Perhaps he might think her diagnosis ridiculous.

But the doctor merely nodded. 'You would make a good doctor, Miss Diamond. And not many doctors would prescribe their own eggs and liver.'

They rounded a corner and were soon approaching the villa belonging to Captain Osborne. What with giving the doctor directions, and clinging to the passenger door as they made the sharp turn through the gates, Beatrice had no time to ponder his words. They bounced up the bumpy drive, designed to accommodate the captain's horses and not the wheels of a car. At one point, as they neared the house, Beatrice thought she might be thrown right out. She held on to her hat and laughed out loud.

The front door flew open as they drew up, and there was Sylvia, standing at the top of the steps in her shawl, a look of amazement on her face. Beatrice stood and waved, beaming, and her sister dashed down the steps.

'A motor car!' There was a sparkle in Sylvia's eyes that Beatrice had missed for too long. Her sister's reaction was everything she could have hoped for. She jumped down.

'This is Dr Lawrence. He's driven me up from Miss Moonshine's.'

In any other circumstances, Sylvia might have frowned a little at the thought of her younger sister driving through town with an unknown young man, but she was standing by the engine, her eyes on the bonnet, transfixed.

The doctor kept the engine idling and climbed out. 'Would you like to look under the bonnet?'

'Oh, wouldn't I!'

Beatrice joined them, though she had no interest in engines. 'Once Sylvia gets sight of an engine, there's no getting her away. I remember the time our parents took us to the funfair, and Sylvia spent the entire afternoon at the merry-go-round, pestering the men who ran it to tell her how the steam engine worked. My mother had to drag her away.'

But Sylvia took no notice. The doctor had folded open the bonnet to reveal a shiny, greasy-looking engine, and she was bending over it.

She pointed. 'Look, Beatrice, these are the pistons. And these must be the spark plugs, which fire up when you crank the handle. What a wonderful invention.' She gave a sigh. 'How lucky you are to own a motor, Dr Lawrence.'

The doctor was standing back a little, his arms folded across his chest.

'I'm afraid I'm more knowledgeable about the human body than an engine. But in any case, the car isn't mine. It belongs to my mother.'

Beatrice and Sylvia turned to look at him as one. His mother – a woman – owned a motor car?

'But maybe you know her,' he went on, smiling. 'Her name is Constance Lawrence.'

Beatrice gasped aloud. *Constance Lawrence!* This smart young doctor was the son of the woman who wrote wonderfully daring books with intrepid heroines and thrilling heroes. The sort of books that made you want to stay up all night, turning the pages. The sort of books Captain Osborne had once said he thought were 'utter bilge'.

'Oh, we *adore* your mother's books,' breathed Sylvia.

'Totally adore them,' echoed Beatrice. 'We've read *all* of them. Miss Moonshine stocks them as soon as they're out in print.' She whirled round to her sister as she remembered. 'And Sylvia, while I was at Miss Moonshine's, you'll never guess what I discovered. Dr Sawbones has it all wrong. We need to bring Evie out in the sunshine.'

The light in Sylvia's eyes dimmed. Her face fell. 'Oh dear, Bea, do you really think...? But Dr Sandbone seemed so sure...'

'Evie isn't getting better with Dr Sandbone's treatment,' Beatrice said gently. 'I'm positive some sunshine and fresh air will do her good.'

Sylvia continued to look uncertain, but Dr Lawrence broke in, 'I have an idea. I'll be taking up a post at the Infirmary soon, but until then I have a free week. Why don't I call in and take you all out in the motor every day? You can bring the baby, and while you show me the sights, Evie can enjoy the sun.'

Sylvia continued to look doubtful, but Beatrice noted how her eyes had brightened at the thought of the drive. She turned to Dr Lawrence.

'Would you really take us out? That would be too good of you.'

'You would be doing me a favour,' he said. 'I don't know anyone in Haven Bridge apart from Miss Moonshine. You would brighten my week by keeping me company.'

Sylvia came to a decision and nodded. 'Thank you so much,' she said. 'And – if you have time,' she added shyly, 'Evie has just had her feed. Do you think we could take a drive with her now?'

Dr Lawrence grinned back. 'Of course.'

Sylvia ran lightly back up the steps to fetch the baby, and Beatrice turned to the doctor.

'I can't thank you enough,' she said earnestly. 'That's the first time Sylvia has shown any interest in leaving the house for weeks.'

Dr Lawrence's brown eyes met hers, serious for a moment, and then he gave another of his warm smiles. 'We must thank Miss Moonshine for introducing us. My mother says she has a gift for making everything come right.'

## *Chapter Two*

For the rest of that week, the sun shone on the heather in bloom on the moors. Every morning, Beatrice and Sylvia would carry a freshly fed Evie in her basket down the steps and into Dr Lawrence's waiting motor. Sylvia had cleverly rigged up a strap for the basket, adapting some of the leather harness from the captain's stables. She would fasten the basket securely onto the rear seat, and then away they would drive, climbing up and up out of the town and right onto the tops of the moors, where Dr Lawrence would park. They would spread a blanket over a patch of heather each day and sit among the drowsy bees and the curious pheasants. They brought a picnic with them and feasted on cheese and freshly baked bread, and ripe tomatoes from the greenhouse. They lay Evie beside them on the blanket, and she'd wave her chubby little arms in the air and gurgle. In just a few days, the pink returned to Evie's cheeks. The doctor leaned over her, pulling faces, and on the third day Evie actually smiled at him. A real smile that delighted Beatrice, but not as much as the smiles of her sister. Sylvia, too, was gradually transformed. The pallor left her complexion, and nothing made her happier than to practise driving the doctor's car, while he and Beatrice looked after Evie.

On the final day of the doctor's holiday, when Sylvia had driven herself quite a way up the road and was happily practising reversing, baby Evie began to grizzle in her basket. The doctor picked her up and cradled her to his shoulder, where she promptly let out a loud burp.

Beatrice laughed. 'I think she's taken to you, Dr Lawrence.'

'For a small creature she has a potent smell,' he said, wrinkling his nose. 'I'm afraid my medical tutors didn't teach us how to change a baby.'

Beatrice pulled a disbelieving expression. She held her arms out to take Evie back. 'It's strange how men are quite capable of academic study, but when it comes to simply changing a baby's napkin, they're helpless.' She drew out a large square of linen from Sylvia's bag and laid the baby down on it. Then she swiftly unpinned the soiled nappy. Evie kicked her legs, delighting in her freedom.

'There.' Beatrice rooted through the bag for clean things. 'Now watch and learn, Dr Lawrence.'

'I wish you'd call me Edward.'

Beatrice lifted her head. The doctor was looking at her with a half-diffident, half-earnest expression. Honestly, Beatrice thought, he's asking me to call him Edward right this moment, just as I'm changing a soiled nappy. But nevertheless, she couldn't help smiling at him. The doctor – *Edward* – smiled back. He opened his mouth to speak, then stopped abruptly, turning to look at the road. There was the sound of the car chugging back up the hill.

'Oh, I'm sorry I was so long,' Sylvia cried. She switched the engine off and jumped down. 'I went much further than I meant. I've had a wonderful time. I drove past Mr Jacks, the farmer. You should have seen the look on his face.' Her eyes sparkled. Then she looked from Beatrice to Edward and back to Beatrice again, and something seemed to dawn on her. 'I shouldn't have left you both alone so long.'

'We won't tell Charles if you don't,' Beatrice said. She pinned Evie's new nappy on and finished dressing her, and rose to her feet.

'Time to get back,' Edward said, drawing out his watch. 'All good things must come to an end.'

The doctor's words were apt, in more ways than one. Dr Lawrence was starting his new job at the Infirmary the next day. There would be no more picnics on the moors. The drive home was a subdued one. Edward was concentrating on the road ahead, a small crease on his brow. Sylvia also was quiet in the back seat, and when Beatrice turned to see how she was, she caught her looking from Edward to Beatrice, a thoughtful expression on her face. She looked away when she caught Beatrice watching her.

After reaching home, and after Beatrice and Sylvia had thanked Edward, and wished him all the very best in his new post, Sylvia pushed open the door while Beatrice carried Evie inside. There was a letter lying on the doormat, addressed in Captain Osborne's strong, distinctive hand. Sylvia snatched it up and began reading at once.

Beatrice carried Evie, who was beginning to grizzle for her feed, into the front room. She was standing by the window, cradling and crooning to her, when Sylvia rushed in, clutching the letter to her.

'Beatrice! He's on his way home!'

Beatrice turned, forcing a bright smile to her face.

'He'll be here in two weeks.' Her sister rushed forward and kissed the top of Evie's head, swooping her into her arms. 'Daddy will be home soon, darling, and he'll get to meet his lovely, chubby little daughter and dote on her as much as Mummy does. Let's come and do your feed, you sweet old grizzly thing.'

She carried Evie from the room, chatting and murmuring to her. The smile vanished from Beatrice's face as soon as the door closed behind them. Of course she was happy Sylvia's husband would soon be home. She was happy he was returning safe from India, and happy for him that he'd finally meet his daughter and be at home with the wife he adored. Captain Osborne was a good man. He was a little rigid in his manner for Beatrice's liking, but he had been besotted with Sylvia since the day they first met, and Beatrice had no doubt the captain would be equally besotted with his daughter.

She turned to the window and gazed out at the rose garden. With her brother-in-law home, she would soon have to leave. She was sure Sylvia would try to persuade her to stay – Charles, too, to be perfectly fair to him. But two was company – three was a family, if you counted Evie – and four was distinctly like a crowd. Sylvia and Evie no longer needed her, in any case. Since their daily drives onto the moors in Edward's car, the sparkle had returned to Sylvia's expression, and Evie's complexion was now pink and rosy. With Charles returning, there was no need for Beatrice to remain.

She rested her head against the window frame. Where on earth would she go? Her stay with Sylvia had been a wonderful taste of freedom after living with their parents. Their mother would love for Beatrice to go back to Lancashire and help them with the farm, but the thought of returning – and of burying herself in the middle of nowhere again – was more than she could bear. Besides, when her father died the farm would go to her younger brother, William, and what would Beatrice do then?

She sighed. If she had been born a man, she would have inherited the farm. She would have given the farm willingly to William, who loved the life, and if she were a man, she would have gone to university to study medicine. Being born a woman was just so *unfair*. Why was it Charles was allowed to join the army and do exciting things like travel to India, and Sylvia, who was so skilful with mechanics, and knew all the workings of every engine, was left at home, unable to practise her talents? Why could Edward go off and become a doctor, and Beatrice couldn't even earn enough money to support herself?

Beatrice ran over her options. She could be a writer, like Constance Lawrence. But Mrs Lawrence was fortunate to earn so much. So few women earned money from writing. In any case, unlike Mrs Lawrence, Beatrice had little imagination. She preferred medical books, where everything was hard, reliable fact. Perhaps she could find work as a teacher. That seemed more likely, but the thought wasn't at all comforting, because she wasn't cut out for teaching, either. But if she couldn't find employment, then the future looked bleak indeed.

## *Chapter Three*

The next morning Beatrice left the house soon after breakfast and began the long walk down the hill to Miss Moonshine's shop. Baby Evie was developing a rash where her napkin rubbed. Beatrice had told her sister she would buy some of the wonderful ointment Miss Moonshine sold, which always cleared the redness like magic. Secretly she was also hoping Miss Moonshine would give her some advice. The wise old shopkeeper always had the answer to any problem Beatrice confided in her.

So Beatrice strode past the terraced houses tumbling down the hills around Haven Bridge, over the bridge and into the town. She ducked under the roses blooming over the shop's archway and came to a halt. The sign on the shop's door said 'Closed'. Miss Moonshine's shop was never closed! But even more astonishing, the entire shop front was decked with banners in the green, purple and white of the Women's Social and Political Union. There were posters in the window declaring 'Votes for Women!' and 'Rally for Women's Suffrage!'

Beatrice stared in amazement. She had heard of the suffragettes' marches in Manchester and London, but never imagined their movement would ever reach Haven Bridge, or that the struggle for equality would touch her life at all. She was standing pondering it all, when the door opened and Miss Moonshine stepped out. She was dressed very conservatively in a high-necked blouse, a trim boater, and a navy skirt, and was clutching an umbrella in one hand and a carpet bag in the other. Napoleon's tiny head poked out of the top of the bag, the side of which was embroidered with the slogan 'Votes for Women!' in large purple letters. There was a resigned expression on the dog's face.

'There you are, Beatrice. I've been expecting you.'

'Really?' Beatrice's mouth opened in surprise, but there was no time to ask how Miss Moonshine knew she was coming, because now another woman was stepping out of the shop, causing Beatrice's jaw to drop further. Constance Lawrence! But of course Miss Moonshine had said Mrs Lawrence was an old friend, and since she was also Edward's mother it was to be expected she'd visit him in Haven Bridge. Nevertheless, Beatrice couldn't help staring, star-struck.

Mrs Lawrence stepped forward to greet her, gloved hand outstretched. She was very different in appearance from her son. Edward was rather tall, but Mrs Lawrence was almost as tiny as Miss Moonshine. She looked like an older version of one of the glamorous heroines in her books. Her hair – still a youthful gold – was just visible beneath her straw hat. She gave Beatrice a wide smile, as though she'd been longing to meet her. Beatrice couldn't help but notice that Edward's mother was wearing lipstick, in a dashing shade of cherry red. Lipstick – how daring! Whatever would Charles say?

Beatrice's shyness fled and she couldn't help a wide smile of her own as she shook Mrs Lawrence's hand. A pair of brown eyes met hers, and now Beatrice noticed the resemblance to Edward in their intelligent gaze.

Mrs Lawrence put her head on one side. 'You must be Miss Diamond.' Her eyes twinkled. 'I've heard so much about you.'

Beatrice felt her cheeks redden a little. Had Edward been speaking of her?

But then Miss Moonshine broke in, 'If you're marching with us, Beatrice, you'll need an umbrella.'

'Marching?' Beatrice glanced at her, aghast. 'Me? You mean with the suffragettes?'

'Yes, of course,' Miss Moonshine said briskly. 'Isn't that why you came? There's a march planned in Hepton. Mrs Lawrence and I are on our way now.'

Beatrice had a fleeting, cowardly desire to say she'd only come for some baby ointment. She thought about the suffragettes, and the enormous scandal there had been about them. She thought of how they'd marched on the House of Commons, chaining themselves to railings, and breaking windows. She thought of how some of them had even been arrested and imprisoned. A frisson of fear ran down her spine. Associating with suffragettes was dangerous. And scandalous, many people might say. Beatrice pictured Charles's shock if he knew Beatrice was marching for the vote.

And then a strange feeling came over her. It started in the pit of her stomach, travelling all the way up, making her lift her head and stand erect. Her eyes narrowed and she set her mouth in a grim line. So what if she got arrested? What had she got to lose? After all, what had the world of men ever done for her? If women got the vote, she'd jolly well vote for the party that allowed women to become doctors and mechanics if they wanted.

She gave Miss Moonshine a smart nod. 'That's right. I'm here for the march.' And then she hesitated. 'But you said I needed an umbrella.' She looked up at the cloudless summer sky. 'Is that really necessary?'

'You should always carry an umbrella in a demonstration,' Miss Moonshine told her, bringing her brolly down with an alarming swish. 'You never know if there might be trouble.'

Napoleon ducked back into the bag. Beatrice, too, was taken aback.

'I don't think I could use an umbrella to strike someone. No matter what happened.' Then she thought again of the marches in London, where the police had brought horses, and there had been so much trouble. She tried to stiffen her resolve and to remember her medical studies and women's rights to a democratic vote. Even so, it was hard not to feel a great deal of trepidation at the thought of violence. How brave these suffragettes were!

Mrs Lawrence patted her arm. 'Don't be anxious, Miss Diamond. Look at us.' She made a gesture that took in her own sober grey jacket and Miss Moonshine's unusually conservative clothes. 'We don't want people thinking we're hooligans. We're just respectable women asking for the right to vote. Nothing to alarm anyone. Now come along!'

She and Miss Moonshine strode off. The village of Hepton lay on the other side of the valley to Sylvia's house. It was a tiny place – no more than a few streets and a pub, and a little church and schoolhouse, perched at the top of a very long, and very steep, cobbled path.

Mrs Lawrence was right, Beatrice thought, as she followed in their wake. They were just ordinary women, causing no trouble to anyone. And what could possibly happen in a quiet village like Hepton? She fell into step beside them. After a few minutes, they reached the start of the path, which lay on the other side of a high stone wall. As they rounded the corner to join it, Beatrice's nerves were jolted again by the incredible sight in front of her. Hundreds of women were already on the march. Women of all ages. Women in clogs, with shawls around their heads. Women tottering slowly on walking sticks, supported by their daughters. Young girls in straw hats and striped jackets, walking arm in arm. Dozens of banners were waving, some neatly embroidered, some with the words 'Votes for Women', crudely drawn. There was a beautiful appliqué of the mill chimneys and the moors, all greens and golds, with the letters WSPU stitched to it. Beatrice had never seen anything like the glorious spectacle of the female crowd in all her life. She turned to find more women were joining them at the rear.

One of the girls ahead began to sing, in a loud and clear soprano.

'Rise up, women, for the fight is hard and long;
Rise up in thousands, singing loud a battle song.
Right is might, and in strength we shall be strong
And the cause goes marching on.'

Miss Moonshine and Mrs Lawrence joined in, and soon all the women were singing, 'Glory, glory, hallelujah!', and Beatrice's voice swelled with theirs.

Slowly, slowly, they made their way up the steep path and precipitous stairs that led to Hepton, their ranks growing. Beatrice glanced around her at the determined faces. In this crowd of women, it seemed anything was possible. The march had grown so quickly, and the streets were so narrow, it was difficult to gauge just how many they were, but she guessed there must have been near on a thousand. Surely people would take notice? Surely their voices couldn't be ignored, and surely things would change for women?

When they reached the top of the climb the women began to spread out. A hush fell. A woman began to address the crowd from somewhere on the other side of the village square, but Beatrice and her companions couldn't catch her words or see beyond the sea of banners and hats. They began to work their way round, dodging through groups of mill girls, who were listening intently.

In the quiet, a man's voice rang out. 'Go 'ome and get yer 'usband's tea!'

The woman speaking to the crowds made some reply Beatrice couldn't catch, and there was a ripple of laughter. Her heart was pumping with a mixture of excitement and nerves. They pushed their way past a group of smirking lads – Beatrice recognised little Alfie among them – and found themselves at the opposite side of the square. They were at the top of a narrow set of stone steps leading back down to Haven Bridge. A strapping policeman stood, arms folded, watching the proceedings.

Beatrice turned to speak to Miss Moonshine, but at that very moment, to her surprise and dismay, one of the boys behind them in the group with Alfie threw a stone.

'Go 'ome to yer wash-tubs!'

The stone flew past Beatrice's head, narrowly missing her, and clattered down the steep steps.

Mrs Lawrence whirled round, umbrella raised.

'Who threw that?' Despite her small stature, Mrs Lawrence had a voice that was enough to quell the boldest schoolboy.

But then a cry came up from all sides of the square. Beatrice discovered later, after all the commotion was over, that the women marchers were being jostled and pushed and harried on all sides in an organised attack by groups of youths. In Beatrice's own small field of vision, the moments that followed passed in swift, terrible chaos. The policeman turned to find out what the trouble was. Beatrice was to remember forever afterwards his red face, sweating under a heavy blue hat, the fierce, bristling whiskers, and his hard expression. He reached out a burly arm to grasp Mrs Lawrence's raised umbrella. As he did so, he jostled Miss Moonshine. Napoleon raised his head from her bag, outraged, his tiny mouth open in a snarl. He snapped at the policeman's arm, nipping the blue fabric.

Miss Moonshine bristled.

'No!' Beatrice cried, but too late. Miss Moonshine raised her umbrella and brought it down smartly on the policeman's forearm, causing him to give an astonished grunt.

'Keep away from my dog,' she said.

'Right, missus.' He clasped hold of Miss Moonshine's arm. 'You're under arrest. Assaulting a police officer.'

'Oh no, please –' Beatrice began, but the policeman's eyes were hard as stones. He began to drag Miss Moonshine away. Her tiny frame was dwarfed beside his massive bulk, but she managed to turn round and give Beatrice a reassuring wave of her hand, still clutching her carpet-bag. Napoleon's head bobbed and fell back inside, and then they were pulled into the crowd and all Beatrice could see was the policeman's hat, moving relentlessly forward.

She whirled round to speak to Mrs Lawrence. Hadn't she seen what had happened? But Mrs Lawrence had problems of her own. Beatrice was aghast to see Alfie and his friends were taunting her.

There was a stifled giggle from one of the boys. She ignored it.

'How many fingers am I holding up?' Beatrice raised her hand.

'Three,' Mrs Lawrence replied.

Beatrice went on asking Mrs Lawrence a question every few minutes – whether she knew where she was, and who she'd come to visit, and what Miss Moonshine's dog was called. She was very relieved when the answers began to come a little more firmly and Mrs Lawrence began to seem more alert. In a little while, Mary came running up with a cup and a jug of water, and a square of faded but clean cotton.

Beatrice lifted Mrs Lawrence's head and let her sip, and then folded the square into a neat sling.

'I'm just going to raise your arm,' she said. Carefully, she lifted the injured arm and slipped the sling around it, reaching under Mrs Lawrence's shoulder with the cloth. Then she unpinned the brooch from her own blouse, using it to fasten the ends of the cloth together.

'There,' she said, sitting back on her haunches. 'That's not a bad job for my first ever sling.'

'Very well done, my dear. And I barely felt a thing.' Mrs Lawrence's voice was still faint, but her eyes had a twinkle to them as she looked up at Beatrice.

Beatrice gave her a rueful smile. She was more relieved than she could say to hear Mrs Lawrence make a joke.

And now there was nothing more to do except wait. The time dragged with excruciating slowness. Around her, the group of boys who had been responsible for throwing stones were still casting anxious glances at the tiny form of Mrs Lawrence, her head now pillowed on Mary Collinge's none-too-clean shawl. When anyone approached too near, the lads were quick to urge them to stand back.

'Give 'er room,' one of them would say, or, 'There's nowt to see 'ere.'

As the minutes ticked by, Beatrice had ample time to ponder the fate of Miss Moonshine, last seen being dragged away by a policeman. What had happened to her?

It was an enormous relief to hear the sound of Edward's car horn. Beatrice jumped to her feet. There were still lots of women making their way up and down the path, chatting excitedly. Edward was forced to take care as they scattered to the side to let him through. Alfie sat beside him in the passenger seat, looking lordly. He was staring straight forward, head held high, as though he were accustomed to driving in cars every day of his life.

Edward brought the car to a halt and jumped out, leaving the engine running. He lifted his bag from the back seat and hurried to where his mother lay. There was a worried frown on his face, but he gave Beatrice a quick smile before dropping down on his knees.

'In trouble again?' He took his mother's uninjured hand in his. The relief on Mrs Lawrence's face at the sight of him was touching. She gave a wan smile.

Edward proceeded to ask the same questions Beatrice had done, holding up his fingers and examining his mother's eyes. He also went through a series of tests to check for injury to her back. Eventually, the stiff set of his shoulders relaxed. He declared his mother fit enough to travel to the Infirmary in the motor, rather than wait for the horse-drawn ambulance that was following, if Beatrice could help support her to the car.

When his mother was safely installed in the passenger seat, her arm in her neat sling, Edward took Beatrice's hand and pressed it.

'Thank you,' he said hurriedly. 'I wish I could take you

home, but I must get her broken bone treated, and I have my own patients waiting at the Infirmary.'

'Don't worry.' Beatrice returned the pressure of his fingers. 'I'll be perfectly fine.'

Edward looked mightily relieved. 'I really can't thank you enough.' He looked about him, as a thought struck him. 'Where is Miss Moonshine?'

'You mustn't worry about Miss Moonshine, Edward dear,' came his mother's voice from the car. 'That redoubtable lady is perfectly capable of looking after herself.'

Edward caught Beatrice's eye and they shared a smile.

## *Chapter Five*

Two weeks after the events of the march, Beatrice was once more making her way down the hill towards Miss Moonshine's shop. That 'redoubtable lady' had been brought before a magistrate and charged with assaulting a police officer with an umbrella. Miss Moonshine had stated in a firm voice that although she did not uphold the legality of the court, since it was run only by men, she was prepared to pay the fine as there was no one to look after her dog if she had to go to prison. She wanted it placed on record that this went much against the grain.

In the meantime, after a night in the Infirmary, Mrs Lawrence was recovering from her accident at Miss Moonshine's. She spent each day sitting in the upstairs room of the shop, scribbling away at her next novel. It was her right arm she'd broken, but by the greatest good luck she was left-handed, and able to write to her heart's content.

Beatrice had seen nothing of Edward in the weeks following the march. He had returned the brooch she'd used to fasten his mother's sling, along with a gift of a beautiful pair of earrings to match. He'd chosen the earrings himself, he explained in the accompanying note, and he wanted her to have them as a thank-you for her level-headed care of his mother. Without Beatrice's presence of mind, Mrs Lawrence might have fared far worse.

Beatrice imagined Edward must be very busy with his patients. She knew she shouldn't mind it, and she told herself she only resented his busyness because she herself was forced to be idle. But deep down, she knew her low spirits were due to the fact that he hadn't found time to visit her at all.

On top of everything, Beatrice's brother-in-law was now home from India. Beatrice had been visiting one of the mill girls when he drove up from the station. On her return, she'd turned into the driveway to find a horse and cart, piled high with baggage. The door to the house stood wide open, and in the doorway were Captain Osborne and Sylvia. They were locked in a wild embrace, oblivious to everything around them. The captain, in his dashing uniform of black and gold, was clasping Sylvia in such a fierce hold, it seemed he might bend her slim body in two.

Beatrice had turned immediately to walk back down the road, where she continued to pace up and down for at least half an hour, giving Charles time to greet his wife and new daughter. She was enormously happy for Sylvia, and of course she was mightily relieved that Charles was safe home. But she couldn't help feeling a little wistful at the thought that no one in her life had ever held her with such passion.

It was in this low frame of mind that Beatrice pushed open the door of Miss Moonshine's shop. The old lady and Mrs Lawrence were standing behind the counter. Miss Moonshine looked none the worse for her brush with the law. In fact when she looked up from her newspaper, her gaze was even brighter than ever.

'Beatrice,' she cried. 'I was expecting you.'

Normally Beatrice would have laughed, but she was feeling too depressed, and so she merely gave the shopkeeper a small smile.

'I've come for some ointment for Evie –' she began.

'Yes, dear, I've got it ready for you.' Miss Moonshine indicated the neatly sealed packet on the counter.

'Oh!' This foresight was astonishing, even for Miss Moonshine, but Beatrice had no chance to ask her how she knew what she wanted, because the old lady was obviously eager to tell her something.

She held up the newspaper she'd been studying. 'Have you seen this?'

Beatrice stepped closer. 'Women Students to Enrol at Manchester Medical College', the headline read. Beatrice let out a gasp. Women at the medical college! Forgetting her troubles, she took the article from Miss Moonshine and read every word. When she'd finished reading, she had to start from the beginning and read all over again.

She lifted her wondering gaze to Miss Moonshine's.

'So,' Miss Moonshine beamed, 'This means you can study to be a doctor, after all.'

A swell of the most tremendous euphoria swept over Beatrice. She was so giddy with the unexpected joy of it, it was several seconds before she could say anything. She imagined stepping through the doors of the college just like the male students. She imagined sitting in a lecture theatre, making notes in her notebook. She imagined going on the medical rounds as a real doctor!

Then cold reality set in. Studying cost money. Undaunted, Beatrice began rapidly going through her various options. She could work as a teacher and save up. Perhaps her parents might be able to help with a loan, which she could repay. Perhaps even Charles –

Mrs Lawrence, who had been standing quietly, now broke in. 'This is where I come in, Miss Diamond. But I hope I may call you Beatrice?'

The older lady came round the counter and took Beatrice's hand in her uninjured one. 'I wanted to thank you for your great presence of mind during the march. Without you, I might have suffered a lot more. I know how long it would take you to save up the fees necessary for your medical training, and I'd like to pay for you.'

Beatrice opened her mouth to protest, but Mrs Lawrence pressed her hand. 'I understand, my dear, and if it worries you to accept a gift, then once you are qualified and earning money as a doctor, you can pay me back. But I have too much money, and I'll only waste it on things like cars. You would make a wonderful doctor, and it would make me very happy if you would allow me to help you.'

Beatrice switched her gaze from Mrs Lawrence to Miss Moonshine, who was watching them both, an enigmatic smile on her face. 'Of course you must accept, Beatrice dear. After all, you and Constance will be family one day.' The old lady clapped her hand to her mouth, an expression of dismay on her face. 'Oh, dear. Perhaps I've said too much.'

Beatrice reddened. She took in Mrs Lawrence's happy expression. Family? What did Miss Moonshine mean?

Mrs Lawrence turned and gave her friend a stern glance. 'Miss Moonshine, really.'

But Beatrice could tell Edward's mother was secretly pleased at the idea of her one day being family. She was secretly very pleased indeed.

## *Chapter Six*

It was a while before Beatrice could take up a place at medical college. These things take time, but the country had waited

**Helena Fairfax is a freelance editor and author. Her novels have been shortlisted for several awards, including the Exeter Novel Prize and the Global Ebook Awards. Helena lives in an old mill village on the edge of the Yorkshire moors with her husband and their rescue dog, Lexi.**

helenafairfax.com

# The Man in Her Dreams

*By Jacqui Cooper*

*Laura*

'I'm sorry, love, I hate to let you down but someone's rung in sick. They need me at work.'

Even as he spoke, James was pulling on a shirt and searching for a tie. He had only just started this new job after being out of work for a while and though Laura knew he was right to go, she couldn't hide her disappointment over missing their day out.

James, as usual, was making a complete hash of knotting his tie and she stepped close to do it for him. 'Do you think you'll be able to get away early? We could still go for a walk.'

'I doubt it. Colin has some kind of stomach bug. He won't be in all day.'

Colin was the other weatherman at the local TV station where James now worked. Laura had met him. He was a nice man. It was a shame he was ill.

*If* he was ill.

James read her doubt. 'It's work, Laura.' His tone

sharpened. 'Do you want to check my call log?' Angrily he offered his phone.

'No,' she said quickly, knowing she had to trust him. Without trust she may as well pack her bag now.

His gaze softened and he pulled her close. 'I won't let you down again,' he whispered. 'I love you too much.'

She loved him too. They might have been through the wringer in recent months but their lives were back on track now. She had to believe that.

'How do I look?' he asked, standing back and flashing his twinkling TV-weatherman smile.

She laughed. 'Great.'

She could tell he was eager to be off now. 'What will you do all day? Carry on with the unpacking?'

They had only moved in a couple of weeks ago. There was plenty to do but the sun was shining and she was tired of being cooped up. 'I'll probably go out.'

'Make something nice for dinner. You know what Mum's like.' He kissed her and was gone.

Laura wandered around the new house. The main rooms were fairly habitable, though there were still piles of boxes waiting to be unpacked. The bed in the spare room still had to be made up for James's mother's visit, and Laura's new studio needed to be set up, but today, the sunshine called. She grabbed her car keys.

The nearest town, Haven Bridge, was pretty and picturesque and, this early in the year, not too full of tourists.

Happily exploring the quirky shops, Laura almost missed Miss Moonshine's boutique. Once spotted, though, the display in the window drew her like a magnet. A bell tinkled as she pushed the door open.

The subtle scent of incense and essential oils reached her and she breathed deeply; her kind of shop.

A tiny woman in a flowing, sleeveless lace gown was dusting the displays with what looked like an ostrich feather. A glittering black hairband scraped her silvery hair back off her face. Her eyebrows were arched and high. Miss Moonshine presumably. She nodded to Laura, who smiled back.

Taking her time, Laura browsed the shelves and display tables. The shop was crammed with things she desperately wanted but knew she didn't need.

A tiny dog, sleeping in an equally tiny basket, drew her attention. It was exquisitely detailed, a toy any child would love –

The dog flicked an ear and she hurriedly backed away. OK, not a toy then.

A collection of jewellery on a table caught her eye next – in particular, a delicate pendant dangling by a fine silver chain from a branch of bleached driftwood. It had an oval outer ring of silver, with a glittering blue fire opal in the centre. The way it caught the light, it resembled an eye, winking at her.

Laura reached for it and as her fingers touched the stone she suddenly saw, not Miss Moonshine's shop but... a garden? A party. She heard voices, laughter, glasses clinking, felt the warmth of the sun on her face, and caught the scent of newly mown grass. A border collie lying under a seat lifted its head and looked right at her, ears pricked. A dark-haired, thirty-something man working the barbecue called to her. 'Daisy? Ready for something to eat –'

The necklace was snatched from Laura's hand and instantly she was back in the shop, blinking in bemusement.

'No touching,' said Miss Moonshine.

Still dazed, Laura glanced at a sign saying, "Browsers welcome."

Miss Moonshine slipped behind the counter and returned with another sign. She replaced the printed, "Browsers welcome", sign with a handwritten one that said, "No touching".

The image of the garden was already fading. 'Sorry,' Laura mumbled.

Miss Moonshine placed the original sign and the necklace on the counter and returned to her dusting. She didn't take her eyes off Laura.

And Laura couldn't take her eyes off the necklace.

She tried. She really tried to like the other necklaces but the fire opal just seemed... better. Miss Moonshine watched with a beady eye.

'Is it for sale?' asked Laura.

'Not to you, dear.'

'I'm sorry?' Only half listening, Laura sidled towards the counter. All she wanted was another look. She wouldn't touch...

Across the shop, Miss Moonshine cleared her throat loudly. Laura jumped, startled to find her hand stretching out towards the necklace.

Miss Moonshine sighed. She walked back to the counter, picked up the necklace and dropped it into a little jewellery box, which she put in a bag and placed in front of Laura.

'Oh, I didn't want to buy it –'

'It's no use to anyone else now,' said Miss Moonshine cryptically, and named a stupidly low price. 'Just be sure to return it when it's done with you.'

'When I'm done with it?'

'You heard me.'

Laura left the shop a few minutes later, the slightly bemused owner of a cheap, but very pretty, necklace.

She had a nice lunch, visited a gallery and got chatting

to the owner, who, once he found out who she was, made a determined bid for his gallery to be allowed to host an exhibition of her paintings. Laura was flattered but non-committal. Of course recognition was always nice but, to be honest, she didn't need the promotion, since she was lucky enough that her artwork was always in demand.

When she returned home, James was already there.

'You haven't made up Mum's room yet,' he said, annoyed.

No, she hadn't. But then presumably, neither had he. 'We can do it now,' she suggested. 'How's Colin?'

'Who?'

'Colin. From work.'

'Oh. Better. He should be back tomorrow. What have you made for dinner?'

'Nothing, I –'

'For heaven's sake, Laura, what have you been doing all day?'

'I went exploring,' she said coolly. 'And if you'd let me finish, I was about to say that since Olivia has found fault with every meal I've ever cooked for her, I bought dinner in the deli. Now, I'm going for a shower, if you wouldn't mind bringing in the shopping.'

'Sorry.' He rubbed his face. 'It's been a long day.'

Standing under the shower, Laura reminded herself that Olivia's visits often led to frayed tempers. James adored his mother and always wanted everything to be perfect, whereas Laura had long since accepted she would never measure up in Olivia's eyes.

Was it simply the stress of Olivia's visit that had him on edge? Or had something else happened to ruin his day?

His phone sat on the dresser. Laura itched to check it.

With sheer willpower she turned away and was putting her makeup on when she remembered the necklace and

He thought she was joking. 'It'll be fun. Do you think Bonnie will need a lifejacket?'

Bonnie had her forepaws on the bed, and was staring intently at Daisy. 'She'll be a public embarrassment if she does. Actually, I was wondering about inviting some others along for part of the time.' Mark was Seth's best friend and business partner. Seth wouldn't find it odd if he was one of the guests.

'Really?' He looked disappointed. 'I was kind of looking forward to having you all to myself.'

Ah well, it would do Mark good to miss her for a while. Absence and the heart and all that.

Surreptitiously she checked her phone again. Nothing.

*Laura*

Laura woke late on Sunday morning, slowly emerging from another weird dream. That made three dreams about Daisy and Seth. Not a repeating dream, but each one completely different, like a soap opera playing in her head.

She rolled over to tell James about the dreams but the other half of the bed was empty. Only then did she become aware of voices downstairs.

When she ambled into the kitchen, James and Olivia were finishing breakfast.

'Sorry, I didn't make you anything,' said Olivia. 'I'm not sure when you normally get up.'

'That's OK.'

'I suppose working from home you get used to sleeping late.'

Laura let that go. Back in London she had frequently been in her rented studio hours before James got up for the office.

'Mum and I thought we'd drive around, give her a feel for the local area,' said James.

'Good idea.' Laura put the kettle on.

'Want to come?' he asked.

'I'm sure Laura has plenty to do,' said Olivia.

'That's right. I do. You two go,' said Laura pleasantly.

They left their dishes. So did Laura, carrying her coffee into the conservatory. There she took her necklace off and laid it carefully on the table. It could not be a coincidence that her "dreams" had started the first time she touched it.

She stared at it from every angle. Poked the opal with a finger and suddenly the image of Seth, bare-chested and sitting up in bed with the Sunday papers, blasted into her mind.

While it was a very nice image, she forced herself to "look" around. She could see Seth and the dog but she had no idea what Daisy looked like. In the visions, she *was* Daisy. Or rather, she could see what Daisy saw and hear what Daisy said, though she only had the vaguest impression of her thoughts.

Even more confused than ever, Laura slipped the necklace into her pocket. Tomorrow a return visit to Miss Moonshine's shop appeared to be very much in order.

*

Laura survived Olivia's barbed comments for the rest of the weekend. On Monday James was up early for work. Olivia rose even earlier to cook his breakfast. Sipping coffee, Laura could feel waves of disapproval coming off her mother-in-law, but James was a grown man. He made his own breakfast every day.

After he had left, Olivia attempted small talk. 'So what are your plans for the house?'

'I'd like to lift all the carpets,' said Laura. 'Once I see what condition the floorboards are in, I'll think about staining and varnishing them.'

Olivia sucked air through her teeth. 'I should imagine that will make the house very cold in winter and expensive to heat.' She looked around the sunny kitchen. 'What about these walls? Magnolia would make the room look bigger.'

Laura had only finished painting the kitchen last week, in time for Olivia's visit. The tin of primrose-yellow paint still sat on the windowsill and you could smell the new paint. 'It's an idea.'

Thankfully Olivia left for her appointment with the estate agent before Laura killed her.

Laura had planned to spend the day sorting out her studio. The thought filled her with anticipation but before starting she put her necklace on and drove into town, disappointed to find a sign in Miss Moonshine's window declaring the shop closed for two weeks.

Heading back to the car, she lingered for a moment on a footbridge over the canal, admiring the intricate artwork on the gaily coloured narrowboats and barges, which reminded her of Seth and Daisy's holiday. Automatically her hand sought the necklace –

*Daisy*

On her way to work Daisy had checked her phone repeatedly, increasingly annoyed that there was still nothing from Mark. Of course, working alongside Seth made things difficult for him.

Daisy loved Seth. He was a good man, thoughtful and generous, good to look at, and a good provider. She would never, ever leave him, but she had never been able to resist the adrenaline rush of an affair. The fact that Seth and Mark were friends only added to the thrill.

She was at work when he finally phoned.

'I miss you,' he said.

'Miss you too. Where's Seth?'

'Gone out to meet a client. What are you doing?'

Daisy dressed windows for a major high-street store. Right now she was up to her knees in summer fashion, sunglasses and beach bags, trying to wrestle a mannequin into a pair of skinny jeans whilst balancing her phone under her chin.

A leg fell off and she swore. Then she dropped her phone. Bending to pick both up, she realised her antics had attracted the attention of the queue at the bus stop.

'Got to go,' she said and hung up.

*Laura*

Laura blinked. She'd just had a very disconcerting moment or two before she figured out that Daisy was dressing a shop dummy.

Who was she talking to? The call seemed... intimate, yet she wasn't talking to Seth. So who?

She lingered, staring down at the canal, convinced more than ever that she was living in a television drama.

At home she opened the door of her new studio with a sigh of deep satisfaction. In London she and her friend Jarrod had rented studio space in an old warehouse. But this was all hers. The building still smelled of the carpentry workshop it had been previously, but soon the intoxicating smells of linseed and oil paint would dominate.

Boxed and crated canvases stood neatly against one wall. Not as many as there should have been but Laura refused to dwell on that. At least the sale had raised enough to bail them out of the mess James had put them in.

She wondered how he was really doing. He said everything was good but she couldn't help worrying. She hoped he was attending his meetings. She hoped the long hours he put in were really at work. But she had done all she could. The rest was up to him.

She swept the floor and washed windows till late afternoon, when hunger drew her back to the house.

Olivia was in the kitchen. Great. James must have given her a key. 'I made you a sandwich,' Olivia said.

'Thanks.' Laura fell gratefully on the food. 'I forget to eat sometimes when I'm working. Hopefully that will improve now I have my own studio.'

Olivia sniffed. 'A luxury if you ask me.'

'It's my living, Olivia. I don't consider it a luxury.'

'If you had a nice office job you wouldn't need a studio.'

Laura had no idea if Olivia genuinely didn't know how successful an artist she was, or if she knew and didn't care. She put her sandwich down.

'I'm an artist. I need somewhere to work.'

'You could try not being an artist. Get a proper job and take some of the burden off James.'

Laura had given up her flat and her friends. She had sold her paintings, used her savings, moved away from everything she knew, all to give James a fresh start. Resentment simmered inside her but she held her tongue.

'When he lost his job, for instance,' continued Olivia. 'He was so stressed, poor lamb and what did you do to help?'

If only she knew. But James had begged Laura to say nothing to his mother and she wouldn't break her promise.

'We both love your son, Olivia,' she said tightly. 'Shall we just leave it at that?'

*

Olivia left on Wednesday with a list of properties to consider and a vow to return in a few weeks when she had arranged some viewings.

'Be great to see more of Mum,' said James after she had gone.

'Mm.'

'Could you two just try to get on?' he snapped.

He'd been irritable lately. 'Is everything all right, James?'

He sighed. 'Of course. Sorry. Just the pressure of a new job, that's all. And you and Mum at loggerheads doesn't help. Everything is fine.'

She hoped so.

He took her hands in his. 'It really is fine, Laura. I won't pretend it's not difficult. But I gave you my word. I won't let you down again.'

She nodded, praying he was right. She had forgiven him once. She didn't think she had it in her to do it again.

*Daisy*

Cruising on the narrowboat was actually more fun than Daisy had imagined; like living in a doll's house. Seth was in his element, happy to do all the hard work. Even though it was only June, the sun shone every day, and Daisy sunned herself on deck in her new bikini.

Seth had packed the fridge full of gourmet foods but most evenings they stopped at a waterside pub to eat. Then they would spend the rest of the evening sitting under the stars drinking prosecco.

Every night before bed Seth walked Bonnie along the bank and Daisy sneaked a quick, furtive call to Mark.

'I miss you,' he said, and she would hug herself and smile.

On the Saturday, halfway through the holiday, Daisy was in her usual spot on deck, smearing on sunscreen, when voices hailed them from the bank.

She felt a frisson of expectation.

'Mark?' She heard the surprise in Seth's voice. 'Rosie? Dylan?'

Daisy hurried to meet the new arrivals. 'Surprise, darling,' she told Seth. 'It seemed crazy to be in Oxford and not call Rosie and Dylan. I couldn't believe it when I heard Mark was visiting, so of course I invited him too.'

Seth smiled as she had known he would, because any other response would be rude.

Mark held up beer, the bottles dripping with condensation. 'We don't come empty-handed.'

Before long they had a party going. Seth and Dylan talked narrowboats and horsepower while Daisy showed Rosie and Mark the living space. Of course the interior was so compact she couldn't help brushing up against Mark. In her bikini. Repeatedly. He was pretty flustered by the time they emerged again.

'I'm sorry, darling.' Daisy leaned into Seth, enjoying Mark's jealousy. 'We haven't seen Rosie and Dylan for such a long time. I know you said no visitors, but I thought it would be nice to catch up.'

'It is,' he agreed.

'It's only a day, Seth. Then it'll be just me and you again.'

He smiled and kissed her sunburnt nose. 'Can I refuse you anything?'

The impromptu party was a great success. By early evening they had run out of beer and Mark offered to make a quick run to the nearest shop.

'I'll come with you,' said Daisy, 'if you give me a few minutes to throw some clothes on.'

Mark flicked a nervous glance at Seth. 'There's no need –'

'Take her,' said Seth, easily. 'She's barely been inside a shop for a whole week. She must be suffering from withdrawal.'

Daisy dressed quickly. They were only just out of sight when Mark made a grab for her. 'You're driving me crazy,' he growled.

'Good.' Giggling, she wriggled away.

He caught her again. And kissed her –

*Laura*

The shock hurtled Laura out of her daydream.

She had been sitting in her garden, sketchpad on her knee, ostensibly looking for inspiration but in reality enjoying a fly-on-the-wall experience of a narrowboat holiday.

Everything had all been fun and relaxing until –

She felt slightly nauseous. What was Daisy thinking? Seth seemed a nice guy, devoted to her. How could she do that to him? And with his best friend too!

Except Daisy wasn't real. Seth wasn't real. She breathed deeply. Not real. All in my head.

She dropped the sketch pad onto the grass. She didn't feel like drawing any more.

Next morning she was outside Miss Moonshine's shop at nine o'clock. She'd been back a few times in the intervening weeks, but either the shop was closed or Miss Moonshine wasn't there, and the teenage goth in charge was no help.

Thankfully, at five past nine Miss Moonshine herself arrived and unlocked the door. Laura followed her inside.

Miss Moonshine listened to her highly agitated tale and nodded sagely. 'The two necklaces were made in the eighteenth century for twin sisters. The young ladies were devastated at the thought of being separated when one of their husbands decided to move the family to the New World. The story goes, they approached a local witch who cast a spell on the necklaces their father had given them. Wearing them, they would always be able to keep in touch with one another. But on the way to the port the young wife's carriage was attacked by a highwayman. She was killed and her necklace was never recovered. Legend has it that both necklaces have been out there ever since, trying to reconnect...'

'Really?' said Laura, agog.

'No. Of course not, dear. It's just a necklace. Probably made in China.'

'But what about the dreams?'

'I can only assume you have too much time on your hands and an overactive imagination.'

'You behaved very oddly when I bought it,' Laura pointed out.

For the first time she saw something flicker in Miss Moonshine's eyes. 'Do you enjoy the dreams?' she asked, finally.

'Mostly,' admitted Laura.

'Then wear it when you do. Remove it when you don't.'

The necklace lay on the counter between them. For all Miss Moonshine's apparent indifference, Laura noticed she hadn't touched it. 'Should I return it?'

'Do you want to?'

No. She didn't.

'Well then.' Miss Moonshine picked up her ostrich feather and began to dust, the matter closed.

At the door Laura paused. 'Are the people in my dreams real?'

'I'd imagine they are as real as you want them to be.'

That was no answer. As she crossed the bridge Laura once more glanced down at the narrowboats, wondering if one of them could be the actual boat Daisy and Seth were renting. She stopped abruptly, apologising to the people who bumped into her.

There was one way she could find out if the dreams were real. She had seen Mark's number come up on Daisy's phone often enough. She could ring it right now...

And then what? If he answered, what would she do? 'Hi, you don't know me but stop sleeping with your best friend's wife, you rat?'

Of course not.

She headed home, the necklace in her pocket rather than round her neck, too wary to wear it for fear of what she might see.

*Daisy*

The Laura dreams were becoming a drag. At any time, no matter what Daisy was doing, the other woman could just pop into her head. Sometimes Laura was watching *her*. At other times, Daisy was watching her. It was the weirdest feeling.

She had witnessed the conversation between Laura and the batty old woman in the shop. She had even seen the necklace in Laura's hand. It was exactly like her own opal necklace which she'd had for years without experiencing anything like this.

Daisy didn't believe it was any kind of eighteenth-century spell but she did have to accept that somehow, the necklaces were connecting her to Laura.

Uneasy, she removed her necklace and didn't wear it again for the remainder of the holiday.

Once she was home she googled Miss Moonshine's shop, which she had the impression was somewhere in darkest Yorkshire. If the shop was real it might mean... well, she had no idea what it would mean.

The shop didn't have a website – and what business didn't these days? – which meant it wasn't real.

Breathing a sigh of relief, Daisy fastened her favourite necklace around her throat once more.

*Laura*

The summer rolled on and though her studio was now ready, Laura's days had not been at all productive.

She tried to blame the ongoing anxiety about James, who remained moody. But the truth was, she was becoming addicted to the Seth and Daisy dreams, living their lives when she should have been living her own.

Then, to crown it all, just this morning James had announced that Olivia was returning to view some shortlisted properties.

Laura was in the garden with her sketchpad, enjoying the peace and quiet while she still could, when a knock drew her to the front door.

'Jarrod?' She shrieked in delight.

'In the flesh.'

He was her oldest friend. 'You have no idea how good it is to see you,' she said, ushering him inside.

He brandished wine and a bunch of flowers she recognised from her own flower beds. 'Some friends were driving up for an exhibition in Leeds so I cadged a lift. I only have a few hours but you've gone so quiet I had to check on you.'

There was genuine concern in his eyes and she immediately felt guilty.

'It's been hectic, with the move and everything.' Laura walked him through the house and out to the back garden, grabbing a couple of wine glasses on the way. 'Come and see my studio and we can catch up.'

When he had done admiring the studio she led him back to the patio, where they sat in the sun, drinking wine.

'So,' he said, 'tell Uncle Jarrod everything.'

She knew he wasn't talking about work. Jarrod had been the one to catch James in her studio, picking through her paintings, looking for what he could sell. He had been there when she confronted James and he broke down, finally admitting his gambling problem.

'James likes his new job,' she said carefully. 'He's going to his Gamblers Anonymous meetings regularly.'

'I'm glad.'

It had been the darkest of times. James had lost his job, not as a direct result of the gambling, but because of the time spent in the casino or racetrack trying to recoup his losses when he should have been at work. His debt was off the scale. Laura's too, since he knew her PIN and had maxed her cards. When the legitimate sources of borrowing had dried up he had turned to dodgy backstreet lenders.

Caught stealing her paintings, it had all come pouring out. He was so very sorry. It was an addiction, an illness. He would seek help. He would never be so stupid again.

Laura had sold paintings that held huge sentimental value, just to bail him out, on the condition that he sought professional help. They'd moved to Yorkshire to give him a fresh start.

'We're doing OK,' she repeated.

The wine was finished. Laura went inside for another bottle and picked up a bag of crisps too.

When she returned Jarrod was leafing through her sketchpad. 'Wow. Who is this?' he said, admiring her many sketches of Seth.

Laura felt her cheeks flame. 'I don't know,' she admitted, wanting to snatch her sketchpad away.

'This is truly excellent. You don't normally do portraits... wait? You don't know?'

So then it all came tumbling out, about Miss Moonshine, and the necklace. About the dreams and Daisy and Mark and Bonnie. But mostly she talked about how angry she was about the way Seth was being treated.

Jarrod listened. When she finished, he eyed the wine. 'Sure you're not hitting the bottle?'

'Of course not.'

'Sniffing paint thinner?'

'That was what James said.'

'So it's a mystical or supernatural experience. Do you think this Miss Moonshine knows more than she's letting on?'

He accepted it? Just like that? She realised he was tipsy. 'She says not. But I'm assuming I'm having these dreams for a reason. I can only hope I find out what that is before they drive me crazy.'

'Can I see the necklace?'

She fished it out of her blouse and held it out. He leaned close, gingerly lifting the pendant. He closed his eyes and screwed his face up in a picture of intense concentration. 'I can't feel anything.'

'Laura?'

They both jumped, banging heads.

Olivia? Oh crap.

Her mother-in-law's sweeping glance took in the empty bottles, and the two slightly inebriated friends. 'I rang but you didn't pick up so I took a taxi from the station. I hope I'm not interrupting your... *work*.' She glared at Jarrod. 'I'll see you inside, Laura. Once your friend is gone.' She turned on her heel.

'Wow. Scary headmistress type. James's mother, I take it.'

She sighed. 'And here I thought her opinion of me couldn't get any worse. Oh well.'

'Does she know what you did for James?' asked Jarrod as she walked him to the gate.

She shook her head. 'No.'

Laura trudged back to the house to face the music.

'Does James know that you are seeing another man?' Olivia demanded immediately.

Laura almost laughed. Jarrod had a much-loved husband at home. 'He's a friend from London.'

'Another artist?' She made him sound like a serial killer. 'Why am I not surprised? Who else would have time to sit about drinking wine all day? I presume he too is lucky enough to have someone at home to pay the bills?'

That was going too far. 'My finances are nothing to do with you, Olivia.'

'Aren't they? Considering I'm paying for this house?'

'What?'

'You heard me,' Olivia spat. 'James has had to take a junior position. Do you think he earns enough to finance your hobbies and pay the mortgage as well? He couldn't even raise the deposit.'

Laura's world went still. 'What are you talking about?'

'I'm talking about my poor boy working himself into an early grave so you can have your own studio and indulge your hobby.'

Blood thundered in Laura's ears. She chose her words carefully. 'Olivia, there is no mortgage on this house. I bought it outright.'

'You?' Olivia sneered. 'With what?'

'I earn a good living as an artist.'

'Stop deluding yourself, Laura.'

'Google me. I repeat – I make good money. I always have. I have never been "kept" by James.'

For the first time, Olivia faltered. 'That makes no sense.'

'Are you giving James money?' asked Laura, her mouth dry.

'Just for the mortgage.' Olivia rallied. 'Just to help him out.'

'Is that why you are selling your house?' Laura's heart felt as if it was being crushed, compacted as cold and hard as a diamond.

'W… what I do with my money is my own business,' said Olivia, but she looked uncertain.

And suddenly Laura saw things clearly. 'You knew,' she said, horrified. 'You knew about his gambling.'

Olivia wouldn't meet her eye. 'There was a bit of trouble when he was at university,' she admitted. 'But he doesn't do that any more. He's better. He promised me he was better. He just needs our support.'

For the first time since Laura had known her, Olivia looked her age. 'You need to speak to James,' said Laura quietly.

Which was exactly what she planned to do.

*Daisy*

Well! Who would have thought that the perma-tanned weatherman had secrets!

Daisy had been kept entertained on her commute home, watching Laura and her gay friend grow more and more merry on the wine. She might even have felt a tiny twinge of sympathy for Laura when the dragon lady appeared to spoil the fun, if not for the fact she'd recently begun to sense a certain level of judgement coming from her, especially where Mark was concerned. Which was rich, considering Daisy had also sensed just how much the other woman liked to look at Seth.

At home, she found Seth in the kitchen.

'Lasagne?' She kissed his cheek and put all thoughts of Laura out of her head. 'You know I'm on a diet.'

'There's a large salad to go with it. And you don't need to diet.'

'Right answer.'

He handed her a glass of wine. 'You look tired.'

'I'm still having these weird dreams.' She'd told Seth about them. 'Do we know any artists?'

He considered. She could actually see his thoughts processing, like the computers he loved so much. 'Can't think of any. You're dreaming about art?'

'She's supposed to be a successful artist but she doesn't seem to do much work. There's a lot of staring at a blank canvas.'

'A message from your subconscious?' suggested Seth. 'Waiting to paint your future?'

She laughed. 'Maybe. How was work?' She kept her tone casual.

'Busy. Mark has a new project. He's out of the office a fair bit but hopefully it's raising our profile so I don't mind the extra work.'

'That's good.'

He nodded. 'It was a brilliant move to partner up with him. It's handy being able to leave someone I trust in charge when I'm not there.'

Daisy kept her gaze lowered.

'I'm pretty sure he's got a woman on the go,' continued Seth.

She almost choked. 'What makes you say that?'

'We shared a house all through uni, remember? I know that look. He's cagey though. I'm beginning to suspect she's married.'

Daisy played with her food. 'But he seems happy?'

'Very. I hope it works out. I'd like to see him settle down. He doesn't have a great track record with women, as you well know. Remember that Spanish au pair?'

Daisy wasn't interested in Mark's previous conquests.

'While I think about it, I'll be away on Friday. Sarah's invited me to see the new baby.'

'Friday? That's a shame. I could have come with you but Mark's out of the office that day.'

'I don't think she's up for too many visitors just yet anyway,' Daisy said quickly. 'But I can't wait to see the baby. I'll probably be late back.'

'No problem.' His eyes twinkled. 'Are we thinking we like babies now?'

Seth had never made any secret of his longing to be a father.

'We'll see how cute this one is,' she said evasively.

*Laura*

At first James had been full of bluster. Then full of anger. In the end he had broken down. He promised to do better. He offered up his second phone. He swore he would actually go to the Gamblers Anonymous meetings she'd thought he was already attending. But Laura had had enough. He had lied to her almost every day of their marriage and now it was over.

After he left, she started painting again. Day after day, portraits of Seth. On the narrowboat. Playing with Bonnie.

Like her, Seth was living a lie. Only he, poor soul, had yet to find out.

*Seth*

On Friday, Seth had forgotten Daisy was away until he let himself into the empty house, Bonnie skipping in front of him. One of the good things about being self-employed was being able to take his dog to work.

He checked his phone. A voicemail from Daisy saying she was on her way home and should be there in half an hour.

Should he make something for dinner? It had been a long day without Mark to lighten the load at work and he decided he was too tired to cook. Fish and chips it was, then. If he left now he should be back just as Daisy got home.

'Fancy a walk?' he asked Bonnie. Stupid question. She leapt and bounced, barking with excitement, and her plumy tail knocked something off the coffee table. Bending down, he found Daisy's opal necklace and he shook his head. Why did she leave things like that lying around? She'd be the first to complain about the vet's bill if Bonnie swallowed it, which she was more than capable of doing.

He put the necklace in his jacket pocket then clipped on Bonnie's lead. 'Come on then.'

*Laura*

Laura was stunned.

She had tentatively tried to tune into Daisy, but suspecting she was spending the day with Mark she had been ready to make a quick exit if necessary.

Time after time she had felt nothing and now, suddenly... *Seth?*

Her shock was so great she almost severed the connection but at the last minute, managed to grab it and hold on. It was tenuous, nothing like the link she had with Daisy, but it was there.

Seth must have the necklace. And somehow she and Seth were connected.

He was talking to the dog, something about a vet's bill, which made her smile.

Laura "walked" with him and Bonnie through a pleasant neighbourhood. A man said hello. A young boy with his mother stopped to pat Bonnie. Laura liked that he seemed to know his neighbours

After ten minutes he stopped outside a fish and chip shop, leaving Bonnie outside where he could see her.

Another ten minutes and he was back out in the evening sunshine, making the same journey in reverse. Somewhere in the distance she heard sirens blaring – a city sound that used to be so familiar but one Laura rarely heard in Haven Bridge.

Daisy still wasn't home. Seth put the oven on to keep their supper warm, then checked his phone. No new messages.

When he called Daisy's number it went straight to voicemail.

'Should we eat ours now?' he asked Bonnie, who thumped her tail in agreement.

The dog barked one second before the doorbell rang. Laura noticed a blue flashing light outside the window.

'I'm coming,' Seth called as the bell sounded again. He took his jacket off on the way to the door. Hung it up –

The connection snapped.

## One year later …

*Laura*

Since the divorce, Laura had entered into one of the most productive phases of her career. Her workshop was filled with new canvases, so many she had eventually agreed to an exhibition at the local gallery.

Today, after calling in to see how the exhibition was going, she popped in to Miss Moonshine's for a chat. They hadn't exactly become friends but Laura had come to enjoy her company, and for her part, Miss Moonshine didn't seem to mind her presence.

Laura hadn't had so much as a glimpse of either Seth or Daisy for over a year now, though her imagination continued to run riot.

'Do you think the necklace is finished with me?' she asked Miss Moonshine.

'Perhaps,' said Miss Moonshine, putting the kettle on.

'I mean, Daisy might just have got fed up with being watched and stopped wearing it.'

'True.'

'Or she could have chucked it away.'

'Also true.'

'Or something might have happened to her.'

'It might.'

Miss Moonshine was like a therapist, listening without ever voicing an opinion.

Laura stood up to leave. 'Do you think Napoleon would like a walk by the canal?' she asked.

The two women looked at the tiny dog, who was, as usual, sleeping in his equally tiny basket. Napoleon's little body didn't move but Laura heard a soft growl.

'I think not,' said Miss Moonshine. 'He rather went off the canal after he fell in during the celebrations for the coronation.' The dog's head snapped up and he glared at her. 'Which is something we don't talk about,' said Miss Moonshine hastily.

'Coronation?' Laura frowned. 'What coronation?'

Napoleon cocked his head at Miss Moonshine, as if he too was interested in the answer.

'Er, the May Queen,' said Miss Moonshine. 'Of course I mean the May Queen's coronation. They have it every year on the canal as part of the flower festival.'

'Oh. Of course.'

Leaving the shop, Laura walked along the canal anyway, since there was nothing waiting for her at home. Finding a sunny bench, she sat down, watching the stately passage of the narrowboats.

The simple truth was, real or imaginary, she missed Seth and Daisy. More than she missed James.

A narrowboat nosed round the bend and she watched idly as it approached. A dog stood on deck, like a figure head, tongue lolling. A collie, like Bonnie, she thought wistfully.

As the boat drew closer the dog began to bark. The man steering called out but the dog didn't stop. In fact the barking grew more frantic. Now the dog was running in excited circles. Laura worried it might fall in the water. Presumably the man did too. His voice sharpened. And then, to Laura's astonishment, the dog launched itself off the boat.

She jumped to her feet in alarm. The boat was too far out for the dog to land safely and sure enough it splashed into the water, surfacing a moment later and doggy-paddling towards Laura.

Still yelling, the man steered to the bank.

The collie had reached the side now but it was too steep for it to clamber out. On her knees, Laura grabbed for it. Luckily it wore a collar and she managed somehow to haul it to safety. Her reward was to be knocked on her backside as the wet dog licked her face.

The man was on the bank, tying the boat up. 'I am so sorry. I have no idea what got into her. She's never done anything like that before.' He dragged the dog off Laura and offered a hand to help her up. 'Your dress! Sorry. Bonnie, that's enough!'

*Bonnie?* Taking the outreached hand, Laura looked up into the greenest eyes she had ever seen. *Seth?*

'I can't believe she just did that,' he repeated, bemused.

*Seth?*

'Are you OK?'

*Seth?* It couldn't be.

Her shocked silence seemed to worry him. Or maybe it was the stupid expression on her face.

'Are you hurt?' he asked anxiously.

'I... I'm fine.' She finally found her voice. 'No harm done.'

Laura wanted to throw her arms around him and hug him like a long-lost friend, but of course she could do no such thing.

Seth? And Bonnie? Bonnie and Seth? She tried to wrap her head around it but couldn't. Seth, in the flesh. The fit, hard-muscled flesh.

She looked beyond him to the boat, searching for Daisy, but saw no sign of her or anyone else.

'I don't know what got into her.'

'It's OK. Really.'

'Look at the state of your dress. Let me pay for it. Or dry cleaning. Or something.'

'It's just a bit damp.'

Bonnie took that moment to shake herself, showering them both with even more canal water.

Seth made a face. 'Then let me at least buy you a drink.'

'There's really no need.' She couldn't take her eyes off him.

'Please. You'll be doing me a favour. I don't think I've spoken to anyone but this crazy dog for days.'

He hadn't spoken to anyone? Again she glanced past him for a glimpse of Daisy.

Seth followed her gaze. 'Some men buy a Harley Davidson. Others a sports car,' he said ruefully.

'Are you saying a narrowboat is your mid-life crisis?'

Emotion flickered in his eyes but he smiled. 'Something like that. I'm Seth, by the way. Now, about that drink?'

'Laura.' There was no way she was turning his invitation down so they walked a short distance to a pub with tables outside. Seth went in while Bonnie rested her wet head on Laura's knee.

'She doesn't always take to strangers,' said Seth, returning a few minutes later with the drinks. 'It's almost as if she knows you.'

Laura thought back to the times she'd been connected to Daisy. The dog had always somehow seemed to know when she was there.

'So,' asked Seth. 'Are you on holiday?'

She shook her head. 'I've lived here over a year now. In another 20 I might be considered a local. What about you?' With effort, she kept her tone casual, but she had so many questions.

'Travelling. Where the fancy takes me.' Again she glimpsed a deep emotion. This time it registered as pain. 'Some might call it drifting.'

'On your own?'

'These days.'

So where was Daisy? Laura was so desperate to know, she was practically hyperventilating, unable to believe he was really here, and at the same time, terrified she would say something that would reveal how much she knew about him.

'If you are free tomorrow, would you have lunch with me?' asked Seth, suddenly. 'To apologise properly?'

Laura felt she knew him well enough to know that meant Daisy was out of the picture. 'I...'

'I'm sorry,' he said quickly, his face colouring. 'That was presumptive. I'm not very good at this.'

'I'd love to,' she said. 'I'm divorced. Oh heck, I didn't mean – I'm not very good at this either.'

'Great. I don't mean great that you're divorced, I mean – oh hell.'

Suddenly they were both laughing.

As they stood up to go, Seth turned serious. 'Laura, I need to get this out of the way, and sooner rather than later. My wife died last year. I'm new to all of this. It's just been me and Bonnie for a while now.'

Her heart stopped. Of all the things she had considered, this was not one of them. 'D – died? H – how?'

'Car accident.' He swallowed. 'Along with my best friend.'

'I'm sorry,' she said, stunned.

'So am I, for telling you like this, but I thought it was only fair. Still want to have lunch?'

She nodded wordlessly and he looked much relieved. 'I'll make lunch on *Firefly* if that's OK? If you give me your number I'll let you know where I'm moored.'

The sun was still shining, but watching him walk away, Laura shivered.

Daisy was dead? And Mark too? Poor Seth. How on earth had he survived a double blow like that?

Her blood ran cold. Did he know about Daisy and Mark?

Laura could barely swallow around the lump in her throat. Seth was real and he was single and he had asked her out.

Yet what she knew could break his heart all over again.

*

She went on the date. Of course she did. She could no more have kept away than she could have decided not to breathe that day.

Bonnie announced her approach and Seth appeared so quickly he must have been watching for her. Her heart leapt as he took her hand to help her on board.

'Sorry,' he said. 'Rain wasn't part of the plan. We'll eat inside if that's OK with you?'

Inside, the narrowboat was as neat as a pin. 'This is great,' she said, and meant it.

'I know. Can't carry much baggage with this as your living space.'

'You live here? I mean, you don't have a home?'

'Not any more. I've been rethinking my life since...you know. Empire building seems a bit pointless these days so I sold my house and my business and bought this.' He grimaced. 'I warned myself not to be maudlin. Should have listened to my own advice.'

The meal he served was simple but delicious. Laura almost asked if he had stocked the fridge with gourmet foods like last time and only just caught herself.

There was no lull in the conversation. Not one. It was the perfect first date. Except standing in the shadows was Daisy. Not literally, of course, but Laura could feel her presence coming between them.

She knew Daisy's secret. And she had a secret all of her own.

And Seth had to know about both before their relationship could go any further.

'Seth, there's something I have to tell you.'

'You don't like boats? Or dogs?'

She shook her head and took a deep breath. 'Remember how you said Bonnie seemed to know me?'

'Yes?'

She gulped. 'This isn't easy.'

He was still only curious. 'Tell me.'

'It's about Daisy.'

Seth went very still. 'I never told you her name.'

Oh Lord. There was no going back now. 'Did she ever mention strange dreams about a woman? An artist?'

'What's this about?' he demanded, face reddening. 'Do you think this is funny?'

She was making a complete mess of this. Unable to think

of anything else, she reached into her blouse and drew out the fire opal.

Seth paled. 'How the hell did you get my wife's necklace?'

'It's not Daisy's. It's mine. My dreams started over a year ago when I bought it.'

'This is ridiculous,' he said curtly. 'I don't know what your game is –'

'You and Daisy had a garden party. Then you went on a narrowboat holiday. She wasn't keen and invited some friends to join you.'

His expression hardened but he said nothing.

'The necklaces somehow connected us. We could see and hear what the other person was up to. I don't understand it. Neither did she.'

Still he said nothing.

'I know it sounds crazy. But there's something else. Something important. It's about Daisy and Mark...'

'About their affair?' he said savagely.

She was startled. 'You knew?'

'They died in his car. I couldn't understand it until one of our "friends" finally took pity on me and explained. Tell me where you fit into all this.' he said coldly.

'I told you. The necklace. Daisy and I were having the same dreams. I mean we were sharing dreams. Sharing lives.'

He stood up. 'I'd like you to leave now.'

Bonnie whined, upset by the tension, as Laura stepped onto the bank. She couldn't bear it. She had found him. And she had lost him.

They couldn't leave it like this.

'There's something I'd like to show you. Will you come with me?'

'You have nothing I want to see.'

'Please, Seth. It's not far.'

'This is a waste of time.' But he shut Bonnie inside and jumped onto the bank.

They walked along the towpath without talking. When they reached the town, she led him to the gallery.

There were a few people inside, probably just sheltering from the rain. They paid Laura and Seth no attention.

Seth looked around, clearly puzzled as to why she had brought him here. She didn't speak but allowed him to find the portrait for himself.

'What is this?' he demanded, glancing from the image of him and Bonnie, to Laura, then back to the portrait again.

He peered at the title. '*Unknown man and dog*?'

'As you can see, the paint is dry. I didn't paint this last night.'

Seth swallowed. 'She, Daisy, said the woman in her dreams was an artist.'

He looked at her, his gaze mirroring her own questions. 'How?'

'I don't know.' And she didn't. But he acknowledged the dreams now.

It was a start.

Miss Moonshine's necklace had brought them to this place. Laura didn't think it was done with them yet.

Reaching for Seth's hand, she hoped not.

**Living on the edge of the Yorkshire moors, Jacqui Cooper doesn't have to look far for inspiration for her writing. Her short stories regularly appear in popular women's magazines, including *Woman's Weekly*, *The People's Friend* and *Take a Break*. Writing has always been her dream and she is thrilled to now be able to do it full time.**

# Take a Chance on Me

*By Marie Laval*

## *Chapter One*

*Friday*

The door chimed as Grégoire pushed it open, allowing the rain and the wind into the shop, along with a handful of petals from the rose bushes at the front of the building. It was dark inside, and he hesitated at the doorway. Perhaps the shop was closed. It was, after all, almost five o'clock.

'Come in, dear, and shut the door,' a woman's voice said from the back of the shop. 'You're letting the bad weather in.'

He stepped forward, but the lighting was so dim he bumped into a display table, causing the odd assortment of tins, cups and saucers, and dainty porcelain figures to clatter. What a strange collection. Were these ancient medical implements? And what about that fossilised crocodile skull, complete with teeth?

He shook his head in dismay. How could anyone want to purchase any of this junk? The name of the shop was misleading. Perhaps Miss Moonshine's Wonderful Emporium should be called Miss Moonshine's Weird Emporium.

'Now, dear, what can I do for you?' An elderly woman with snowy white hair cut in a surprisingly trendy asymmetrical bob appeared at his side. She moved fast. Only a few seconds before she'd been at the back of the shop, hadn't she?

Grégoire looked into the woman's hazel eyes. He must be more tired than he'd realised after the flight from Paris and the drive from Leeds airport in the pouring rain across bleak, empty moors. For a second, he completely forgot why he was there.

She smiled and cocked her head to one side. 'So?'

'Ah yes, sorry. I believe this comes from your shop.' He extracted the tiny music box in the shape of a piano from his coat pocket and cranked the mechanism at the side. The last bars of *La Javanaise* tinkled above the sounds of the wind and rain hammering against the shop's arched windows.

The woman gestured towards the box as soon as the music died down. 'May I?'

Grégoire handed it to her. She switched an art deco lamp on, turned the box upside down and traced the contours of the faded sticker with a fingernail painted a dark purple. 'Yes, indeed. I remember this music box very well. I bought it from a French dealer a few years ago. It's vintage 1970s. Still in perfect working condition, so quite rare, I believe.'

The knot in his chest loosened. He was on the right track. 'Can you tell me who you sold it to?'

The woman shook her head. 'I'm afraid I can't give the names of my customers to just anyone.'

He was so close. How could he fail now? He raked his fingers through his hair, still wet from the rain, and flinched when pain lanced through his hand and wrist. Lowering his arm, he flexed his fingers a few times until the pain receded.

'Are you all right?'

The woman's eyes shone with kindness, but anger and

pride made him want to curl his fist, punch the wall and finish the job that the car accident had started. He took a deep breath and gave her a curt nod.

'I'm fine, but it's very important that I find who bought this music box.'

'Why would that be?'

'It was left on my grandfather's grave in Paris, I believe by someone who knew him well. I came here especially to meet them and... thank them.' That's all she needed to know.

'You're French, aren't you?'

He nodded. 'My name is Grégoire Beaufort.'

She arched her thin, white eyebrows. 'The concert pianist? I thought you looked familiar.'

His agent must have been doing something right if an elderly woman who ran a junk shop in a small Yorkshire town knew of him. Perhaps he could use his notoriety to his advantage. At least now she wouldn't suspect him of being a dangerous stranger with sinister motives.

Honesty, however, pushed him to correct her. 'Ex-concert pianist. I don't perform any longer.' In fact, he hadn't touched a piano in the three months since the accident and had no intention of ever playing again.

She smiled and extended her hand. 'Delighted to meet you, Monsieur Beaufort. I am Miss Moonshine, and a great fan of yours. Your renditions of Liszt and Chopin are among the most beautiful and sincere I've ever heard, and I have heard many in my time.'

Her handshake was surprisingly firm for such a small woman. Then again, she wasn't exactly your typical little old lady, more a mixture of old hippy, avant-garde fashion designer and something else – something he couldn't quite put his finger on... but he was daydreaming again.

'*Merci*, but like I said, my performing days are over.'

'I am very sorry to hear that. Did you know Liszt stayed at The White Lion Hotel, not five minutes' walk from here, whilst on a tour of England? He was such an extraordinary, vibrant young man.'

'I had no idea.' Liszt was the composer he had most enjoyed playing, the one whose music touched his soul and made it fly as high as the stars, or pushed it down to the cold depths of despair. All that was in the past.

'I believe your grandfather was Henri Beaufort, the famous pianist and conductor. I was very sorry to hear about the accident. It must have been dreadfully hard to lose him.'

He nodded, a lump forming in his throat.

'How long are you planning to stay in Haven Bridge?'

'I'm not sure. I don't fancy driving back to Leeds in this weather tonight. Can you recommend any local hotel?'

'The Old Bull is very nice. You will find it after the bridge, on your left.'

'About the music box, are you sure you can't help me?'

'I am sorry. I can't, but I hope you have a pleasant stay at The Old Bull. They have entertainment on Friday night. I am sure you'll enjoy it.'

Entertainment? Did she mean stand-up comedy, or dancing? He repressed a sigh, wrapped the music box back in the protective plastic and put it in his pocket. 'Perhaps. Well, goodbye, then.'

She closed the door behind him. It was blowing a gale now. Clouds turned the sky almost black, rain bounced off the pavements. He started walking in the direction of The Old Bull. The shops and cafés in the main street were closing for the day. A few cars drove by and a handful of people ran past him to escape the rain.

Grégoire pulled up his collar and dug his hands into the pockets of his jacket. He should be used to being alone in strange, foreign places. He'd travelled the world often enough. This time, however, was different. He wasn't there to perform, or give a piano masterclass, but to fulfil his grandfather's dying wish.

## *Chapter Two*

*Friday evening – The Old Bull*

'Do you need anything before you start?' Barry called from behind the counter.

Jane dropped her bag next to the piano and shook her head. 'I'm all right, thanks, although I could do with a cup of tea.'

'I take it you want your usual brew, without milk or sugar?'

He pulled a face and the overdramatic look of horror made her laugh. She opened the piano's fallboard and looked around. It was just before seven on a Friday night. The pub should be full, but the bad weather and the football match on the television meant many regulars had chosen to stay at home.

'Let me know when you're ready and I'll turn the music off.' Barry set a steaming mug on the table beside the piano.

Jane took a sip and sighed. 'That's the first cup of tea I've had since breakfast. It's been crazy busy at the café all day, and when I got home I had to bake a birthday cake for Arthur's party.'

'How old is your Arthur now?'

'Three already! I remember the night he was born as if it was yesterday. I was in such a state, Grandma held my hand all night. I hope the weather improves so we can have the party in the garden. It'll be more fun.'

'I've not seen your grandma for a while. How is she doing?'

Jane frowned. 'Soldiering on, and ignoring the doctor's advice to take it easy.'

'Joyce was always a very determined lady.'

'She's stubborn, you mean. Since she decided to help with the choir's performance at the summer fete, she's been driving everybody crazy, including the dogs.'

Barry's hearty laugh boomed. 'She'll have your choir in good shape in no time. She is a great musician, like you. In fact, you two are very similar, give or take a few years, of course. You have her eyes, her smile, even her hairstyle.' He pointed to Jane's short blonde hair.

'I wish I was half as talented as she is.' Jane ran her fingers up and down the keyboard, and her thoughts wandered as she settled into her usual playlist – Elton John, Adele, Sinatra, Kings of Leon, followed by some Leonard Cohen and a couple of ABBA songs.

There was no woman she admired more than her grandmother. As a girl, she had followed her every move at the farm, copied the way she sang, the way she dressed or did her hair. When all her friends were growing their hair, straightening or curling it, she'd kept hers short and smooth, Twiggy-style, and never mind if girls at school sniggered and said she looked like a boy.

It was her grandmother who had brought Jane up. She had taught her to play the piano, sing and read music, as well as helped with her homework, and tended to her grazed knees or bruised heart when she'd fallen in love with unsuitable boys. Her mother had never shown any interest in music, the farm, or her only daughter. She worked in a community centre in London and came to Haven Bridge twice a year, made a lot of noise about the state of the farm, or her daughter's lack of ambition, and disappeared again, leaving behind a cloud of patchouli and promises which everybody knew would remain unfulfilled.

A few more people drifted into the pub. Red-cheeked from the wind and dripping with rain, they didn't look in the mood for a singalong.

Barry walked past, a couple of empty pint glasses in his hand. 'Why don't you go home? It's not going to be a good night.'

She nodded, and finished with the old French song she always played at the end of her set.

*

Grégoire watched the rain bounce on the road from the window of his bedroom on the first floor of the pub. Clouds swallowed the hills and the houses that clung to the slopes. If this was summer, he dreaded to think what winter was like in this place.

Downstairs in the pub someone was playing the piano. This must be the entertainment promised by Miss Moonshine. He unzipped his bag, pulled out a fresh pair of trousers and a shirt, and stepped into the bathroom to take a shower. Ten minutes later, refreshed and changed, he sat down on the bed and was reading the tourist information leaflets he'd picked up from the pub downstairs when his mobile rang. He glanced at the call display.

'Hi, Cassandra.'

'At last! I was starting to believe you were avoiding my calls. We're supposed to have dinner together tonight. Remember?'

He cursed under his breath. The dinner date with Cassandra had completely slipped his mind. 'I'm sorry. I can't make it.'

'But we need to talk about the recital at Salle Pleyel.'

He sighed. Would Cassandra ever accept his concert pianist days were over, and that he'd never play at Salle Pleyel, or anywhere else for that matter?

'I won't perform again, I told you. I'm sure you won't have any trouble finding another pianist.'

'I don't want anybody else. I want you. Listen, Grégoire, we don't have to go out if you don't want to. I'll grab some takeaway dishes from a restaurant and come over.'

'You can't. I'm not in Paris.'

There was a pause. 'Where are you?'

'In England. Yorkshire, to be exact.'

'What? What are you doing there?'

'Chasing after a ghost.'

'You're not making any sense. My poor darling, I know the accident, your injuries and your grandfather's death hit you hard, but you need to pick yourself up. I am worried about you. You're acting very strangely.' Her voice was softer now, almost cajoling.

'There's no need to be worried. I'm taking a holiday, that's all.'

Cassandra said something, but he wasn't listening. Perhaps she was right and he should be worried about his mental health. He could swear the pianist downstairs was now playing *La Javanaise*. But it was impossible! The song might be a classic in France, but who would know it here?

Nobody... except perhaps the person who bought the music box from Miss Moonshine's shop and left it on his grandfather's grave – the woman he was chasing after.

'I have to go.' He ended the call, snatched his keys from the bedside table and ran out of the room.

Grégoire raced down the stairs to the main part of the pub, but by the time he got there, the music had stopped, the fallboard was down and the stool tucked under the piano. Had he imagined it all?

'Hi there.' The landlord, who had introduced himself as Barry, looked at him, puzzled. 'Is everything all right?'

Grégoire cleared his throat and pointed to the piano. 'I thought I heard someone playing, a minute ago.'

Barry nodded. 'That was Jane. She plays here Friday and Saturday nights. You just missed her. She's good, isn't she?'

Grégoire made a non-committal sound. The pianist had been skilled enough, he supposed – at least enough for a backwater pub – but she had played *La Javanaise* with just the right amount of melancholy.

'The last song was very nice.'

'She always closes her gig with that old song. She says it's a French hit from the sixties. Perhaps you know it, being French yourself.'

'I certainly do. It's a classic.'

Barry's face lit up. 'She'll be delighted to hear that. It's a nice tune, but a bit too sad, in my opinion. Most people prefer ABBA to sing along to.'

'Did you say she would be back tomorrow evening?'

'Unless she's too tired after Arthur's birthday party.'

'Arthur?'

Barry laughed. 'Her baby. He's three years old tomorrow. Actually, she calls him her baby but he's not really a baby. He's –'

A woman's piercing shriek from the kitchen interrupted him. 'What the heck was that? Sounds like my new barmaid is being murdered in there! Take a seat. I'll be back in a sec.'

Grégoire sat at the bar, feeling a lot more optimistic about his quest. Jane could be the woman he was looking for – the woman who had left the music box on his grandfather's grave. It was a pity he'd missed her tonight, but he would try to get her address or contact number from Barry later. Failing that, he could always wait for tomorrow...

## *Chapter Three*

*Saturday*

Jane recognised him the moment he stepped in. He had been in the news a lot after his car accident, and of course, with his brown hair and dark eyes, he looked just like a younger version of his grandfather.

He scanned the cake counter and the display of collars, leads and dog toys before looking at the customers enjoying coffee and cake. Dogs stretched at their feet, or wolfed down a biscuit or a bowl of doggy ice cream.

She had been expecting him since Miss Moonshine called that morning, but her heart still beat too fast for comfort. Her fingers shook as she piled up the pup-muffins she'd just colour-coded with icing so that Dixie, the café's Saturday girl, would no longer get mixed up between the blueberry, apple or carrot flavours. There had been several customer complaints lately, although not from the dogs.

The cakes formed a colourful pyramid almost as high as her, and the thought of ducking behind the counter and escaping through the back door was suddenly very tempting. It would, however, be irresponsible, as well as cowardly. Dixie could not be left alone without causing chaos, selling dog cakes to humans and vice versa. What's more, if Grégoire Beaufort had come all this way, he wouldn't leave until he had answers. She'd better sound convincing.

She took a deep breath, wiped her hands on her apron, and forced a smile. 'Hello. Can I help you?'

He narrowed his eyes to look at the paw-shaped name badge pinned to her apron. 'Are you Jane Bowland?' He sounded surprised – disappointed, almost.

She nodded. 'I am.'

He took something out of his pocket and handed it to her. The music box, of course.

'This may sound a little strange,' he started, 'but could you tell me if you bought this music box from Mrs Moonshine's shop?'

It had been stupid of her not to realise that the music box could be traced back to the shop, and Haven Bridge. She should have ripped the label off before taking it to Paris.

She tilted her chin. 'Yes, I did.' There was no need to mention she had bought it at her grandmother's request.

Once again, he looked taken aback. 'I see. May I ask why you left it on Henri Beaufort's grave at the Père Lachaise? He is – I mean, he was my grandfather.'

Now came the tricky bit. She wiped her hands on the sides of her apron. It was hard to make up stories when a man with eyes as deep and dark as a moonless night stared down at her.

'I grew up listening to your grandfather's music. I was very sad to hear about his death and I wanted to pay my respects.' At least *that* was the truth.

Grégoire Beaufort frowned. 'But why choose this particular music box, with that particular song?'

She lowered her gaze and started rearranging the pup-muffins. 'It was the only one in Miss Moonshine's shop, and I happen to love the song.' It sounded lame, but with luck he would believe her.

'You played it last night in the pub, didn't you?'

She looked up. 'How do you know?'

'I'm staying at The Old Bull, and I heard you from my room upstairs. I thought you played it well.'

She gasped and her heart bumped to a stop. Grégoire Beaufort, the world-famous concert pianist, who had performed in the most prestigious concert halls in the world, said she played well?

'Really? You're not just saying that to be kind?'

He smiled, a dimple appearing at the side of his mouth, and her heart skipped another beat. It was no wonder her grandmother had fallen for Henri Beaufort if he had smiled at her that way.

'I never say things I don't mean,' he said. 'I thought you played with great feeling.'

She had no time to bask in the compliment because Mrs Graham walked into the café with her bichon frisé in tow.

'Jane, love, can I have a cappuccino and one of your apple muffins for my little Oscar? And try not to make any mistake this time. The carrot cake Dixie sold me last week gave him dreadful wind.'

'I'll bring them over straightaway.' Jane smiled apologetically at Grégoire Beaufort. 'I'm sorry. I need to see to the customers.'

'Of course. Thank you for taking the trouble to go to Paris and pay your respects to my grandfather. It was very thoughtful of you. I will put the music box back on his grave. Goodbye.'

He looked so sad suddenly that guilt tightened her chest, and she almost called him back to tell him the truth. She bit her tongue, reminding herself she had lied for a very good reason. The trip to Paris had almost killed her grandmother. Meeting Henri Beaufort's grandson may cause her to suffer another heart attack, one which could be fatal.

## *Chapter Four*

Grégoire stood on the pavement outside the café, hardly noticing the shoppers who brushed past him, the busker belting out an old Bob Dylan song near the packhorse bridge and the children feeding bread to squabbling ducks on the riverbank.

This trip to Yorkshire had been a waste of time. He should pack his bag, return to the airport and fly back to Paris, but the thought of his grand piano standing like a silent reproach in his apartment, and the long list of emails and phone calls from his agent that he had to return, turned his heart to ice.

Looking around, he spotted the sign for The White Lion pub where Miss Moonshine said Liszt had once stayed and resolved to go there for a drink before leaving, in tribute to the old master. Right now, however, he fancied a walk to clear his head, so he started towards the canal.

The towpath was busy with joggers, dog-walkers, and families. Barges painted cheerful reds and deep greens lined the canal, with people out on deck, watering plants, carrying out repairs or sunbathing, a mug of tea or a can of beer in hand.

Sunlight sparkled on the water. Trees and overgrown bushes swayed in the gentle breeze, letting out scents of earth and vegetation, and their reflection rippled on the surface of the canal. Overhead the sky was a pure blue. If it weren't for the muddy puddles on the path, he could think he had dreamt the torrential downpour the previous day.

He dug his hands into his pockets, and his fingers touched the music box. He had been a fool to come here. When Barry had told him where to find Jane Bowland the night before, he had truly believed he had found the woman his grandfather had loved so much. It wasn't the name his grandfather had mentioned, but people changed name sometimes, especially artists and performers.

But Jane was only another of his grandfather's groupies. A surprisingly young one, with her bright blue eyes, smooth pink cheeks and pixie-styled blonde hair, but a groupie nonetheless.

His grandfather had always had a lot of female fans. A charismatic pianist and conductor, he had, in his heyday, been a playboy. Women had followed on tour, forcing their way into his hotel rooms, throwing themselves at him at parties or swooning in his arms after his concerts. Henri used to joke that his life as a classical musician had been a farce, and in many ways as outrageous as that of a rock star. His funeral service had been a bit of a circus too, with crowds of tearful elderly women gathering at the Père Lachaise, holding single white roses – Henri's favourite – in their black-gloved hands.

'Hi there. Or should I say *Bumjor*! Oops, that sounded a bit rude, but I was never any good at French at school, even though it's a sick language.'

Grégoire looked at the young woman in front of him. She had a head full of dreadlocks and piercings sticking out of her ears, lips and nose. Her leggings and top were black, tight, and slashed to shreds.

'You're the French guy who was in the café earlier, aren't you?' The girl's lip-piercings moved in the most disturbing fashion as she spoke. Grégoire repressed a shudder and focused on her kohl-lined eyes.

He nodded. 'Yes, that's right.'

'I work at the café, although not for much longer if I carry on mixing up the pup-muffins. The dogs aren't bothered, though, it's their owners who make a fuss.'

Confused, he stared at her. What was this talk of dogs and muffins?

Then he understood. Of course! That explained the name of the café – Man's Best Friend – as well as the strange smell and the dog paraphernalia for sale. 'You sell cakes for dogs.'

'Yep. Jane bakes them. She bakes biscuits too.' She counted on her fingers. 'Cheese, sausage, bacon –you name it. The dogs love them. She got an award last year, you know. She took me to the ceremony. We got dressed up and I even got an awesome new piercing. There.' She pointed to an arrow sticking out from the side of her ear and looked at him expectantly.

Grégoire forced a smile. 'Hmm. Yes. Very nice.'

'Did you meet Jane when she went to Paris with her gran?'

He held his breath. 'Jane went to Paris with her grandmother?'

The girl nodded. 'Poor Joyce had a heart attack when they came back. It was touch-and-go for a while, but she's all right now.'

'Jane's grandmother is called Joyce?'

The girl rolled her eyes. 'That's what I just said.'

'Then I must return to the café and talk to Jane at once.'

She shook her head, her dreadlocks swinging around like Medusa's snakes. 'She has gone home to the farm for Arthur's party. She made him a sick cake. You should see it. She must have used at least two kilos of carrots.'

It sounded revolting, but perhaps Jane's son loved carrots. He remembered Barry had mentioned that it was his third birthday today.

'Where is the farm?'

'It's on the top road. You can't miss it. There's a big gate with Bowland Farm written in white above it. It's not a proper farm anymore, mind. Jane and her gran only have rescue animals now.'

'Thank you very much, *mademoiselle*.'

She beamed him a smile. 'Oh, that's so chic, but you can call me Dixie.'

He'd better hurry back to town and find a toyshop. Bringing the boy a present might help Jane and her grandmother overlook the fact that he was gate-crashing their party.

An hour later he parked by the side of the road near the entrance to Bowland Farm and grabbed the bag with the wooden train set he had purchased. In front of him fields stretched in the sunshine, dotted with grazing sheep and covered with a carpet of buttercups, red clover and meadowsweet. Stone walls criss-crossed the hillside, a tower rose on the hill opposite, and clumps of trees nestled in dips and recesses. The warm breeze carried sounds of sheep bleating, leaves rustling and tractors humming. On a warm and sunny day like today, this was a glorious place to be.

Echoes of voices singing 'Happy Birthday to You' reached him, and he hurried down the muddy track towards the farmhouse.

The front door was closed, but the voices came from the back garden. He made his way around the house and reached the garden gate as Jane carried the most hideous birthday cake he'd ever seen across the lawn. Almost a foot high, and made of compacted brown mush, it was decorated with what looked like mint sweets and gingerbread men.

Poor kid, he thought, shaking his head. There weren't even any candles on that ugly cake, just three huge carrots. Come to think of it, where was the boy? There were no children running around or playing in the garden.

Jane set the cake on the garden table, turned away to pick up a glass of champagne, and saw him. Her smile vanished at once.

Behind her a donkey ambled across the lawn and stopped dangerously close to the cake. Grégoire opened his mouth to shout a warning, swung the garden gate open and walked in. He didn't see the pile of dung until it was too late. His foot sank into it with a wet, squelching sound. He slipped, lost his balance, and fell backwards. The train set flew up in the air and landed on the grass with a thudding noise.

Everybody turned to stare as he cursed in French and scrambled to his feet, his hands covered in muck, his trousers soiled, his dignity dented. And from what he could see, it had all been for nothing. The donkey's muzzle was now buried deep in the birthday cake.

Jane rushed to his side. Her blue eyes sparked with fury. 'What are you doing here? You have to go.'

'*Et bien*...thanks for your concern,' he replied stiffly. 'I don't think I broke any bones.'

'I don't care if you broke all the bones in your body. You have no business being here.'

She was right, of course.

'Who is this, darling?' A woman called from the other end of the garden.

Jane whirled round. 'It's all right, Grandma. It's just someone asking for directions.' Turning back to him, she pulled on his sleeve to drag him out of the garden and hissed, 'You must leave now.'

Ignoring her, he bent down to pick up the present. The colourful wrapping paper was ripped and stained, showing the picture of the wooden train set.

'Here. I'm sorry the paper is soiled. It's for Arthur. I hope he likes it.'

She looked at him as if he had lost his mind. 'What are you talking about? What would Arthur do with a train set? Never mind. You must go.'

He handed her the present anyway. 'I am sorry to intrude on your party, but I need to talk to your grandmother.'

'She doesn't want to talk to you, and I don't want your stupid present. My donkey may be clever but he doesn't play with trains.'

'Your donkey? *Non* – you don't understand. This is for your son. Arthur.'

She pointed to the donkey, which had by now eaten its way through half the cake. 'This is Arthur. It's *his* birthday. He's three today. Now please come with me. I don't want my grandma to get upset.'

'Why would I get upset, love?' an elderly woman asked. She had short white hair, and bright blue eyes – the same as her granddaughter's.

Grégoire took one look at her and swallowed hard. He had found her–the woman he'd been looking for.

## *Chapter Five*

Jane looked at her grandmother. Her face was pale, but her breathing sounded even and she wasn't clutching at her chest.

'Are you Joyce Granville?' Grégoire asked in a hoarse voice.

Jane's grandmother nodded. 'That was my maiden name. I'm Joyce Bowland now.'

'I am Grégoire– Henri's...'

'Grandson, yes, I gathered that much. You look just like him.' Joyce's eyes softened and she pointed to his trousers. 'Look at the state of you. Come into the house with me, and we'll get you cleaned up.'

She held out her hand. 'Help me. I am not as strong as I used to be.'

Grégoire looked at his dirty hands. 'But I'm filthy.'

'I've run a farm for the best part of forty years, my lad. Muck doesn't bother me.'

He smiled, took her hand and linked arms with her.

'Jane, my darling, please see to our guests, and tidy up your donkey's mess. Oh, and put that train set away,' her grandmother instructed as she walked past, looking suddenly very small and frail as she leaned on Grégoire Beaufort's arm.

Jane picked up the broken biscuits and chewed carrot stumps Arthur had left on the lawn and shoved them into a rubbish bag.

'Who is Mr Gorgeous? Do tell.' Sandra Haworth's eyes shone with curiosity.

The other women flocked around her, asking questions. He sounded foreign. Was he French? Did Joyce and Jane meet him during their trip to Paris? Why did Joyce look so tearful? And who was the train set for?

Sandra was one of the town's chief gossips. Her brother-in-law worked for the local newspaper, so Jane must take care not to reveal too much. Should the press get wind of the story that Grégoire Beaufort, the world-famous pianist turned recluse and grandson of a music legend, was at Bowland Farm, they wouldn't have a moment's peace. Not to mention that Joyce's past could be splattered all over the news.

'He's nobody special, just an old friend of Grandma's visiting from Paris.'

'He looks pretty special to me.' Sandra clicked her tongue. 'Very dark and handsome, even covered in muck.'

'Especially covered in muck!' Pauline Thompson patted her brown curls. 'I like my men dirty.'

Brenda Roberts drained her glass of prosecco. 'I wouldn't mind cleaning him up with my own fair hands. Do you think he needs help showering?'

'Shh!' Jane's face was burning. What if Grégoire heard them?

'Oh, give over playing the prude.' Sandra poured herself the last of the bubbly wine. 'You have eyes like the rest of us. The man is a dish.'

'I hadn't noticed.' It was a lie. Of course she had noticed his soulful eyes, the cute dimple at the corner of his mouth when he smiled, and his tall, athletic figure. She had even noticed that his aftershave smelled like a summer garden after the rain. Right now, however, he must smell of Arthur's droppings.

She faced the three women. 'Ladies, thank you so much for coming. Pauline, are you all right driving Brenda and Sandra back? Great. Then I'll see you all tomorrow at the rehearsal. Two o'clock sharp.'

Ten minutes later, after more laughing, innuendo and salacious jokes about sexy French men and steamy showers, the three women left. Jane picked up the train set and walked into the farmhouse, where Joyce sat at the kitchen table, drinking a glass of water.

'Grégoire is getting changed. I gave him a pair of your granddad's trousers and put his in the washing machine. He can have them back tomorrow when they're dry.'

Jane put the train set on the table and crossed her arms. 'I'm sure he can sort out his own laundry. Why is he even here? I don't want him upsetting you. I don't want you to get hurt.'

Joyce smiled but there were tears in her eyes. She cradled her glass in her hands. 'I have hurt ever since I left Henri over fifty years ago, my darling. Don't get me wrong, I loved your granddad. We had a good life here, and I don't regret a moment of it, but part of me always wondered what it could have been if I had stayed in Paris. If only I had taken the chance...'

'He never forgot you either.' Grégoire stood in the doorway, wearing khaki corduroy trousers that were too big for him. He glanced at the train set and smiled. 'I hope I didn't ruin your birthday party, even if I made a complete fool of myself.'

Jane couldn't help but grin back. 'And I am sorry for shouting at you when you slipped in Arthur's poo. It was rude of me.'

They looked at each other and her breath hitched in her throat. The kitchen with its pine units and green walls receded and became blurred, until all she could see clearly was him. Her heart beat fast and hard, her body tingled all over.

'Please sit down, both of you, you're making me dizzy,' Joyce said, breaking the spell. She turned to Grégoire. 'How did you find me?'

'I traced the music box you left at the Père Lachaise to Miss Moonshine's shop. She wouldn't tell me who bought it, but recommended I stay at The Old Bull. That's where I heard Jane play *La Javanaise*.'

'She did it on purpose,' Joyce whispered. 'She knows Jane always closes her set with the same song. Why have you come here? It's been so long since Henri and I were...friends.'

'He told me about you in hospital. He wanted me to find you and give you this.' Grégoire pulled his wallet out of his breast pocket and extracted a gold and mother-of-pearl pendant in the shape of a rose.

'He had it made especially for you.'

Joyce's fingers shook as she took the pendant. 'A white rose, Henri's favourite. He used to say I was his white rose.'

'It's also the symbol of Yorkshire,' Jane remarked. 'Would you like to wear it now, Grandma?'

Joyce nodded and Jane fastened the clasp behind her neck. Her grandmother touched the pendant with the tip of her fingers and seemed lost in her thoughts for a while. The only sound in the kitchen was the tick-tock of the clock on the wall. Then Joyce started talking.

'I met Henri at the Conservatoire. It was an exciting time to be young in Paris. There were clubs and bars, concerts and impromptu gigs, poetry readings, café-théâtre. One of our favourite artists was Serge Gainsbourg, and *La Javanaise* became our song.'

'My grandfather loved that song,' Grégoire said. 'He often played it in the evenings, when he thought we were asleep.'

'Why did you split up?' Jane asked.

Joyce sighed. 'It was my fault. I was insecure, I suppose. When Henri's career took off, he started travelling a lot. He met people, went to parties. I was afraid he would find me dull and grow tired of me. I didn't want him to feel that he was stuck with me, that I was holding him back... so I finished it first, before he did. I never thought he would remember me, or the song, after all these years.' She squeezed Grégoire's hand. 'Please tell me all about him, about you, and your family.'

## *Chapter Six*

*Saturday afternoon, one week later*

'How long is *Monsieur* Gorgeous staying at the farm?' Sandra clipped her dog's lead onto the table leg and pulled a biscuit out of her handbag for him to chew on.

Jane arched her brows. 'You mean Grégoire?'

Sandra laughed. 'Who else?'

'Grandma told him he could stay as long as he wanted.' Jane spread the music sheets on the table and sighed. Grégoire had fitted in very well at the farm. So well, in fact, that he seemed to have become indispensable to her grandmother. He took her out, did chores around the farm, and even helped look after Arthur and the other rescue donkeys. Above all, he made her grandma smile.

Sunlight streamed through the windows of the community centre. She should be at the farm, doing jobs or baking a batch of biscuits and muffins for the café, but with the summer fete less than a week away, and the choir far from ready, an extra rehearsal had been arranged for that day.

There was also the issue of Grégoire and the unsettling effect his thoughtful eyes and seductive smile had on her system. She blushed so hard every time he was near, she feared she might spontaneously combust. It was safer to spend as much time as possible away from him.

Pauline patted her labradoodle's head and said in a dreamy voice, 'I think I'll call round tomorrow. I want to take another look at him.'

Brenda nodded. 'So do I. Actually, my French is a little rusty. Perhaps he can give me private tuition.'

'My French isn't the only thing that's rusty,' Pauline retorted.

Jane put her fists on her hips and shook her head. 'You two are impossible.'

'What's going on?' Dixie strolled in with Lady Madonna, her Irish wolfhound. She had weaved ribbons in the dog's hair and it looked like it had dreadlocks, like its owner.

'We're talking about Jane's *Monsieur* Gorgeous,' Pauline said.

'He's not *my* Mr Gorgeous!' Jane protested.

'But he is gorgeous,' Dixie retorted. 'I love his eyes and his sick French accent.'

'There's nothing sick about his accent,' Jane snapped, remembering too late that Dixie meant it as a compliment.

The rest of the choir ladies arrived with their dogs, and the conversation about Grégoire continued, much to Jane's mortification.

'I hear your grandma has taken a handsome French lodger,' one woman started. 'When are you going to introduce him to us?'

'Paws off, I saw him first,' Brenda said.

Pauline hissed an annoyed breath. 'I did!'

Miss Moonshine strode in with Napoleon, her ancient chihuahua, in her arms. 'Actually, *I* saw him first,' she said, bending down to put the tiny dog on his blanket. 'He came into my shop on the day he arrived, and I sent him over to see Jane at the pub.'

Jane gasped. So they'd been right. Miss Moonshine had sent Grégoire to The Old Bull on purpose.

'Never mind who saw him first,' Sandra retorted. 'I'm the one who's going to teach him about Yorkshire hospitality and bake him a batch of my fat rascals.'

Brenda sniggered. 'I think he'd rather sample some of Jane's muffins. They may be for dogs but they taste a lot better than your fat rascals. What's more, I saw the way these two looked at each other at Arthur's party. There'll be romance in the air before long, you mark my words.'

A chorus of *oohlalas* followed, and Jane was about to call everybody to order when her grandma walked in with Grégoire.

'Grandma! You didn't say you were coming.'

Joyce seemed surprised. 'Didn't I? It must have slipped my mind. Grégoire, be a good lad and bring me that chair over there.'

'Of course.' Grégoire fetched the chair and looked at the women petting the dogs at one end of the room, a frown creasing his forehead. 'I thought you were joking when you said it was a choir for women and their dogs.'

Joyce laughed. 'Why do you think the choir is called "Barking Mad"? Jane set it up last month to raise money for our local hospice. She thought it was an unusual idea.'

'It is certainly unusual,' he said. 'Don't the dogs howl and mess about?'

'Only when we sing badly. They're perfectly well-behaved the rest of the time. They will be good as gold when you play the piano for us.'

Grégoire shrank back. 'No! I told you. I don't play anymore.' He looked down at his hands. 'I *can't* play anymore.'

Joyce shrugged. 'Of course you can. Besides, we need your expertise.' She patted his arm and pushed him towards the piano.

'Grandma!' Jane hissed. How could her grandmother be so insensitive?

Her grandmother ignored her. 'Come on, ladies. We'll start with something nice and cheerful from our ABBA medley. What about "Take a Chance on Me"? Jane, my darling, give Grégoire the music in case he doesn't know the song.'

## *Chapter Seven*

Sweat beaded on Gregoire's forehead as he lifted the fallboard and stared at the black and white keys.

'Are you all right?' Jane whispered.

He tried to answer, but his throat was so parched it hurt even to breathe, let alone speak.

He looked at his hands, the backs crisscrossed with scars, and the fingers surgeons hadn't managed to straighten. What if he couldn't even manage one ABBA song? What if the dogs started howling and Jane and the other women laughed at him?

'Grégoire.' Jane's hand on his arm gave him a jolt. 'You look like you're about to faint.'

She moved closer and her warm, sunny fragrance reached him. It was the scent that had been driving him crazy all week when they'd bumped into each other in the farmhouse's kitchen first thing in the morning, her skin and hair still damp and fragrant from the shower, and wearing a t-shirt with the logo of that weird café she managed. She baked a batch of dog cakes every day as he came down hunting for coffee and company. For the first time in his life, he had enjoyed talking about all kinds of silly things he knew nothing about, like donkeys and recipes for dog muffins.

Jane's blue eyes were filled with worry and kindness. 'It's all right. I'll play.'

And then it hit him. He was behaving like an idiot – worse, a diva. This wasn't about him losing face because he couldn't manage Liszt or Rachmaninov anymore. It was about Jane's weird choir and the summer fete. What did he have to be nervous about? His audience today consisted of a bunch of dogs who wouldn't know the difference between Chopin and "Chopsticks", and a group of women who would be grateful for any help he could give them.

He let out a long breath. 'I'm fine.'

Sitting down, he hesitated as his fingers made contact with a keyboard for the first time in months and launched into a fast jazz tune. The conversations stopped and everybody, dogs included, turned to look at him.

'Not only is he gorgeous, but he can play too.' One of the women licked her lips and stared at him as if she wanted to eat him alive.

Joyce winked at him. 'The boy has many talents. Come on now, ladies, let's make a start.' Gesturing towards him, she added. 'Maestro, whenever you're ready.'

*

Two hours later, the dogs and their owners left in a chorus of yapping, chattering and laughter. Miss Moonshine invited Joyce to try a new restaurant. Brushing aside Jane's concerns for her health, Joyce accepted. It was time she enjoyed herself again, she decreed, and moderation was all very well and good, as long as you didn't overdo it.

The woman who had been staring at him during the rehearsal came up to Grégoire and laid a possessive hand on his forearm. 'Why don't you come for a bite to eat at my house?'

Immediately, her friends protested that they, too, needed a crash course in French. The three of them looked at him like he was a tasty morsel. Words to decline the invitation failed him.

Jane saved him. 'I'm sorry, ladies, but Grégoire is coming to The Old Bull with me tonight.'

'Thank you,' he mouthed as the women turned away, arguing between themselves.

'They are very nice, really,' Jane said after they left. 'They're just a bit –'

'Scary? Forceful? Desperate?'

She laughed and shook her head. 'They're curious about you and... they fancy you.' Her cheeks blushing bright pink, she gathered the music sheets into her huge handbag.

'By the way, don't feel obliged to come to the pub tonight,' she added as they left the community centre. 'I only said that because it was the first thing that sprang into my mind.'

'I'd love to come.'

She smiled and a ray of sunlight shone on her hair, her skin... on his heart, and it took his breath away.

'I'm not due at the pub until seven,' she said. 'Shall we go for a walk?'

'Only if you let me carry your bag. It's far too heavy for you.'

She laughed. 'But it's a handbag, and it's pink!'

'So what?' He reached out for the bag and slung it on his shoulder and they started in the direction of the canal.

They walked without talking for a while, stopping every so often to point at shiny dragonflies flitting over the water or duck families paddling in line. Golden sunlight glinted on the surface of the canal, and the sky was a perfect, delicate shade of blue. Scents of hawthorn and wild flowers filled the air.

He took a deep breath. It was like a weight had been lifted off his chest, and he felt free at last, and not just because he had finally put his pride aside and managed to play again. It felt good to be here, strolling with Jane in the sunshine.

It felt even better when Jane took his hand, leant against him and whispered excitedly. 'Look over there, by the bridge. A kingfisher!'

All he saw was a splash in the water followed by a flash of bright blue as the bird flew away – the same blue as Jane's eyes. He gave her hand a squeeze. 'Wonderful. This place is magic.'

'I bet you weren't saying that the day you arrived.'

'True. I didn't know it could rain so much.'

Her hand trembled in his. 'We had terrible flooding here a while back, you know. It was awful... so many shops, houses, lives ruined. Most of us pulled back, thankfully. The pub, Man's Best Friend café, and Miss Moonshine's shop were cleaned up, refitted and reopened, but many didn't.'

'I am so glad Miss Moonshine's Emporium did, or I would have never met you.' He realised it was true, and not just because he wouldn't have been able to fulfil his grandfather's dying wishes and find Joyce.

She blushed again but didn't pull her hand away. It was getting late so they turned and walked back, still hand in hand. As they reached the bridge, a gang of youths blocked their way. 'Look at him, showing off with that pink handbag,' one of the boys sniggered.

'Nice handbag, mate!' another shouted.

Jane turned to him, alarm in her eyes, but he only laughed.

'Thanks, lads. I think pink suits me, don't you?'

The boys muttered something derogatory and strode away, hoods up despite the heat and hands stuffed in the pockets of their baggy pants.

Happiness fizzed inside him, like a big, warm smile, and he couldn't help himself. He lifted Jane's hand to his lips and kissed it, once, twice, and once more for good measure.

Yes, it felt good just to be here, in a balmy summer evening. And to fall in love.

## *Chapter Eight*

*Saturday evening*

The pub was packed inside and out, and the patio doors were open so that patrons could hear Jane's music and sing along.

Grégoire stood next to the piano, sipping his half-pint of bitter.

'Hurry up, or it'll get cold,' Barry said as he walked past.

Jane laughed when Grégoire looked puzzled. 'It's a joke,' she explained. 'People always say we drink warm bitter up here in Yorkshire.'

Amazingly, she was still smiling after playing and singing for over two hours.

'Is it usually this busy in here?' he asked as she finished a Coldplay number.

She nodded. 'If you think this is busy, you should be here at Christmas and New Year.' She launched into 'Hello' by Adele. Everybody started singing, and he realised he would indeed like to celebrate the end of the year here with Jane.

It was late when they left the pub and walked to his car. He was still carrying her pink bag, even heavier after Barry had slipped in a couple of bottles of locally-brewed beer for him to sample.

Jane looked up. 'I was wondering if you would stay

until the summer fete and see the choir through its first performance. The rehearsal was wonderful with you at the piano today. Even the dogs were well-behaved. But please don't feel obliged to accept,' she added quickly. 'You must be busy, and your family must miss you.'

He shook his head. 'They don't - not really. My parents live in the South of France so I don't see them very often. I would be happy to help, now I seem to have conquered my nerves.' *And my stupid pride*, he added silently. 'The only thing I would ask is that you don't tell anyone who I am. I don't want journalists pestering me.'

'I would never dream of it.' She cocked her head to one side, and added in a mischievous tone, 'Even if it would bring the choir lots of publicity and more funds for the hospice.'

'Good. Are you sure you don't mind me staying at the farm?'

'Grandma loves having you here, and Arthur too, even if he still can't play with your train set.'

*What about you?* he wanted to ask. Thankfully, his phone rang before he could make a fool of himself. He fished it out of his jeans pocket and tightened his mouth when he saw the name flashing on the screen. Cassandra. Again.

'Hi, Cassandra. What is it now?'

'I have great news for you. My agent booked the reception room at the Ritz for a concert next Saturday. And before you complain, there will only be fifty guests, so you needn't be anxious.'

His fingers gripped the phone. 'How dare you go ahead with this without consulting me?'

'I only want to help you overcome your phobia of performing in public. If you don't like the Ritz, we could try the George V or -'

He closed his eyes. 'I told you I wouldn't do concerts anymore. Actually, Saturday isn't possible anyway. I'm helping a choir perform at the local summer fete.'

'What? You'd rather be with a bunch of old crones than with me?'

He looked at Jane. 'They're not all old crones, and the dogs are rather cute.'

'What dogs?'

'It's a choir for ladies and their pooches, so the dogs get to sing too. Please get your agent to cancel the booking, or find another pianist.'

## *Chapter Nine*

*Two days before the summer fete*

'What should I wear for the fete?' Jane glanced at the clothes strewn upon her bed. It was only seven thirty in the morning but she had been up for an hour already, trying clothes when she should have been baking a tray of cakes for the café.

'What's wrong with the tunic you're wearing now?' her grandmother asked. 'It's a lovely colour. It brings out the blue in your eyes.'

'I should be wearing something dramatic and sexy.' She pulled the tunic over her head, threw it on the bed and slipped on her work t-shirt with its *MBF* logo.

'You don't wear sexy clothes, my darling. It's just not you.' Her grandma narrowed her eyes. 'Does this have anything to do with Grégoire, by any chance? He will like you in anything, you know.'

Jane's cheeks heated, and tears pricked her eyes. 'No, he won't. He's used to beautiful women wearing designer evening dresses. I'm just...me. A pub musician who works in a café, lives on a rundown farm, and bakes cakes for dogs to make ends meet.'

'Don't you dare speak about yourself and my farm in that way.' Joyce's sharp tone made her look up.

'I'm sorry, Grandma, about the farm. Everything else is true, though.'

'No, it's not. You are the most beautiful, the most talented and creative granddaughter I have.'

Jane shrugged. 'Huh! You mean I'm the *only* granddaughter you have.'

She couldn't hold the tears any longer and buried her face in her hands as she slumped on the bed.

'What's brought this on?' The bed sagged as her grandmother sat next to her, wrapping her arm around her shoulders. 'Are you worried about the performance? Grégoire said everything is going really well and the choir only needs a little tweaking.'

Jane shook her head. 'It's not that.'

'Then what is it?'

'He's going to leave after the summer fete, and I'll have to forget him. But I don't think I can ever forget him.'

'Oh, love. You have it bad, don't you?'

Jane nodded. 'And there's this Cassandra Lloyd who keeps phoning and texting him all the time. I googled her. She's beautiful, Grandma, a real star.'

Joyce gave her back a comforting pat. 'Star or not, it seems to me that if he really wanted to see her, he'd have gone back to Paris days ago instead of making himself at home here.'

Jane heaved another shaky sigh. 'Do you really think so?'

'Of course I do. He's already out in the fields with Arthur this morning. He's taken a shine to that donkey. And an even bigger shine to you.'

The phone ringing downstairs interrupted her.

Jane glanced at the alarm clock. 'I wonder who it can be? I'll get it.' She wiped her eyes, jumped to her feet and ran down the stairs.

'Hi sweetie,' Derek's voice boomed. Sandra's brother-in-law was the editor of the *West Yorkshire Times*. 'I know it's early but I'd like to speak to your famous French guest and get an exclusive before somebody turns up on your doorstep and steals my scoop.'

Her heart felt like it had stopped. 'What famous French guest? What scoop?'

Derek laughed. 'We had a tip that Beaufort was staying at the farm, and for once our Sandra is speechless. She can't believe the French guy she's been lusting after is a world-famous pianist in hiding.'

Feeling dizzy, Jane swayed against the dresser. 'Grégoire isn't hiding.'

'Really? The world media, the paparazzi and his famous American girlfriend have been after him for weeks. Now, be a good girl and get him for me. You owe me for that article I did on your dog cakes last year.'

In a panic, she slammed the phone down. It immediately started ringing again. She had to tell Grégoire he was no longer safe at the farm.

She opened the door and ran across the courtyard towards the field where Grégoire was feeding Arthur carrots.

Too late! Half-a-dozen vans bearing logos of television channels and radio stations were driving into the courtyard. Tyres screeched. Doors slammed. Voices called,'He's over there!'

Grégoire turned. The smile froze on his face as he spotted the vans, and he let the bag of carrots slide to the ground.

Jane tried to catch her breath. 'They know you're here.'

'BBC Television? ITV? Sky News? What's going on, Jane? You told the media I was here?' Grégoire stared at her, incredulous.

Jane shook her head, the words sticking in her throat.

How could he think she would betray him?

'Mr Beaufort!' a journalist called. 'Feeding donkeys at dawn and running an amateur choir, is that your new career path?'

Grégoire hissed a breath then narrowed his eyes to look at her. 'I didn't think you wanted publicity for the choir that badly.' He shrugged. 'Never mind. I guess it was time I faced the music anyway.'

Forcing a smile, he picked up the bag of carrots and added, 'I will leave after I've spoken to the reporters.'

## *Chapter Ten*

*The evening of the summer fete*

'So now we're in a mess because Mr Gorgeous had a tantrum and left in a strop?' Sandra took a swig of alcopop.

Jane sighed. 'We're not in a mess. We're ready. And Grégoire didn't have a tantrum. He had a good reason to be angry.'

'I still can't believe you knew about him all along and never breathed a word. We're supposed to be friends. Derek wasn't impressed when you put the phone down on him.'

'I panicked. Did he say how he found out about Grégoire?'

'Does it matter?'

Jane's shoulders sagged. 'No, I suppose it doesn't.'

Grégoire had left, looking dark and angry, barely giving her a backwards look before getting into his rental car and driving off. And now her heart ached so much she couldn't breathe.

Her grandmother walked into the marquee with Miss Moonshine, who was carrying Napoleon in the crook of her arm. Both women were dressed in shiny silver dresses, and the chihuahua sported a matching bow around his collar.

It should have been a happy occasion, especially since

the publicity generated by Grégoire meant they had already collected their target money for the hospice. All Jane felt was emptiness and desolation, and she couldn't wait for the evening to be over so she could hurry back home.

Miss Moonshine gestured for her to come over. 'Jane dear, can I have a word? Grégoire bought this for you earlier this week. I had to take it to a jeweller friend to get it fixed. I'm sure he would want you to have it tonight, for good luck.' She handed Jane a small box with a shiny blue bow.

'What is it?'

Miss Moonshine patted her hand. 'Open it. And please allow a very old lady to give you a bit of advice. I'm sure your Grandma would agree if I told you daylight always follows even the darkest night, and that everything will sort itself out.'

Perhaps it was Miss Moonshine's kind words, or the expression in Napoleon's big brown eyes, but Jane clutched the box and turned away with tears blurring her vision. Sitting at the piano, she pulled on the ribbon, lifted the lid of the box and gasped in wonder. Inside was the most exquisite gold brooch of a kingfisher encrusted with shimmering blue crystals.

Images of golden sunlight reflecting on the canal and of a kingfisher diving into the water flashed in front of her eyes. That was the day Grégoire had had his first rehearsal with the choir; the day they'd held hands as they walked in the late afternoon sunshine. After that, she had dared to hope that they were friends– perhaps even more than friends. What hurt the most was that he believed she had betrayed him, and their friendship.

She wiped her tears and pinned the brooch onto her tunic. People were coming in and sitting down in the marquee. Soon all the chairs were taken and it was standing room only at the back. She'd better pull herself together and focus on the music and the singing.

Her grandmother gathered the choir and the dogs at the centre of the stage and turned to the audience. 'Ladies and gentlemen, we are delighted to perform in aid of our local hospice, so please give generously.' She turned to Jane. 'This choir was an idea of my darling granddaughter's and if some of you think that it's barking mad –' People in the audience laughed and Joyce carried on, 'Then you would probably be right. We hope you enjoy tonight.'

She nodded to Jane, who played the first bars of "Thank You for the Music". The lights dimmed, leaving only a spotlight on the singers.

The singing went remarkably well, the only incident being when Napoleon started howling during "Waterloo". Miss Moonshine gave him a bacon biscuit to keep him quiet.

At last it was the final song, and Jane was about to start "Take a Chance on Me" when a disturbance at the back of the marquee made her look up. A tall, dark-haired man dressed in a black dinner suit strode down the main aisle. Her heart skipped a beat and her fingers missed a couple of keys. Grégoire was there. He had come back!

He nodded to Joyce as he climbed onto the stage, walked straight to the piano and bent down towards her.

'Ever played a duet?' he whispered.

She looked at him, too stunned to reply.

'Move over,' he added.

Obediently, she shuffled her bottom along the padded piano stool, and he sat down beside her. There wasn't much space for two at the piano, so his left shoulder and leg touched hers, and their fingers brushed as they played. He left the main accompaniment to her whilst he improvised. How could he have wished never to play again, she wondered, as his fingers flew over the keys? He was the most gifted musician she'd ever heard.

When the song ended she hardly heard the cheering from the audience, and the barking from the dogs. She only heard the beating of her heart.

Joyce marshalled the choir, the dogs and the audience out and soon the marquee was empty.

Grégoire rose to his feet. 'It looks like the concert went well.'

She nodded. 'It was fine. The dogs behaved, apart from Napoleon who had a bit of a wobble during "Waterloo". He hates that song.'

'Not surprisingly, I should say.' He smiled. 'I'm so glad I caught the last song. I wasn't sure I would make it. The plane was delayed.'

She turned to look at him. 'Why did you come back?'

'Because this is where I want to be. That's if you can forgive me for being an idiot and leaving in a churlish manner. I know you didn't phone the press. I knew it straightaway, but seeing all those journalists and television crews at the farmhouse made me feel...' He sighed.

She tilted her chin. 'You were embarrassed to be seen with us at the farm.'

'Not at all – or if I was, it was because I knew I should have given a press conference long ago instead of hiding like a coward. Will you forgive me?' He looked at her, his dark brown eyes serious, almost anxious.

Hope blossomed inside her. He said he wanted to stay in Haven Bridge. He was asking for forgiveness. And he looked at her as if he really cared.

There was one thing she wanted to know.

'Who alerted the media?'

'Cassandra. She wanted me to come back to Paris and do a series of recitals with her.'

He looked at the brooch she had pinned to her top and his face lit up. 'It reminded me of your eyes and the day we walked along the canal.'

She touched her fingers to the brooch. 'I love it. It's beautiful. Thank you.'

He held out his hand. 'It's still daylight. Shall we go to the canal to see if we can spot the kingfisher?'

She beamed a smile and slipped her hand inside his. 'Good idea.'

**Originally from Lyon, Marie Laval now lives in the beautiful Rossendale Valley in Lancashire, and writes contemporary and historical romance with a French twist, including bestselling romantic comedy, Little Pink Taxi, published by Choc Lit.**

facebook.com/marielavalauthor

# The House on the Hill

*By Helen Pollard*

Hettie Brown sat in the oak-panelled solicitor's office in Haven Bridge on a drizzly Monday afternoon, still in her black dress from the morning's funeral. Glancing around at the old-fashioned furniture and the rain spattering the narrow windows, Hettie felt like she'd been dropped into the set of an old black-and-white movie. She half expected an Alastair Sim lookalike to be in charge of her great-uncle's affairs – someone starched, stuffy and grey.

But the real-life solicitor who breezed in and introduced himself as Steve Cooperman was hardly that.

If he'd sounded nice over the phone, Hettie had to admit he looked rather nice in person, too. Somewhere in his thirties, with short brown hair and a light tan (where did he get *that* up here in the chilly north?), he wore no suit, instead opting for a creased linen jacket without a tie. Hettie wasn't sure whether to appreciate the informal wear that put her at her ease or to find it disrespectful when discussing a deceased person's affairs, but the friendly light in his blue-grey eyes swayed her towards the former.

He reached out to shake her hand, and as she took it, Hettie felt a jolt of ... something. Must be nerves.

'How did the funeral go?' he asked, glancing at her sombre dress and boots.

'Very well, thank you, Mr Cooperman.'

'Please. Call me Steve.'

'Steve.' Hettie smiled at him. 'Uncle Alex had a good innings, as they say. Ninety-five, after all!'

Hettie's great-uncle had been a stubborn man and an acquired taste – someone you either loved or hated. The feeling was usually mutual. But Hettie's own memories of Alex were purely fond ones. She'd spent many a school holiday at his huge old stone house here in Yorkshire, high on the hill climbing out of Haven Bridge towards the moors – holidays shared with Charles, her second cousin once removed. Or was it third cousin twice removed? Hettie had no idea how that stuff worked.

Hettie hadn't been able to take time off work to organise the funeral, so Charles had jumped in. Now he had gone back to his job in Glasgow, leaving Hettie to tackle the next stage of proceedings.

'Mr Harris isn't joining us today?' It was as though the solicitor had read Hettie's wandering thoughts.

'No. Sorry. He had to drive straight back. I'm sorry I couldn't meet with you sooner. Busy patch at work. But I have the rest of this week off, so I'm all yours now.'

Steve raised an eyebrow. 'Better make the most of it, then.' He cleared his throat. 'So, as executor, you'll –'

Hettie sighed. 'I still don't understand how you can make someone an executor of a will without their permission. It's ridiculous! Didn't it occur to Uncle Alex that I might not *want* the responsibility?'

Steve gave her a sympathetic look. He had been kind

on the phone after Alex had died, coping calmly with her shock at finding herself co-executor, along with Charles, of Alex's will. But the list of executors' responsibilities he had explained to her could have made Hettie's hair stand on end if it wasn't already a frizzy halo of strawberry blonde around her head.

'Alex knew you might refuse if he asked you, Miss Brown,' he said now.

'Hettie. Please.'

'Hettie, then. He also knew you probably wouldn't or couldn't refuse once he was gone. Would you rather some stranger went through Alex's papers? His house and possessions? A house clearance without a by-your-leave?'

'I could still do that – get someone in to clear the lot.'

'Indeed, you could,' Steve agreed. 'But your great-uncle entrusted your cousin and *you* with this.'

'Trust or no, I live in London, for heaven's sake. Over two hundred miles away.'

'You have this week off,' Steve reminded her. 'The house and its contents need to be valued before we apply for probate. There'll be inheritance tax. I can organise that, but it would be helpful if you could get the place in order first. You can do the bulk of it in a week, surely? Take any paperwork down to London with you?'

Hettie snorted. 'If that house is in the same state as the last time I was there, it'll take more than a week. Have you ever seen it?'

'No. By the time I inherited Alex as a client, when my partner Jed retired, he was in the hospice.'

Frustration got the better of her. 'Then I suggest you see for yourself before spouting your mouth off about how long it'll take!' she snapped, immediately tagging on a heartfelt, 'I'm so sorry. This is hardly your fault.'

'That's OK. You've had a stressful day. Tell you what. I'll come and see the house with you now.'

Feeling sheepish, Hettie said, 'There's no need. I shouldn't have snapped. I'm just stressed with everything there is to do.'

'I understand.' He looked at his watch. 'Give me ten minutes, then we'll go up there together.'

*

Half an hour later, Steve stood by Hettie's side in the weed-invaded driveway of the house, staring at the large edifice of blackened stone.

'I didn't expect it to be so big,' he admitted. 'Jed told me Alex never married or had a family.'

'He inherited it decades ago, but he never downsized. He needed the space.'

'What on earth for?'

'You'll see.' With a smirk, Hettie pushed open the wooden door, cringing as it creaked.

'Wow. It *is* big.' Steve gazed around the cavernous entrance hall, his eyes lighting on an umbrella stand full of antique golf clubs covered in cobwebs. 'And ... *untouched*.'

Hettie grinned. 'We haven't even started.'

She led him into the large kitchen with its scrubbed pine table, tall dressers cluttered with mismatched china, an old Aga stove, and blackened saucepans hanging from a wooden rack.

Steve picked up a can from a dusty, crowded shelf. 'Marrowfat peas.' Turning it in his hand, he glanced at her in alarm. 'Best before October 1995.'

'Alex wasn't stupid. He wouldn't have eaten them. He just wasn't one for clearing out clutter.'

Passing everything from an old, battered cast-iron mincer

fixed to the worktop with a vice, to a state-of-the-art electric yogurt-maker, Hettie led a bewildered Steve through to the utility room.

He pointed at a mangle. 'I haven't seen one of those outside of a museum.'

'Don't let it fool you. He only kept it because it was his mother's and he admired the simplicity of its design. Alex *loved* his mod cons.' She gestured at the modern washing machine and tumble dryer; the fancy steam iron hanging on the wall. 'This house is a real juxtaposition of old and new. It always has been.' She smiled at a memory. 'I could tell you some tales. Maybe some other time.'

Over the next hour, she led Steve on a whistle-stop tour of the house. He gaped and commented at sixties-patterned wallpaper clashing with antique Turkish rugs; ancient four-poster beds in guest rooms versus Alex's own push-button adjustable bed; seventies stereo equipment next to an old gramophone; ugly antique vases dotted amongst remote controls for every viewing or recording gadget ever invented.

'Incredible,' he said when they were back in the hall. 'Jed told me it was a fascinating place, but I had no idea.'

'Glad you enjoyed the tour.' Hettie raised an eyebrow. 'Do you still think it'll only take me a week?'

Steve laughed. 'OK. I take that back.' The mahogany grandfather clock at the foot of the stairs chimed six. 'It's late. You've had a long day. Why don't you let me take you to dinner?'

Taken aback by his offer, Hettie found herself smiling and nodding before any sensible thought process could make its way through her brain.

As Steve drove them back into Haven Bridge, she told herself it *was* late and it *had* been a long day. She'd barely eaten anything, so she needed to eat now – and if a kind man wanted to help her with that, she couldn't find a good enough reason to object.

Steve chose a pub in the centre of town. 'I hope this is OK? I presumed you'd be too tired for formality.'

Hettie smiled. 'This is perfect.'

After the chill of the big house, the pub was warm and cosy, and Hettie was content to relax with a glass of wine.

'Where are you staying?' Steve asked her once they'd ordered.

'At a B&B. I'll move up to Uncle Alex's tomorrow.'

Steve spluttered on his beer. 'You're kidding!'

'Why not?'

'It's freezing up there, even in June.' He reached across the table and held chilled fingers against her cheek to prove his point.

'I'll only be using a few rooms.' Hettie did her best to ignore the speed of her pulse. 'I can put the heating on, if I have to.'

'And it's isolated.' Steve looked dubious. 'If you need anything, you'll let me know?'

'Yes. Thank you.'

He smiled, and her stomach flipped, making her wonder if wine on an empty stomach had gone to her head.

'You're obviously attached to the place,' Steve said. 'How come you spent so much time there?'

'I grew up near Leeds. My mother was a single parent working two jobs. She couldn't drop everything to take care of me in school holidays, and she couldn't afford childcare. Alex offered to take me, and Mum jumped at the chance. She got some breathing space, I got the freedom a child is rarely given, and Alex got some company.' She laughed. 'Although I suspect he was relieved when we were retrieved by our respective parents.'

'We?'

'Charles and me. His dad's job meant they moved around a lot, so it gave Charles stability, spending holidays there. And, of course, he loved having a doting tomboy following him around, agreeing to all his hare-brained schemes - which Alex encouraged, by the way.'

'Sounds like Alex was a great bloke. By the time I met him, he was very frail.' Steve frowned. 'But he must still have been fairly ancient when you two stayed there, surely?'

'That was why we got the freedom of the place - he couldn't run around after us. Alex rounded us up for meals and spent the evenings reading adventure stories to us - which only encouraged exploring and building unstable treehouses, as I recall.'

Hettie was aware that the conversation had been all about her, so when the food arrived, she asked Steve about himself, discovering he'd embarked on his legal career at a big, fancy firm in Manchester, only to realise that his forte - dealing with people sympathetically - might be better put to use in a smaller practice.

'Isn't it all house purchases and divorces?' she asked.

Steve smiled. 'Not always. You'd be surprised. Even a will can contain a little interest and excitement. Take your great-uncle, for example. Alex said I'd enjoy meeting you, and he was right. Anyway, I'm content. The big-time was never for me. How about you?'

'I wouldn't say I aspire to dizzy heights in university administration, but I enjoy my job and the department I'm in. A higher pay scale wouldn't go amiss, though.'

'When Alex's affairs are sorted, you'll get a portion of the house. I know he shared it amongst quite a few relatives, but still, it's something.'

'I haven't thought much about that yet.' Hettie made a

face. 'There's a lot of water – or, rather, paperwork and hard graft – to go under the bridge first.'

*

In bed at the B&B that night, Hettie felt unsettled, and she had a sneaking suspicion it wasn't all down to the funeral or her legal responsibilities.

It was disconcerting to be back in Haven Bridge. A decade had gone by since she'd last stayed there, and yet it was like yesterday. She hadn't had time to explore yet. Maybe she could do that in the morning, before she moved up to the house and began to assess what she needed to do.

She would have to phone work and extend her leave for another week – she had plenty of holiday owing. But she suspected that a second week would make little difference. She might as well resign herself to coming up north every weekend for the next five *years*, by the looks of the house.

From out of nowhere, a tiny voice asked her if that would be so terrible, with a handsome solicitor seemingly willing to hold her hand through the whole process. She hadn't expected to find him so amenable, so empathetic, so – *oh, admit it, Hettie* – so damned attractive.

As she punched her pillow and tried to settle down, sleep felt a long way away.

*

The next morning, Hettie took the exploratory stroll around town she'd promised herself. Haven Bridge was a lovely place, with its old stone buildings and eclectic mix of shops and cafés. Uncle Alex used to take her and Charles for daily walks around the town or along the canal, and Hettie remembered trying to peer through the barge windows, wondering what it was like inside. She and Charles always managed to entice

Alex into the sweet shop, and he would always pretend to fight against it, making their hard-won mint choc chip ice cream or bag of sherbet pips taste so much better, somehow.

Wandering the streets, she couldn't help comparing it with London. Here, you could walk along without being jostled. The air seemed fresher. Noticeboards outside shops advertised local book clubs and yoga classes and meditation groups. It would be easier to make friends here, Hettie thought; to connect with people, maybe find a niche for yourself.

She noted what had changed and was pleased to see there was still a traditional sweet shop in town. Eventually, she found herself outside Miss Moonshine's shop on Market Street.

It hadn't changed a jot. The handsome stone building had been here since 1777, according to the date above the door. Set back from the road, with roses dotted between the stone slabs in front and growing up an arch over the doorway, it looked more like a fine old house than a place of business. Hettie and Charles had spent many happy hours rooting through Miss Moonshine's amazing selection of goods, old and new – a cornucopia of fascination for curious children.

Alex had stated in his will that all his unwanted tat – er, that is, vintage valuables – should go to Miss Moonshine to sell, with half the profits for charity. Since the old lady hadn't been at Alex's funeral, Hettie felt she should reintroduce herself.

If the shop hadn't changed, then neither had Miss Moonshine. Birdlike, with white hair piled loosely on her head, she had always had an *interesting* sense of fashion, which today had resulted in black leggings, a floaty dress and a scuffed leather jacket. No growing old gracefully for Miss Moonshine, Hettie thought, smiling as she approached her.

The old woman recognised her immediately, her hazel eyes shining. 'Hettie Brown. How the devil are you?'

'Fine, thank you, Miss Moonshine. It's good to be back in Haven Bridge, despite the circumstances.'

The old lady's eyes dulled. 'I'm sorry about Alex. And I'm sorry I wasn't at the funeral, but I don't do them nowadays. I've attended too many over the years to count.'

'I understand.' Hettie breathed in the citrus scent from an oil burner behind the mahogany counter. 'You know about Alex's will?'

'Yes. That handsome young solicitor came to see me.'

Hettie glanced dubiously around the crowded store, its shelves and tables and niches bulging with anything and everything. 'There'll be a ton of stuff for you.'

'Don't worry. I won't let Alex down. You'd be surprised how much you can fit in this place.'

A bundle of chihuahua fur stirred in a basket next to the counter, and doleful eyes stared up at them as if to say, '*More* stuff? You must be joking!'

Miss Moonshine patted his head. 'Go back to sleep, Napoleon. This doesn't concern you. Would you like a cup of tea, Hettie?'

'Thanks, but I'd better not. I've already wasted the morning wandering aimlessly, reminiscing. I need to get on.'

'Some other time, then. You'll drop in again?'

'Of course.' Hettie turned to go.

'Oh, and Hettie?'

'Yes?'

'Time reminiscing isn't time wasted. Memories are important. They're not always firmly in the past. Sometimes they lead you to your future.'

*

By the following evening, Hettie was satisfied with how things were going up at the house. She'd moved into a guest bedroom, and otherwise she mainly occupied the kitchen and the sunroom. And she'd made a start on the rest.

Since the larger items and furniture would be cleared by a specialist, Hettie concentrated on everything else – the contents of every shelf, every cupboard, every drawer. Alex had been a serious hoarder, so the only way to tackle it was room by room – and be ruthless.

That was the hard part. Hettie tried to be objective, but sometimes memories overwhelmed her, and the years would fade until she was a child again, exploring every room, every corner of the garden, never bored. Sometimes she found herself clutching some item or other, staring at it as her mind drifted to the past – not with melancholy, but with a smile on her face. People often looked back on their childhoods through rose-tinted glasses, Hettie knew, but her holidays here with Charles and Uncle Alex really had been a glorious time of freedom and learning and exploration.

The downside was that the memories made her realise how unexciting her current existence was. She'd been in London for a couple of years, renting with flatmates she got along with but couldn't call best friends; not much of a social life to speak of; a job she loved and excelled at, but in a city she had no ties with. Spending time at Uncle Alex's reminded her how important those ties could be. Haven Bridge was a proper community.

When Steve arrived unexpectedly mid-evening, he found her cross-legged on the floor of one of the many bedrooms with a large pile of stuff behind her, three smaller piles in front of her and a thoughtful frown on her face.

'Tell me there's method to this madness,' he said from the doorway.

Hettie jumped a mile (if it's possible to jump from a cross-legged position). 'Oh! I didn't see you.'

'Nor did you hear me come through the *unlocked* door and up the stairs.' He moved into the room and placed a hand on her shoulder. 'Hettie, I worry about you being here on your own. At least you could save me from grey hair by locking the door.'

'Sorry.' Hettie stood and dusted down her jeans. 'Although I can't imagine anything happening all the way out here.'

'That's what every victim in every horror movie says.' He sighed. 'Sorry. I don't mean to pass my heebie-jeebies onto you. You're obviously more comfortable in this mausoleum than I am.' He pointed to the teetering piles around her. 'Why don't I make us some tea, then give you a hand?'

'Oh no, I couldn't expect you to.' Hettie's tone didn't hold much conviction. She'd been alone with her thoughts enough over the past couple of days. His company was welcome.

'See it as a favour to Alex, if you're worried about me doing *you* a favour. Besides, this place holds a certain fascination.' Steve gave a mock shudder, making Hettie laugh, and set off for the kitchen.

When he came back with steaming mugs of tea, she explained her system. 'I'm only allowing myself three piles – one for Miss Moonshine and the charity thing, one to chuck and one to keep. I'm trying to keep the "keep" pile small. But...'

'Some things have too many memories?'

Hettie was pleased he understood. 'I begged another week from work.'

'You're going to need it.' Picking up an old seventies cassette recorder, Steve frowned. 'What made Alex such a hoarder? He wasn't a proper collector, was he? Jed said he worked in the mills.'

'That's right. He loved the textile industry. Loved the history, how the machinery worked. He loved knowing how *anything* worked.' Hettie pointed at the recorder in Steve's hands. 'One evening, he took that apart just to show me and Charles how it worked. Then he helped us to put it back together again. He missed his job when he retired, so he surrounded himself with this stuff and tinkered to his heart's content. He was thrilled when Charles became an engineer.'

'I bet.' Steve hesitated. 'You speak very fondly of Charles. He was the same about you when I spoke to him. Do you see him much?'

'With him in Glasgow and me in London, it's not easy. We meet up for weekends when we can.'

'Does he ... have a girlfriend? Partner?'

'Not at the moment. They come and go. But someone'll grab him for good one of these days. I know I'm biased, but he's quite a catch.'

*

Hettie was surprised when Steve turned up again the following evening, but she certainly wasn't complaining. She'd worked her way through two more rooms during the day.

Steve glanced at the 'keep' piles and nudged her playfully. 'I thought you were keeping those down.'

Hettie shrugged, sheepish. 'I'll go through them again when I'm feeling more detached. And there could be things that Charles might want, so he'll need to go through it sometime, too.'

'Is he planning on coming up here again?' There was a strange expression on Steve's face.

'Of course. He can't expect me to make all the decisions on my own, can he?'

Steve sipped at his tea. 'It'll be nice for you, having some company. Somebody to help.'

Hettie gave him a pointed look. 'I already have that. Don't you have a social life?'

Steve laughed, erasing his earlier frown. 'I'm having a couple of pints with some mates on Saturday, and I'll be out for my usual group ramble on the hills on Sunday. Does that count?'

*So that's where he gets his tan.* 'Of course it counts. There's no ... girlfriend?'

Steve watched her through the steam rising from his mug. 'I'm taking someone out for dinner tomorrow night.'

Hettie suppressed a pang of disappointment. 'Lucky girl. What's her name?'

'Hettie.'

'Hmmm?'

'Her name's Hettie.' When she stared at him blankly, he rolled his eyes. 'You need to eat, don't you?'

'Oh! You mean me? Well. Thank you.' But he still hadn't answered her question. 'I won't be treading on anyone's toes?'

'I have three women on the go, but I reckon I can juggle a fourth.' He gave her a look. 'No. No-one's toes.'

'Good. Well. That's lovely. Dinner, I mean, would be lovely.' Flustered, Hettie put down her tea, plucked a clockwork monkey from the bed and wound it up so it clashed its cymbals, opening and closing its mouth in a maniacal grin. 'Chuck, keep or Miss Moonshine?'

Steve shuddered. 'Anything but keep. That thing would give me nightmares!'

*

The following evening, as Hettie showered off dust and cobwebs before her dinner with Steve, she was glad she'd popped out for a quick shopping spree. All she'd brought with her were jeans and t-shirts, and the black funeral dress was hardly appropriate for a date – er, that is, a meal out with a friend. In town, she'd found brown linen trousers and a lacy cotton top in a copper that flattered her hair colour. Inspecting herself in the mirror, she was pleased with the result. Less frizz would be good, but Hettie had long since given up her war with it.

Steve clearly approved. 'Wow! You look...'

'Cobweb-free?'

'I was going to go with gorgeous.' With a shy smile, he ushered her to his car and drove down the winding hill to park in town. They walked to a Mediterranean restaurant, enticing with fairy lights twinkling and candles flickering on the tables. Had he intended the romantic atmosphere, Hettie wondered?

As they studied the menu and ordered, she realised it was too long since she'd eaten out with a man. In London, it wasn't easy meeting someone. All the blokes at work were middle-aged, and the few dates instigated by her flatmates with friends of friends had come to nothing. Just because her last serious relationship had fizzled out didn't mean she didn't have hopes for the future.

'Penny for your thoughts?'

Hettie jolted. 'Sorry. I was thinking –' *Ah.* Perhaps it wouldn't do to let Steve think she saw this as a proper date. It certainly felt like one, but she'd been out of the dating game for a while, and she didn't trust her own instincts. Besides, were solicitors allowed to get involved with their clients? 'I was thinking how much easier it must be to make friends somewhere small like Haven Bridge.'

'Not easy in London?'

Hettie shrugged. 'I get on with my flatmates, and I go for drinks with colleagues, but everyone at work is younger or older or married with kids.'

'Do you enjoy your job?'

'Yes. Or at least, it's so busy that I don't have time to worry about it.'

'Do you like being in the city?'

'I was desperate to get away from the suburbs,' she told him, smiling. 'And, if I'm honest, I was also trying to escape a boyfriend I'd been going out with for a year before I realised he was horribly dull. He couldn't accept we were finished, and London seemed far enough away to persuade him. I had plenty of good intentions – to visit museums and galleries and soak up the culture – but it soon tailed off. Nowadays, all I want to do at weekends is catch up on sleep and binge-watch the latest series.'

Steve sipped his wine. 'If you have a hectic job, you need to relax at weekends. That's why I like it here. There's enough to do if you want to mooch around; have a coffee with friends. But if you're feeling energetic and want fresh air, there's plenty of good walking.'

The waiter brought their plates, and Hettie sniffed appreciatively at her fragrant lamb.

'Do I get the impression you're not entirely happy in London?' Steve asked as he tasted his food.

'I thought I was, but coming back here has stirred up memories.' Hettie sighed. 'You mentioned fresh air. I never saw myself as outdoorsy, but it turns out I do miss it, after all.' She smiled. 'Alex used to take us to the woods sometimes. We played hide-and-seek and built dens with branches and pretended to fish in the stream with twigs. I loved the burble of the water. And I loved the trees swishing all around us; a whispering, green fairyland.' She rolled her eyes. 'Sorry. I'm being fanciful. Perhaps I only enjoyed it because I was a kid with no worries.'

'I don't know about that. I like to walk in the woods; sit by the stream; let my mind wander. I could take you up there sometime, if you like.'

'That would be nice.' Hettie's face fell. 'But I don't think I can spare the time.'

A flicker of disappointment crossed Steve's features, but he nodded. 'You'll be up here for the odd weekend, won't you? Perhaps we could go then. Make it a working walk to save time.'

If there was one thing Hettie was sure of, it was that if she was on a woodland walk with Steve, she wouldn't want to be having a serious discussion about her great-uncle's affairs. She would want to hold hands and chatter and find out more about him, maybe even paddle in the stream and... *Oh dear, Hettie.*

Forcing herself back to the real world, she asked, 'Was it the countryside that made you decide to move here?'

'I couldn't put my finger on why I wanted to move. I only knew I wasn't happy with city life. It was like having a mental weighing scale – pros and cons on either side.' He used his knife and fork to demonstrate. 'One side drops and you don't notice, then it drops a bit more. It's only when it tips too far that you realise.'

Hettie was quiet for a while. How far had her scales tipped without her noticing?

'The last time I visited Alex at the hospice, he was in a probing mood,' she confessed. 'Did I love my job enough to stay in London? Couldn't I get a job I loved somewhere I liked better?'

'Was he suggesting you move back to Yorkshire?'

'He didn't *say* that, although I suppose he was hinting. He said he only wanted me to be happy. That I should do whatever it takes to make it happen.' Hettie's voice hitched. 'Sorry. I'm being sentimental.'

'That's understandable.' Steve reached out to touch her hand, transmitting warmth and friendship. '*Are* you happy?'

'Not ecstatically. But I'm not *un*happy.'

He cocked his head to one side. 'Alex would have been disappointed if you settled for that.'

'I know.' Hettie sighed. 'He told me I'd lost my way.'

Steve lifted her chin with a forefinger. 'That's not fair. You don't always realise you're on the wrong path until you're halfway along it. And then you can't choose the right path until one comes into sight.'

Hettie was aware the atmosphere between them had become charged with emotion. Time to lighten things up.

'I'll remember that, oh Wise One. Now, what should I do with a thirty-six-piece coffee set in sickly green?'

Steve smiled, and Hettie's pulse speeded up. He had an incredible smile.

'Hettie, I have a favour to ask.'

Emboldened by the wine and keen to move away from serious discussion, Hettie said, 'Fire away.'

'I'm going to a wedding a week tomorrow in Halifax. An old university mate. When I replied, I was seeing someone, so I accepted with a "plus one". We broke up, but I forgot to alter it. I hate going to weddings on my own. Would you take pity on me and come?'

Hettie's eyes widened. She had no reason to refuse, other than... 'I don't have anything to wear. I wouldn't know anyone. It would cost me a whole day's work at the house. And what if Charles decides to come up that weekend?'

Steve's crestfallen expression made her immediately sorry for the string of excuses. 'I'd like to help you out, but...'

'I understand if you don't fancy it. But if you are willing, I'm sure you'd find an outfit here in Haven Bridge. As for the house, I can help most evenings. And Charles?' The warmth left his tone. 'If he does come up that weekend, you'd have most of the Sunday together. He's meant to be helping, isn't he? It'd give him the house to himself.'

Hettie chewed her lip. 'I suppose.' And before she could listen to any more negative voices in her head, she accepted.

*

Hettie was delighted when Charles arrived the next morning to spend the weekend helping. Making decisions alone had been hard, and she wanted to go through everything with him.

Steve seemed somewhat less delighted. When he showed up with two takeaway cups of fragrant coffee, he looked dismayed as Charles and Hettie opened the door, giggling over a jigsaw that had caused them much amusement as children, due to the topless Spanish lady in the background.

'I brought coffee,' Steve said stiltedly. 'Sorry – I didn't know you'd be here, Charles.'

Hettie frowned. 'Didn't I tell you?'

'No. You said maybe next weekend. Here. You two have these. I came to help, but there's no need now.'

'Steve, stay and –'

But he'd already handed over the coffees, turned and headed back down the drive.

'*Well!* What was that about?' Charles asked.

Hettie watched Steve's receding back. 'I'm not sure.'

'What, it's normal for your solicitor to bring you coffee on a Saturday morning?'

'No, but... He popped by on the odd evening to give me a hand. And we've had a couple of meals together.'

'Oh?' There was a wealth of suggestion in Charles' tone.

Hettie punched him on the arm. 'He's worried about me being here on my own. And he's fascinated by the house.'

'It couldn't be the current *occupant* of the house he's fascinated by?'

'What? No!' Hettie felt her cheeks heat. 'We get on well. There's nothing more to it than that.'

Charles chose a coffee and took an appreciative sip. 'If you say so, Hettie.'

*

When Charles left on Sunday afternoon, Hettie felt lonely in the house on her own.

Steve didn't show up on Monday evening as she'd half expected, and Hettie couldn't help feeling disappointed – unfairly, she knew. He was under no obligation to turn up evening after evening to help her. It wasn't as though he was her boyfriend. A couple of dinners, a few evenings chatting and getting dusty together... It was hardly a serious relationship, for goodness' sake.

And yet when he finally showed up on Tuesday night, she was relieved; a relief that soon faded as she realised things between them were a little stilted. Hettie had a distinct feeling Steve hadn't taken to Charles, and she felt the need to smooth things over. She just wasn't sure how.

It was Steve who broached the subject. 'Did you enjoy your weekend with Charles?'

Hettie glanced warily at him, but his tone had been casual. 'Yes. Very much.'

'Get much done?'

'Lots. Amidst the exploring and reminiscing.'

'Good.' Steve nodded. 'Good.'

Did that mean that things were back to normal between them?

Steve changed the subject. 'Found an outfit for the wedding yet?'

Hettie winced. Despite a quick foray into town, she hadn't found anything that would fit the bill.

'Not yet,' she said. 'But I will. Don't worry.'

'Don't get anything you don't like, Hettie. And don't spend too much. You'll look great in anything.' He stared at his feet. 'I've put you in a bit of a jam.'

'Not at all,' she lied. 'It'll be fine.'

*

When Hettie went into Miss Moonshine's shop the next morning with a long list of items the old lady would be landed with to fob off onto an unsuspecting public, the shop owner picked up on her agitation straight away.

'Is something wrong, dear?'

'No. Just busy,' Hettie hedged. 'The sorting's hard. My "to keep" piles are getting out of hand.'

'If it helps, I have a general rule I stick to – that my possessions should either be useful or bring me joy. Preferably both.'

When Hettie's eyes strayed to take in the inordinate amount of clutter – however fascinating – around them, the old lady chuckled.

'I'm talking about personal possessions, not the shop. But there's something else troubling you. What is it?'

Sighing, Hettie explained about the wedding invitation.

Miss Moonshine switched on her kettle and produced a herbal teabag from an ancient caddy. When it had brewed, she handed the cup to Hettie.

'Why is that a problem? Steve's a lovely young man.'

'Yes. And I accepted because I didn't want to let him down. But I don't know him well enough for a long day like that.'

Miss Moonshine's eyes narrowed. 'You and Steve are getting to know each other pretty well, if you ask me. I gather he's spent quite a few evenings with you. That's more than some dating couples see of each other in a month.'

Hettie refrained from asking Miss Moonshine how she knew. The woman had always seemed to know things, a talent Hettie hadn't appreciated when she was a small child with mischief in mind. Instead, she whined, 'I have no idea what to wear. I've had a scout around town, but nothing felt right.'

'I'd go with something outside the box. Something unusual. That way, you'll either stun everyone's socks off with your originality, or if it's the wrong thing, it'll look as though you *deliberately* chose to be different. Can't lose.'

Hettie took in Miss Moonshine's outfit today – a long, tie-dyed skirt in indigo; a loose, lacy top; elbow-length, white gloves and shiny black biker boots. And yet somehow she pulled it off. Hettie wasn't sure she could do the same.

Miss Moonshine beckoned her towards the back of the shop. 'Let's see what we can find.'

As the older woman rummaged through rails of vintage clothing, Hettie began to regret bringing the subject up. She doubted that formal wedding wear could be found on a second-hand rail. Napoleon looked doubtful, too. He sat watching from a threadbare velvet stool in the changing room – a corner of the shop roped off with a heavy brocade curtain.

Half an hour later, Hettie was eating her – thankfully unspoken – words. After a false start with a stretchy red dress that made her look like a lumpy vampire bride and a flouncy cream number that brought a demented meringue to mind, Miss Moonshine came up trumps.

Hettie gaped at her reflection in the gilt-framed mirror. The crushed-velvet dress skimmed rather than clung to her figure in a shimmering multitude of purples and silvers and blacks, ending mid-calf. Hettie *knew* her black suede boots with spiky heels that she'd brought for the funeral would look great with it. Miss Moonshine handed her a pair of looped silver earrings with amethyst centres – 'On loan, Hettie dear, no need to buy them' – that went perfectly. And when she used two Victorian black jet combs to sweep Hettie's hair into a messy up-do that made it look like the frizz was intended all along, Hettie kissed her papery cheek.

'If I didn't know better, I'd say you had magic in you. How on earth did you put this together out of…' She wafted a hand at the shambolic array of clothing around them '…this?'

Miss Moonshine shrugged. 'It's a knack. And I know my stock.'

'It's a knack I'm grateful for.' Hettie studied herself in the mirror again. 'Although I'm worried I might stand out.'

'Only in a good way, Hettie. If you feel good in it, it will give you the confidence you need to get through the day, and that's what matters most.' Miss Moonshine's eyes twinkled. 'You'll turn a few heads, I reckon. Especially Steve's.'

Hettie harrumphed. 'I'm not out to turn anyone's head, Miss Moonshine. Most especially Steve's.'

*

That evening, Hettie was pleased to be able to tell Steve that she had finally found something to wear on Saturday.

'Was it expensive? It's my fault you had to buy it. I could help.'

'It didn't cost much,' Hettie reassured him. 'And I'd wear it again.'

Relieved, Steve turned back to the oak cupboard he was clearing and reached to the top shelf for a musty, dusty pile of papers.

'Shall I shove this lot into boxes for you to take back to London, to go through at leisure?' he called.

'Leisure? What's that?' Hettie retorted, laughing as Steve lost control, and sheaves of paper tumbled onto his head and down to the floor. 'Here. Let me help.'

She crouched beside him, shuffling the papers into piles, suddenly conscious of their nearness – and, disturbingly, the way his jeans moulded to his thighs.

*Inappropriate thoughts, Hettie. Control yourself.*

'What are these?' Steve showed her a handful of yellowed sketches of detailed, coloured grids.

'Designs for cloth.'

'Alex drew them out like this?'

'Yup. A long time ago now. Pre-technology and all that.'

Steve sat back on his heels and studied them. 'Things were so different back then. In kind of a nice way, I reckon.'

'Maybe. But Alex also said it was dangerous and noisy and ... ha!' Caught by a memory, Hettie burst out laughing.

Steve smiled at her. 'What?'

'I just remembered the story about the foreman sneezing.'

'And that was funny because...?'

Hettie grinned. 'It's funny *because* the man's false teeth flew out when he sneezed and slid right under one of the machines, and he couldn't get them back because it would've been dangerous. The factory cat shot after them amidst all the fluff and filth and brought them back out licked clean, and the foreman put them straight back in!'

Steve joined in her laughter, making Hettie feel warm

inside. It was good to have someone to laugh with her; to share her memories and not seem to mind the endless supply of them. Someone to keep her company in the evenings after she'd spent a long day working on her own. It was *really* good.

*

Hettie might have told Miss Moonshine she wasn't out to turn Steve's head with her outfit, but turn it she most definitely did.

His jaw almost hit the floor when she opened the door to him on Saturday morning.

'Hettie. You look stunning.'

She managed to turn a self-satisfied smirk into a gracious smile. 'Thank you. I'm still not sure it's the right thing to wear.'

'It is. It most definitely is.'

Hettie took in his grey suit. 'You scrub up pretty nicely yourself.' *Most definitely.*

Hettie turned a few heads at the wedding, too. Yes, she stood out from the more conservatively dressed guests, but as Miss Moonshine had predicted, she didn't care. She just felt so damned *good* in the outfit.

Steve obviously thought she felt good in it, too. As the daytime reception segued into the evening dancing, he became more tactile, holding her close, his hand around her waist unable to remain still, skimming the fabric as they moved to the music.

Tired from the long day and the strain of chatting with people she didn't know, Hettie was simply happy to be with someone she *did* know as they moved slowly to the smoochy numbers.

'You have no idea how grateful I am that you came,' Steve murmured. 'Everyone's dancing with their wife or girlfriend or a convenient cute niece or grandchild. If you weren't here, I'd've had to sit all on my lonesome, watching everyone's coupledom. I would've been *very* forlorn.'

He smiled, and Hettie's pulse stuttered.

As she smiled back, she wondered if *his* pulse stuttered the same way. 'Glad to be of service. Although you wouldn't have been alone for long. Quite a few women have their eye on you.'

Steve pulled her closer, so their bodies moulded together, and Hettie rested her head on his shoulder and drifted. How was it possible to be this content whilst being so *aware* of the two of them?

Maybe it was getting to Steve, too. 'How about a little fresh air?' he whispered. 'See if there's any moonlight out there.'

Disappointed at breaking the contact, Hettie allowed him to lead her off the dancefloor, out into the grounds where lamps illuminated a halo around the building before petering away into darkness.

Steve headed for the darkness. On the edge of it, he turned her to face him. 'It was a little public in there for what I had in mind.'

'What *do* you have in mind?'

His hand cupped her face, while the other slid around her back. 'This.'

Hettie's breath caught as his head lowered, his lips landing lightly on hers. He waited a moment, allowing her time to resist, but Hettie had no intention of resisting as his mouth began a gentle but powerful onslaught that left her unable to do anything other than go along with it. She wound her arms around his neck, pulling him closer.

A noisy group catapulting onto the patio from the ballroom jolted them apart.

'I thought I was only supposed to be your plus one,' Hettie chided.

The corners of Steve's mouth twitched. 'You shouldn't believe everything you're told.'

She poked him in the chest. 'You're a solicitor. You're supposed to deal with the truth.'

'It was the truth. I needed a plus one. I also wanted to spend a whole day with you, away from the dust and chaos of the house. I hadn't bargained for the added bonus of seeing you dressed like this.' He ran a finger under the dress at her shoulder, sending a tingle that rippled out much further than where he'd touched.

'You don't like me in filthy jeans and baggy t-shirts?'

'On the contrary, I love you in jeans. You have an excellent backs– er, figure. But you look amazing in this, Hettie.'

Hettie smiled widely, silently sending thanks to Miss Moonshine through the ether.

'You feel good in it, too.' One of his hands slid down her side while the other moved over her shoulder and down her back, both heading south.

Hettie stopped him gently, rewarding him for his restraint with another kiss.

'The dancefloor was safer,' she pointed out.

With a lingering look at her mouth, Steve reluctantly nodded. 'Yeah.'

Back indoors, the band were on a break and the noise of laughter and chinking glasses grated. Hettie knew the magical moment was broken – but they couldn't have carried on like that in a dark garden all night, could they?

In silent agreement, they left the party and drove home in contemplative quiet. When Steve dropped her at the house, she declined his offer to see her indoors.

'You don't trust me?' he asked, hurt in his eyes.

She placed a gentle kiss on his lips. 'I don't trust myself.'

*

If Saturday was an unexpectedly enjoyable dream, then Sunday turned into a miserable nightmare.

It started out well enough. Charles asked Hettie about the wedding, teased her about Steve and demanded to know what information she was withholding (most of the evening and especially the kisses). To her relief, he gave in gracefully with his loveable, boyish grin and proceeded to show her what he'd been up to while she was being romanced.

They ate lunch in the sunshine on the back patio – so far, so good – and then Charles glanced at his watch.

'I have to leave in an hour or so. How about a game of tag? Work off lunch?'

'*Tag*?'

'Why not? You used to love it when we were kids.'

Hettie was about to point out that they weren't kids anymore, but the wistful look in his eyes stopped her.

'Fine. But I'm not as quick as I used to be. I need a head start. Count to ten first.' She eyed his long legs. 'Make that twenty.' Without waiting for a reply, she was off, streaking across the sloping, overgrown lawn like a hare.

When Steve appeared twenty minutes later, Hettie and Charles were embroiled in a red-faced tussle on the grass at the back of the house, Charles pinning her underneath him as she wriggled to get away.

'Tagged you!'

'Didn't!'

'Did!'

'Didn't – Oh! Steve!' Hettie brushed hair back from her face in an effort to appear civilised. 'I wasn't expecting you.'

'Clearly.'

Hettie took in his expression. It wasn't friendly.

'I've spent ten minutes searching the house for you,' he said curtly. 'I was getting worried. The screaming didn't help.'

'Ah. Sorry. We were –' Still out of breath – crikey, she'd allowed herself to get unfit lately – Hettie wafted a hand vaguely.

Releasing her, Charles picked up the slack. 'Reliving childhood memories. Playing games.'

'Games. Yes. So I see.'

'I'd better get ready.' Casting a quick glance at Hettie, Charles skirted widely around Steve and scarpered into the house.

'I assumed he'd have already gone.' Steve's voice was tight.

Hettie frowned. What on earth had come over him? 'He's about to go.'

'What time are you setting off for London?' It sounded more like a police interrogation than a question from a friend.

Disconcerted, Hettie mumbled, 'In a couple of hours. Did you come for a reason?'

'I came to say goodbye.'

'Well, I'll be back next weekend, I suppose.' Hettie's good mood had dissipated rapidly. It felt like there was a wall of ice between them. 'Steve, what's wrong? Is it – is it to do with last night?'

'It's not about last night!' His outburst startled her. 'Well, yes, it is. But it's more about that cousin of yours.'

Hettie stared at him. 'What has Charles got to do with anything?'

'Don't you know?' Exasperated, he said, 'You and I have been getting pretty close, Hettie. Especially last night. But whenever Charles is around, you're giggling and hugging and – I don't know how to even begin to describe what that was just now.'

'It was a game of tag.'

'It all looks rather familiar to me.'

Hettie's eyes narrowed. 'Are you *jealous* of him?'

'Would that be so unnatural?'

Taken aback, Hettie lost her cool. 'It would be *stupid*.' But even as she said it, she realised he was serious. 'Steve, all those tales I told you about my childhood holidays here with Charles... Did I *ever* suggest there was anything other than affection between us?'

'Childhood is one thing. Now you're adults. Very affectionate adults.'

'Yes, but that's rather different to what you're suggesting. I can't believe you're so upset about it.'

'I thought we had a connection, Hettie. Something special.' He dragged in a long breath. 'OK. I accept that the jealousy is stupid, but I can't help feeling it. What you and Charles have is solid and unbreakable. What you and I have is new and fragile. It's hard, the idea of you going back to London while I fade into a distant memory.'

'You know I'll be back for the odd weekend. Besides, I – I had no idea you felt that way.'

Steve threw his arms out in frustration. 'What *did* you think?'

'I thought we were becoming good friends.' *With tingles whenever you smiled at me. A racing pulse whenever you laughed with me.*

'You never had a relationship born out of friendship?' Steve demanded. 'Isn't friendship the best basis for a relationship? And what about last night?'

*Ah*. 'I suppose I put that down to the moonlight and music.' Although she'd spent a restless night reliving it.

'That's all? Was it in my imagination, the attraction between us?'

'No! It's there for me, too. But…' Hettie sighed. 'I didn't think you'd want it to go anywhere. We'll be living separate lives again soon.'

He ran a hand through his hair. 'We should have talked. And I suppose I didn't know what I wanted.'

Hettie's heart thudded against her ribcage. 'Does that mean that you know now?'

'Maybe. But I'm not sure it makes any difference. You're leaving, and I'm staying.'

A hollowness gnawed at Hettie's insides. 'Wouldn't we keep in touch?'

'The odd e-mail or text? That's not what I had in mind, Hettie.'

'Then *what*?' Hettie almost shouted, frustration getting the better of her.

'Look, I'm glad we're friends. But I want more than that. After yesterday, I hoped you did, too. Long-distance relationships are hard, though, and we'd *both* have to be committed. I get the impression you're not so keen. So, I guess it can't be helped.' He shook his head. 'It can't be helped.'

And without giving her a chance to reply – not that she had any idea what she would say – he turned on his heel and left, shoulders sloping, chin down to his chest.

'Well!' Hettie slid onto the nearest chair, her head reeling.

Steve was right about one thing – it was no use envisaging a relationship. What he was wrong about was her perceived indifference. She'd loved his company. Her responses to his smile, his laugh, over the fortnight she'd been in Haven Bridge should have warned her well before they danced together that he was becoming more than a friend.

When Charles came downstairs with his bags, he didn't say anything, for which she was grateful. After waving him off, she packed her own stuff on automatic pilot.

The drive back to London was too long a time to be alone with her thoughts.

And the following week back in London was too long to be without Steve. At work, she managed to ignore the pangs by keeping busy. The evenings were another matter. Chatting with her flatmates over cups of tea, watching TV, trying to concentrate on reading a book... The way she usually spent her evenings paled when she remembered the warm laughter and animated chatter she'd shared with Steve at Alex's house.

*

The following weekend saw Hettie once more at the house in Haven Bridge. All the hard work she'd put into sorting things out meant it didn't feel lived in any more. Alex's presence was already fading. And Steve's.

He hadn't been in contact all week, despite the fact they had things to discuss with regard to Alex's estate. She'd even e-mailed Charles to see if he'd heard anything as co-executor. He'd said not and asked if everything was OK. She'd lied and told him it was.

But it wasn't, and here she was spending her Saturday mooching unproductively about the house. Huffing, she put the kettle on for yet another so-called soothing cup of chamomile tea that soothed nothing at all.

A knock at the door made her jump.

'Cooey! Hope you don't mind, Hettie, dear.' Miss Moonshine breezed in, today in tight jeans that showed off her svelte figure, a vest-tee covered with a giant flapping man's shirt, and her favourite biker boots.

'Miss Moonshine. What can I do for you?'

'I was passing, so I thought I'd pop in. I wondered if you could give me any idea how much more junk Alex has let me in for?' She cocked her head to one side. 'A cup of tea would be nice. And a chat.'

Uncomfortable under her gaze, Hettie turned back to the kettle.

She knew. The woman knew something was wrong. It was like she had a sixth sense.

Hettie carried the tea to the sunroom, and they sat genteelly sipping from the old china tea set like ladies in an Oscar Wilde play.

'How did the wedding go last week?' Miss Moonshine's voice was casual, but her hazel eyes were sharp.

'Very well, thank you. The dress was perfect. Oh, wait. I still have your earrings.' Keen to avoid interrogation, Hettie ran upstairs to retrieve them.

'Thank you,' Miss Moonshine said as Hettie handed them over. 'I have a customer with a reserve on them.'

That was a shame. Hettie might have bought them for herself. Ah, well.

Miss Moonshine clicked her tongue and put her teacup down. 'Isn't there anything you want to talk about, Hettie?'

Caught like a rabbit in headlights, Hettie stuttered, 'Like what?'

'Like how you've been getting on with Steve like a house on fire and now you're conflicted because you think it could go somewhere, but it can't because you live so far apart and neither of you is in a position to do much about it?'

'You can't know that.'

Miss Moonshine gave her a look. 'Any idiot with eyes could see the attraction between you two. As for the rest, put it down to logic or intuition – whichever you believe in more – aided by the way Steve has been stomping along the street past my shop every day, temper and misery emanating off him.'

'Ah.' Hettie sighed. 'Anyway, there's no solution.'

Miss Moonshine wagged a finger at her. 'Rubbish. You could start out with a long-distance relationship. Test the water.'

'I'm not sure either of us wants that, Miss Moonshine. Too tiring. Too painful if it doesn't work out. Even more painful if it does.'

'Why could neither of you move?'

'Steve's not a city boy. I couldn't expect him to go back to something he hated. And it's taken him time to build up a reputation here. It would be unreasonable to expect him to start all over again.'

'I understand that. But do *you* love London so much?'

Hettie fell silent for a moment. 'I thought so,' she finally said. 'But it's so nice here, the way people know each other and nod to each other on the street. It feels comfortable. Still, I do love my job.'

'Couldn't you find something similar here?'

'Vacancies like that will be few and far between,' Hettie said.

Miss Moonshine reached into her bag, pulled out a piece of paper and handed it over. On it were online links to two admin vacancies at the University of Bradford.

When Hettie merely stared at them, Miss Moonshine filled the silence. 'Would it be so hard for you to change course a little, Hettie? Perhaps it's time to decide what matters to you and to chase after *those* things instead of the things you've conditioned yourself to want.'

'Maybe.' Hettie's voice was small. 'Maybe.'

*

Steve didn't come to the house at all that day. Hettie still felt sick at the way things had been left between them the previous weekend.

She couldn't resist looking up the links Miss Moonshine had given her. One job wasn't her area of expertise. The other was. It would be a pay grade higher, too. Even so, Hettie wasn't sure she wanted to uproot herself on the faint promise of a romance. What she did know was that moving to Haven Bridge appealed in its own right, and that was important. If she did move, and it didn't work out between her and Steve – a possibility, despite Miss Moonshine's predictions – she had to want to be there for *herself*.

Sleep was elusive that night.

*

Hettie was steeling herself to phone Steve the next morning, hopefully to clear the air between them, if nothing else, when there was a knock at the door.

That was a bad sign, she thought, as she opened it to find Steve standing there. He'd always let himself in before.

'Hi.'

'Hi.'

The awkwardness was painful.

'Coffee?'

'Please.'

She made them both a strong one, and he followed her to the sunroom, perching awkwardly on the edge of a cane chair.

'I came to apologise for last Sunday,' he said. 'I lost the plot a bit.'

Hettie shook her head. 'You said things that needed to be said. If you hadn't, I would have gone back to London not knowing how you felt.'

'But I was abrupt. I left so suddenly because I didn't want to say anything I'd regret.' He dug into his pocket and pulled out a small package wrapped in tissue. 'I brought you a present.'

'Thank you.' Hettie unwrapped the tissue to reveal the silver and amethyst earrings Miss Moonshine had lent her for the wedding. '*You* bought these?'

'You looked so beautiful that night, and they suited you so perfectly, I couldn't imagine anyone else wearing them. I thought you might like them as a reminder of your time here.'

*And of me.* His unspoken words hung in the air between them.

'They're beautiful.' Hettie fingered the hammered silver and the smooth polished stones, knowing they were her favourite piece of jewellery already. A jolt of happiness ran through her fingers, as though sent by the stones themselves.

She closed her eyes as Miss Moonshine's words came back to her. *'Would it be so hard for you to change course a little, Hettie? Perhaps it's time to decide what matters to you and to chase after* those *things instead of the things you've conditioned yourself to want.'*

Hettie reached out to take Steve's hand. 'What would you say if I told you there's a vacancy at the university in Bradford?'

Steve stared at her, hope in his eyes. 'I'd say, "Go for it".'

'I might not get it.'

'You can only take one step at a time, Hettie. You're really thinking of moving up here?'

'Yes.'

'You know I wouldn't ask you to do that for me, don't you? I couldn't bear the idea you might move here for us and then be unhappy.'

'I'm doing it for me. Haven Bridge is where I want to

be. As for "us"?' She took a deep breath. 'Steve, we haven't known each other long...'

'That doesn't make any difference, if there's something there. You know there is. I know there is.' His eyes twinkled. 'Even Miss Moonshine knows there is.'

A sudden thought came to Hettie. 'You know, Alex had an awful lot of relatives he could have chosen to be executors. I assumed he chose Charles and me because we loved the house so much. But... Steve, you don't think he did it because he was trying to get you and me together, do you?'

Steve smiled. 'Would you put it past him?'

Hettie thought about it. 'No. But it was a heck of a long shot.'

Steve moved across to sit next to her on the sofa. 'Well, I for one am glad he played it.' Pulling her close, his hand curled around the back of her neck and his other arm tightened around her waist. 'Go for the job, Hettie,' he murmured against her mouth. 'Move up here. Give us a chance. You won't regret it, I promise.'

As his lips closed over hers, his heart beating steadily against her own, Hettie knew he was right about that.

She would have no regrets.

**As a child, Helen had a vivid imagination fuelled by her love of reading, so she started to create her own stories in a notebook. Now a bestselling author of contemporary romance, she believes that good characterisation is the key to a successful book and loves infusing her writing with humour and heart.**

amazon.co.uk/Helen-Pollard/e/B00O2E0BRC

# Miss Moonshine Says, 'Go!'

*By Angela Wren*

*Saturday*

In the early morning sunshine, Charlotte's gleaming black bodywork shone. There was just something about a rally day and the sight of the 1936 4-4 two-seater Morgan that made Maddie's heart beat faster. Strictly speaking, the Morgan was her dad's car, but she had worked on it alongside her father since she was a teenager. Now, at the age of 28, Maddie was co-owner with her dad of a repair and bodyshop that specialised in work on old vehicles. Business was good, and that same business enabled Maddie and her dad to take advantage of tours and rallies like The North Yorkshire Oldies' Tour of the Dales. At least, that was how it was supposed to be.

Maddie broke into a steady trot, her eyes focused on the car in its designated spot in the paddock. To everyone else in Haven Bridge, the paddock was just the station car park – used every working day of the week by commuters.

I hope Raych makes it on time, Maddie thought, as she drew level with the car. As always, she circled it, patted the bonnet and let a self-satisfied grin spread across her face.

'Well, old girl, it might be just you and me today, if Raych doesn't get here.'

A tall, athletic man in overalls and a padded jacket strode from the officials' table across to one of the cars a few spaces away.

Maddie moved swiftly around her open-top car, releasing the fastenings on the cover that protected the interior. Once folded, she laid the cover on the passenger seat, before reaching behind for the two small ramps that would enable her to get under the vehicle to check the suspension and brakes. She placed the ramps in front of the wheels and drove the car slowly into position. Then she pulled her arms out of her dad's black, full-length driving coat and left it on her seat. Another reminder that her father couldn't be there.

With the car up on its portable ramps, Maddie quickly located the spanner she needed for the checks on the brakes and suspension. She glanced across the paddock. The man in the overalls was now standing beside a car she also recognised, talking to someone else. Yup, that's him, she thought. She lowered herself onto her trolley and pushed herself under the car to begin her usual work.

About ten minutes later, with just a couple of checks left, she became aware of a presence.

'Hello, Mr Townsend. It is Mr Martin Townsend, isn't it?'

Maddie thought she recognised the voice. Her concentration was interrupted and her irritation level rapidly began to rise. Her feet, clad in her favourite and most comfortable pumps, were sticking out from under the car. Beside them was another pair of feet, definitely male and clad in heavy black safety boots. She sighed, tucked the spanner in her overalls pocket and slid herself out.

'It's Maddie Townsend, actually. Short for Madeleine.'

Her tone was more cutting than she intended.

The man smiled. 'I guess the flowery pumps did kind of give that away. I'm Simon Walker. We competed against each other last year, if you remember.'

'Yup. I also remember that you took first place to my second.' She crossed her arms, stood her ground and stared at him, wondering what was coming next.

'That's true, but you and your dad didn't exactly make it easy for me and my co-driver. Surely you realised that at the time?'

Maddie shrugged. 'Maybe.' She rocked back and leaned against the car. 'This year I'll be even more difficult to beat.' She raised her left eyebrow in challenge.

Simon smiled. 'Maybe,' he said. 'And your dad? Is he driving or navigating this year?'

Maddie let her bravado slip a little. She tidied a stray strand of blonde hair behind her ear. 'Unfortunately, Dad can't be here this year. He's not too well at the moment and he's... umm...' She bit back the tears that always appeared when her father was in her mind. 'He's got to take things easy for a while. So, umm... I will be driving for both days of the tour.' She blurted out the last statement and looked her competitor straight in the eye.

Simon nodded. 'Well, may the best driver win.'

'I will,' she stated. Having regained control of her composure she realised the paddock was almost silent and significantly fuller than earlier. A train pulled out of the station and Maddie noticed Simon was now looking past her. She turned. Strutting towards the paddock was a tall, willowy brunette in tight white jeans, with a dusky pink blouse cinched in at the waist, wheeling a lilac suitcase behind her. As the woman sashayed between the cars, all work on engines, bodywork or tyres stopped. Dozens of pairs of eyes followed her route until she halted at Maddie's parking space.

'Hi, I'm Raychelle Decoursey,' she said, addressing Simon, her right hand proffered for him to shake.

Maddie cleared her throat. 'My navigator,' she explained.

Simon nodded and shook Raych's hand. 'Simon. And may the best team win.'

When her fellow competitor was out of earshot, Maddie turned to her companion.

'Could you really have been any more obvious, Raych?'

Raych ran her hand through her flowing and perfectly coiffed locks and smiled knowingly. 'I don't know what you mean.' Her dark brown eyes were open wide in mock wonderment. 'I'm a free agent now, he was gorgeous, and it was an opportunity not to be missed.' She tossed her hair back over her shoulder.

Maddie sighed.

'Oh... Umm, I haven't stamped on the beginning of a beautiful – ?'

'No. Hell, no.' Maddie rifled in her pocket for the spanner. 'He's nobody. Just the guy I've got to beat this year, that's all.'

Raych gave her friend a questioning look. 'But you don't deny he's gorgeous, then?'

Maddie dropped down onto her trolley and disappeared under the car. 'Hadn't even noticed.'

'Really, is that so? Well you don't fool me, Madeleine Townsend, so just get yourself back out from under that damn car and tell me all about him.'

'Raych. Ouch! Damn it.' Maddie emerged from her hiding place, her left hand cradling her temple, which was now sporting a greasy splodge over the beginnings of a lump. Upright again, she wiped her grubby hands on an equally grubby cloth that she kept in her pocket.

'You may think he's cute or whatever, but I can't afford to be distracted. I've got a rally to win, Raych, and I need your help to do that. So cute or not, Simon is off the menu.'

Raych gave her friend a who-do-you-think-you're-kidding look.

Maddie let her guard down and, hands shoved deep in her pockets, she let out an exasperated sigh. 'OK, you win. Be my guest, but at least wait until the tour is over and that trophy is in the bag for my dad.' She could feel a tear beginning to well in the corner of her right eye.

'It's OK. I get it.' Raych reached out and gently squeezed her friend's upper arm. Unable to be serious for long, she let a broad smile spread across her face. 'And as for Simon, well, now you're talking. And it's an absolute promise – no hanky-panky until we cross that finish line on Sunday afternoon.'

They both broke into spontaneous laughter. 'Deal. Now we need to get organised. The officials' table is over there, so take your suitcase to the hotel and dig out only what you'll need tonight.' Maddie had booked rooms for them both at The Old Grange in Asby. 'When you get back here, we need to sign on and get the Tour Road Book and Time Cards, and the sooner you get to grips with the paperwork, the better.'

Raych saluted and grinned. 'Aye, aye, Captain.' Gaudy case in tow, she resumed her sashay across the remainder of the paddock, followed by yet more pairs of male eyes.

Maddie moved to the front of the car and unstrapped the bonnet. She was once again lost in her world of grease and oil and engine components. The only place she ever really felt completely at ease. Here she could happily lose herself and put off having to deal with the rest of life's more difficult stresses and strains.

*

With no more than a few minutes to go, Maddie pulled on her father's coat and fastened it from top to bottom. Helmet on and goggles sitting on top of her head, she climbed into the driver's seat.

'Where's your cagoule or raincoat or whatever?'

'It's July! It's a beautiful and bright sunny day. I won't need a coat.' Raych examined her carefully painted nails.

'We're on a tour of Yorkshire. It rains a lot here. Especially up in the Dales.' Maddie put the car in gear.

'Well if it rains we can stop and put the hood up, can't we?'

Maddie looked behind as she reversed out of her parking spot. 'This car has all the up-to-the-minute technology of a vehicle of its age. An electrically operated hardtop wasn't part of the design.'

Raych drove a modern convertible, and the idea that other cars were not as comfortable as her own would never have occurred to her.

The first course car left, followed by Simon and his co-driver, James, in their Delahaye135. On the signal from the marshal, Maddie trundled down the exit route from the paddock and onto Station Road. At the end of the road she followed the other cars round to the right and along a lane that crossed the rails and ran behind the station. In her rear-view mirror – an old one her dad had rescued from a slightly younger model of a Morgan – she noticed the green Bugatti that had come third the previous year. The driver, who was too close for comfort, had a smug look on his face.

And you can eat my smoke, mister, Maddie promised him as she blipped the accelerator. The resulting throaty hum from the Morgan's engine brought a satisfying smile to her face.

'Oh, what lovely properties.' Raych tossed the road book

in the footwell. 'I bet they've got a fabulous view over the valley. I wonder how much these places cost?'

Maddie glanced across at her. 'Raych, I know this isn't really your thing and I am grateful to you for joining in, but I need you to concentrate. At the moment I do know where I'm going, because I checked the route to the formal start as soon as I got here yesterday.' She halted at the junction, checked both left and right, shifted into first and crossed onto Ingleborough Lane. Each side of the lane was lined by local spectators, with marshals at regular intervals.

'I'm ready for my close-up now, Mr DeMille.' Raych plumped her hair and posed as the car passed a serious photographer with a camera on a tripod.

Maddie followed the Delahaye through a pedestrian precinct, cordoned off for spectators only, and into a small car park that was being used as the second paddock and the formal start. The ten cars lined up beside each other. Maddie pulled on the brake and switched off the engine.

'We've got speeches for about twenty minutes now, so it's a good opportunity for us to go through the first few pages of notes for the route and –'

The passenger door slammed shut and Raych was already on her way across to Simon's car.

Maddie sighed. So much for having an agreement. She reached down for the paperwork. Flipping open the first few pages, she realised Raych hadn't even looked through the route. She grabbed the Ordnance Survey map and began to align the tulip diagrams to it, jotting down occasional notes in the road book. Glancing across at Raych, she shook her head in disbelief. Her navigator was perched on the bonnet of the Delahaye, surrounded by other competitors, and as always, she was enjoying the attention.

A small rostrum for the dignitaries had been erected

at one side of the parking area. The Mayor tapped on the microphone to draw everyone's attention to the fact that the formal proceedings were about to begin.

'Ladies and gentlemen, welcome to this, the twelfth visit to our little town of The Yorkshire Oldies' Tour of the Dales. We are delighted to host the start of this prestigious event and to have the privilege of holding the gala dance and awards presentation here in Haven Bridge on Sunday evening. I hope you've all got your tickets.' The Mayor let out a deep baritone laugh, which wasn't echoed by anyone else. Pulling his robes further up his shoulders and straightening his chain of office, he continued, his voice clear and his vowels deep and Yorkshire.

'And now it gives me great pleasure to declare this event open and to call on my very special guest to take on the role of Celebrity Start Official for the first ten cars.' He turned to the elderly, white-haired lady who was sitting on his right. 'Miss Moonshine, owner of Miss Moonshine's Wonderful Emporium here on Market Street.'

To rousing applause, Miss Moonshine stood, adjusted her fur stole and tucked her dog further under her arm. In two elegant strides she took the Mayor's place at the microphone.

'I'm so pleased to have been granted this great honour on behalf of our town. Napoleon and I feel blessed that we have been chosen…'

'Who's that?' whispered Raych. 'And hasn't she got gorgeous skin? Wonder what products she uses. That fox stole wouldn't be my choice, of course, but with that fabulous 1940s dress, it looks absolutely perfect on her.'

'Raych, shush. She's a really nice lady and she is always really kind to my dad when we have an event here.'

'And I love her little dog. So cute.'

'Raych, be quiet and get in the bloody car.'

'... and so, I'm just here to do what the lovely man in the yellow jacket tells me to.' Miss Moonshine tickled Napoleon's ear. 'And darling Napoleon is going to help me, aren't you, dear?' The dog directed his sad brown eyes towards his owner and delivered a low two-tone moan from the back of his throat.

'OK Raych, you need to concentrate now. Here's the road book and you just follow the tulip diagrams and call out the instructions.' Maddie started the car.

Raych looked at the page in front of her, a deep frown on her face. 'Tulips? Why do we need pictures of tulips?'

'Just follow the diagrams. An arrow is a direction either left, right or straight on, and a circle is a roundabout.' Maddie nosed the car forward.

Raych searched through the first half-dozen pages and then turned back to the first. 'So, this bent arrow is what?' She shoved the page in front of Maddie's face and pointed.

'That's a tulip diagram and it means we're turning right out of the start paddock and the next diagram means that we are then turning left at the junction just ahead of us. Got it?'

'Funny-looking tulips to me. If a guy presented me with tulips looking like that, I'd send him packing.'

'OK, it's us, Raych.' Maddie pulled forward to where the marshal stood, stopwatch in hand.

Miss Moonshine circled the car. 'Maddie Townsend, how lovely to see you here again. I think you will do well today and tomorrow. Good luck to you, Raychelle.'

Raych frowned and was about to ask a question when Miss Moonshine looked from one to the other and then gently rested her hand on Maddie's shoulder. 'Nothing is ever as bad as it seems, my dear. And take this,' she added, holding a small pink stone in the palm of her hand. 'Rose quartz. It will bring inner calm for the difficult days ahead and is good for the heart.'

Maddie looked at the object glinting in the sunshine. 'Thank you, that's very kind, but I don't –'

'Yes, you do, my dear.'

Miss Moonshine's eyes twinkled, and without being fully aware why, Maddie took the stone and dropped it into the top pocket of her coat.

'That's right, dear. Keep it close to the heart, where it can do most good.'

'And five seconds and counting.' The marshal held up his left hand and in unison with Miss Moonshine counted down. '...three... two... one... and go!'

Maddie's attention snapped back to the race. She let out the clutch and the car rolled forward and they turned right onto the street. At the junction she turned left.

She shouted above the roar of the engine. 'At the lights we take another left. I'll be concentrating on the traffic and my driving, so you need to call out the notes. So, the next call is, "traffic lights left". OK?'

'Got that, but there's no need to shout.'

The lights were at red and Maddie stopped. When the lights changed, she set off immediately. 'Where was the call, Raych?'

'Sorry, I forgot. I was trying to work out –'

'Raych, I have to make every second count to beat those guys. I had to check the road book myself because you hadn't. It's your job to call out the instructions for every turn, junction, roundabout, OK?' She looked at Raych, who nodded. 'OK, so what's the next call?'

Raych studied the page. 'I think I need a pen so I can strike out the diagrams as I make the calls.' She began foraging in her handbag.

Maddie pulled up at a T-junction. 'Raych, where am I going? What's the call?'

'Well, the arrow's pointing that way,' she said, indicating right. 'So that's a left.'

Maddie moved the car around the corner and picked up speed on the long, straight road. 'And that was actually a right.' Maddie accelerated up the gentle climb.

'Well, I always do have problems remembering which is which.'

*And you also have a driving licence.* Maddie filed away the thought without verbalising it. 'Just a suggestion, but maybe you should put a capital L and R at the top of each page of notes, just in case you get it wrong again.' Maddie stole a look at her friend.

'Great idea. Good to know you're still the sensible and practical one.' Raych started scrawling letters in each corner of the notes. The required calls for the next few junctions were never made.

*

The first time-control and check-in on the tour was at a pub on one side of the village of Kirkgrove. Maddie was directed to a parking spot in the small car park at the side of the building. Carrying the road book and the maps, the girls went into the pub. The crew from the Delahaye were both sitting at the bar.

'You made it in one piece, then?' James, Simon's navigator, grinned and took another sip of his pint. Maddie scowled. Her only reply was to ask for two coffees. Raych went straight to the Ladies to do something about her wind-blown hair and smudged make-up.

Alone at a corner table, Maddie checked her phone for messages. There were plenty of supportive texts from friends and customers of the garage waiting in her inbox, but the one she really wanted to see wasn't there. She scrolled through her contacts list until she found the number she wanted. The call connected almost immediately, but the tone at the other end indicated the switchboard was busy. Maddie shoved the phone in the top pocket of her overalls as Raych took a seat opposite and tried the insipid-looking liquid in front of her.

'Ugh. This coffee most definitely is not Arabica.' Raych dumped the cup back on the saucer with a clatter.

Maddie was poring over the maps and the tulip diagrams.

'Are you OK?' Raych asked.

'Yup, I guess so.' Maddie slumped back in her chair. 'I wanted to know the result for this first leg, but the guy at the time-control said they won't advise drivers of anything until all competitors have been through.'

'That's as clear as a foreign language to me.' Raych regarded her friend for a moment. 'But that's not what's really bothering you, is it?'

Maddie shook her head. 'I can't get through to the hospital.' She scraped her thumb and forefinger across her eyes and pinched the bridge of her nose.

'Any missed calls?'

'Nope.'

'And I suppose they told you they would be in touch if there was any change, didn't they?'

'Yup.'

'And you do know that your dad is in the best place with the right people who can help him, don't you?'

'Yup.'

'And if you were there instead of here, what would you be doing?'

'Climbing the walls, probably.'

'So, we've got this rally thing to win and you need to help

me with all of this.' Raych dropped her hand and started shuffling the maps and pages of notes around.

'You're right.' Looking at the sea of paper on the table, Maddie began to gather it into some sort of order. 'Pull that next table across, will you? I need more space.'

A few moments later, the two coffees discarded and tepid, Maddie was her intense and focused self again.

'This next section here is for regularity.' She indicated two points on the map. 'That means I've got to maintain a steady speed and make the distance in exactly the right time. If I arrive early, I get a penalty of a minute. If I'm late I get a penalty.'

'How do we do that?'

'There's an average speed that we must maintain.' Maddie flipped over to the relevant page in the notes. 'There, that's the instruction, so from that point on we need to keep tabs on our time and our speed, and you'll need to keep me constantly updated on our time so that I can balance our speed.'

'But there are those funny bent arrows and stuff, which means turns and junctions and things.'

'Exactly. It's not meant to be easy. It's a competition, Raych. I'll need you to call out all the corners, junctions, etc, along with the distance to each one, so that I can maintain my optimum speed by approaching each turn or junction as efficiently as possible.'

Maddie noticed the bewildered look on her navigator's face and smiled. 'It's really not that difficult, you know. I can run through all of the calls for the next section if you want.' She glanced at her watch. 'We've just about got enough time.'

Gradually moving through each of the notes, Maddie specified the call and Raych wrote each one down. They were so intent on the work that neither of them noticed that James had been taking a keen interest and had gradually moved across the room with the dregs of his pint.

'Sweeping 30 right, hairpin left, 90 right – not done this before, then?' He perched himself on the edge of the next table, his face a perfect picture of smugness. 'I guess the best team is going to win after all.' He downed the last of his pint and, as Simon emerged from the Gents, left his empty glass on the table and joined his driver as they both walked out.

*

A vast old mansion, now a hotel, stood on the edge of the village of Asby, overshadowed by Grange Scar. Built in the local stone, with small, low windows deep-set in the thick walls, it made an imposing presence in the bleak and windswept landscape of Cumbria. Rain had pelted down as they drove the length of the Closed Road section through the forests of the national park, but now it had lessened to a steady drizzle. Maddie pulled into the short drive and followed the arrows round to the side, where a marshal was waiting to show her to her parking spot. She reversed in, while Raych went to the time-control to sign in.

Maddie got their tiny overnight bags from behind the seats and dumped them on the ground. She was anxious to get the car covered and protected from the drizzle as soon as possible. As they made their way round to the front of the hotel, the green Bugatti pulled off the road. The driver sped through a large puddle, showering their feet and legs with muddy water. Raych glowered and turned, about to shout, but Maddie stopped her.

'Don't. I know those two. They're not real car enthusiasts. If I had to label them, I'd say they were a pair of parent-indulged petrolheads. Anything you say will just pass through the space in each of their skulls that they call a brain.'

Raych released a heartfelt and frustrated sigh. 'With a description like that – I think you're right. Such inconsiderate idiots just aren't worth the attention or effort.'

The girls exchanged a sobering nod of agreement and marched into the hotel.

'Good evening, ladies. Are you with the car event that's staying – ? Ah, Miss Townsend, lovely to see you again. And Mr Townsend? Is he not driving this year?'

'Nice to see you too, Robin, and no, Dad's not too well at the moment. It was a last-minute change of plan and he's... umm... taking some time out from competing. It's just me and Raychelle Decoursey this year. You'll need to sign in, Raych,' Maddie added.

Robin presented Raych with a form and a pen. 'I've allocated the rooms you and your father usually have,' he said, turning to the board behind and retrieving the keys. 'Perhaps Miss Decoursey will take the room you would normally have, and you can use the room your father would have had. Would that be all right?'

Maddie nodded and, paperwork complete, they followed Robin up a short flight of wide stone steps to where a tall stoneware vase filled with grasses stood on a landing. Another short flight of stairs and they reached the first floor. The corridor was dark, with walls lined with paintings. Robin strode into the darkness and within a few seconds the lights came on. The floor of the corridor sloped downwards slightly before rising again and, when they reached the end, another wide stone staircase awaited them. Maddie looked up, as she always did, just to remind herself how many more stairs there were. The ornate ironwork of the banister curled round and round, and a glass chandelier hung from a small dome above.

On reaching the third floor, Robin went to the door on his left and swiped the key over the censor.

'Miss Decoursey, this is your room.' He held the door open wide for her. Raych trooped in, dumped her bag and flopped onto the bed.

'Great room, thanks.' She looked around. 'Just one thing. Where's the en suite?'

'I'm sorry but this room doesn't have an en suite. This part of the building dates from the seventeenth century and we –'

Raych stood. 'NO EN SUITE!' Hands on hips, she glowered at Robin. 'What do you mean there's no en suite?'

'If I could –'

'Don't "if" me. Today, I've been rained on. I've been shouted at. I've been lectured. I've been muddied on. And, just to make my day absolutely complete, as I arrived here I was puddled on by two single-celled car-geeks. All day my hair has been winded on to the point of destruction and you tell me there's no en suite!'

Robin, having gradually edged himself backwards as Raych advanced statement by statement, now found himself wedged against the wall.

'Raych.' Maddie stepped into the room. 'It's true there is no en suite in this room. But,' she raised her hand to silence a further tirade, 'there is a small bathroom just across the hall and only the occupant of this room has access. Isn't that right, Robin?'

Robin mustered his most winning smile. 'Exactly so, Miss Townsend.' He nodded to Raych and slid out of the room.

*Sunday*

Maddie was up at six. Her first thought was her father and she checked her phone. There were no messages, nor any missed calls. She phoned the hospital.

'Cardio-thoracic, please.' She drummed the fingers of her left hand on her leg as she waited to be connected. 'Yes, hello, I'm enquiring about my father, Martin Townsend.' More waiting. 'Yes... OK. But he's stable... Yes, I understand that... And someone will let me know if there's any change, won't they? OK. Thank you.'

*Just wake up, Dad, and get better.* Dumping her phone on the bed, she went to get showered and ready to face the rest of her day. There was one thought that constantly circled through her mind. *I shouldn't be here. I should be at home.*

Later she stood in front of the mirror, scraping her wet hair off her face and pulling it into a tight ponytail.

'I shouldn't be here,' she said to her reflection. Her decision made, she threw her things in her bag, pulled on her overalls, grabbed her coat and raced down the stairs to Raych's room.

'Raych, it's me.' She knocked on the door. 'Raych, are you there?'

'Morning.' Raych held the door open, a beaming smile on her face, as Maddie brushed past her. She let the door click shut by itself. 'Something wrong?'

Maddie paced the room. 'I've been in touch with the hospital and they say there's no change. I keep thinking that I shouldn't be here. That I should be at home. That I should be doing something useful. That I –'

'Woah. Slow down, girl. And quit pacing.' Raych poured the remainder of the coffee from the pot on her breakfast tray into a clean cup and handed it to Maddie. 'Sit, drink, and then tell me what this is all about.'

Maddie took a sip of the coffee and for the first time noticed the state of the room. The bed was already made. The small table by the window to her right was covered with maps and pages from the road book, all of which had been annotated with the calls. Maddie turned to Raych. Her hair was neatly arranged in a plait and she was wearing a pair of blue overalls.

Maddie frowned. 'Overalls! Where did you get those?'

Raych grinned. 'From Robin. Umm, after my tirade yesterday I thought I owed him an apology and an explanation. So, we got chatting and he helped me with the road book. Which means that today I can be a much more useful navigator for you.'

Maddie hesitated, a look of distress on her face. 'Thanks, Raych, and I really appreciate you agreeing to step in at the last minute, but I've decided to chuck the competition and go home. That's where I should be.'

'OK. If that's what you really want, then we'll do that. But don't forget what you told me on Thursday. About your dad picking up a lot of business from the other competitors. That is why you asked me to help, isn't it?'

'Yes, but that was before I found him collapsed on the bodyshop floor on Friday morning.' Maddie wiped her hands across her face.

'Just a moment ago, you said there had been no change in his condition. Remember our conversation yesterday in the pub in Kirkgrove?'

Maddie nodded.

Raych sat down on the bed beside her friend. 'I just want to remind you that your dad is in the right place with the right people. And yesterday you said that if you were back in Leeds rather than here, you would be climbing the walls.'

Maddie sighed.

'And what was it that strange lady said?' Raych went on. 'That Miss Silvershine, or whatever her name was? Something about inner calm?'

Maddie picked up her coat and started rifling through the pockets. 'The pink stone!' She held it in her hand and gazed at it for a few moments. Miss Moonshine's words from the previous day echoed through her mind. 'Her name is Miss

Moonshine. And she was right.' She dropped the stone in the top pocket of her overalls. 'I just need to focus and remain calm and we –'

The phone on the bedside table rang. Raych answered the call. 'Yes, she's here, Robin.'

Alerted, Maddie motioned to her friend to give her the phone. Raych shook her head.

'Yes, I'll tell her.' She replaced the receiver and let out an exasperated sigh. 'Robin says one of the tyres on your car is flat and he thought you would want to know as early as possible.'

'Well, whatever we're doing today it won't be until I fix that tyre.' Maddie checked her watch. 'I'll get something to eat and I'll meet you outside in half an hour, OK?'

*

Maddie stood in front of the car. 'Damn it. Both tyres are flat.'

Squatting down, she ran her hand over the front offside tyre and frowned. Moving to the other side, she did the same with the nearside tyre. They were both smooth, with no indication of where the damage may have been. She took a step back and regarded the car.

'Well, Charlotte, old thing, you've definitely been in the wars,' she said. 'Must have been the forest roads, but... odd that I can't feel the damage on either tyre.' She shook her head in confusion. Forest roads were notorious for giving tyres a very hard time... unless... She moved to the rear of the car and her anger began to simmer. She prodded the spare mounted on the back. It was spongy under the pressure she exerted. Every single tyre was flat. Had the spare been intact she might have been able – only just – to accept that it was one of those things. But the spare was flat too, when it hadn't even touched the ground since she fitted it to the wheel three months ago. That was downright deliberate. That was mean and it was cheating. Maddie circled the car again and again as she tried to control her rage.

Breakfast forgotten, she dumped her stuff on her seat, retrieved her jack and set to work to put the components together. A realisation made her pause for a moment.

I'm going to have to check every tyre to make sure there really are no punctures, she thought. She nodded in response to herself, got down on her knees, fitted the jack under the body and started to raise the car.

'Congratulations. You finished yesterday with no penalties,' said Simon, striding by on his way to the Delahaye. He stowed his bag and then came across to Maddie. 'That looks a lot of work. Want a hand?'

Maddie's dark, accusatory look made him take a step or two back.

'Hey. I didn't do this. I would never do this.'

'Is that right? According to the results posted this morning, you're trailing in fifth position and yes, I did come in first yesterday and I intend to keep that position today, too.' She gave him a hard stare before getting on with her work.

Simon hesitated for a moment and then disappeared. A few moments later he was back. 'I didn't do this, Maddie. But considering some of the comments in the bar last night, I think I might know who did.' He placed his own jack in front of her. 'It might be quicker and easier if we divide the job between us, don't you think?'

Just as she acknowledged his presence, the team from the green Bugatti walked by. The two of them sniggered to each other.

Maddie leapt to her feet and followed them. 'You want funny? You want something really funny?'

They stopped and looked at her.

'Well, that got your attention, didn't it?' Maddie stood her ground, arms crossed, and glared at them. 'You see those cameras up there?' She turned towards the wall of the hotel. 'That's Robin's CCTV. Now I haven't the least idea whether it was you or someone else who let down all my tyres. But someone did. And guess what? Now they, whoever they may be, will feature in footage that I can pass on to the Motor Sports Association. I don't know if the Association will take any action or not, but that would be the right place to go to in the first instance, wouldn't it? After that, there's always the internet, isn't there?' Maddie looked from one to the other. 'But, as I say, I don't know if it was you two or not, but you might want to do me a favour and pass on to the other drivers that there is a cheat on this tour. OK?' Maddie marched back to her car.

'Well said.' Simon smiled at her. 'They needed pulling up. Last night in the bar they were causing trouble. My navigator, James, and those two almost came to blows at one point.'

'They're just a pair of – never mind.' She cast her eye over the second jack and the second air-pump that had joined it on the ground. 'Are you sure you don't mind helping?'

'You're a genuine car enthusiast, and from what I've heard, a great mechanic. I like to think that others would help me if I found myself in a situation like this. So, yes, I'm very happy to help out.'

Maddie looked at the Morgan and thought through how best to undertake the work. 'OK. I can use my ramps as stops at each back wheel and we'll jack up the front, and if you check the offside, I can do the nearside. We can then do the same with the back and hopefully we will both make our starting timeslots for today's event.'

Simon nodded. They moved to their respective sides of the car and set to work.

*

The weather for the drive back to Haven Bridge was more clement than the day before, and although there were patches of cloud, the sun shone throughout. Maddie and Raych had checked in at every passage control and had been exactly on time in the regularity section of the return journey. The forest road, which had been used as a Closed Road section for the day, had been an opportunity for Maddie to finally let out all her frustration and anger. With Raych's more informed preparation and concentrated approach, she had been able to maximise her speed on corners and at junctions. On the straights, Charlotte had been pushed to her engine's limits.

Raych shouted the call. '0.4 miles, T-junction 90 right.'

'OK.' Maddie checked the speedometer and slightly lifted her foot off the accelerator. She changed down and swept round the bend.

'Fifty yards hairpin left into Ingleborough Lane.'

'OK.' Maddie took the turn. The road was lined with spectators and marshals. 'I've got the route from here,' she shouted. 'Get ready to sprint to the officials' table as soon as I pull up. OK?'

'OK.' Raych collected the necessary paperwork for the officials together and dumped the road book in the footwell. As they roared by the waving and cheering spectators, she waved back.

Maddie turned into Station Road and then into the station car park, where the finish line was set. Once across, she pulled up in the space she had been given at the start. Raych jumped out. Maddie let the engine run for a few moments before pulling on the brake and switching off. Seconds later she was at the officials' table, signing in with her navigator.

Strolling back to the car, Maddie cast her eyes over the paddock. An Austin Healey 3000 was parked to one side, as though it had never left its space. She scrunched her eyes up to read the number plate. She thought so. It was Robin's car. Hmm, what was he doing here? A short distance away the green Bugatti was being loaded on the back of a tow-truck, the driver and navigator standing around talking.

'Would you just look at that?' Maddie pointed to the Bugatti.

'There is justice in the world, after all.' Raych laughed. 'What about striding over there and giving them your business card, Maddie?'

'Raych, you are unbelievable at times.' Their roar of laughter was drowned out by the arrival of another competitor, the sound of the car engine and the exhaust echoing across the paddock.

'Well?'

Maddie shook her head. 'It might feel good to be able to do that, but I'm not going to.'

Back beside the Morgan, Maddie dug her phone out of her overalls and checked it.

'Two voice messages,' she said, holding it up for Raych to see. She quickly clicked through and listened. The first message brought an irritated frown to her forehead. The second a smile of relief and tears. 'He's awake. He's going to be OK and they expect to be moving him onto an ordinary ward tomorrow.'

Raych ran around the car and hugged her friend. 'That's great news. That's the best news,' she said, wiping away tears from her own eyes.

Maddie pulled away. 'Look at us,' she said. 'Weeping

like babies in front of all these blokes.' She pulled out her handkerchief and blew her nose. 'I've got a reputation to maintain and – a business to run for the next few months all by myself.'

'You can do it. You know you can. And talking of business, give me one of your cards.'

Maddie reached into a storage pocket under the dash and pulled out a small box from which she extracted a card. 'If anybody asks, I know nothing.'

Accepting the card, Raych nodded and made her way across the paddock to the green Bugatti.

Slipping back into the driver's seat, Maddie dialled a number in response to the first voicemail message she had picked up. 'Hello, Mr Fox-Sanderson. Maddie Townsend. I'm responding to your message. What can I do for you?' She slid down in her seat. Fox-Sanderson was a regular customer and he always made a point of dealing with no one other than her father. She grimaced as she listened to his usual whingeing and waited for an appropriate moment to interrupt him.

'I'm certain we can fit that work in. I will need to check our calendar at the garage when I go into work tomorrow but... No, unfortunately it won't be Dad who will rebuild the engine for you, he's taking a well-earned break and... I will have Olly do that work for you... He's a very capable mechanic, Mr Fox-Sanderson. I would trust him to work on Dad's Morgan if I wasn't able to find the time to do the work myself... No, it was Olly who did the work on the Sprite that you brought us last year... No, it was Olly who did the work on the Mark 1 Cortina and I can assure you he is more than capable of completing the work you require on a 1965 MGB...Yes... I will... first thing tomorrow... Yup, be in touch tomorrow. Bye, Mr Fox-Sanderson.' She stabbed the end-call button, rested her head on the steering wheel and closed her eyes.

A car pulled up in the next but one space to the Morgan. Maddie looked up. It was the Delahaye, and inside it Simon and James were talking. The windows were wound up and she couldn't hear what was being said, but there was no mistaking the look on Simon's face as he spoke to his navigator. James was turned away from her, with his back wedged up against the door. His hand gestures, the way his back was arched and the slamming of the car door when he subsequently got out led Maddie to one undeniable interpretation. Their driving relationship had just come to an end.

'Oops!' Maddie watched, but Simon was staring ahead unaware. She decided to let him have his space.

*

The first-floor bar at The Old Green Wicket hotel in Haven Bridge had been transformed. Bunting using small replica red, green, blue and chequered flags adorned the picture rails the length and breadth of the room. At one end, a long table was set out with numerous cups, plaques and awards, all polished and gleaming.

Behind the awards table, a projector was displaying pictures and photographs of the good and the great from all aspects of motorsport. Interspersed with these shots were photos of cars of all ages, including, Maddie noted, some wonderful coach-built vehicles dating from the last few years of the Victorian era and the first decade of the 20th century. She watched with keen interest as the reel repeated and noticed Miss Moonshine at the wheel of a 1928 LaSalle, her dog on the passenger seat beside her. Maddie shook her head. Her grandfather had worked on that car in the late

1930s and 40s. She recognised the number plate. In their old family photograph albums, it was the car that had fascinated her as a child. If pushed, she would sometimes admit that the LaSalle was probably her primary prompt to join the family business.

'A penny for them?' Simon, tall and elegant in a blue suit, stood at the opposite side of the dining table from Maddie.

'Sorry... Oh, they're not worth even a groat,' she said smiling.

'Do you mind if I join you?'

'Nope. Table's set for six, but I think there will only be Raych, me and Robin from the hotel at Asby. So, take your pick.'

Simon moved round the table. 'I'll take the spare seat next to you, then.' He put down his pint of bitter. 'Raych not staying for the dinner?' He grinned at her. 'Was the experience of being a navigator too much?

Maddie studied the tablecloth to hide her smirk. 'Raych wouldn't miss this for the world. She's over there.' She nodded towards the bar where Raych, in a full-length fitted chocolate brown dress, hair beautifully dressed and curled, was sipping a glass of prosecco and talking to Robin.

'Can I get you a drink?'

'It should really be me who gets you a drink. I owe you a pint at least for helping me this morning with the flats. But I see you've already got one.'

Simon smiled. 'Have you always been this fiercely independent?'

'Yup.'

'Well, just for this evening, how about we forget that we are normally competitors and mechanics. Instead of our usual overalls, I'm wearing a suit and you're... well, wearing a dress and – '

'I think the description you're looking for is that I've scrubbed up reasonably well.'

Simon laughed. 'I'm not going to be able to win, am I?'

Maddie shook her head.

'So, a glass of fizzy stuff like Raych, or something else?'

'I've checked the wine list and they have an excellent white sauvignon. A glass of that would be very nice, Mr Walker, thank you.' She gave her best echo of Raych's breathy tones.

'Sauvignon coming up. And I like fiercely independent better.'

Maddie watched him as he moved across the room to the bar. The place had begun to fill up, and some of the VIPs and officials had arrived for the formal part of the evening. A flutter of applause spread around the room as the Mayor and his wife walked in. They were greeted with complimentary drinks from a waiter near the VIPs' table. Next, Miss Moonshine – without her dog on this occasion – appeared at the top of the stairs, dressed in a sleeveless silver-grey evening gown and carrying a matching shrug and purse. She paused and took in the scene. A bright smile on her face, having spotted the Mayor's wife, Miss Moonshine took her place with the other dignitaries.

Maddie checked her watch. It was almost seven and there was no sign yet of Simon's navigator, James. She scanned the room full of people. The soft music that had been playing when she arrived was drowned out by a myriad of conversations. At the bar, Raych and Robin were deep in conversation. Simon was slowly picking his way back through the tables.

'Thanks. Is James not staying for the awards and dinner?'

Simon shook his head as he sat down again. 'Let's just say that as far as motoring is concerned, James and I have decided to declare our partnership at an end.' He took a gulp of beer.

'Ah. I kind of thought that might be the case. In the paddock at the finish, you two didn't look too pleased with each other.'

'It wasn't mutual.' He sighed. 'Basically, I sacked him. At every stop yesterday, he took the opportunity to have a beer. Last night he got hammered in the hotel bar. Today he was like a zombie, and at lunchtime it was clear to me that you couldn't be beaten. I drove to maintain my fifth place. As I'm sure you know, driving and navigating at the same time in these kind of events isn't easy.'

'Hmm.'

The VIPs assembled in front of the awards table and the Mayor tapped on the microphone. Raych and Robin took their seats at Maddie's table. The lights were turned up and the hum of spoken words died down.

'Good evening, ladies and gentlemen. Welcome to the final event of this fabulous weekend. I hope you've noticed the photos behind me, showing points on the tour among all the historic pictures. A wonderful show, I think. I also can't help noticing that one particular car, a Morgan, seems to have been photographed quite a lot over the past two days.'

The Mayor picked up his crib-sheet, placed his spectacles on the end of his nose and studied it for a moment or two. 'My wife's just reminded me that dinner is to be served at 7.30, so I don't want to keep you hungry people waiting any longer than necessary. Miss Moonshine is here to present the awards, so let's get on with it, shall we?' The Mayor looked at his audience in anticipation of a response, and was rewarded with a light applause.

'So, in reverse order, the award for overall third place across both days goes to car number 17, the 1938 Alpha Romeo driven by John Newton with navigator Darren Lessing.'

Polite applause followed as the team collected their awards from Miss Moonshine. The driver gave a nod and a wave to those gathered in thanks.

'The award for overall second place goes to car number 5, the 1935 Riley Imp driven by Will Jordan with his navigator wife, Liz.' The couple made their way to the front, collected the trophy and plaque and shook hands with Miss Moonshine. Mrs Jordan then approached the microphone.

'Thank you everyone for organising a great event. We've both thoroughly enjoyed it. Maybe next year we'll be first, who knows?'

A round of applause along with some barracking ensued.

'Ladies and gentlemen, please.' The Mayor held up a hand to quell the disturbance.

'Just two more awards. The prize for overall first place, with no penalties, goes to car number 3, the 1936 Morgan 4-4 and driver, the talented and expert mechanic Maddie Townsend, and her lovely navigator, Raychelle Decoursey.'

A roar of applause went up as Maddie and Raych made their way across the room.

'Well done,' said Miss Moonshine as she handed the cup to Maddie and a plaque to Raych. 'With the difficulties you've had you both deserve this.'

'I think it was your good luck that won this for us,' said Maddie, as she accepted the trophy. 'And I need to give you this back.' She offered the piece of quartz in the palm of her hand.

'You keep it, my dear,' said Miss Moonshine, folding Maddie's fingers over it. 'And when you get back home, use it to help your father recover.'

Shouts of, 'Speech!' were coming from the audience, giving Maddie no time to think about, or question, what the old lady had said.

She turned to face the room. 'Thank you, everyone. And especial thanks to Raych, who stepped in as my navigator at the last minute, having never done the job before. I think I put her through hell on Saturday, but today she did a fantastic job. I can now go home and present this to my dad. Everyone, I think Raych deserves her own round of applause.'

The room erupted with cheers and shouts of, '90 right!' and 'Sweeping 30 left!', as the girls negotiated their way back to their table.

Simon and Robin were still clapping as they took their seats.

'Well done.' Simon reached out, took Maddie's hand and squeezed it. 'I don't suppose you would like to partner me on the White Rose Tour next month, would you? Robin's competing and Raych has agreed to navigate for him.'

Maddie was about to refuse when she felt her attention drawn to the other end of the room. Miss Moonshine, the projected images playing behind her, took a couple of steps forward and smiled.

'Well, what do you think?' asked Simon.

Miss Moonshine nodded at Maddie and turned away.

'Yes,' she said. 'I think I would like that.'

**Angela Wren is an actor and director at a theatre in Yorkshire, UK. She loves stories and reading and writes the Jacques Forêt crime novels set in France. Her short stories vary between romance, memoir, mystery and historical. Angela has had two one-act plays recorded for local radio.**

angelawren.co.uk

# The Angel Stone

*By Sophie Claire*

Lola was in the cereal aisle restocking the packets of cornflakes when Greg appeared. He was grinning so hard that she immediately stiffened, sensing trouble. He never shopped in Supersave, and he'd never dropped by to see her in all of the twelve months they'd been together. His mate Barry appeared too and gave her a brief nod, but hung back near the muesli, his gaze fixed intently on his phone.

'Hey Lola,' said Greg, loudly, and gripped her by the shoulders.

Lola glanced at his hands, perplexed by the way he'd clamped them around her. The smell of aftershave bit at her. 'Hey,' she murmured. 'I thought you were working tonight.'

He was the night guard at the scrapyard, which meant he was usually asleep at this time.

'I am,' he said, and glanced back at Barry.

'Is everything OK?'

He nodded – a little too enthusiastically – but didn't say anything.

'Greg,' she said quietly, 'I can't talk long. Pat's on my case. I've got to get all this lot out by four o'clock.' She pointed to the trolley stacked high with cornflakes boxes.

He knew what an ogre her boss was, yet his response was to shoot her another goofy smile. She frowned. Was he drunk?

'Forget about those for a minute,' he said, and his tattoos blurred as he swept his arm through the air. 'This is important.'

He rooted around in his pocket, and Lola looked anxiously about. If Pat caught her chatting, she'd be in huge trouble. She'd already been interrupted six times this afternoon by customers asking where things were.

Greg pulled out a tiny velvet box and cleared his throat. Barry stepped forward and Lola suddenly realised he wasn't looking at his phone - he was filming them.

Her heart slugged as Greg dropped to his knee. She stared at the top of his head, and a prickling sensation spread from her throat up into her cheeks. His brown hair was neatly combed and he was wearing his leather jacket. He looked like he was dressed up for a night out, she thought faintly.

'Lola,' said Greg, opening the box and presenting it to her. Inside was a minuscule diamond protruding from a shoestring of silver. 'Will you marry me?'

She blinked. How could he put her on the spot like this? They'd never talked about marriage. Not once. They weren't even living together. The longest they'd ever spent together had been a weekend in Wales. Something inside her kicked out in panic. Marriage was for later, for people with kids and a house and a -

Did she want to marry him?

The clawing in her stomach told her everything she needed to know.

'Well?'

The fluorescent lights above span and her head swam. How was she going to get out of this?

'Lola?'

She glanced at Barry, whose phone was still pointed at them like a gun. Behind him a cluster of customers had paused, baskets in hand, to rubberneck. This would be all over Facebook by tonight – if it wasn't already being beamed out live.

'I – I wasn't expecting this,' she whispered.

Greg grinned up at her. 'I know. I wanted to surprise you.'

She tugged at the collar of her uniform. The pea-green polyester suddenly felt prickly and tight. She didn't want to get married, but if she said no, how humiliating would it be for him? She couldn't do that to him. A memory sprang up of the humane mouse traps her mum had put in the kitchen a few years ago and the way the mice's eyes had bulged, too big for their bodies, when she'd found them in the plastic cage. Trapped.

She sucked in air. There was only one way to get out of this.

'Yes.' She forced the word from her lips.

'What was that?' He darted a look over his shoulder at the camera, then turned back and grinned. 'Say it again, flower. A bit louder.'

She stretched her lips into what she hoped was a convincing smile. 'Yes.'

*

Two hours later, Lola shut the front door and heeled off her shoes. She had unloaded all the cornflakes in the end, but only because she'd stayed late to finish the task in her own time. From the kitchen came the sound of a pop song, and the sweet smell of onions cooking. She pushed the door open and her mum and sister both looked up from the laptop.

Mandy jumped up and threw her arms around her, squealing in her ear. 'We've seen it! It's on Facebook and everyone's talking about it. OMG, I can't believe it - who knew Greg was so romantic? I'm so happy for you, Lo!'

She stepped back, flicking her long dark hair back over her shoulder. 'Show us the ring!'

Lola felt the knot in her chest tighten as she held out her left hand.

'Congratulations, love,' said Mum, and hugged her too.

'It's on Facebook? Let me see.' He hadn't wasted any time.

Her stomach plunged as the video played out in front of her. Barry was good with computers and she could tell he'd been heavily involved in putting the film together. It began with a photo of her, labelled 'The Unsuspecting Bride', then switched to a video following Greg, 'The Groom', from the car park into Supersave. Lola winced at the unflattering shot of her bum as she bent to pick up cornflakes boxes. The tinny supermarket music had been replaced with the upbeat rhythm of Bruno Mars' 'I Think I Wanna Marry You'.

She sat down heavily. Why had he rushed to post it online? This was moving too fast.

'...did you know he was going to propose?' She realised Mandy had been firing a stream of questions at her, most of which Lola hadn't heard. 'You look so shocked - was it a complete surprise?'

'I had no idea.' Lola groaned. 'Oh God, it's so awful...'

Mandy put her arm around her. 'It's not that bad, Lo. True, a bit of lipstick would have been better and you could have brushed your hair - but you look...sweet. Natural.'

Lola smiled at her sister, whose make-up was always immaculate. 'I mean it was horrible to be put on the spot like that...'

Her mum, who had been drying pots, stopped and looked at her.

Mandy's heavily pencilled brows pulled in a frown. 'But you said yes.'

'I know, but –'

'So it all ended happily. When's the wedding?' She clapped her hands. 'You will let me do your hair, won't you?'

Lola shook her head. 'That's just it. I can't do it, Mands. I'm going to have to get him on his own and explain.'

Her mum sat down next to her. 'You mean you don't want to marry him?'

Mandy's eyes widened, the effect exaggerated by her false lashes. 'But you said yes! You're wearing his ring.'

'What else could I do? They were filming it.'

Mandy blinked.

'But I don't feel ready. I'm too young.' It was a relief to say it out loud. She was lucky that the three of them could talk about anything. They'd always been close. Family was everything.

'You're twenty-five. Why is that too young?'

'Mands, can you make us some herbal tea?' Mum took Lola's hand. Her touch was warm and it calmed her a little.

Her sister went to fill the kettle.

'I was twenty-five when I had you,' Mum said gently.

'I know, but...' She tried again to picture herself married to Greg: standing beside his canal boat, smiling for the camera, his muscular arms wrapped around her. But each time the image vanished, as if someone had erased it.

'When are you going to speak to him?' asked Mum.

Lola looked up at the clock on the wall. 'I don't know. His shift has started now. It'll have to be tomorrow.'

'You two are perfect together.' Mandy planted two mugs of chamomile tea in front of them. 'You all small and blonde, and him all hunky and hard-looking.'

Was that a wistful edge to her sister's voice? Lola's eyes narrowed. 'We're not perfect. I don't feel like I know him all that well, even after a year.' Their days off rarely coincided, and when they did he preferred to spend time in The Packhorse with his mates. Lola went along when she could, but it wasn't the same as being alone together. 'And he can't know me very well. I mean, look at this ring.' She yanked it off her finger and held it up. 'He's seen the jewellery I make. This is so - so...'

Supersave had strict rules about jewellery, but her fingers were usually decorated with big, bright rings. Her work had an exotic feel, with geometric patterns and bold colours: it was different, unusual. Whereas this diamond was conventional. Bland. '...it's just not me.'

The kitchen became quiet. The only sound was the thump of the boiler and the heating clicking on for the evening.

Mum watched her with concern. 'So you're not happy with him?'

Lola thought about this. Mandy wasn't the only one who thought Greg was hot. He'd arrived here on his narrowboat three years ago, so he still had the exotic allure of a newcomer, plus he was a bit older, and his solid physique complemented his softly spoken manner. He held doors open for Lola, he insisted on walking her home after dark, and sex with him - well, it made up for any flaws in their relationship.

'I'm not unhappy,' she said finally. 'It's just... I don't want to marry him. I'm not sure I want to get married at all. I mean, you managed fine on your own, Mum.'

The cat flap squeaked and Elton appeared. His black fur glistened, and he left a trail of wet paw prints on the tiles as he hurried through into the house.

'It's a lot easier with a partner, Lo.'

The bleak look in her mother's eyes made Lola want to bite back her words. She knew it had been hard for Mum when their dad had died. 'But you loved Dad. You always say he was your soulmate. Greg isn't mine.'

Mum and Mandy exchanged a look.

'And I can't believe this is it. That I'm going to get married now and never –'

'Never what?'

Lola looked up at the naked bulb hanging from the ceiling and tried to find the words to articulate this feeling, this fear that had been eating at her ever since Greg had got down on one knee. There must be more, surely? 'I just hoped I'd achieve...more. Be someone.'

'Be someone?' Mum's eyes narrowed. 'Don't go getting fancy ideas like the contestants on those television talent shows. All dreaming of record deals and hoping to become overnight stars.'

Lola realised too late that she'd touched a nerve. Everyone knew Mum was bitter because of her own experience. 'I don't mean I want to be a celebrity.'

'What, then?'

'I... I'm not sure.'

'Dreams don't keep a roof over your head,' Mum continued. 'In the real world there are bills to be paid, and there's no fairy godmother or Simon Cowell going to do that for you.'

Lola fiddled with a loose thread dangling from the hem of her tunic. She pulled at it and wound it around her finger. 'I know.'

Mum was right. She had to be practical. Realistic. And she was, normally.

'I know Greg isn't rolling in it, but two incomes are better than one,' said Mum.

'I like Greg.' Mandy winked. 'And you've always said he's good in the sack.'

Lola forced a smile.

'Why don't you sleep on it?' said Mum. 'You don't need to make a decision today.'

'What if he's the only man who ever asks you?' said Mandy.

Lola shrugged.

'Think about it, love,' said Mum, 'but watch you don't get carried away, wishing for the impossible, setting your sights too high. He might not be perfect, but then none of us are.'

*

Her mum's warning hung over Lola like hill fog as, next day, she trailed into town. Was she wishing for the impossible? She should know better. Take the travel magazines and Pinterest boards she liked to pore over, for example. She was drawn to the pictures of deserted beaches and mountain trails, but she knew she'd never be able to afford a trip like that. Each month she entered their competitions to win exotic holidays, but she never expected anything more in return than junk mail from the tour operators.

She rubbed her bare finger, thinking of the ring beside her bed. Now she wasn't sure what she'd say to Greg when she saw him. His proposal had been a shock, but should she be making more effort to consider it?

She checked her phone again. She'd texted, asking him to call her when he woke up, but there was no reply yet. In the meantime, she was searching for a gift for Mandy. It was her sister's birthday in a couple of weeks and she needed inspiration for what to buy.

Lola paused beside a rose-covered archway. Set back

from the road, the shop door was ajar. 'Miss Moonshine's Wonderful Emporium', the sign read. The building itself looked like it had once been a grand house, with tall windows and a gleaming black door, although the rampant shrubs and silver birch concealed much of it and gave it an air of mystery.

Strange. Lola had never noticed the place before. Curious, she headed for the door, glancing up at the arch. She didn't know much about gardening, but did roses normally flower in April?

Inside, her shoes tapped on the stone floor. The shop was deserted, and she wove her way through the displays of eclectic objects, old and new. Woodland creatures made of felt perched on tables and high shelves, and they tracked her movements. The bare brick wall was a mosaic of mirrors and paintings and carvings.

Lola passed a curtained doorway and wondered idly what would Mandy like? Perhaps this pretty, hand-stitched cushion for her room? Or that vintage birdcage? She looked at her own beaded bracelet. She'd made her sister jewellery before, but Mandy didn't share her taste.

The sound of Bruno Mars playing made her still. The music came from behind a blue curtain, and the back of her neck prickled. Last night her phone hadn't stopped buzzing with messages from friends. It seemed everyone in Haven Bridge had seen the video on Facebook, but Lola didn't want to discuss it. She hurried away, heading for the door.

'Hello, dear.'

The woman's voice stopped her, and Lola span on her heel. A tiny, pale-faced lady with startlingly dark lipstick smiled at her, and the curtain she had just stepped through twitched and trembled, then stilled.

'Hi,' said Lola, and turned away quickly, in the hope she

wouldn't be recognised. Her heart thumped heavily as she pulled out her phone. The music reminded her she had to speak to Greg – as soon as possible.

'I would resist the temptation if I were you.'

Lola stopped and turned. 'What?'

The lady stood behind the counter, filling a basket with timepieces, but her piercing hazel eyes were fixed on Lola. Her white hair bobbed as she nodded. 'Don't let others sway you, dear. You're young. You have plenty of time to follow your heart.'

Lola blinked. There were lines of pink drawn around the lady's eyes, and her thin lips were painted a dark shade of plum.

'I don't know what you mean. You don't know anything about me,' she said irritably, and moved to leave.

'Lola, isn't it? Lola Brown.'

'Just because you've seen me on Facebook doesn't give you the right to judge me.'

'Face – ?' The lady looked puzzled.

Fierce heat stole into Lola's cheeks. This was Greg's fault, damn him, for posting that stupid film online. Now even strangers were butting in, telling her what to do.

The blue curtain shook and a tiny dog appeared. He trotted over to a basket in the corner.

'Have you asked yourself, what are your dreams?' the shopkeeper went on. 'It can be easy to lose sight of them.'

Dreams don't keep a roof over your head. Lola liked to think she had her feet on the ground. Unsettled, she fiddled with the zip of her coat.

'If it feels like a risk, that's when you're truly living,' the lady went on.

Clearly, she was referring to Greg and his engagement ring. It seemed everyone was pushing her to marry him. 'I didn't ask for advice,' Lola snapped, and made for the door.

But the shopkeeper blocked her way. A delicate perfume trailed in the air. Confused, Lola glanced back at the counter. How had she moved so fast?

'Here.' The lady dipped her hand into a bowl of gemstones. She wrapped one in a slip of brown paper and held it out. 'Keep this with you at all times and it will help you find your path.'

Lola sighed. 'I don't want to buy –'

The lady seized her hand and put the tiny parcel in it. 'It's yours,' she said firmly. 'Take it.'

Her eyes creased with kindness as she smiled, but they had a steely glint which warned Lola not to argue.

Lola mumbled her thanks and left, pushing the stone deep into her pocket, telling herself she'd dispose of it later.

*

'Greg?' she called, ducking her head as she stepped down into the canal boat.

The smell of bacon rose up to greet her and made her nose wrinkle. Greg emerged from his cabin. His hair was damp and ruffled, as if he'd just towel-dried it, and he grinned when he saw her. He pressed her to him and his lips were warm and soft as he kissed her. She'd been relieved when he'd finally returned her calls and arranged to meet her, but now she was here relief gave way to trepidation.

'Want coffee?' he asked as he poured one for himself.

She shook her head. He might have just got up, but it was late afternoon. 'We need to talk, Greg.'

'Oh yeah? About the wedding? You want to fix a date, don't you?'

'No!' she said quickly. 'About the video – it's all over Facebook.'

'I know.' He grinned and bent to open the grill. He pulled out a tray of bacon rashers, which had singed at the edges.

'I wish you'd told me beforehand.'

Her sharp tone made him look up at her. 'It wouldn't have been a surprise if I had.'

Didn't he see? She didn't like surprises. In fact, she hated them. Especially when they concerned her future. She'd lain awake all night, trying to calm her panicked thoughts.

He dropped the bacon into a couple of bread rolls and slathered them with brown sauce. 'I haven't got anything veggie in. You want a bap?'

'I'm not hungry.'

She followed him over to the small table and sat opposite him. He picked up a roll, then stopped and frowned. 'Where's your ring?'

Lola swallowed. 'I – er, I left it at home. Listen, Greg. This has all happened –'

'Did you like it? Wasn't cheap, you know.' He took a hungry bite.

Her lips pressed flat. 'Greg, I'm not sure about any of this.'

He licked sauce from his fingers. 'You want a different ring? I don't think they'll take it back, but we could ask to exchange it. So about the date – I was thinking next spring.'

'I'm not sure about getting married...'

He stopped.

'...to you,' she added quietly.

'What do you mean?' He put the sandwich down. 'You said yes. It's on film, it's on the bleeding internet – you said yes!'

'Because you put me on the spot! I didn't want to show you up in front of all those people.'

'So you're saying no?' He was incredulous.

'I'm not sure. I – I need time to think.'

He stared at her. 'I can't believe this. What will everyone think? I'll be a laughing stock.'

She looked down at her lap, feeling the sting of guilt. But it was kinder to be honest with him, no matter how brutal it felt now.

'Well, how about you move in with me instead?'

Her earrings jangled as she looked around the place, trying to swallow down her horror at the thought of the two of them being squashed in this narrow cabin with its low roof. Her skin prickled. 'I'm not sure about that either.'

'Why not?'

'I don't feel we know each other well enough.' She reached for her necklace and her fingers squeezed the wooden beads.

'It's been a year.'

'Yeah, but –'

'And we're good together.' He nodded towards his bedroom and threw her that lopsided grin which always made her melt. 'You don't have any complaints in that department, do you?'

She felt spots of heat burn her cheeks as she smiled. 'No, I don't. But Greg – that's not enough, is it?'

His smile faded and he raked a hand through his hair. 'I'm thirty-two, Lo. I'm not getting any younger. How long do you expect me to wait?'

'I – I don't know,' she finished quietly.

'I see.' He pushed his empty plate away. He looked angry. Hurt.

The air in the boat seemed to weigh heavily.

'I should go.'

He didn't reply, and she was in such a rush to climb the steps to daylight that she bumped her head. Rubbing it, she stepped off the boat onto solid land and hurried away down the towpath.

As she walked, her fingers found the unfamiliar package in her pocket. She pulled it out and unwrapped it. Moon white, it felt smooth and cool in her cupped hand. The slip of brown paper bore a description:

*Angel Stone*
*Nurturing stone associated with personal growth and insight*
*Opens the mind to new possibilities and opportunities to realise your full potential*
*Can help break unwanted patterns of behaviour and bring inner strength and courage*

Lola shook her head. The eccentric shopkeeper might believe in crystals and horoscopes, but Lola didn't.

Still, it was a beautiful stone. Too beautiful to throw away. She used beads and gemstones all the time in her jewellery-making, but she'd never seen one like this before. She shoved it back in her coat pocket and put it out of her mind.

*

'Lola, a word in my office please?' said Pat in the staff room.

Lola was pushing her raincoat into a locker. 'Sure,' she said. 'What is it?'

But her boss had already vanished. Lola followed and watched with a sick feeling as Pat shut the office door. She never closed that door.

'Is something wrong?'

Pat ignored the question. 'Have a seat.'

She did so, watching warily as Pat swivelled her laptop round. Lola came face to face with an image of herself frozen on the screen, Greg on one knee before her.

Pat's lips were pinched, her eyes as hard as stone. She said quietly; 'This happened in work time.'

'I didn't know he was going to do it,' she said quickly. 'I didn't know anything –'

'I'd already warned you, Lola. Your efficiency is below standard.'

Lola swallowed and smoothed out a non-existent crease in her green trousers. 'I'm sorry.' She made herself meet her boss's gaze square on. 'It won't happen again.'

'Correct. It won't. You'll get your P45 in the post.'

She sat up as a rush of heat swept through her. 'You're sacking me?'

'I'm letting you go, Lola. You've had warnings already. This was the last straw.'

'But – but I need the money!' Mum relied on her help. When she'd first set up the salon and business had been slow, they couldn't have managed without Lola's wages. 'You can't –'

'I don't pay my staff to stand around daydreaming or being *serenaded* by their boyfriends.'

Pat's mouth twisted around the word serenaded and, too late, Lola remembered how her boss's partner had left her for a younger model last year. She glanced at the frozen image on the computer screen. Was Pat jealous?

'I'll see you out.'

Lola stood up and mustered as much dignity as possible as she left the premises.

Outside she walked head down against the rain. A bus drew up, but she stepped back. She'd walk instead. Why not? It was only a couple of miles, and goodness knew she had time on her hands. Tears stung her eyes.

Her shoes kicked up water, and her trousers were soon soaked through, but she didn't care. What would she do? She and Mandy were expected to pay their share of the bills, and the rent around here wasn't cheap. She'd have to find another job. Her heart sank at the thought of waitressing or working in Mum and Mandy's beauty salon. What about her jewellery-making? No. It didn't sell.

Her fingers curled around the crinkly brown paper in her pocket, surprised because she'd forgotten it was there. She opened it and examined the pale stone. Despite the cold rain, it felt warm and solid in her fingers. What was it the old lady had said? *If it feels like a risk, that's when you're truly living.*

At the time, Lola had been so angry with everyone telling her to marry Greg. She crested the hill and looked down over the chimneys and rooftops of Haven Bridge. But what if that wasn't what the old lady had meant?

Perhaps she should pay the shop another visit.

*

The scent of perfume hit her as she went in. The bell tinkled as Lola closed the door, and the chandelier danced a little before settling. Tourists in raincoats and walking boots milled about the place, and Lola spotted the shopkeeper behind the till serving a customer.

Lola climbed the stairs to the second floor. It was quieter up here. Old wooden chests were filled with folded blankets, and glass baubles strung from the windows caught the sun and scattered rainbow shards around the room. A wicker basket spilling over with balls of wool sat in the brick fireplace. Lola paused in front of it. She could tell the fireplace was original, and wondered what it had witnessed over the centuries. How many people had walked past it or gazed into its flames?

'Not as many as you might think.'

Lola span round. The white-haired lady was standing behind her, calm and unruffled, not even slightly out of breath despite the steep stairs.

'This place used to be a chapel – before it passed to me and I opened this shop.'

Lola nodded politely. Had she really spoken her thoughts out loud? Crikey. She was losing it.

The lady straightened a pile of greetings cards. Her fingers were crooked, her skin pale as marble. She wore a curious outfit; a tweed skirt and a red blouse with ruffles around the cuffs and throat. Her heels were at least three inches high yet she moved around with the grace of a ballerina.

'Who – who are you?' asked Lola.

The lady beamed and bobbed a curtsey. 'Why, Miss Moonshine, dear. Pleased to meet you.'

Lola couldn't help but smile. It was strange; she had grown up in this town where everyone knew everyone, yet she'd never heard talk of this eccentric lady before.

She felt in her pocket for the stone. 'When I came in yesterday you gave me this.'

Miss Moonshine's thin lips stretched in a plum-coloured smile. The creases around her eyes spoke of a full life, rich in experience.

'I – I just wondered why you gave it to me?' said Lola, feeling the pinch of guilt for the way she'd reacted.

'Because you needed it.' The lady's hair glinted like pearls as she looked at Lola. 'Has it made you rethink?'

'About what?'

'Your future, of course.'

Lola didn't reply. She'd thought of nothing else, but had only gone in circles.

The lady peered at her. 'Everyone has a dream, a goal, a wish they'd like to come true.'

The stone seemed to glow in her hand, and a gentle heat seeped into her bloodstream. Lola looked out of the window at the mill by the river and pictured herself in a workshop making jewellery, taking commissions for bespoke pieces.

But that was silly. She'd tried displaying it in her mum's salon and once she'd taken a stall at the market, but people had barely glanced at it.

'Ah, so you do have a dream,' said Miss Moonshine, stepping forward to peer at her more closely. 'But you're afraid.'

A shiver travelled through her. Afraid?

'There's no need to be. When you find your true path everything will simply fall into place. It's a magical feeling, as if the universe has realigned itself just for you.' The lady turned and busied herself, straightening piles of folded tea towels and plumping up cushions with surprising strength. 'Try it,' she added. 'Follow your heart.'

Lola bit her lip. 'What if I don't know where my heart wants to go? I mean, we all have dreams, don't we? But real life gets in the way.'

Real problems, like losing your job. Frustrated, she turned away. She hurried downstairs and across the shop, but as she reached for the door, Miss Moonshine's voice stopped her. 'I've always thought real life was overrated, don't you agree?'

Lola did a double take. The old lady was wearing a full-length ballgown, and the green satin shimmered like a mermaid's tale. Tucked under her arm was the tiny dog.

'How did you do that?' asked Lola.

'What, dear?'

'Get changed so fast?'

Miss Moonshine looked down at her dress as if she herself wasn't quite sure. She shook her head. 'Anyway, what was I saying?'

'You said real life was overrated.' Which might work as the old lady's mantra, but in the last forty-eight hours Lola's life had turned upside down, and she didn't have a clue how to put it right. 'It's not always that easy, though, is it? I mean, it's not just about me. There's Mum and my sister – and Greg…' She bit her lip. Was she making excuses? She sighed. 'I just don't know what to do for the best.'

Miss Moonshine tilted her head in a look of sympathy. 'Let the stone guide you.'

*

Mum had been chopping carrots. Hearing Lola's news, she put the knife down. 'She did what?'

'Mum, please. Don't overreact.'

'Overreact? She sacked you because the love of your life asked you to marry him!'

Greg wasn't the love of her life, thought Lola, but Mum was already snatching at the strings of her apron, saying, 'I've got a good mind to go over there right now and –'

'Mum, don't.'

'Who does she think she is? Debbie turns up late every day but I haven't given her the push.'

Lola cringed to be compared with the salon's moody and argumentative receptionist. 'It wasn't just that,' she said quickly. Her mum stopped. Lola took a deep breath. 'She had given me a warning already. Two, actually. About my efficiency. I sometimes got distracted.'

Her mum frowned. 'That doesn't sound like you, Lo.'

'It was just so boring stacking shelves or sorting through best-before dates. Sometimes I did daydream. A bit.' The glimpse of a customer's hairclip or some bright new packaging could be enough to trigger ideas for jewellery she wanted to make. Pat had caught her jotting notes and quick sketches more than once.

'I see.' Mum sat down.

Lola wished she would be cross, rather than looking so disappointed.

'So what are you going to do?'

She shrugged as if it was no big deal. As if that stone wasn't burning in her pocket and Miss Moonshine's words weren't filling her ears. *You don't have a dream?*

'I'll look for something else.' There were always waitressing jobs going in the town's many cafés and pubs. She added hesitantly; 'And I might try again to sell my jewellery.'

Mum lifted a brow. 'That won't pay the rent.'

Lola felt a shot of hurt. 'How do you know?'

'Well, how much do you earn from it at the moment?'

'Not much, but if I had more time and promoted it, I might sell more. I was thinking I could join one of those online craft stores. And could you display it again in the salon?'

'I can,' Mum said carefully, 'but remember last time? It didn't sell, love. It's too colourful, too chunky. Round here people want copper, wood, glass. Natural materials, muted colours. And all those designers in the mill, they have degrees and things. They're not like you and me, Lo.'

Lola blinked hard and looked away.

'I just don't want you to raise your hopes and be disappointed again.'

Alone in her room, Lola opened her jewellery case and picked out her favourite necklace. The turquoise and coral beads rippled through her fingers, making her think of ancient civilisations and exotic places where the sun was fierce and the colours intense.

But Mum was right. Jewellery-making was for people with all the qualifications and letters after their name. Lola had left school with the bare minimum of exam passes. She mustn't lose her head to a silly dream just because of an eccentric old woman.

Still, she loved creating it, and right now she needed cheering up. There wasn't space in her small bedroom, so she laid out her beading mat on the kitchen table and started arranging and rearranging beads until she got a pattern that pleased her. She found it therapeutic, all the bending and clipping of metal, the stringing of beads and stones, the alchemy of combining colours in different ways and watching the results emerge like a butterfly from a chrysalis.

She noticed her mum kept popping back into the kitchen and glancing her way. When she came in for the fourth time Lola told her; 'I'm fine, you know.'

Mum turned in surprise.

'You don't need to keep checking on me.' She threaded a bead onto the wire and picked up her round-nosed pliers to twist the metal into a loop.

'I wasn't –'

'Honestly, Mum, I'm good.' Lola's tone softened. She put the pliers down. 'I hated that job anyway.'

'Did you?'

'Yeah. I fell into it because there was nothing else at the time and you needed help with money while you set up the salon, but I never meant to stay there so long.'

Her mum's forehead creased with guilt. 'Money isn't so tight now I've built up a list of regular customers.'

'I know.'

She *was* fine, Lola assured herself. OK, so she was still angry at the injustice of losing her job over Greg's proposal, and she may have squeezed her pliers tighter than was necessary while she'd enjoyed a little mental fantasy that she was snipping Pat's head rather than a metal headpin. But the more she thought about it, the more she saw what had happened as a release. This was her chance to try something new. To really think about what she wanted to do with her life.

'Mum, do you know Miss Moonshine?'

'Who?'

'She owns the shop next to the bank.'

'The emporium?'

'Yes.'

'I've seen it but never been in. I'm not sure when she's open. Why?'

Lola shrugged. 'Just wondered.'

Mum nodded at the laptop. 'Have a look if her shop is on our community web page.'

It was, but the photos looked really old and grainy. Curious. Lola wondered if the lady had used a black and white filter.

Lola glanced at the earrings she'd just finished. Making jewellery might not be something that would pay the rent, but there was no harm in setting up an online store, was there? And while she had time on her hands, maybe she'd catch the train to Manchester, check out what was happening there, too. She touched the small lump in her pocket. She'd never dared before, but now what did she have to lose?

*

She found the craft centre in a former indoor market which had been divided into workshops and stalls. Research had told her that the owner was a jewellery designer himself, and Lola had emailed to ask if he'd consider selling her pieces. He'd replied with a terse and non-committal message telling her to drop by so he could take a look at her work.

After speaking to a couple of stallholders, she found him in a workshop, soldering.

Lola cleared her throat.

He turned. 'How can I help you?'

His eyes were the most startling shade of blue. Pale and clear, like a summer sky reflected in a raindrop. He was much younger than she'd expected. Around Greg's age, at a guess. Her heart skidded. Oh God, she was so nervous. What if he laughed at her? Or worse, pitied her?

She reached for the Angel Stone, which now hung from a long silver chain. She'd taken to wearing her new pendant all the time, and at night she slept with it under her pillow. Of course, she didn't believe for a minute that it would do anything, but it was reassuring somehow.

'I'm looking for Scott Allen?'

'You've found him.'

His voice was deep and velvety – or was it simply his Australian accent she found so enchanting? He wiped his hands on a rag and stepped forward to shake hers.

'I'm Lola. I emailed you.' She handed him one of the business cards she'd designed and printed.

'Yes, I remember.' He looked at the small card. 'Lola. Nice name.'

'Thanks.'

'Unusual.'

'Mum was a Barry Manilow fan.'

'Ah. What was the song called – Copacabana?' His lip curved a fraction. 'How big a fan are we talking? Did she throw her knickers at the poor guy?'

She giggled. 'No, but she sang backing vocals for him once.'

'She's a singer?'

He watched her intently, as if nothing were more important than what she had to say.

'Not any more. When my dad died she had to give it up and get a steady job.'

'I'm sorry.'

She shrugged. 'I don't remember him. I was very small.'

'Lola.' His lips twitched. 'Gotta admit, I'm feeling the urge to break into song, but I bet everyone does that, right?'

She nodded. 'Please don't. I can't stand his music.'

He laughed. 'Could have been worse,' he said. 'My Dad was a film buff. If he'd had his way I'd have been christened Woody. Woody Allen, see?'

With his broad shoulders and solid build, he couldn't be more unlike the actor. She laughed, and her shoulders dropped as she relaxed a little.

'Luckily,' he went on, 'my mum put her foot down.'

Lola smiled. The air seemed to fill with a static buzz.

'So you have jewellery to show me, Lola?'

'Oh – er, yes.' She flicked open the catches of her case and pulled out a selection of earrings, necklaces and rings, crossing her fingers he'd like some of them, at least.

He picked up an Aztec-style bracelet and examined it. The beads glinted crimson and black. She watched for his reaction, but he gave nothing away. She pushed her hands into her pockets and found her gaze lingering on his blonde lashes and the strong lines of his jaw. Her jewellery was chunky, but in his hands it looked small and delicate.

'These are unusual,' he said finally. 'I've got to be honest, though, I'm not sure my customers will go for these styles.'

Lola's heart sank. She almost reached for her case. Then capitulation gave way to something else. Something fierce.

Why did no one have faith in her? She loved her pieces. Miss Moonshine's smiling face hovered in her mind, and her left hand made a fist around the Angel Stone pendant. She glanced behind at the displays of pewter and pearl. Her work would stand out here.

'You don't know unless you try.' She smiled, feigning

confidence. 'I love the colours and styles of ethnic art and I try to use them in my work.'

His brow lifted. 'So I see. Have you been to Australia? I think you'd love Aboriginal art.'

She shook her head. 'But I've studied it.'

All those hours spent gazing longingly at pictures on the internet and in magazines had to count for something, didn't they?

'You're right, we should give it a go. And don't get me wrong – I like it. I'm just not sure what Joe Public will make of it. How about a month's trial and I'll return anything that hasn't sold? Agreed?'

Relief rushed through her. 'Agreed.'

On the train home Lola sat by the window, and as the apartment blocks and warehouses rushed past to be replaced with emerald and bronze hills, chaotic hopes began to unfurl. In her head she cradled the image of Scott bent over the soldering iron in concentration. What would it be like to make jewellery full-time? To have a workshop of her own? A place where she could hammer and solder and have space to come up with even more imaginative designs. Oh, she knew it was a dream, but it made her blood fizz to think –

A dream.

She glanced down at the Angel Stone and a fiery determination spread through her. Suddenly she knew what she wanted.

To make jewellery for a living. And one day to travel, to see the places which inspired her so much, to work with people and learn new techniques. One vision interlocked with the next, and it blossomed, this dream of hers, as if for too long it had been denied light and air. Perhaps it was unrealistic, impossible even, but she held on to it nevertheless.

As the train pulled up at her station, Lola stood, her spine straight with resolve. Tomorrow she'd really get to business making a quantity of jewellery, and she'd make a list of all the other outlets she could approach too.

*

'Lola, is that you?'

'Yes, I'm home!' She pushed the door shut and shook off her coat, impatient to tell Mum and Mandy about her trip.

But before she could say a word, Mum appeared in the doorway. 'You won't believe what's happened.' Her face was pale, her eyes raw. Mandy hovered behind her, jittery too.

Lola stopped. 'What?'

'Debbie walked out.'

'Debbie?' It wasn't a complete surprise. The receptionist had always been volatile. 'Why?'

'We had words because she's been coming in late again. She got in a huff, waited until we were busy with clients, then left and never came back.'

'Oh Mum, I'm sorry –'

Mum's bracelets jangled as she waved a hand through the air. 'That's not all. She ripped out pages from the appointment book. Can you believe it? It's already causing pandemonium. Eight years it's taken me to build up my business and now I could lose it all.'

'Oh no.' Lola bit her lip. 'Have you called her?'

Her mum nodded. 'She won't answer.'

'It's been mad,' said Mandy. 'We didn't know who was booked in when or what for so we couldn't prepare and we've been running late all day.'

'The customers have been very good about it,' said Mum, 'but I don't know what I'm going to do. The phone hasn't stopped ringing and we can't answer when we're with clients.'

Lola reached to hang up her jacket. When she turned

back, she suddenly realised the two of them were watching her expectantly. 'What?'

'I need to advertise for a new receptionist,' said Mum.

Mandy nodded.

So did Lola.

Mum went on, 'But I don't have time to do interviews while I'm coping with all the chaos she's caused.'

Silence filled the hall. Then realisation dawned on Lola. 'You want me to – ?'

Her heart plunged as she thought of the plans she'd made on the train home.

'Well you're not working, are you? Please, Lo. If you could cover on reception – just until I find someone...'

Their pleading looks were too much. Lola closed her eyes, feeling all her resolve crumble and fall away.

But what choice did she have? Her mum had sacrificed so much for her and Mandy. Lola couldn't turn her back on her own family, could she?

She swallowed a sigh. 'OK,' she said, feeling a weight like concrete in her chest.

Her mum beamed. She turned to Mandy. 'I told you we could depend on Lola.'

*

Lola put the phone down and immediately it started to ring again. It seemed Debbie had meddled further by spreading rumours that the salon had closed, so all day Lola had been fielding perplexed enquiries and reassuring customers that their appointments would not be cancelled. She tried to ignore the ringing while she dealt with the small queue of customers in the shop and the postman.

'Lola! I have a special delivery for you. Can I have your signature?'

She scrawled her name, took the envelope, then scuttled off to prepare a foot spa for the next lady's pedicure. The phone seemed to give up and finally fell silent, much to her relief. While the hot water ran, she wiped the beads of sweat from her forehead. Her gaze drifted to the window and the hills which loomed over the valley. She'd been silly, on that journey back from Manchester, to raise her hopes, to believe her life could be different. This was home. She was needed here. That trip had felt like an escape, but immediately on her return she'd been sucked back into real life, swallowed up by her obligations. It was all well and good an old lady talking about chasing your dream, but Lola prided herself on being dependable, and right now her mum needed her. As she closed the tap, she had the sensation of a small flame being extinguished. Her shoulders sagged.

She carried the foot spa to the treatment room, and wiped her hands down over her tunic. The envelope fell out of her pocket. She bent to pick it up. The holiday company's logo suggested it was more junk mail. But special delivery?

The phone's shrill ringing started up again. She glanced over her shoulder, then tucked it back in her pocket to open later and hurried back to reception.

'Lo, it's me.'

'Greg?'

'I heard what happened - about your job.'

'Yeah,' she said, waving goodbye to a customer as they left.

'I'm sorry.'

'Yeah, well.' She didn't know what to say, especially after the way they'd left things last time she'd seen him.

He cleared his throat. 'I - ah - would you like to come for dinner? At my place.'

She blinked. 'Dinner?'

In all the time they'd been dating, he'd never once made her dinner.

'Are you free tonight? Say, seven-thirty?'

'But it's Friday. You always go to The Packhorse on Fridays.'

'Yeah, well... you've had a tough time of it lately, what with losing your job and then all the stuff at your mum's salon. I haven't really been there for you like I should. I want to make it up to you.'

She frowned. This didn't sound like him at all.

*Don't be so cynical, Lo.* 'Dinner would be lovely,' she said. 'Thanks.'

And as she hung up, her heart beat a little faster at the prospect. It would be just the two of them. They could make a fresh start. She smiled to herself. Perhaps there was hope for them after all.

*

'Wow! This looks amazing!'

Wide-eyed, Lola turned full circle, taking in the table set for two, the candles, the fairy lights strung around the cabin. It was so unlike Greg to go to this much trouble that she couldn't prevent the tiny suspicion a female hand had been involved in this.

She brushed the thought aside. He was making an effort to repair their relationship, and he deserved she do the same instead of being suspicious. Her thoughts turned to the letter in her bag, and she felt a secret lurch of excitement.

Greg smiled and went back to stirring a pan. 'Nearly ready,' he said. 'Why don't you open the wine?'

Lola followed his gaze to the bottle of Beaujolais and two glasses beside it. She'd never seen him drink anything but stout.

'You don't mind me having steak, do you?' he asked as he brought the plates over.

The smell of meat wafted past her, making her feel queasy. 'No, of course not.'

'Don't worry. Yours is veggie.'

Lola looked down. On her plate were roast potatoes, boiled potatoes, mash and a smattering of boiled carrots. 'Potatoes – my favourite,' she joked.

He smiled proudly. 'Tuck in.'

He pushed a big piece of steak into his mouth.

Lola looked at the fairy lights strung up behind him. White and rose-shaped, they looked incongruous next to his bulky shoulders. 'Those lights look familiar.'

'They're your sister's.'

'Mandy's? Why –' The penny dropped. Her eyes narrowed. 'Was this her idea?' she asked, gesturing at the candles, the wine, the food.

He shot her a sheepish grin and nodded.

Lola forced herself to smile. Her sister had only been trying to help, yet the gesture was much less meaningful now she knew Greg hadn't thought of it himself.

'So, what are you going to do about your job?' he asked.

Lola looked up. For a fraction of a second she considered telling him about her trip to Manchester. Then she changed her mind. Making jewellery full-time felt like a pipe dream now she was back home. And the crisis at her mum's salon had been a brutal reminder that she couldn't just up sticks and leave.

'I'll look for something in town,' she said. 'Waitressing, something like that. When Mum doesn't need me at the salon any more, that is.'

The prospect of looking for a new job would be postponed, however, thanks to the unexpected letter she'd received. Excitement bubbled up inside her. 'Greg, I won a competition.'

'Oh yeah? What did you win?'

'Tickets to go round the world.'

He paused, his fork halfway to his mouth. 'What?'

'A trip – round the world.'

He put the fork down. 'On a plane?'

'Well it wouldn't be much of a prize if you had to walk.'

He didn't return her smile.

She added, 'It's a trip for two. We could go together.'

She'd thought about this long and hard. It would be a second chance for them, a test. If they didn't get on, then she'd know marriage wasn't right for them. And if they did – it would cement it.

Plus, she might feel differently about settling down after seeing the world.

'I get travel sick,' he said.

She waited for him to wink or laugh – but he was deadpan. 'On planes?'

'Trains, planes – the lot.'

'I – I didn't know that.' How did she not know that? He'd never mentioned it before.

And yet he lived in a canal boat. Her eyes narrowed.

'Apart from boats, obviously,' he added quickly. He stabbed a potato. 'This old girl is due a trip, actually. We could do that instead.'

It took her a moment to realise he was referring to the boat.

'Instead?' She made herself breathe. 'The prize includes accommodation.'

He carried on chewing.

She smoothed out her sequinned top, playing for time while she regrouped because she hadn't expected him to react like this. Her fingers touched her pendant and curled around the stone's fiery heat. A month ago, what would she have done? She would have worried about getting permission for two months' leave from Supersave, she would have felt guilty about leaving Greg. She would have timidly accepted his verdict.

Now, though, her chin went up.

'Greg, I really want to do this. I want to see other continents, other ways of life.' She pictured icy peaks and canyons, platinum beaches, caves, temples, ancient inscriptions. 'This is a dream come true. The chance of a lifetime.'

A flash of surprise crossed his face, then he scowled. 'Don't let me stop you,' he said, but his eyes glinted like metal cutters.

'Don't be like that.'

'How do you want me to be? You don't want to marry me, you want to go to the other side of the world without me. What does that say about your feelings for me?'

The blood rushed to her face. 'Perhaps it says more about *your* feelings that you don't understand.'

'I don't understand?'

'You expect me to marry you when you've never even taken the time to get to know me. We hardly see each other because you prefer to be out with your mates than spend time alone with me.'

'We're alone now, aren't we?'

She shook her head and laughed. 'Only because my sister suggested it.'

Why hadn't she seen how selfish he was before? Wouldn't a man who really loved her want her to be happy? Wouldn't he be encouraging her to travel and get her job sorted before settling down? The pendant glowed warm against her chest. Well, she was all the more determined now to go, even if it meant travelling alone.

They cleared the plates in silence. When Greg grudgingly

offered her dessert, Lola shook her head and looked at her watch. 'I've got work in the morning. I'd better go.'

He nodded. 'I'll walk you home.'

'There's no need –'

'I'll walk you home,' he insisted.

Outside her front door, he turned to her and his eyes brimmed with regret. He dipped his head and kissed her. A light brush of the lips, which felt like an olive branch.

'Thanks for tonight,' she said, choosing her words carefully. 'You went to a lot of trouble, and I appreciate it.'

He looked at her for a long moment, his expression unreadable in the shadows. The street was still and silent. On the other side of the road a cat darted past, its eyes shooting stars in the night.

'I thought we were good together, Lo, but now...' He sighed and shook his head.

She stiffened. 'Now?'

'It seems like you're changing,' he said finally. 'You want different things.'

Lola blinked, but before she could respond he'd turned and left. She watched him stride away into the dark, shoulders hunched.

Had it lain dormant in her all along, this wish to do something with her life? Or had Greg's proposal been a wake-up call making her question the path she'd taken? Her fingers squeezed the Angel Stone. Or had something else triggered the change in her?

*

The salon door opened and a lady came in.

She glanced at Lola and frowned. 'Oh. I must have got the wrong place.'

'The wrong place?' asked Lola.

'I was chatting to the lady in the emporium and she said you were looking for a receptionist after the last girl left at short notice. I'm looking for work, you see.'

'Oh. Right. Yes, you're in the right place. I'm just filling in until Mum finds a replacement. Can you just wait there a minute?'

Lola darted into the back room where Mum was laying out fresh towels for her next treatment. 'There's a lady at the front asking about the job.'

Her mum sighed. Lola knew what she was thinking. She'd been interviewing for three weeks now, but none of the candidates had been suitable. One had turned up wearing ripped jeans, another had been barely out of school with a mouth like a sewer, and the last one hadn't even bothered to wash her hair. Lola had begun to despair that she'd have to stay on indefinitely and perhaps even miss out on her trip. Unless their luck had just changed.

'She's smartly dressed,' said Lola, 'and well spoken. Says she's done reception work before and she can start straight away. She even smells of perfume.'

Ten minutes later, the lady emerged with Mum, the two of them laughing like old friends.

'I'll see you first thing tomorrow, Bridie,' said Mum.

'I'm looking forward to it.'

The lady left, carefully closing the door behind her.

Mum smiled. 'Can you believe Bridie and I knew each other in London?'

'Really?'

'Yeah. She sang too. Still does, apparently. She hasn't changed a bit. She'll be great to work with.'

'You won't need me any more, then?' Lola's spirits rose at the thought of being released. She could start making preparations for her trip.

Her phone rang. She glanced at the number, and hastily accepted the call.

'Lola? It's Scott Allen. Just calling about your jewellery.'

She braced herself for bad news. 'Oh yes?'

'It's sold really well, mate.'

Her heart soared. 'It has?'

'Yeah. Listen, could you come over here again? I'd like to talk to you about having your own stall here, if you're interested?'

Interested? 'Sure. When were you thinking?' she said breathlessly.

Her pulse sped like a runaway train and her cheeks, for some inexplicable reason, were burning.

Once they'd arranged a date and time, she asked; 'I'm curious to know which items sold. The necklaces or the earrings, the colourful pieces or the plain...?'

There was a moment's pause before he answered. 'It all sold, Lola. Everything you left with me has gone.'

*

Lola willed the Manchester train to go faster. She was so excited she felt like the River Calder after heavy rain when it was brimming full and threatening to burst its banks. Her jewellery had sold: people wanted to buy it. For the first time in her life, it seemed possible she could do the thing that made her happy – and earn a living from it.

'Lola!' Scott's deep voice hooked itself around her. 'Good to see you again.'

His blue eyes lit as he smiled and he held his hand out. She shook it, and tried not to show how pleased she was to see him while her heart hammered against her ribs.

He reached into a drawer and pulled out a wad of notes. 'Your profits.'

Lola grinned. 'Thanks.'

He showed her the stall which had become free, and her head began to spin when she realised it contained a small workshop. They sat down to discuss the cost, and made rough calculations of how much she could earn if she did this full-time. Even excluding the possibility of online sales, it was easily double what she'd been earning at Supersave.

'So when can you start, Lola?' Scott sat back in his chair.

She bit her lip. Should she ask? He'd told her he was keen to fill the stall as soon as possible.

*Follow your heart.*

She sucked in air. 'I wondered... can you wait a month or two? It's just I won a round-the-world ticket. It's the chance of a lifetime. Something I've always dreamed of doing.'

His brows lifted. She held her breath.

Then his eyes creased and he smiled. 'That's how I ended up living here, you know? Took a gap year, went travelling, came here and decided I wanted to stay. You're going to have the time of your life. I hope you take the opportunity to visit Australia.'

Relief cascaded through her. 'It's top of my list,' she grinned. 'Has been ever since I watched *Crocodile Dundee*.'

He laughed. The blood rushed to her ears. 'You'll find it really inspirational for your work. When you come back, I expect you'll be bursting with ideas.'

*

Walking home from the station, she squeezed the stone. She still had to break the news to Mum.

'So you're going to work in Manchester?'

Lola nodded. 'I'll commute for a while, see how it goes, but it might be easier to live there.'

Mum nodded. 'What about Greg? You haven't had second thoughts?'

'None at all. We agreed it was over and I gave him the ring back.'

'Good.'

Lola stepped forward and touched her mum's arm. 'How do you feel about me leaving home?'

'I'll miss you, but this is your chance, love. I'm so excited for you.'

'What about the bills? Will you manage? What if the salon goes through another quiet patch?'

'The salon's doing better than ever since Debbie left – and I don't want you to worry about that, anyway. It's my responsibility. I'm grateful for the help you've given me, Lo, but you need to think of yourself and your own life.'

She smiled with relief. 'I'm glad you feel that way.'

'I love you. I want you to be happy. It's fantastic that your jewellery is selling so well. How about I nip out and get a bottle of cava to celebrate?'

Lola smiled.

Mum picked up her handbag. 'By the way, I popped in to see that Miss Moonshine lady.'

'Did you?'

'Yeah. The postman delivered her mail to my shop – I don't know how he got it mixed up when our address is nothing like hers. Anyway, I took it round in my lunch break and –' Mum's brow furrowed. 'It was really strange.'

'What was strange?'

'It was almost as if she was expecting me. She welcomed me like an old friend, but I'm sure we've not met before.' She looked pensive. 'Then I spotted this...'

She reached into her bag and pulled out a glittery black band with a yellow feather attached.

Lola peered at it. 'What is it?'

Mum slipped it onto her head. 'I used to wear something like this in my singing days. It took me back...' She smiled at the memory.

'Right,' Lola said carefully. It looked a bit tacky.

'It got me thinking, maybe I could try a bit of singing again. Just for fun, you know? Bridie's in a band and they sometimes need an extra singer.'

'Mum, that's a great idea!'

'You don't think it's silly? I mean, I'm hardly the young girl I once was.'

Lola thought of how hard it must have been for Mum to lose her husband so young, to suddenly find herself alone with young children, and to be forced to give up her singing and take the first job she'd found in order to pay the bills. She'd been denied the chance to follow her dream back then. But now what was to stop her? Lola touched her pendant and smiled.

'It's not fanciful at all. You have a great voice.'

Mum smiled and her eyes took on that dreamy look again. It made her look ten years younger.

'There's just one thing, though, Mum.'

'What?'

'Promise me. No Bruno Mars.'

**Sophie Claire writes emotional stories set in England and in sunny Provence, where she spent her summers as a child. Previously, she worked in marketing and proofreading academic papers, but now she's delighted to spend her days dreaming up heartwarming contemporary romance stories set in beautiful places.**

sophieclaire.co.uk

# The Girl Who Didn't Win

*By Kate Field*

It was raining – of course it was. Clare had just spent her last £20 on her first cut and blow dry in over six months, so what else had she expected? The weather had already ruined her life. It was hardly going to baulk at messing up a hairstyle.

She dashed along the pavement towards the bus stop, fat dollops of rain pounding on the top of her head and squeezing down the gap between her neck and the collar of her jacket. A taxi roared past, too close to the kerb, drenching her in the dirty water that was bubbling back up from the drains. She hadn't seen rain like this since January, not since the floods that had washed away the final traces of her life with Ed...

Stopping to empty water from her shoe, Clare leant on a gate outside a shop she'd barely glanced at before – Miss Moonshine's Wonderful Emporium. Lights glowed in the tall windows, brightening the gloom of the afternoon and drawing her in with the promise of warmth inside. She headed down the path to the door, which creaked and jingled as she pushed it open.

'Oh my dear, whatever happened? You're soaked through!'

A lady of indeterminate age, with a shock of white hair and a kind smile, approached Clare as she stepped into the shop.

'I was caught in the rain,' Clare began, but as she gestured at the window, instead of the rain-speckled glass she had intended to point out, a streak of sunshine filtered through the dusty pane.

'This summer weather is so fickle, isn't it?' the lady said, holding out a towel that she seemed to produce from nowhere. 'Here, rub yourself down. You'll soon dry off. Why don't you take your time and have a little browse? There's something for everyone here.'

Clare thought it unlikely that there'd be anything for her, unless Miss Moonshine was giving things away, but after the kindness with the towel she felt obliged to feign some interest. Only she didn't have to feign it. As she wandered through the higgledy-piggledy rooms that made up the shop, table after drawer after cupboard held something to catch her eye: vintage clutch bags in vibrant jewel colours, pretty glass perfume bottles, exquisitely embroidered samplers, cases of glittering costume jewellery... It had all been laid out with obvious love and care.

She wandered upstairs and through to the furthest room, under the eaves. A gate-legged mahogany table filled the centre of the room, and on top of it stood a magnificent Georgian-style doll's house. And beyond that... Clare's feet were irresistibly drawn to the bookcase in the corner, where every space was crammed with old books: some antiquarian with their plain spines and elegant gold lettering, others more modern with a rainbow of glossy dust jackets. She picked out a book and flicked carefully through the pages, inhaling the faint, musty smell and letting the memories unfurl around her.

'Ah, you're interested in the books?' Miss Moonshine had followed her without her noticing.

'This is valuable. It's a first edition.' Clare opened it and showed it to Miss Moonshine. 'You should be selling this for at least ten times as much.'

'Really? I had no idea. You know your books. Are you a collector?'

'I sell them. Sold them.' Clare sighed. Six months on, and the pain and disappointment were no less acute. 'We had a second-hand bookshop, down in the Cotswolds.'

'How lovely! But you no longer have it?'

'No.' Clare tried a shrug, but grief lay too heavily on her shoulders. 'Everything was lost in the floods last January.'

Everything in the shop, and every hope of replacing it, because Clare had discovered that they didn't have insurance for the stock, or for the interruption to the business. Her fiancé, Ed, had always sorted out the insurance, and last year, without him, she had simply renewed the same policy without giving it a thought. Losing all they had built together had been like losing him all over again.

She was dragged back to the present by a gentle pressure on her arm.

'You've had some bad luck,' Miss Moonshine said. 'It won't last, my dear. I'm very grateful to you for telling me about this book. Is there anything I can tempt you with?'

'No, I'm sorry, not today.'

Clare wandered back downstairs to the front of the shop. Weak sunshine still filtered through the windows.

'I know what might suit you.' Miss Moonshine opened an ornate walnut cupboard to reveal several boxes piled on shelves. 'I call these my Lucky Dip boxes. There's all sorts in them, and only £20 a box. I have one here that's mainly books.'

She picked out a box and put it down on the counter, next to a tiny chihuahua that had curled up to sleep in a patch of sun. The top item was a slim volume of love poetry, identical to one Ed had given Clare many years ago at university, and that had been lost in the flood. She reached out to stroke the cover.

'I'm sorry, I really don't have the money...'

She pushed her hands into her pockets to prevent the temptation to rummage further through the box. Her fingers snagged on a crumpled piece of paper. She pulled it out and stared at the screwed-up £20 note in her hand.

Miss Moonshine laughed.

'It's almost as if it were meant to be...'

*

Half an hour later, Clare returned to her parents' house, Miss Moonshine's Lucky Dip box in her arms. She had lived here for four months now, boomeranging back when it was clear that her business – her life – had no future.

'Hello love, how was your day? Your hair looks nice.' Michelle, Clare's mum, met her in the hall. 'What have you got there?' She peered in at the top of the box. 'Books? Ooh, does this mean you're thinking of getting back on your feet again?'

The hope on Michelle's face was hard to bear. Clare's parents had taken her in without hesitation when she had needed them, devastated first by Ed's death and then by the loss of the bookshop. They tiptoed round her despair, cheering her on as if she were an unsteady toddler, needing encouragement to walk after taking her first tumble. Her head told her how lucky she was. Her heart was too numb to feel it.

'No. I don't know...'

She couldn't if she wanted to. She had no money. All her savings were tied up in the shop, which no one wanted to buy now it was a known flood risk. And even if she'd had the money, how could she ever replace what she'd lost? There could never be another Ed. The bookshop had been their dream; they had worked long hours in jobs they hated for years to save up the money to buy it. She had already experienced the best that life could offer. How could she follow that?

'Well, there's no rush, is there? We love having you here.'

Her mum was still smiling as Clare hurried up the stairs to her room. She put the Lucky Dip box in the centre of the bed and started to take out the items, starting with the poetry book, which she carefully laid to one side. There were five other books, mainly of nominal value, although one first edition easily justified the price of the box. Below the books lay a bizarre collection of odds and ends: a pack of Royal Wedding playing cards, a tarnished compact mirror with beaded case, and buried right at the bottom, almost hidden below the base flap of the box, was a small sequinned purse. It looked like something belonging to a child, and Clare was about to toss it to one side when she felt something heavy inside.

The teeth of the zip were bent, and it took several forceful attempts to open the purse. The zip finally gave way and a splash of silver flew out and landed on the bed. It was a charm bracelet, real silver according to the hallmark, but it only had one charm attached in the shape of a lucky four-leaf clover.

Clare fastened it onto her wrist. It was a perfect fit, and the clover shone as it caught the sunlight bursting through the window. It could have been made for her. Her conscience prickled. Miss Moonshine couldn't have known this bracelet was there, or she wouldn't have left it to languish in a box of scraps. Perhaps she ought to take it back... But she knew, as she ran her fingers over the intricate chain, that she wouldn't. Perhaps, as Miss Moonshine had said, this was meant to be. She was due some luck at last, wasn't she?

*

The following Friday lunchtime, Clare headed to the newsagent's opposite the Haven Bridge Picture House. It was her regular end-of-week indulgence: one scratch card, in the hope that she would win the jackpot. She hadn't thought through what she would do if she did win. The money wasn't even the point; since the first time, buying a card had become an addiction, the tiny flare of hope like a needle prick, reminding her that she was still capable of feeling something.

She arrived at the door of the newsagent's at the same time as a glamorous young woman, beautifully made up and with straight blonde hair as glossy as a mirror. They reached for the handle at the same time, clashing hands.

'Sorry,' Clare said, automatically drawing back. She opened the door and stepped aside. 'After you.'

'No, it's fine, after you.'

'No, I insist.'

The other woman smiled and entered the shop, heading straight to the counter at the back. The shop assistant nodded in recognition at Clare, while the woman dithered over her selection of chocolate bars.

'And I'll take one of those scratch cards as well,' she said with a pretty laugh, pointing at the roll of scratch cards that Clare always chose. It was a special contest, with a top prize of £100,000, which always seemed just the right amount to do something with, even if she didn't know what that something would be. 'You never know your luck, do you?'

Clare had a pretty good idea of her luck, but nevertheless as the blonde woman moved to one side to put her change away, Clare handed over her money for a scratch card and immediately scratched away at it, the charm bracelet banging against her wrist as she did. The weekly flicker of hope soared and then died, and she crumpled up the card.

'Better luck next week,' the shop assistant said, as he always did. 'It will –'

Whatever else he had planned to say was drowned out by a shriek. The other customer was staring at the card in her hand.

'I think I've won,' she said, but from the puzzled frown on her face she clearly doubted her own words. 'Is this right? Can you check?'

She held out the scratch card to Clare, who took it in stunned silence. How unbelievable was this? She had bought a scratch card from the same shop at the same time every Friday for the last four months, without ever coming close to winning, and now, on the day she had let – no, *insisted* – that someone went before her in the queue, she had missed out on what – £50? £100?

But it was so much worse than that. Clare looked at the card, then at the woman, then handed it over to the shop assistant.

'Blimey,' he said. 'You've only gone and won the jackpot. A hundred grand? That's all right, innit?' He looked at Clare and grinned. 'Could have been yours if you'd got in first. Bit unlucky there, weren't you, love?'

*

Clare wasn't going to bother going to the newsagent's the following Friday – what were the chances of finding two winning scratch cards in the same shop? – but Nicky, Clare's boss at the pharmacy where she worked, took one look at the drizzle and asked Clare to pop out and pick up the latest edition of her favourite magazine. Of course, this Friday there was no rush for the door, no queue for scratch cards, Clare noted, twirling the lucky charm bracelet on her wrist in a way that had become a habit already. In fact, the shop was empty except for the usual shop assistant and a tall, dark-haired man flicking through the magazines.

'Here she is!' the shop assistant cried as Clare walked between the shelves of confectionery to the counter. 'Didn't I tell you she'd be in? She's not missed a week these last four months.'

Was he talking about *her*? But who was he talking to? Clare looked round. The other customer shoved his magazine on the shelf and walked over.

'Hi, I'm Ben Murphy from the *West Yorkshire Times*.'

Clare didn't need the introduction. She knew exactly who he was. He was Ben Murphy from Haven Bridge High School; that wide, slanting smile was instantly familiar, even though it must be almost sixteen years since she had last seen him. Clearly she had no features worth remembering, or perhaps grief had stained them beyond recognition. She took a step nearer the counter, sure that there must have been a mistake. What could he want with her?

'Hang on, I know you, don't I?' he said, frowning. 'Were you in my year at school? Chloe...?'

'Clare. It's Clare.' There had been a Chloe in their year: riotous blonde curls, a bust to rival the South Pennines, and a father who owned an off-licence – all irresistible attributes to teenage boys. Including Ben Murphy, if Clare remembered rightly, from what she had glimpsed from behind the safety of her books.

'Of course! You were the bright one of the year, weren't

you? Spent your time working hard, unlike me. I never concentrated unless there was a ball heading my way.'

Ben hadn't needed to work. He had been destined to take over the family business, a successful construction company, so exam results were a bonus, not a necessity. But hadn't he said he was from a newspaper? Clare shrank even further from him. The press had crawled – or waded, more accurately – all over the ruins of her bookshop and the other buildings that had been damaged in the flood, hunting down "human interest" stories. They had homed in on her, somehow discovering that the loss of the business had come barely 18 months after losing Ed, reducing her personal tragedy to a story that would be forgotten within hours...

'What do you want?' she asked.

His smile froze at the ill-disguised aggression in her voice.

'You!' He laughed, and his face creased into well-worn lines that testified to a happy life. Lucky him. 'Or I think it is. Were you here last week when the winning scratch card was bought?'

'Yes, but I didn't buy it. You've got the wrong person. *You* can tell him,' Clare said, appealing to the shop assistant. 'I'm not the winner, am I?'

'No, it was the pretty blonde lass. But he knows that.'

'Kitty has already given an interview,' Ben said. 'That's the girl who won. Haven't you seen the paper?' He delved in his bag. 'We're trying to find the girl who *didn't* win.'

The girl who didn't win! That could be the title of her autobiography, Clare reflected. It certainly summed up the last two years. She peered at the paper that Ben held out to her. There was a large photo of Kitty, holding one of those over-sized fake cheques and smiling ecstatically, as well she might. She had a hundred thousand reasons to smile, didn't she?

The headline below the photograph read, 'Do you know the unluckiest girl in Yorkshire?' Clare skimmed the article. The whole tale was there: how the two of them had arrived at the shop at the same moment; how she had held the door open and allowed Kitty to go first; how that one act of politeness had cost her £100,000. Clare tossed the newspaper onto the counter.

'How did you find me?' she asked.

'Easy. I asked Kevin here if he knew you.' The shop assistant nodded and grinned, clearly enjoying his 15 minutes in the spotlight more than Clare was. 'He didn't know your name, so he suggested that if I came here today I'd be sure to catch you.'

Because her life had become so small, so predictable, that the only date in her diary was the weekly intimate encounter with a scratch card? It was humiliating and true.

'And why are you so keen to catch me?'

Ben grinned at that, and Clare pressed against the shop counter, mortified. She hoped he didn't think she was flirting. Nothing could be further from her mind.

'Because it's a great story,' he said. 'It's always good to show both sides of the coin – the winners and the losers. Readers love a human-interest story.'

'No.' As if calling her a loser wasn't bad enough, he sealed his fate with that phrase. 'You mean you want to rake over my life, show the world how miserable it is, and how devastated I am not to have won the money. You'll sacrifice anyone to sell a few papers. Well, you're not sacrificing me. I've lost far more important things than money. I don't give a stuff about that.'

She turned to go, but Ben caught her arm.

'Clare. Wait –'

There were no laughter lines about his face now. There

'You probably won't remember me, but I found this in one of your Lucky Dip boxes,' she began.

'Of course I remember you, my dear. You're the girl who knows books.'

It was better than being the girl who didn't win, Clare supposed.

'Is there something wrong with the book?' Miss Moonshine asked. 'No returns on Lucky Dips. You take the box as you find it.'

'No, the book's fine. Only I found a couple of things tucked inside it, and I'd like to return them to the owner if I can. Do you have any record of where it came from?'

'There have been so many things over the years...' Miss Moonshine shook her head. 'I'm sorry I can't help. Was it something important?'

'Maybe. Only to the owner.' Something held Clare back from saying more. The note seemed too intense, too private to discuss in a busy shop. She reached in her bag and brought out the photograph. 'I don't suppose this rings any bells?'

Miss Moonshine peered at the photograph.

'That man...' she began, and Clare's hopes rose. 'But no,' Miss Moonshine said, shaking her head. 'I thought he favoured someone, but I can't place who it is at the moment.'

Clare held out her hand for the photo, but Miss Moonshine started tapping at it. 'I can tell you where this tree is, if that helps.'

'Really?' Clare moved closer and inspected the tree in the background of the photograph. She hadn't noticed before that the trunk was split in two, and only one half was bearing leaves. 'Is it local?'

'I believe so. It looks very much like the Lightning Tree on the moors to the west of town, on the way to the ruined chapel. It was struck by lightning back in 1922... or was it 23?

I can't be sure. I'm so sorry I can't be of more help.'

'No, you have been. If the photo was taken locally, it suggests that the people in it might have been local too, which could make them easier to find.'

Clare reached for the photo again, and the charm bracelet glinted on her wrist. She still wore it every day. It hadn't brought her any luck, but she found a curious comfort in feeling the chain against her skin.

'That's a pretty bracelet,' Miss Moonshine said. 'Is it a clover for luck?'

'Yes.' Clare hesitated, but her conscience had been pricked. The truth rushed out. 'It was in the Lucky Dip box, under the books. Didn't you know? I wondered if it might have been a mistake, because it must be far more valuable than the cost of the box. You should have it back...'

Clare started to remove the bracelet, but Miss Moonshine covered her hand and stopped her.

'No returns on Lucky Dips,' she repeated, smiling. 'The bracelet is yours now. Maybe it once belonged to the same person as the book and the photograph?'

Clare hadn't thought about that and determined to go through the contents of the box again, to see if there might be other clues about the owner. She had taken a few steps towards the door when Miss Moonshine called after her.

'Have you thought of contacting the local newspaper?' she asked. 'I would guess the photograph dates back to the early 1950s from the hair and dress. It would be worth checking the archives. Perhaps there might be a record of the couple marrying? You never know your luck.'

*

Clare did her best to ignore Miss Moonshine's suggestion, but after a weekend of fruitless searching on her own, she had to face the obvious. The newspaper was an excellent place to look, and Clare already had a contact at the *West Yorkshire Times*. Could she really ask a favour of him, when she had been so rude before? She had to. Returning the note to its owner had already become personal, as if restoring this final message could somehow make up for the loss of her own. So on Monday morning she rang the newspaper office and asked to speak to Ben Murphy.

She had almost lost her nerve, and was about to cut the call, when Ben's warm voice stole into her ear.

'Hello, it's Clare,' she mumbled. There was no reply. 'Clare Sampson. From school. From the newsagent's. The girl who didn't win,' she added in desperation, mortified to have been forgotten again.

'I know which Clare,' Ben replied, and she could hear amusement in his voice. 'I'm just surprised to hear from you. You made it pretty clear when we met that you didn't want to talk to me.'

'Sorry about that. It was a shock, that's all...' She stopped. She didn't want him to think she'd changed her mind about the scratch card story. 'Is there any chance we could meet? I wondered if you could help with something.'

'Sure. Do you work in Haven Bridge? I'll be there this afternoon actually. Why don't we meet on the packhorse bridge at one?'

Today? She hadn't expected him to agree so easily, or to be free so soon. She glanced in the mirror. She wasn't looking her best; it was hard to find the motivation to make an effort nowadays. Still, what did it matter? It wasn't a date. There had been no dates since Ed. There would be no more dates, because she had already loved and lost the man who was meant for her. Nevertheless, when she left the pharmacy to walk to the packhorse bridge just before one, she had acquired a slick of lipstick and mascara from the samples on the pharmacy shelves.

Ben was already waiting on the peak of the old stone bridge that straddled the river in the centre of town, leaning over the side to watch the ducks as they paddled around the small island that divided the water below. He lifted a hand in greeting as Clare approached.

'This was one of my favourite spots as a child,' he said. 'I used to pester whoever was looking after me to come here and feed the ducks.'

A shadow crossed his face, and Clare wondered about his turn of phrase. Who had looked after him? His parents had been alive when they were at school: it had been impossible to miss their arrival at every concert or Parents' Evening in the biggest, most expensive car. Before she could ask – if she dared – he smiled.

'Lunch?' He gestured towards the café beside the bridge, and without consciously agreeing, Clare found herself ushered through the door and to the one free table in the window.

'Spot of luck, wasn't it?' Ben said. Clare nodded, and without thinking she touched the charm bracelet on her wrist.

They ordered lunch and spent a while reminiscing about their schooldays, although they had been part of such different groups within their year that they shared few common memories. Clare had thought it might be awkward – she would never have dared to speak to Ben at school – but it was easier than she had expected. In fact, it was good. He was funny, told a story well, and listened as if he was genuinely interested. She sat back in her chair, realisation striking her. Was he just acting as a journalist? Was he still fishing for information about the girl who didn't win? She stared at him suspiciously.

'How long have you been a journalist?' she asked, interrupting his tale about the Sixth Form prom.

His laughter abruptly died.

'About twelve months.' It was the shortest sentence he'd spoken for some time. He looked away, through the window. Clare was intrigued.

'Why journalism? I thought you were heading for great things in the family business?'

'I was. I did.'

'Didn't it work out?'

Ben looked back at her, frowning.

'You mean you don't know?'

'Know what?'

'The business went bust. Two years ago. We lost everything.'

The previous warmth in his voice had gone, replaced by a flat, unemotional tone that was achingly familiar to Clare.

'I'm sorry,' she said, the trite words inadequate, as she well knew. 'I wasn't living here then. I hadn't heard.'

He shrugged and pushed his plate away, abandoning half his sandwich.

'It's old news now. Just another business lost to the recession.'

But it wasn't – it was his family business, the one that was supposed to provide his future. She wanted to reach out, explain that she understood, but the words wouldn't come; she wasn't ready to share her story.

'How did your parents take it?'

He grimaced.

'Badly. Forty years of work disappeared overnight when the bank pulled the plug. It destroyed them.'

'And you turned to journalism?'

He sighed and rubbed the side of his face.

'It was what I'd always wanted to do, given the choice. But it's not easy starting at the bottom at my age. The pressure's on to make it work, so my parents can stop feeling they've let me down.'

He sat back as the waitress approached and filled their coffee cups. By the time she left, he had found a smile, but with her new knowledge Clare could see the edges to it, note the lack of spontaneity behind it.

'So why do you need my help?' he asked. 'Please tell me you have a fantastic story that I can sell to the nationals and get my name out there...'

Clare took the photograph from her handbag, feeling awkward now that she only wanted to take his help, not give any.

'Remember this photo?' she asked, passing it across the table. 'I'm trying to find out who these people are, if I can.'

Ben studied the picture.

'Like I said, the man looks familiar, but I still can't think why. I don't know the woman. Should I?'

'No. But I think the photo was taken locally, and I wondered if there was an archive at the newspaper and an easy way to check it...' Clare trailed off, having second thoughts about asking him now. She hadn't minded using him when she dismissed him as a mere journalist. Now she had been reminded that there was a man behind the job, a man who hadn't had the easy life she'd assumed. 'Don't worry about it,' she said, plucking the photo from his hand. 'I shouldn't have asked. You must be far too busy for this.'

'I am busy. I'm interviewing a dog who can ride a scooter in half an hour.' He laughed. 'The junior reporter gets all the best stories.' He looked at her across the table. 'Is it important that you find out who this is?'

'Maybe. I have something that belongs to them that they might like to have back.'

'That sounds mysterious. Aren't you sure?'

'I'd want it back if it were mine.'

She willed him not to ask any more questions. She didn't want to mention the note, not here, against the backdrop of shouting toddlers and with expectant customers hovering near their table, eager for them to leave. She didn't want to risk him asking why it meant so much to her. He studied her in silence, then nodded.

'I don't have time today, but I'll have a look as soon as I can. Have you done a reverse image search?' Clare shook her head and Ben smiled. 'I'll try that first. With a bit of luck, the answer will only be a couple of clicks away.'

*

It was three days before she heard from Ben, and when he eventually rang Clare could tell from his voice that he'd found something. Infuriatingly, he wouldn't tell her what it was.

'Meet me by the canal bridge next to the locks on Sunday morning,' he said, laughing off her questions. 'All will be revealed.'

He was already waiting when Clare arrived, a steaming takeaway coffee cup in each hand.

'Hello,' he said, holding out one of the coffees. 'Black, no sugar, right?'

'Right,' she replied, smiling back, and feeling an unexpected nugget of warmth that had nothing to do with the drink now heating her hands. 'Well remembered.'

'Observation skills,' he said, laughing. 'First thing they teach at journalist school. Shall we head to the park?'

They strolled along the towpath by the canal, past the

colourful narrowboats and on through the gate into the park. Ben led the way to a bench that was catching the morning sun.

'So what have you found?' Clare asked, the moment they sat down. 'Do you know who the people in the photograph are?'

'I know who the man is.' Ben took out his phone and pulled up a photograph. 'What do you think? The same man?'

'Definitely.' Clare smiled, but peering at the photograph again, began to frown. 'But he looks different in this one. More... groomed,' she concluded, struggling to find the right word. The picture on Ben's phone was a head and shoulders shot, and the man was wearing a jacket and tie. He was leaning to one side, smiling straight into the camera, and it almost looked as if he were wearing make-up.

'Who is he?' she asked. Something else about the picture niggled her. He looked familiar, and not because of the original photo. She felt as if she should know his name, but that couldn't be right, could it?

'You're not going to believe this.' Ben paused. 'It's Randall Hunt.'

'Randall Hunt?' Clare repeated. 'Wasn't he an actor?'

'Not just any actor.' Ben tapped at his phone. 'He was part of the Golden Age of Hollywood. At one point he was tipped to rival Cary Grant as a leading man.'

'He *was*?' Clare's heart sank at the use of the past tense. 'You mean he's dead?'

'I'm afraid so. He died about 15 years ago. But his career ended well before that, back in the fifties. Probably not long after your picture was taken.'

'Oh! Why was that?'

'No one knows. It's a mystery.' Ben leaned closer to Clare, and she could see the curiosity lighting his eyes.

'Look, it's all on Wikipedia. He just vanished from the public eye.'

Clare scrolled through the Wikipedia entry. It was exactly as Ben had said. Randall Hunt had been set for super-stardom, after his first two films had made his name, and he was widely feted as the new darling of Hollywood. But then he had abruptly retired from the movies, and very little more was known about him until his death was announced. There weren't even any details about whether he had ever married or had children.

Clare handed back the phone.

'Did anything come up for the woman in the photo?'

'No. I've not found a match for her yet, and no other photos of them together.'

Clare sipped her coffee, watching a pair of dogs chasing across the grass.

'So it's a dead end, isn't it?' she said eventually, disappointment stretching from her scalp to her toes. 'She could be any woman, from anywhere in the world. I was told it might have been taken beside the Lightning Tree up on the moors, but that can't be right, can it? Why would a Hollywood actor have been in Yorkshire?'

'Actually, he was.' Ben showed Clare a different page on his phone. 'His last movie was filmed on location around Hardcastle Crags. He was in the area for several months. There are quite a few articles about it in the archives. But I suppose that doesn't mean she was a local woman. You don't even know what the relationship was between them. She could be someone who worked on set, or even his sister.'

'Definitely not his sister, not if he wrote the letter to her,' Clare said, then stopped as Ben turned those curious eyes on her. She hesitated, and then put down her cup and fished the letter out of her handbag. 'Here. I think this belongs with the photo.'

She watched as Ben read the words, saw the rueful smile soften his lips as he reached the end.

'So that's what you wanted to return,' he said, passing the paper back. 'A love letter. You're a secret romantic, aren't you?'

'No, it's not that.' Clare turned towards Ben, drawing back when their knees brushed. 'It isn't just any love letter. It's a *last* love letter – the final memento of a love affair.'

'And you really think it's so important that someone would want it back? Over sixty years later?'

'Yes! This might have been it, their one chance of happiness, and for some reason it was snatched away. You don't get over something like that. Even a goodbye is precious when you know there can't be anything more. It must have been devastating to lose this,' she added, looking down, feeling the weight of her own loss crushing her all over again. Only it wasn't all she felt; briefly, Ben's knees pressed against her own again.

'What happened?' he said, and the gentleness in his voice stole through her usual reserve. 'What have you lost?'

'Everything,' she replied, and when Ben frowned, not understanding, she found herself telling him it all. About the bookshop, and how they had dreamed of a life spent working together; about Ed, and how his death had taken away the certainty of her future; about how the floods had destroyed what little she had left and burdened her with a shop she couldn't sell and debts she couldn't pay. The words tumbled out. It was a relief to speak of it at last, after months of bottling up her misery.

'Do you wish you could have interviewed the unluckiest girl in Yorkshire now?' she asked, referring to the headline he had shown her in the newspaper when they first met. 'Would that have made a good story?'

'No. It's not a good story,' Ben said, and for barely a second, he placed his hand over hers and squeezed it.

Clare shivered as the sun disappeared behind a cloud. Ben stood up. 'Shall we carry on walking?'

They returned to the towpath and headed back towards the locks.

'There were bad floods here a few years ago,' Ben said, stuffing his hands in his pockets. 'Perhaps you could speak to some of the businesses that were affected. They might be able to give you some advice about your shop and on starting again.'

'No,' Clare said, stopping as they reached the bridge by the theatre. 'There's no point. I had everything I wanted, and now it's gone. I've had plenty of pep talks about second chances, but it would always be second-best, wouldn't it?'

'Not necessarily. I know the situations can't compare, but being a journalist is my second chance, and I can't regret it. I share a crummy house, drive a clapped-out car, and have a precarious bank balance but I've never felt so lucky.'

'I think we've already established that I don't have luck like that.'

'Perhaps you need to start making your own luck. It's simple, isn't it?'

It did sound simple when he said it, and for a moment Clare's habitual gloom wavered, and she wondered what might be possible... but then a gust of wind blew away her fragile hope, and she huddled into her coat, the familiar despair wrapping round her again.

*

Two weeks went by, and the initial excitement of identifying

Randall Hunt fizzled away as they came no closer to finding out who the woman in the photograph was. Ben sent Clare regular text messages about his search – funny, warm messages that unaccountably brightened her day – but there was no disguising the lack of progress. He had suggested publishing the photo in the newspaper, and it was an obvious solution, but Clare held back. The couple in the picture had preserved their privacy for sixty years; she didn't want to be the one to ruin that.

With options running out, Clare showed the photograph to Nicky, her boss at the pharmacy.

'I don't suppose you recognise this woman, do you?' she asked, holding out the photo and carefully covering Randall Hunt's face.

'What?' Nicky glanced at the image. 'It's black and white! How old do you think I am? I could only have been a baby when that was taken.'

'I mean do you recognise her as a customer? If you try to imagine what she looks like now...'

'If she's still alive, she must be in her late eighties by now, at least. One grey perm looks the same as another to me. Is it important?'

'Not really, only...'

The loud beep of Nicky's mobile phone interrupted.

'That's all I need,' Nicky said, throwing down her phone. 'Brian tripped over the cat last night and has sprained his ankle. He can't drive, so he can't do the prescription run.' She looked across at Clare. 'Lucky I have you now. You'll have to do it. I have a list as long as your arm of prescriptions that need delivering today.'

'Me? I don't know how to do it.'

'It's hardly rocket science. You drive to a house, you drop off a prescription. There's even a satnav in the van. If Brian can manage, I'm sure someone with your qualifications can.'

The day didn't prove to be a highlight of Clare's employment at the pharmacy. It was murky and miserable – a clear reminder that the summer was over and autumn on the way. The rain was so heavy she could barely see through the windscreen, even with the wipers on the fastest setting. She leaned forward in the driver's seat, gripping the steering wheel so tightly her fingers went numb as she tried to negotiate the steep and twisty lanes around town. At last she reached the final delivery on the list and followed the satnav's directions onto a narrow track, holding her breath as she squeezed the van between the bushes lining either side. She was beginning to wonder if she'd gone wrong when a huge black-stoned house came into view around the next bend. Clare lost concentration for a second, the van hit a pothole and skidded into a bank of mud.

Clare climbed out and inspected the damage. Not only were there clear scratch marks down the side of the van, it was well and truly stuck in the ditch. It was just her luck, wasn't it, that Brian had to be absent on the day the weather turned? Nicky was going to be furious. The charm bracelet peeped out of the bottom of her sleeve as she gave the van a half-hearted shove. She didn't know why she was still wearing it. If anything, her luck had been worse since she'd found it.

The local garage was too busy to rescue her for at least an hour. Deciding she might as well finish the delivery, Clare trudged along the track, rain soaking through her clothes and puddles splashing over the tops of her shoes, until she reached a weathered oak door and banged on the knocker.

It must have been a couple of minutes before the door opened, to reveal an old man with thick white hair, tartan slippers and a warm smile.

'Is it raining?' he asked, peering past Clare and looking up at the sky. 'What are you doing out in this weather, lass? Only fish and fools enjoy this much water.'

'Mr Wardle?' Clare asked, holding up the pharmacy bag, which was rapidly disintegrating in the rain. 'I've brought your medicine.'

'But you're not Brian.'

'No, he's not well today.' Clare held out the bag, but the man made no effort to take it. He looked past Clare again.

'Nay, you didn't try to drive up the track in these conditions, did you? Brian knows better than that. You'll end up stuck!'

'I am stuck. Someone's coming to help me out.'

'Well, you'd best come in while you wait. You look like you could do with a cup of tea.'

She could actually do with a large glass of red, but tea was a close second, and after only a moment's hesitation, Clare followed Mr Wardle into the house. He shuffled through a wood-panelled hall that was large enough to hold a fireplace and two wing-backed chairs, and into an old-fashioned but spotless kitchen. Glossy purple cupboards with metal trim handles had clearly survived for several decades, and a large, scrubbed pine table filled the centre of the room.

Mr Wardle opened a cupboard and took out two mugs. He popped a teabag in each one.

'Don't tell my sister,' he said, tapping the side of his nose. 'She's a stickler for the full works, cups and saucers and teapots. Do you mind it the simple way?' He didn't wait for a reply, but wandered over to Clare and held out his hand. 'I'm forgetting my manners,' he said. 'I'm Bert. How do? Who might you be?'

'Clare.'

'A proper, solid name.' He nodded in approval, although

Clare wasn't too sure she liked being called solid. 'I once knew a Clare. Good teeth and trim ankles. Almost asked her to dance once at the Astoria in Todmorden but I lost my nerve and next thing you know she's engaged to some fella from Burnley. Takes all sorts,' he said, handing Clare her mug. 'Come on through to the parlour, the fire's going in there.'

The parlour was a dark but comfortable room next to the kitchen at the back of the house. A Victorian tiled fireplace dominated one wall, and Clare headed towards it, craving its warmth and reluctant to leave a wet patch by sitting down on any of the chairs.

'This is an amazing house,' she said, looking round. 'Have you lived here a long time?'

'Almost ten years.' He gestured towards a row of shelving to one side of the fireplace, which was filled with picture frames. 'It's my sister's house. She's been here for over sixty years, and I moved in when we were both left on our own. It's not been a bad arrangement, bar the odd disagreement now and again. It certainly beats being alone.'

Clare managed a small smile and turned away to look at the photographs. They were typical family photos – babies, children, weddings – clearly chronicling the passing years in both the faces and the fashion. She was about to speak to Bert again when an older photograph caught her eye, a black and white image of a teenage girl and boy. She pulled it forward and stared at it.

'Is this you?' she asked Bert, holding out the frame. He smiled.

'Aye, I've not changed a bit, have I?' He tugged at his hair. 'Still all my own, and not many can get to my age and say that.'

'But who's this with you?' Clare asked, pointing to the girl at his side.

'That's my sister. That's our Nancy. A real beauty, wasn't she? You could have scoured the whole of Yorkshire and not found one to match her.'

But Clare had seen one who matched her – on the photograph in her handbag, looking with love into the face of Randall Hunt.

*

'I've found her.'

Clare telephoned Ben as soon as the van had been rescued, and she was safely back in Haven Bridge. 'Her name is Nancy Wardle.'

She told Ben the story of her afternoon, hardly able to contain her excitement, and apart from a few interruptions to laugh at her driving skills, Ben seemed equally thrilled.

'How sure are you?' he said. 'Did you ask her brother?'

'No. He might not know anything about it, if it was a secret affair. I'm almost certain, though. She had the same eyes and smile.'

'It's unlikely there were two girls who looked like that around the same area at the same time. She was stunning.'

It was true, but for some reason Clare's excitement dipped a little on hearing that, which was ridiculous, because what was it to her if Ben did consider someone stunning? It wasn't as if she had any interest in him herself.

'What do you want to do next?' Ben asked, interrupting the confused swirl of her thoughts. 'Are you going to visit again and return her things?'

'She's in the Peak District for a few days, visiting friends.' Clare had managed to weasel the information from Bert. 'I suppose it gives us more time to double-check. Would you mind looking into Nancy, see if you can find anything else? I promise it will be the last thing I ask of you,' she added, belatedly conscious that she had referred to "us" automatically.

'No problem,' he said. 'I'm happy to help. I want to hear this story as much as you do.'

*

Ben phoned Clare later that evening, when she was curled up in bed with a book.

'I think you're right,' he said, cutting straight to the point. 'I can't believe I missed this before. Randall Hunt visited the Haven Bridge Picture House in 1953 and guess who worked there?'

'Nancy?' Clare didn't need to wait for confirmation; she could sense Ben's smile down the telephone. 'Is that where they met? Did you find a photo of them together?'

Ben laughed. It was an oddly intimate sound to hear in her bedroom, when she was wearing only her pyjamas; oddly comforting too. It reminded her of the long, late-night conversations she had shared with Ed before they moved in together. She snuggled further under the duvet.

'Nothing quite that good,' Ben said. 'I found an article about his visit, and there are two photos. One is of Randall on the steps of the Picture House, and the other is of members of staff lining up to meet him. Nancy is in the line. The timing fits, doesn't it? What do you think?'

Clare didn't hesitate.

'I think we need to meet Nancy.'

*

Ben parked his car on the road and together they wandered down the track to the house on the moors, while the early autumn sun warmed their heads and the curlews circled high in the sky. Clare felt a curious sense of anticipation – positive anticipation, not the usual gloomy dread she had lived with for so long.

Breaking all sorts of rules, she had looked up Bert's telephone number in the pharmacy records and arranged to visit him and Nancy this morning. She'd mentioned vaguely that she had found something that might belong to Nancy, but Bert hadn't seemed to care. He'd said they were always glad of visitors, and of an excuse to break into a new packet of biscuits.

Bert answered the door, shook their hands, and led them straight to the parlour. A lady was standing by the window, and she turned as they entered the room. Clare knew at once that it was Nancy: the eyes and the smile were unmistakeable. But this wasn't the Nancy she had expected. She had imagined a tiny old lady, bowed with age, with permed grey hair and shapeless, comfortable clothes, shuffling around in her slippers like Bert. The real Nancy was slim and tall, her white hair styled in a pixie cut and wearing elegant trousers and a silk blouse that made Clare look the dowdy one.

'How very good to meet you,' Nancy said, shaking Clare's hand with a firm grip. There was no trace of a Yorkshire accent, and her voice was redolent of old films. 'Bert tells me that you might have something of mine. This is quite the mystery. I don't recall having lost anything recently.'

She gestured at them to sit down. Clare perched on the edge of the sofa and Ben took a seat by the fire while Bert brought in tea and biscuits. Clare glanced at Ben and he nodded, confirming that he agreed this was the girl in the photograph, although the raised eyebrows that followed the nod suggested that Nancy wasn't what he had been expecting either.

'So why don't you tell me what this is about?' Nancy asked, after a few minutes of small talk while they made the most of the tea and biscuits.

'Do you know a shop in Haven Bridge called Miss Moonshine's?' Clare began. The atmosphere changed at once; Nancy stiffened and sent her brother what appeared to be a warning look.

'I'm aware of it,' Nancy said. 'I believe it's even older than I am. But I've never been in it.'

'Oh.' Clare didn't know if this was bad news or not. She reached in her bag and took out the book of poetry. 'A few weeks ago, I bought a box of bric-a-brac from there, and found this book inside.'

She held out the book and Nancy took it. Her hands shook as she held it, inspecting the front cover. Then she opened it, flicking through the pages, too fast to be reading the words – almost as if she were looking for something. She reached the end cover and let the book drop to her lap.

'Yes, this could well be mine. I used to have a copy just like it. But how could you know? My name isn't in it.'

'I found this inside the book.' Clare delved inside her bag and brought out the photograph. 'I recognised you when I delivered Bert's prescription.'

She passed the photograph to Nancy, and any lingering doubt was washed away when she saw the emotion ripple across the older lady's face: surprise, followed by a flash of tenderness, finally replaced by wariness as Nancy looked up at Clare.

'Have you shown this to anyone?' Nancy asked.

'No.' Clare decided not to mention Miss Moonshine and Nicky.

'And why are you showing it to me?'

'Well...' Clare was confused. Wasn't it Nancy in the photograph? 'I thought you would want it back. There was this as well,' she added, feeling like Mary Poppins as she rooted in her bag again and brought out the note. 'I wouldn't have wanted to lose them. If it had been me in the photo, if someone had written this note to me, I would want to keep it forever.'

Nancy studied Clare for what seemed a terrifyingly long time and then she smiled.

'Forever?' she repeated. 'Yes, I suppose you're still at an age where forever seems possible, and even desirable. May I?'

She held out her hand for the note. When Clare passed it over, Nancy glanced at the words, too briefly to read them, as if she knew them off by heart.

'If you managed to track me down, I dare say you had easy work to discover the identity of the man?'

'Randall Hunt,' Ben said. 'A rising star from the Golden Age of Hollywood until he disappeared. Do you know why?'

Clare shot him a warning glance. What was he doing? She wanted to hear the story as much as he did, but they had agreed not to interrogate Nancy. It was up to her whether she chose to tell them the story or not.

'I do,' Nancy said. 'I'm probably the only one left now who does. Apart from Bert, of course. He always knew everything. He took that photograph, you know. The only one we ever had taken together. It was too risky, you see.' She turned the note over in her hand. 'I can't tell you what a relief it is to have this back. Dear Bert, who had kept our secret so well for almost sixty years, decided to spring clean one day and took piles of old goods to Miss Moonshine's shop. He had no idea that I was using this book as a hiding place. I have lived in dread that it might fall into the wrong hands.'

'It hasn't,' Clare said. 'I only wanted you to have these things back because they must be precious. You don't need to tell us anything. Whatever secrets you have are safe.'

Nancy studied her and then nodded and relaxed back in her chair.

'We met at the picture house in town,' she said. 'I worked there, and he visited when he was filming out on the moors near Hardcastle Crags. Something clicked at once, the magical way it sometimes can. Perhaps you know?'

Nancy glanced from Clare to Ben.

'Oh, we're not –' Clare began, only to be silenced by the sight of Ben's smile.

'We met up whenever we could over a long, glorious summer. We took whatever was available: minutes or whole days, early mornings or late nights. Every moment was precious because this was it, we both knew that. The thing we had seen in the romantic pictures. The real thing.'

'So why did it end?' So much for not interrogating Nancy. Clare had to know more.

'Because his wife found out.'

'His wife?' Ben repeated, sounding as surprised as Clare felt. 'I haven't seen anything about his wife on the internet.'

'They married long before he was famous, when they were mere teenagers,' Nancy said, with a dismissive wave of her hand. 'The studio felt it was better for his image to be single. His wife never accompanied him on set. But somehow she found out about us and came up here to confront him.'

'What happened?' Clare asked, fearing the worst.

'She didn't make it. There was a terrible accident on the way, and her car collided with a tree. She survived, barely. She suffered a head injury and was left needing constant care.'

'And that's why he couldn't leave her,' Clare said, recalling the words of the note.

'He did the right thing,' Nancy replied. 'He gave up acting, withdrew from the limelight and devoted all his time to looking after his wife. I would never have expected him to do anything else. I always knew it was a gamble to become involved with a married man, and it was a gamble I didn't win.'

'You must have been heartbroken. How do you get over losing a love like that?' It was a rhetorical question. You didn't get over it, Clare knew that. But to her surprise, Nancy smiled.

'Why would you focus on the loss? We had four wonderful months, and I learnt what love was all about, and how marvellous it could be. Two years after Randall left, I met another lovely man. We were married for over fifty years before he died. We have four children, ten grandchildren, and two great-grandchildren. I thank my lucky stars for every day I had with him. What a wonderful life I would have missed if I hadn't moved on from Randall.'

'But wasn't your husband second-best?' Clare asked, edging forward in her seat.

'Certainly not. And my current beau isn't third-best either. Is there a better tribute to the dead than to want to recreate the happiness they taught you was possible?'

Was that true? Clare's head reeled. Perhaps she could have hope for the future; perhaps she could contemplate starting over...

Nancy stood up, distracting her from her thoughts. Clare watched as the elderly lady walked over to the fire, the note and photograph in her hand. She hesitated for only a moment, and with one final look at the picture, she threw them both into the fire. In seconds, they were gone.

'There. I promised Randall that I would protect his privacy. The secret is safe now, isn't it?'

Clare nodded and turned towards Ben. His hand was in his pocket and it looked as if he was quickly pushing something out of sight... a small metal device... Her stomach churned. Had he recorded the conversation? She'd trusted him, thought he had accompanied her today as a friend, not as a journalist. How could she have been so stupid?

She stood up quickly, though it felt as if her heart was filled with lead, weighing her down.

'I think we should go now,' she said, unable to look at Ben. 'Thanks so much for telling us.'

She held out her hand to shake Nancy's, and the charm bracelet slid down her wrist.

'Randall's bracelet,' Nancy said, reaching out to touch it.

'This was his?' Clare asked.

'Mine. He gave it to me. An inexpensive gift – anything more might have aroused questions.' Nancy smiled and fingered the clover charm. 'He added this to reflect how lucky we were to have found each other. We thought we would have a lifetime to collect more charms...'

Clare began to unfasten the bracelet.

'Here, you should have it back.'

'No.' Nancy reached out and clasped her hands over Clare's. 'I've had more than my share of happiness. I've no use for it now. You keep it, with my blessing. I hope it brings you luck.'

They had taken barely a dozen steps away from the house when Clare rounded on Ben, her heart thumping with feeling in a way it hadn't done for months.

'Did you record that conversation with Nancy?'

She had expected a denial – what else would a slippery journalist do? – so she was surprised when he nodded.

'How could you? You knew I only wanted to return her things. You knew that this secret has been protected for years. How could you even think of betraying her? What has happened to you?'

'Failure happened, that's what. I told you. I need to make the journalism work. I don't have qualifications or a degree like you. This is it, my second chance, and if I blow it there's nothing else. At least I'm willing to risk starting over.'

'Unlike me?' Clare stepped away, stung by his words, ready to be furious... but the fury wouldn't come. Instead, there was a precious memory, of one of the last conversations with Ed, when they had lain together on his hospice bed, hip to hip and hand in hand. 'Don't you dare sit around feeling sorry for yourself,' he had told her. 'Live. Remember me by living as fully as you damn well can.' Tears sprang to her eyes. What would he say if he could see her now, too afraid to live at all?

'I'm sorry,' Ben began, but she shook her head.

'So am I,' she said. 'I thought I could trust you. I thought –' She stopped. Never mind what she had thought. She'd clearly been wrong. She walked away.

'Clare, wait.' Ben ran in front of her, forcing her to a halt. He held out the dictation machine. 'Here. Listen to it.'

'Why? I've already heard it. And no doubt I'll be able to read all about it in the tabloids soon enough.'

'You won't. Listen to it.'

He pushed the machine into her hand and she pressed what she thought was the play button. Nothing happened.

'It's not working.'

'Yes, it is,' Ben said. 'There's nothing on it. I started recording but then I wiped it. You're right. I couldn't do it to Nancy. The mystery of what happened to Randall Hunt is probably the greatest story I'll ever uncover, but it's not mine to tell. It's hers, and Randall's, and it will stay theirs, as they wanted. Some things are worth more than money.'

Clare's relief was immense: relief that Nancy's secret was safe, but more fundamental relief too, that Ben was who she had begun to hope he might be. She managed a tentative smile.

'I have to believe that, don't I, as the girl who didn't win?' she said.

Ben laughed.

'But if you'd won on the scratch card, we'd never have met. I wasn't important enough to interview the winner. Only you.' He stepped closer, and his smile washed over her. 'I actually think it was lucky you didn't win...'

Clare's phone rang, breaking the intensity of the moment. She moved away to take the call, and then wandered back, feeling dazed.

'What's the matter?' Ben met her halfway.

'Nothing. I mean, it's good news.' Clare shook her head, still finding it hard to take in. 'Amazing news. A cash buyer has made an offer on the bookshop, for the full asking price. I can't believe it. This means I can clear all the debts, maybe have some money left over...'

'To start again?' Ben looked at Clare, but she didn't know how to reply. Was that what she wanted? While she'd thought the shop would never sell, she'd been able to carry on drifting, avoiding decisions about the future. But now... was it time to live again, and to live fully?

'Sorry,' Ben continued. 'I didn't mean to push you. I know you've had a rough time – the worst. But I just want you to know that if you do feel ready to try again – with a bookshop, or anything else – I'm here. As a friend, or a shoulder to lean on, or anything else you want me to be...'

He broke off, rubbed the side of his face, and looked away. A faint breeze ruffled his dark hair, and Clare felt something loosen inside her, as if the bandages around her heart were finally coming off.

'I'm ready to try,' Clare said, and Ben's gaze landed on her again.

'A new business... or...?'

'Everything.'

Ben took a step nearer, a cautious smile lighting his face.

'Second-best?' he asked. 'Or second chance?'

'Definitely a second chance,' she said, and she smiled and held out her hand.

**Kate Field writes contemporary women's fiction, mainly set in her favourite county of Lancashire, where she lives with her husband, daughter, and hyperactive cat. Kate's debut novel,** *The Magic of Ramblings*, **won the Romantic Novelists' Association Joan Hessayon Award for new writers.**

amazon.co.uk/Kate-Field/e/B00J18F3PY

# The Last Chapter

*By Mary Jayne Baker*

*Chapter One*

Callie prodded the rusty beer can with the tip of her trainer, lip curling with distaste. It always amazed her that people could come for a day trip to a place like Haven Bridge, presumably because of its reputation for tranquil, unspoiled beauty, only to do their best to ruin it for everyone else. Honestly, what was the point?

At least that was one good thing about her hobby, she thought, reaching for the can with one Marigold-clad hand and chucking it into the bin bag she was carrying. She could do her bit keeping the town tidy at the same time.

Her face lit up when she spied something poking out from the long, wildflower-starred grass that furnished the river bank. Bending, she picked it up and examined it.

It was a glass pebble, broad and round. Callie could tell it must've done its time on the riverbed from the perfectly smooth edges. And now, glinting envy-green in the sunshine, it had made its way to her.

What had it been in a previous life? Beer bottle? Ornamental bowl or vase? She liked to think about such things, to make stories for the items she found. In the past, the emerald pebble had been something functional, part of the unnoticed furniture of day-to-day life. In the present, it was litter. But in the future, next week perhaps, it would be something beautiful.

*

'Callie Fox.' Miss Moonshine, enveloped in a huge tartan kilt-dress paired with her favourite bovver-boy Doc Martens, didn't crack a smile. The flat northern vowels didn't lift a notch. But from the sparkle in her hazel eyes, Callie could tell she was pleased to see her.

The old lady came out from behind the shop counter and gave Callie's cheek a pinch. 'Show me something beautiful.'

'Ow,' Callie said, rubbing her cheek.

Miss Moonshine eyed her expectantly, head tilted, birdlike. 'Well? What do you have for me?'

'Nothing now.' Callie tilted her nose in mock offence. 'You don't deserve it, Nippy the Crab Lady.'

Miss Moonshine clicked her tongue, but her eyes twinkled. 'Don't listen to the bad girl, Napoleon,' she crooned to the elderly chihuahua wheezing in his bed. 'Mummy knows she doesn't mean it.'

Callie smiled. 'Go on then, I'll show you. But only because these're too good to keep to myself.'

She made her way past the assorted bric-a-brac lurking in the hollows and shadows of the fusty little shop. A plastic Transformer, not unlike one she'd played with herself as a child, nestled incongruously against an ancient-looking, feverishly ruddy china doll. A dressmaker's dummy in a white lace corset cast its long shadow over the piles of shabby paperbacks teetering precariously in every unfilled inch of space. Tat and treasure, mingling like a mismatched couple's wedding list. The only thing they had in common was that each item there was *chosen*. Everything on sale had been personally selected by Miss Moonshine.

When Callie arrived at the old mahogany table that served as a counter, she reached into her pocket and drew out four small objects wrapped in tissue paper. She placed each one gently on the table.

'Ah!' Miss Moonshine let out a sigh of satisfaction. 'I had a feeling you'd bring me something special today. Let me see.'

Callie carefully unwrapped one of the little parcels and handed it to Miss Moonshine to examine. The old lady held it up before her, squinting at it with a critical eye.

It was a small pebble, emerald green river glass, painted with a tiny yet intricate buttercup motif.

'Beautiful things,' Miss Moonshine whispered to herself.

'I did four in the same style,' Callie said with a modest blush. 'A wildflower theme for the summer. Cornflower, lavender, primrose and buttercup.'

'Where did you find them? Did anyone see you take them?'

Callie had been selling her rivercombed craft pieces to Miss Moonshine for two years now, ever since she'd first moved to Haven Bridge, and she'd become accustomed to the shopkeeper's eccentricities. At first, she'd wondered why Miss Moonshine always wanted to know where she'd found the materials used for each item, and who had been around at the time. Now, she just answered the questions. When you'd known Miss Moonshine a while, you started to realise this was someone who didn't need to make sense.

Still, it was odd. She always asked Callie to bring her beautiful things, yet it was often the items Callie was proudest of, that she'd put the most work into, which Miss Moonshine showed the least interest in. A beautifully carved and painted driftwood peacock Callie had spent months on, vibrant in jewelled blues and greens, got barely a second look. Miss Moonshine had offered a tiny fee that Callie had refused, taking the peacock back home to occupy pride of place on the mantelpiece. Whereas one of her earliest efforts, a laughably crude bottlecap collage unworthy of a playschool kid, had rendered the shopkeeper practically giddy. She'd handed over a £50 note for that piece without question. Too frightened to spend it in case Miss Moonshine realised what a massive mistake she'd made and asked for it back, Callie still had it, tucked away at the bottom of an old money box. It was that note which had given her the confidence to keep going.

'I found them on the river, by the bridge,' Callie said. 'All four pebbles on the same afternoon. They must've washed up when it burst its banks last month.'

'Who saw?'

'Plenty of people. It was near The Packhorse pub. Sunny day so the beer garden was packed.'

'Show me the others.'

Callie unwrapped each little ornament. Miss Moonshine held the tip of one finger briefly against each, her eyes falling closed.

'The primrose, £5. The cornflower and the lavender, £10 each,' she said at last, opening her eyes. 'Oh yes, and the buttercup. £20 for the buttercup.'

Callie frowned. 'What? But the primrose is the best one.' She drew a finger along the carefully delineated pink petals, feeling a thrill because it was her own handiwork. 'I spent a week on that.'

'Primrose, £5,' Miss Moonshine repeated stubbornly.

'But why so much more for the buttercup? It isn't even that good, the petals went squiffy. I almost didn't bring it.'

'That's my offer. Take it or leave it,' Miss Moonshine said with a shrug.

Callie sighed. 'You know I'll take it. I need the money, as usual.' The pittance she earned as joint owner of The Caf on the Canal was certainly never going to make her fortune. Not with business the way it was at the moment anyway.

Miss Moonshine opened up the till and handed over £45 in notes. It wasn't much for all the work she put into each piece, Callie reflected as she tucked it away in her jeans pocket, but it helped pay the bills. Plus it sent a shiver of delight through her to think of her pieces out in the world, being beautiful, making happiness.

'Come back when you've got more,' Miss Moonshine said. 'Oh, and here.' She grabbed a tatty paperback from the top of one teetering pile. 'Take this as part of your fee. I think you'll enjoy it.'

'Oh, no.' Callie backed away, raising her hands in protest. 'I'm not taking anything off you.'

Miss Moonshine smiled. 'You've been listening to stories, Callie Fox.'

Stories. Yes, she'd been listening to stories. You couldn't help it, when you'd lived here long enough. There were a lot of stories about Miss Moonshine.

Her friend Megan Archer, for example, the other part-owner of the narrowboat that housed The Caf on the Canal. Megan had bought a vintage Matchbox car from the shop for her young son one rainy day. Weeks later, she'd been tracked down by Jackson, a gorgeous lawyer from Nebraska who'd been given the car by his GI grandfather as a little lad. Now they were engaged, Megan was selling her half of the café and the whole family was moving to America.

Then there'd been long-widowed Charlie Chipchase. He'd come in for a book on how to trace his family tree. Well, no, he'd come in for a new lampshade, but Miss Moonshine had sold him a book on how to trace his family tree all the same. The Chipchase family weren't too impressive, but the librarian who'd helped Charlie find their records online had been. Now she was Mrs Chipchase.

They weren't all love stories though. One man had bought a pair of antique silver candlesticks that had turned out to be stolen goods. When police tracked them down, they'd found evidence he was responsible for stalking dozens of local women. These days, he gave his home address as HMP Manchester.

There were bagfuls of tales like that, going back, ooh, years – local folk who'd bought things from Miss Moonshine's shop and whose lives had changed irrevocably. It was coincidence, of course. It had to be. And there were plenty of other customers who bought things and carried on just as humdrum as they had been before, only humdrum with a new tablecloth.

But for all that Callie liked to consider herself a sensible, healthily sceptical modern woman of thirty, she couldn't stop the bite of superstition in her gut. Miss Moonshine. Her oddities, her fashions. Her... eyes.

'I don't want it,' Callie said again, waving the book away. 'I'm fine as I am.'

'It's only a book, dear.'

'It might be jinxed.' Callie shot a suspicious look at the yellowing cover, which bore a lurid illustration of a busty woman with long red hair not unlike Callie's own (hair, sadly, not bust). The woman was spilling from a torn dress, her fringe falling seductively over one eye. She held a telephone receiver in one hand and a man lay prone at her feet while a sinister-looking yellow bird watched from a cage. 'It might be a load of old tosh as well. Looks it.'

Miss Moonshine turned it around to read the back. '"*Budgerigars Don't Talk*. A page-turning whodunnit to keep you awake into the small hours. Femmes fatales! Murder! Sex! Intrigue!"' Her mouth flickered. 'Surely even a sensible girl like you enjoys being kept awake into the small hours every once in a while.'

'But –'

'Callie. It's only a book.'

Refusing to listen to further protest, Miss Moonshine tucked the book into Callie's handbag and pushed her towards the door.

## *Chapter Two*

Callie picked her way carefully down the precarious steps that led into her narrowboat café.

'Get much?' Megan asked. She was mixing a cappuccino for the customer on the other side of the hatch, who looked like he was in a hurry to be somewhere else.

Callie shrugged. 'Forty-five quid and a free book.' She retreated into a hidden corner where she couldn't be seen through the hatch while she put her pinny on. 'Better than a kick in the teeth, I guess.'

'It'll keep you in pinot grigio for a week or two, at least.' Megan smiled at the customer, a good-looking young man in paint-stained overalls, as she placed the coffee down in front of him. 'There you go, you. Go on, get back to work.'

'Cheers, Meg.' The man took his coffee and wrap, and Callie noticed how his cheeks dimpled when he smiled. He treated Megan to a familiar wink before dashing off.

'Could you try not to make me sound like a wino in front of the customers?' Callie said, glaring at her friend.

Megan grinned. 'Whatever will you do without me here to embarrass you, eh?'

Callie glanced through the hatch at the tables and chairs set out on the grassy area at the edge of the towpath and sighed. There was seating for at least thirty people out there, and another two dozen or more could sit inside. The sun was blazing, the swans and their cygnets were playful, the food was top-notch and the teashop-on-a-boat thing was unique in the town. So why were there only four customers out there? All the ingredients were right for the perfect business, but somehow it just wasn't working.

'Honestly, Meg? I've got no idea what I'm going to do without you.' Callie helped herself to a fresh-baked muffin, threw herself into a chair and started picking out the chocolate chips. 'I'll miss you to bits, you know.' She took in their cosy café with its lacy tablecloths and floral curtains, the smell of the fresh pink roses on each table - Megan's joy - mingling deliciously with the scent of hot currant teacakes and melting butter. 'The whole place'll miss you.'

'Come on. You don't need me.' Megan sat down in the chair opposite and reached out to squeeze Callie's hand. 'You're the genius behind this operation. You source the cakes, the stock, the... you know, boaty things. I'm just a glorified waitress.'

'The hell you are. You're the heart.'

Callie swallowed, staring down at her muffin so her friend wouldn't notice the tear welling in one eye. The truth was, she didn't know how she was going to keep the place going without Megan. She needed the camaraderie, the friendship, the support. The feeling that they were, literally, both in the same boat. And on a more utilitarian note, she needed the money. So far, there'd been no interest from anyone in buying Megan's half of the struggling business, and as Callie couldn't afford to either buy her out or to pay the bills alone, that meant they could soon be closing their serving hatch for good.

But she couldn't say any of that to Megan. Not when her friend was so blissfully, sickeningly happy with Jackson, all excited about the wedding and their new life in America. It wasn't fair.

'You'll be OK, you know,' Megan said gently. 'I promised I wouldn't leave you in the lurch and I won't. We'll work something out.'

'Yeah.' Callie summoned a smile. 'Yeah. Something'll come up. And if not... well, I'll just have to move on, I guess. The sale of the boat'll set me up in something, if it has to come to that. It was nice while it lasted, eh?'

Megan was silent. But there was a twitch at the corner of her lips that Callie knew all too well.

'Meg, what is it?'

'Nothing.'

'Come on, I know that face. There's something you aren't telling me.'

Megan let the twitch spread into a grin. 'OK, there is. But I'm not sharing yet. It's a surprise.'

'I hate surprises. Tell me.'

'Nope. I'm not saying a word till I get back from lunch.' She tapped a finger to her nose when she clocked Callie's worried expression. 'It's something good though, I promise. Something I –' She stopped herself. 'But I've said too much. We'll talk after I've grabbed a pasta pot and stretched my legs.'

'You've not had interest from a buyer?'

Megan pulled an imaginary zip across her lips. 'You'll get nothing out of me, Cal, so I'd save your breath. If I tell you now you're going to want all the details and I'm starving.'

'But –'

'Look, just man the hatch for an hour. There's someone I need to talk to before I spill the beans anyway. I'll be back before you know it.' Casting off her frilly pinny, Megan grabbed her jacket and disappeared up the stairs.

What could it be? What could it *be*? Callie went into autopilot as she served the thin smattering of customers who stopped by over the next hour, her head in a whirl.

She so badly wanted it to be a buyer. No one could replace Meg, of course, but a new partner was realistically the only way she could keep the business going. But she didn't see how Megan could have had interest without it getting back to her. She was the contact on the ad they'd placed seeking enquiries.

Ten minutes after the last customer had disappeared, Callie was leaning on her elbows at the serving hatch, staring into space. She'd run through every possibility she could think of. Secret buyers. Lottery wins. Megan cancelling the move to America and bringing Jackson into the business as some sort of naked butler. Nothing added up.

She checked her phone to get the time. Meg was late back, as usual.

Callie had propped herself on her elbows again and was preparing to resume her fixed stare when she spotted something poking out of the mud on the towpath.

There was no mistaking it, glinting in the sun. It was only surprising she hadn't noticed it sooner. A shiny Edwardian penny, hers for the looting. It was just what she needed to finish her latest craft piece.

She glanced furtively from side to side. The canal was quiet, locals back at work, tourists lunching in their favourite tearooms or pubs. She could easily nip out, grab the penny and be back before there was even the sniff of a customer. Anyway, Megan would be here any minute.

Callie jogged up the stairs and jumped off the boat. She looked around, but the penny, so clear a moment ago through the hatch, seemed to have disappeared.

Then she saw it, further away than it had seemed from inside, sticking out of a muddy slop a little way down the path. She fixed her gaze on it as she made her way over, a human magpie, her focus entirely held by the sparkling copper.

Her focus was so entirely held by the penny, in fact, that she completely failed to notice the dog. That is, until the tiny thing hurtled into her ankles, tripping her and sending her flying towards the canal.

Time seemed to slow as Callie careered out of control. She closed her eyes in panic, arms flailing but with nothing to grab hold of, unable to stop, preparing any minute to find herself up to her neck in dirty brown water. But, thank God, her progress was impeded by something soft in her way.

Something soft. Warm. Tall, she noticed when she'd plucked up the courage to open her eyes. With dark hair and attractive dimples and a seriously irritated expression on its face.

It was the good-looking customer in the overalls, the one Megan had served a cappuccino to earlier. Callie just sagged there against his body, confused and disorientated, until he pushed her impatiently away.

'What the hell do you think you're doing?' he demanded.

'Sorry. Accident. I was – there was a penny.' Callie glanced at the muddy patch and frowned. No glint of copper. The penny was nowhere to be seen. 'At least, I... thought there was.'

The man snorted. 'Seriously? You were striding along like a woman possessed for the sake of a damn penny? You've just cost me a day's work worth a couple of hundred quid.'

He nodded to the narrowboat he was standing in front of, and for the first time Callie noticed what he was doing. A selection of paint pots and brushes were at his feet, and against the deep blue of the boat was an intricate pattern of flowers, wet and shining new. It bordered the boat's name, *The Naughty Nell*, carefully written out in impressively detailed carnivalesque lettering. Callie's eyes widened as she saw the huge streak of paint across the letters where she'd knocked into the artist, sending his brush arm off course.

'Oh my God, I'm so sorry!' she whispered, horrified. 'Really, I didn't – I tripped on a dog. There was a little pug or a chihuahua or something, I never saw it coming.' She glanced around, but the dog and its owner, like the penny, seemed to have disappeared without trace. 'It was here a minute ago,' she mumbled weakly.

'Right. I'll just tell that to my client then, shall I? "Sorry, sir, but there was this invisible dog and this invisible penny and this insane woman who can't watch where she's going... well, you really had to be there."'

'I'll pay,' Callie said desperately. 'I mean, I'm not rich or anything, it might have to be in instalments, but I will cover your fee.' She looked again at the ugly paint smear spoiling what must have been hours of painstaking work. As a sort-of artist herself, she could imagine exactly how devastating that must feel. 'Honestly, I'm really so, so sorry.'

Despite her faltering apology, the man's anger showed no sign of abating.

'This was an urgent commission,' he snapped. 'The client paid me extra to fast-track it for him, and he promised recommendations to boat-owning friends, guaranteed future work. I've travelled up from Manchester to do it.' He glared at her. 'And it's not just the money, it was some of my best work too. All day that's taken me, and now it's lost. All day!'

Callie frowned. 'Look, it really was an accident. I've said I'm sorry, and that I'll do what I can to compensate you. I'll speak to your client too if you like, explain it was all my fault. I am genuinely mortified, I swear, but what more can I do?'

'Dunno, can you turn back time and maybe not ruin the best work I've ever done for the sake of your coin collection?'

'If I could, I promise you I would.'

But the man just continued to glare, a paintbrush gripped menacingly in one fist. Callie, irritated at his refusal to meet her halfway, glared right back.

'Oh. Hello,' a bright voice called from further down the towpath. Megan was making her way towards them, waving.

'Ah right, brilliant,' she said when she reached them, smiling broadly, seemingly oblivious to the dense school-dinner-custard atmosphere she'd just dunked herself into. 'You two've met then. Well, that saves me half a job.'

Callie blinked. 'You what?'

'Sorry, didn't he do the introductions properly?' Megan nudged the man in the ribs. 'Can't trust you with anything, can I, Rich? Cal, this is my annoying big brother, Richard. He'll be relocating here from Manchester in August.'

'Your... sorry, did you say your brother?'

'Well, not just my brother.' Megan beamed in the face of Callie's puzzled stare. 'He's your new business partner too.'

## *Chapter Three*

There was one thing to be said for being single, Callie thought as she stretched luxuriously the diagonal length of her double bed. As much leg room as she liked, and she could wear the huge, frumpy bedsocks that kept her feet cosy without anyone to comment.

After her confrontation with Narrowboat Dick, as she'd mentally nicknamed Megan's grumpy brother Richard, a relaxing, stress-free evening thinking about absolutely nothing felt like just what she needed. Worrying about the mess she was in at work, with her best friend moving to America within the month and a new business partner who hated her guts, could definitely wait until the morning.

She reached for her Kindle to pick up the mind-numbingly worthy book club read she'd been struggling to get immersed in, then groaned when she went to switch the thing on. Dead battery. And God knew where she'd left the charger.

OK, paperback it was then. It was nice to go a bit old school sometimes, she reflected. You couldn't beat the smell and feel of old paper.

Old paper... oh yeah, she'd nearly forgotten. The tatty detective thriller Miss Moonshine had slipped into her bag earlier was just visible in her eyeline, the corner of the loud illustrated cover poking out. She didn't have much in the house older than that. In fact, she could practically smell the book's musty beige leaves from her bed, faintly perfumed with the cheap scent and tobacco of decades of previous owners. Its smell suited it. It was enticing.

What was it called – *Budgerigars Don't Talk*? Daft title. Still, it saved her going downstairs. She leaned over the bed and pulled her bag towards her.

The book had obviously been well-read in its life. The spine had long since peeled away, replaced by a couple of layers of Scotch tape, and when she flicked through, nearly half the pages had come loose from their binding. They were covered in scribbles and doodles too. Callie realised now there was nothing mystical or otherworldly about Miss Moonshine offloading this particular bit of stock onto her. She'd certainly never manage to sell the sad-looking thing.

Callie flipped to the first page and started reading. The opening line was everything she'd been expecting.

*The luscious redhead who sashayed into Kurt's office that morning had more curves than the Chicago Cubs' best pitcher, topaz eyes that snapped like the fourth of July, and mile-high legs wasted outside a can-can chorus line.*

'Unless she thought she might use them for, oh, I dunno, walking?' Callie muttered to herself. 'You dirty old sod, Kurt.'

The anonymous annotator who'd owned the book once upon a time seemed to agree. *Does Redhead get a name, Kurt? Or is she just a hair colour on top of a pair of legs?* they'd scribbled in the margin.

*Kurt Constantine had a list of enemies as long as the Mason–Dixon line and twice as dirty,* Callie read on in a mental voice that sounded more like Humphrey Bogart than Humphrey Bogart. *Every hood he'd put away. Every girl he'd cast aside. Two ex-wives, one ex-partner, one dead partner's beauty-queen daughter, and those pen-pushing saps at City Hall who just hated how untidy things got when Constantine was on the case.*

'Well blow me. A maverick, womanising private detective who gets up the nose of The Establishment,' Callie muttered. 'Who saw that coming?'

Her gaze skimmed to a note in the margin, and she smiled. Her reading companion had really gone off on one over this bit.

*Do they always have to be hard-boiled, cynical old buggers who throw the rule book out the window?* he or she had demanded. *Just for once, I'd like to meet a teetotal, non-smoking, touchingly naive gumshoe who always does as he's told. Bonus points if he's still a virgin and devoted to his dear old mum.*

Impulsively, Callie grabbed a biro from her bedside drawer and scribbled her own note underneath.

*Midnight, and DI Timothy Biggins stalks the mean streets of Milton Keynes…*

A few chapters on, Callie had decided her phantom reading buddy had to be a he. For all his sarky comments on Kurt's casual lechery, the sketch he'd done of flame-haired femme fatale Lucinda on page 21 – and in particular the attention to detail around the cleavage – suggested a distinctly male and heterosexual perspective. Callie decided to christen her new friend Algernon, or Algie for short.

It was the name she'd always planned to give the cat her landlord wouldn't let her have.

It was a good drawing, very detailed for a doodle. Algie had some serious artistic talent. It was also clearly based on Jessica Rabbit, with perhaps just a smidge of Rita Heyworth thrown in.

Callie scribbled another comment.

*Ouch, Lucinda. You're going to take someone's eye out with those things. Chilly in Chicago, is it?*

She found herself wishing that Algie, whoever he was, could write back.

A sudden thought struck her. This book was old. It looked old, it smelled old, and it sure as hell read old. It must date from long before the radical notion that women were anything more than a heady mix of lipstick-ringed cigarettes, push-up bras and dangerous yet compelling sex appeal. Would Algie still be alive?

Hurriedly she flicked to the page bearing the publisher's details. Publication date of 1966. So even if Algie was still around, he'd be - she did a quick calculation - at least in his seventies. That was a sobering notion.

But then... Jessica Rabbit. He'd drawn Lucinda like Jessica Rabbit. No, not just *like* Jessica Rabbit - this *was* Jessica Rabbit, pretty much. And that character hadn't existed until the 1980s.

Oh, what was the point dwelling on it? There was no chance she'd ever meet the real Algie, or recognise him if she did. What did it matter if he was an old man or not?

She smiled at a pair of cartoon eyes doodled in the margin, launching from their sockets on springs as, in her big seduction play, Lucinda left Kurt to "slip into something more comfortable". *Awooga ha cha cha! Kurt, you dog!* Algie had written underneath. Callie knew she probably never would meet Algie. But if she did, she definitely needed to buy him a pint.

Two hours later, Callie was hooked, both on the story and her one-sided conversation with Algie. To be honest, without Algie she probably would've abandoned the book in chapter two. It really was pulp fiction at its most pulp-worthy. But with him to keep her company, it felt like fun. Like watching a cheesy film with an old friend you know is on your wavelength, always happy to yell at the screen along with you.

By now, Kurt Constantine was in serious hot water. He was on the tail of an elusive Chinese opium gang led by an old enemy nursing a grudge, wanted by Interpol in a case of mistaken identity involving smuggled rubies, being pursued for alimony by both ex-wives, and Luscious Lucinda, the client he was falling hard for, had very possibly killed up to four men – five, if you counted the sniper she'd accidentally knocked off the Empire State Building during a passionate clinch in chapter seven. All the while trying to babysit the suddenly mute budgie who'd been the only witness to the original murder, which Lucinda claimed had been pinned on her by her double-crossing former guardian. So he was coping admirably, considering.

Callie (and Algie) were glued to the page as Kurt tiptoed, catlike, down the Chinese lantern-lit corridor leading to the secret Soho dope den – and to his nemesis, disgraced District Attorney Johnny LaMancha.

Callie grabbed her pen and started writing.

*Kurt, mate, what're you thinking?! Never, ever,* ever *agree to meet the bad guy without backup. It's a trap, you massive div!*

Algie agreed. At the top of the next page, an impressive caricature of his vision of Kurt as a mouse, in a long mac and fedora with a goopy expression on his whiskered face, was about to nibble a piece of Acme-branded, dynamite-stuffed cheese strapped to a giant mousetrap labelled *WORLD'S MOST OBVIOUS TRAP.*

Just then, as Kurt was about to confront Johnny and exchange Pavlov the Budgie for the photographs that would clear Lucinda's name... the doorbell rang. Cursing, Callie put Kurt, Lucinda and Algie to one side, dragged on a dressing gown and traipsed downstairs to answer it.

'Oh,' she said. 'It's you.'

'Um, hi.' Narrowboat Dick was hovering on her doorstep, clutching a bottle of wine. 'I hope you don't mind me popping round. Meg gave me your address.'

'Did she?' Callie pulled her dressing gown tighter around her, fully aware that her scoop-cut pyjama top and lack of bra weren't leaving much to the imagination. 'What for?'

'Well, because I asked her to.'

'Oh.'

*...let's see. It couldn't be Johnny LaMancha, that was a given. He had a watertight alibi due to being in bed with both Kurt's ex-wives at the time of the murder. It might be Lucinda, except that seemed just a bit too obvious. And she was right-handed – Kurt had already worked out the murderer led with his left, unless it was a double bluff. But the Chinese opium dealer, Lo Chan Tan – there was an idea...*

Richard was staring at her. She shook her head to clear her thoughts.

'Sorry, I was miles away. Did you say something?'

'Yeah.' He nodded to her calves. 'I said that if you don't mind me saying so, those are some seriously impressive bedsocks.'

'Thanks. You should see the matching suspender belt.' She stuck out one leg and gave it a little jiggle, just to make sure he got the full effect. Callie was willing to bet Kurt's femme-fatale girlfriend Lucinda didn't have a pair of sexy bedsocks like hers.

Richard smiled, his cheeks dimpling.

'I came round to apologise, Callie,' he said. 'We got off on the wrong foot today, didn't we? Totally my fault for being such a touchy, miserable sod, and – well, I brought you this.' He held out the wine, his green eyes wide and appealing. 'I'm really quite nice, most of the time. Please don't ask my sister to corroborate that.'

'Thank you.' She smiled as she took the wine. 'OK, you're doing the adorable eyes thing on purpose, aren't you?'

'Yep. Is it working?'

'Might be.' She examined the white wine he'd brought her. It looked like good stuff. Not that she was any kind of connoisseur. 'You really didn't have to do this, Richard. I should be the one apologising to you. I bet ten cases of wine wouldn't cover what you lost in earnings today because of me.'

'Don't worry about it, I managed to get things sorted out with my client,' he said. 'Told him what happened, and he said no worries as long as the work's done by the weekend. I can paint over it, redo that section of the design and it'll be finished by end of play tomorrow.'

'A whole extra day's work though! And all your beautiful lettering, ruined. I am *so* sorry, truly.'

'No, I am,' Richard said in an earnest tone. 'I overreacted. I should never have had a go at you like that when I could see it was an accident. It was out of order.'

'It wasn't at all. I paint too – I mean, not like you, just a hobby. But I'd have been the same if someone had spoiled my best work.'

He smiled. 'So are we going to stand on your doorstep apologising to each other all night or are you going to invite me in?'

She hesitated. 'Now?'

'It's not all that late for a Friday, is it? You can split your bottle of wine with me and we'll have a chat about plans for the caf.'

'It's just... I was kind of in the middle of something,' Callie said, grimacing apologetically.

A Soho opium den, to be precise. The drink was tempting, when Richard was being all friendly and funny – and, unless she was sorely mistaken, more than a little bit flirty – but she couldn't abandon Algie now. Not when Kurt was so close to finally unmasking the killer.

Richard glanced at her pyjamas. 'Oh. Sorry, rude of me. You were obviously having a duvet evening, you don't want me galumphing in.'

He was quite charming really, now he wasn't angry at her any more. And he'd brought her wine, and the dimples were endearingly cute. Callie felt guilty for having misjudged him. He obviously wasn't grumpy by nature, she'd just caught him at a bad moment. And whose fault had that been?

'That's OK,' she said. 'I'll hold onto the wine and we'll do it another night, eh?' She wiggled her foot. 'I might even put my sexy bedsocks back on for you, since you're such a fan.'

'I'm forgiven then?'

'You're forgiven. And I'm sorry I called you a dick.'

'Don't worry about it. I had it coming.' He frowned. 'Did you call me a dick?'

She couldn't help grinning. 'Well, no. Not to your face.'

He laughed. 'Glad we got things sorted, Callie. I'll be in touch about the caf and the drink.'

She felt a stab of worry. 'Richard, are you sure about taking on the caf? You're not just buying out your sister as a favour? Because I'd rather sell up than be partners with someone who isn't fully committed.'

'Are you kidding? I've always envied Meg her working

day on a narrowboat. You paint enough of them, you start to hanker after one of your own.' He flashed her a reassuring smile. 'Callie, don't worry, please. I'm going in with my eyes wide open. Yes, I know about the finances. Yes, I know it'll be an uphill struggle. But it's a great little business. With an injection of fresh ideas, I know that between us we can get her back in the black.'

Callie smiled back. 'I hope you're right.'

'I know I'm right.'

'You're not taking over the waitressing too, are you?' She scanned Richard's broad chest and well-defined shoulders. She couldn't quite see him in Megan's lace-bordered floral pinny, somehow.

'Well, I'll be more of a silent partner for the first month or two. I'm still based down in Manchester at the moment, then I'll be moving into Meg's old place. We'll have to talk about whether we need to hire someone for the interim period. But after that, yeah, of course I'll do my share.'

'No need for a temp, I can cope on my own for a bit. I mean, if it's only for a couple of months.'

It wasn't like they were overrun with trade, Callie thought glumly. It'd be pretty lonely though, just her. She'd miss Megan something rotten. Fleetingly she wondered what it would be like, working alongside Richard day after day instead of Meg.

'OK. We'll thrash out the details another time,' Richard said.

'Right. Another time. I'd better get back to Algie.'

Richard frowned. 'Algie?'

'It's short for Algernon.'

'Oh. Right. Your boyfriend.'

She smiled, wondering if the look of disappointment in his eyes was really there or her wishful thinking. 'No, just a friend. We were actually in the middle of a reading date when you called.'

Richard looked puzzled, but she didn't bother to explain. Always leave the two-bit Charlies wanting more, as Lucinda would've said. Although it might be a bit late for Callie to start cultivating an air of aloof mystery now, given the bedsocks.

'Night, partner. Thanks for the wine.' Callie treated Richard to a warm smile before she closed the door.

## *Chapter Four*

As soon as Richard had gone, Callie hurried back to her book. But there was a disappointment waiting for her when, around midnight, she reached the last chapter.

The problem wasn't the finale, which packed a shocking twist as Pavlov the Budgie finally sang like a canary to reveal that the murderer wasn't Lucinda or Johnny or Lo Chan Tan, but Babs, the beauty-queen daughter of Kurt's dead partner. No, it was Algie who'd let her down. His annotations had suddenly disappeared, leaving Callie to experience the final showdown between Kurt and Babs alone. It wasn't the same, somehow.

Callie wondered what could've happened to stop him commenting. Surely he had something to say about Babs's cry of, "You'll pay for this, Constantine! You and your goddam tweety bird!" as the cops hauled her off to Sing Sing.

Under the final paragraph, Callie wrote *That's all folks* and doodled a morose-looking Porky Pig doing a thumbs down, a poor imitation of Algie's more polished cartoons. She sucked the end of her pen, and as an afterthought added, *Algie, I owe you a beer.* Then she tucked the book away in her bedside drawer, feeling deflated and mildly bereaved. It felt like she'd been on a date that had been going amazingly, really building a connection, only for the bloke to suddenly disappear before pudding.

She checked her phone for the time. Half-midnight, and well past her bedtime. Callie flicked off the bedside lamp and tried to settle down to sleep.

But sleep wouldn't come. The story she'd just finished whistled around her brain – shadowy images of Kurt, Lucinda and the rest, looking like Algie's caricatures. Uneasy thoughts about where the book had come from, and the identity of the mysterious man – she was still certain it was a man – who'd kept her company as she'd read it, stopped her from relaxing. Algie's annotations had really lifted the experience, from a straightforward night in bed reading to something social and fun.

Giving up on getting any rest that night, Callie grabbed her phone again and pulled up Google. She typed in the name of the book to see what information there was online about it. She didn't really know what she was looking for, but it was something to do.

There wasn't much. A couple of references on forums dedicated to the art of pulp fiction, with an image of the cover, but no real detail on the work itself. In fact, none of the people posting in the forums had ever seen an original copy. They were so rare that anyone who did have one in good condition could apparently get up to £600 for it from private collectors.

Shame hers was covered in graffiti and falling apart, since she could really have done with £600.

So it seemed like she and Algie were some of the only people in the world to have actually read *Budgerigars Don't Talk*. Eventually Callie gave up looking for information about the book and typed in the name of the author, Sidney Farrier, instead. That was a bit more helpful, and she soon found an entry for him on a wiki of crime writers. A single paragraph seemed to be enough to summarise his career.

He was English, she discovered, which wasn't much of a surprise. No one who tried that hard to keep his similes American could really hail from the land of baseball, hot dogs and Mom's apple pie. Plus Kurt Constantine's habit of saying, "Crikey, toots!" to Lucinda when they found themselves in a tight spot was a dead giveaway.

*Sidney Farrier was a British pulp fiction author of the 1960s,* the terse paragraph noted. *His debut novel,* Budgerigars Don't Talk, *sadly failed to make its mark on the reading public. After abysmal sales, the publisher recalled and pulped all remaining unsold copies. Any that survive are now highly prized by collectors. Mr Farrier never published another book, and his current whereabouts and career status are unknown.*

So it had been one of a kind, pulp fiction in a very literal sense. Poor old Sidney Farrier. It must be depressing, watching all that hard work end up as a pile of mulch. It made Callie think of Richard and the beautiful, intricate canal boat signage she'd managed to ruin. She still felt guilty about him having to do it again.

She glanced once more at the paragraph about Sidney Farrier, then switched off the phone. It hadn't really given her any closure. She wasn't sure what would have done, really, except a useful note at the end saying "By the way, Callie Fox, your copy was previously owned by..." followed by Algie's real name and his address so she could look him up. Sighing, she tried to settle down again and managed to fall into a fitful sleep.

She slept for a good half-hour before sitting up with a jerk.

'That's it!' she muttered. 'I've got it!'

*

Callie marched into Miss Moonshine's shop the next day, her

copy of *Budgerigars* tucked under her arm, and rang the silver service bell smartly. A curtain behind the counter billowed, and, as if by magic, the shopkeeper appeared.

'Callie Fox. Again.'

'Miss Moonshine.' Callie kept her expression fixed. She'd come here with one aim in mind. Well, two aims in mind. OK, maybe three. But she had a job to do and no enigmatic old ladies with weird dress sense and funny eyes were going to stop her.

Miss Moonshine examined her for a second, smiled, and bent to tickle little old Napoleon between the ears.

'You didn't bring me anything.'

'Sorry, are you talking to me or the dog?'

'To you. The dog's as deaf as a post.'

'Oh, but I did.' Callie slapped the book on the mahogany counter. 'I brought you this back. And I want to know who donated it. Um, please,' she added as an afterthought, noticing the sparkle in Miss Moonshine's hazel eyes seemed to have taken on a dangerous quality.

'Your heart's not in it, my Miss Fox. Try again.'

'Right.' Callie picked up the book again and this time practically slammed it down. 'Miss Moonshine, I demand to know who donated this book you very suspiciously gave me yesterday for free. Right now.'

Miss Moonshine's lip twitched. 'Much better.'

'Well?' Callie said. 'You're going to tell me you don't remember, aren't you? I bet you are.'

'How much do you bet?'

Callie met the old lady's gaze, and thought better of it.

'I withdraw my bet.'

'I'm very glad to hear it. I only ever play for keeps, you know.' Miss Moonshine picked up the book and locked beady eyes with the budgie on the cover. 'Yes, I remember.

This came in a box of paperbacks owned by a lady who's moving abroad.'

'A lady?' Callie felt her heart sink. That didn't sound right. She was certain Algie was a man. One hundred per cent certain. Could it have been a wife, maybe? A daughter? She felt a jolt in her chest. She knew Miss Moonshine got a lot of her stock from house clearouts after people had... passed on.

'Where are the others?' Callie asked. 'Do you still have them?'

'Certainly.' Miss Moonshine nodded to a pile of paperbacks stacked up in no particular order next to her table. 'These all arrived with that one.'

Callie scanned the pile. It was an eclectic mix. Thrillers, romances, children's books, all relatively modern. Nothing in the same style as *Budgerigars*.

She extracted one of the thrillers and flicked through the pages, feeling a stab of disappointment when she found they were blank. Well, not blank – they were covered in type, obviously. But there were no annotations. She picked out a couple of others, but Algie hadn't felt inspired to say anything about them either.

'Not what you were looking for?' Miss Moonshine asked softly.

'No.' Callie looked up to meet her eyes. 'But I'll take them.' She gestured towards the other piles of books filling up floorspace around the shop. 'In fact, I'll take the lot.'

'So it's happened,' Miss Moonshine said in the same low voice. She walked over to Callie and stood on tiptoes to squint into her eyes, putting one finger under her chin. 'Yes. I see.'

'What's happened?'

Miss Moonshine let Callie's chin go and looked away.

'I'm sorry, my dear,' she said. 'I won't be able to take any more beautiful things from you. The ornamental pebbles were our last bit of business together.'

Callie frowned. 'What? I thought you liked my things.'

'I like them very much. But I can't sell them. Not now, not any more.'

'But people buy them, don't they?'

'They do. And they'll buy them from you just as well.' She gave Callie's cheek a rough pinch. 'Take them. Sell them in your little boat with your teas and your buns and your books. I think the new idea should bring in a lot of customers, don't you?'

Callie stared at her. 'How did you know I'd had a new idea?'

Miss Moonshine smiled. 'Goodbye, Callie Fox.'

## *Chapter Five*

'Here you go, ladies.' Callie placed the cream-tea-for-two tray down in front of a couple of elderly women at one of the indoor tables on her boat. She gestured around the shelves she'd had installed down one side, specially designed to make the best use of the space and bursting at the joints with old books. 'Oh, and feel free to take a look at our books while you enjoy your teas. Just chuck a donation in the honesty box if you'd like to read one, and help yourself to a free Book Defacers' Club pen.' She nodded to the little pot full of branded pens, all different colours, in the middle of the table.

One of the ladies frowned. 'I'm sorry, dear – did you say Book *Defacers'* Club?'

'That's right.'

'Oh, what a horrid idea,' her friend said, shaking her head. 'To deliberately damage a book! It's a terrible thing. I used to be a librarian, you know.' She shot an accusing glare at Callie, who smiled.

'It's not what you think, I promise. We don't spoil them. Just the opposite, in fact.' Callie grabbed a book from a nearby shelf and flicked to a random page. She turned it around to show the women the notes and sketches dancing down the margin in multi-coloured biro. 'This is the kind of vandalism that helps get folk reading, you see? Three people have taken this book away, read it, made notes and brought it back. Then the next person who checks it out can see what the other people made of it. Like reading with friends.'

The ex-librarian stared. 'So it's like... a reading group?'

'A little. But more irreverent.' Callie pushed the book, which was called *Sex Secrets of the Mitford Sisters*, towards the lady. 'Give it a go, eh? You never know what you might find.'

She moved through the packed tables, filled with people chatting or reading as they guzzled their tea and cakes, to a young couple. The girl, Eden, was a regular and Callie knew her well.

'You tracked him down, then?' Callie said.

Eden flushed. 'Yes. On Facebook.'

The lad she was with smiled at Callie. 'Thanks to this place, it seems. I scribbled my name in the back of that book I borrowed from you. Couldn't believe it when Eden got in touch out of the blue saying how much she'd enjoyed my comments and asking if I wanted to meet up.'

'And now we're onto our fifth date.' Eden beamed at him. 'Thanks, Callie.'

'Don't thank me. Thank Algie,' Callie muttered as she headed to the hatch to deal with the lunchtime queue. She owed that man at least a dozen beers by now. One for all the enjoyment his notes on *Budgerigars* had given her, and another eleven for inspiring The Book Defacers' Club, the idea that had given new life to her business. Good old Algie. If only he'd thought to scribble his name in the back of the book they'd shared too.

She served the first two customers waiting at the hatch, lunchtimers who grabbed their sandwiches and darted off to eat them in the sunshine before they were due back at work. The third, though, was a familiar face.

'Howdy, partner.' Richard held up his palm for her to high-five.

'What're you doing in the queue?' she asked, smiling as she slapped it with her own.

'Undercover bossing you.'

'Yeah. You're not actually my boss though, are you?'

'All right, undercover partnering you then.' He glanced through the hatch into the packed café. 'Looks like it's going well. Can I come in?'

'You don't need to ask, you know. It's half your boat.'

He shrugged. 'Seems only polite.'

He disappeared, materialising at her side a minute later, and Callie noted how happy she was to see him. It felt like a gap was being filled, whenever Richard was up this way and came to help out. A gap Megan had left, yes, but a gap that in her mind had become very much Richard-shaped in the six weeks since his sister had been gone.

He'd been popping up more and more frequently while he moved his things into Megan's old house, with Callie helping him out where she could. They usually went out for a drink and a chat when he was in town, to discuss the business and other things. Things like books, films, music. The difference between toads and frogs. Why rough was pronounced rough but through was pronounced through. Anything that popped into their heads, usually. It had certainly made the pain of coping with Megan's move away more bearable. Without her really noticing, Callie realised that from a pretty inauspicious start, she and Richard Archer had become good friends.

He leant down to give her a kiss on the cheek. 'Good to see you, love.'

'You too. Welcome back, Rich.'

He smiled. 'You mean welcome home.'

'Oh my God! Is this it? Have you moved in for good?'

'Yup. Notice is up on my old flat. I am now an official resident of Haven Bridge and full-time waitress with his very own frilly pinny.' He cast a glance around the bustling café. 'Just in time too, by the look of things. This place is swamped.'

'I know. Ace, isn't it? Best idea I ever had, the book club thing. It's really pulling in the crowds – that and the new signage you did for us,' she added with a grateful nod. 'The old girl's the smartest she's ever looked.'

'These probably help too.' He wandered over to her crafty shelf and picked up a photo frame decorated with pebbles and coins she'd salvaged from the river. 'Still can't believe I'm business partners with a professional Womble.'

She smiled and took the frame from him, trailing her fingers over the highly polished coins. 'This is the bit of wombling that got me in so much trouble a few months ago.'

'Trouble?'

'Yeah. I saw this old penny that would've been just the thing for the photo frame I was working on. Seriously upset some diva-ish painter bloke when I tripped and knocked into him.'

Rich grimaced. 'Ever going to stop reminding me about that?'

'No time soon. Sorry.' She nodded to a bookshelf near

the window. 'Oh, we've got some new stock in since you were up last, by the way. There's always a few who prefer to hang onto the books and don't bring them back. Not really in the spirit of the thing, but heyho.'

'Let's take a look then.' Richard ambled off to examine the shelf as Callie busied herself clearing a recently vacated table. Like her he was a big reader, and always took an interest in the books they had on offer.

'Goodness me!' a voice from behind her exclaimed.

Callie turned to see a respectable-looking elderly gent in a tweed waistcoat and spectacles holding her battered copy of *Budgerigars Don't Talk*, staring at the cover.

She frowned. Where had that come from? She could swear she'd left it at home.

'Oh, I'm sorry, sir,' she said, approaching the man. 'That's not stock, I'm afraid, it's my personal copy. I couldn't part with it.'

'My dear, you don't understand. This is my book.' He blinked at it, as if he couldn't believe he was really holding it. 'Crikey. It's a very long time since I last saw *Budgerigars Don't Talk*.'

No. Surely not. Algie... was this him? This old man, with his crystal-glass accent and his round glasses and his beard? It couldn't be.

Could it?

'*Your* book?' Callie repeated.

'What was that?' Richard was still by the window, examining the new stock. His head jerked up. 'Did someone say *Budgerigars Don't Talk*?'

'Er, yes,' Callie said. 'This gentleman was just –'

Before she could finish, Richard had darted over and grabbed her urgently by the shoulders. 'Who did it?' he demanded. 'Do you know who did it? Was it Lo Chan Tan?'

'No,' Callie said, feeling dazed. 'No, it was Babs. The dead partner's daughter.'

'Miss Dairy Queen, I knew it! Was she behind the ruby-smuggling ring then?'

'Yeah. She was sleeping with Johnny LaMancha.'

'Heh. Wasn't everybody?'

Callie stared at him. 'I don't believe this. It was you, wasn't it? You're... *him!*'

The old man looked puzzled. 'So do I take it you've both read it?'

'Apparently.' Callie shook her head and turned her attention to him. 'Sorry, did you say this was your book?'

'Oh, I didn't mean it was my copy,' the man said. 'That's at home, one of the last of its kind. I mean it's my *book*. I'm the author.'

'You're Sidney Farrier?' Richard said.

'Loath as I am to admit it.' The man smiled, looking down at the tacky cover illustration. 'It's the most dreadful tripe, isn't it? I was raised on *Boys' Own* stories and Raymond Chandler. In my twenties I had the rather deluded idea I could do better.'

'Well it kept me awake till after midnight.' Callie shot a sideways smile at Richard. 'I actually turned down the offer of a drink with rather a nice young man just to finish it.'

Richard smiled too, his gaze holding hers for a moment.

'You're one hell of a storyteller, Mr Farrier,' he said. 'I'd like to shake your hand, if I may.'

The old man blushed as Richard grabbed his hand and pumped it vigorously.

'You know, it was rather disheartening when my publisher made the decision to pulp the unsold copies,' Sidney Farrier said. 'I couldn't help being proud of it – "a poor thing but mine own", if you like. Seeing it again today, hearing how much you two young people enjoyed it... well, it's really made my year. Thank you.' He squeezed each of their shoulders in turn. 'Thank you.'

'Um, you're welcome,' Callie said. 'And thank you.'

'Do you know, I'm almost encouraged to start something new,' he said. 'Yes. Yes, I really think I might.'

Beaming, Sidney Farrier handed the copy of *Budgerigars* back to Richard and nodded goodbye.

'Cal, where did you get this?' Richard asked when Sidney had gone, holding up the book. 'I've been looking everywhere for it.'

'Bric-a-brac shop on the high street. Miss Moonshine's. She used to buy craft pieces from me for her stock sometimes. Do you know the place?'

'Yes, I know it. I dropped off a couple of boxes of books there for Megan when I was helping her get ready for the big move.' He slapped his forehead. 'That's it, isn't it? I must've accidentally got my book mixed up with the rest. I was right up to the last chapter as well.'

'I bet you've been going mad trying to work out who did it.'

'Just a bit.' He smiled. 'You know, I'm not sure that wasn't why I was in such a bad mood the day you knocked into me painting. I finally thought I'd got it all worked out when this crazy girl cannoned into me and I completely lost my train of thought.'

He opened the book and flicked to the last page.

'"You and your goddam tweety bird"?' he said, quirking an eyebrow. 'Really, Babs?'

Callie smiled. 'I thought you'd like that.'

He skimmed down the page and frowned. 'Who drew this?'

Rich turned the book around and held it up. The little doodle she'd sketched to end the book, thumbs down Porky

Pig with his *That's all folks* caption, stared back at her.

'I did,' Callie said, flushing. 'This is kind of the book that started it all, you know. The Book Defacers' Club. I saw your notes and I started adding my own and... I don't know, it just made it so much more fun, somehow. Sharing it with someone.'

Richard started flicking through the book, looking at her additions. He was soon smiling, and, occasionally, snorting with laughter.

'You know, you're funny,' he said.

'So're you. What made you think of writing in it?'

'Dunno. I never did before. Farrier's style just heightened my sense of absurdity, I think.'

'Yeah. I know what you mean,'

He looked up at her. 'So did you buy this from the old lady in the shop? Miss Moonshine?'

'Actually she gave it to me. It was part of my fee for some craft pieces. Floral ornaments made of glass river pebbles.'

'Heh. Did she now?' Richard reached into his pocket and took out something small, round and very familiar. 'Funny, she gave me something too. In payment for the second box of paperbacks I brought in.' He held the green and yellow pebble up to examine the pattern. 'I don't know why I've been carrying it around. Perhaps I thought it might bring me luck.'

Callie took it from him. 'The buttercup,' she whispered.

'I picked it out of the four. Not sure why, there was just something more... charming about it, I suppose. Unique. Never occurred to me it might be one of yours.' Richard started looking through the book again. 'Who is Algie, Cal?'

'Well, you are,' she said with a slight blush. 'That's the name I gave him, the phantom doodler. I'll be honest, I got kind of attached to him.'

'It says here you owe him a beer.'

She glanced around the busy café, full of folk reading at their tables over hot beverages, or standing while they examined the books and craft pieces for sale.

'I'd say I owe him a fair few,' she said. 'All this is thanks to him.'

Richard took her hand and gave it a gentle squeeze.

'Could he claim them tonight?' he asked softly, his eyes moving over her face. 'Maybe over dinner? I think he'd like that.'

Callie flushed, looking down at her fingers pressed in his.

'I think I would too,' she said.

Miss Moonshine, arranging Callie's three remaining pebbles in her window display at the other end of town, smiled to herself.

*That's all folks…*

**Author bio Mary Jayne Baker is a novelist from Bingley, West Yorkshire. She writes romantic comedies as Mary Jayne Baker and uplifting women's fiction as Lisa Swift, and has also recently completed her first historical novel. Her book *A Question of Us* won the Romantic Novelists' Association's Romantic Comedy of the Year Award 2020.**

maryjaynebaker.co.uk

Thank you so much for reading *Miss Moonshine's Emporium of Happy Endings*. We hope you enjoyed our collection of stories. If you did, please consider telling your friends or posting a short review on Amazon or Goodreads. Word of mouth is an author's best friend, and much appreciated!

# AND IF YOU'VE ENJOYED THIS ANTHOLOGY, YOU MAY ALSO ENJOY...

## CHRISTMAS AT MISS MOONSHINE'S EMPORIUM

**When the magic of Christmas is just what you're looking for...**

There's something magical about Miss Moonshine's Wonderful Emporium, and at Christmas she brings an added sparkle to the inhabitants of the pretty Yorkshire town of Haven Bridge. Customers who step over her threshold find an eccentric collection of gifts, but Miss Moonshine has a rare knack for providing exactly what they need: a strange Advent calendar whose doors give a glimpse of a happy ending; a vintage typewriter that types a ghostly message from Christmas past; a mirror in a silver case that reflects the person you'd like to be.

Step inside Miss Moonshine's quirky shop, and the thing you need most for Christmas will be right there, waiting for you...

Available on Amazon, both in print and for Kindle.

## *ABOUT THE AUTHORS*

*Miss Moonshine's Emporium of Happy Endings* is an anthology put together by a group of romantic novelists and short story writers from Yorkshire and Lancashire, in the north of England. The group meet regularly in the little town of Hebden Bridge, and this location, lying as it does on the moors near the border between the two counties, led to the group name Authors on the Edge, and to the inspiration behind this collection.

Much cake was consumed by these authors in the making of this anthology.

**Top: Mary Jayne Baker, Sophie Claire, Jacqui Cooper**
**Middle: Helena Fairfax, Kate Field, Melinda Hammond**
**Bottom: Marie Laval, Helen Pollard, Angela Wren**